"Jackson, did you take a blow to the head? In case you haven't noticed, we're in a heap of trouble here."

"I suppose."

"You *suppose*? First there's the swim to the beach, where we might either drown or be gobbled up by sharks. Then once we get to the beach we have no supplies, no flares, no nothing." And no shoes for her, now that she'd kicked off the second one. But she was used to being barefoot.

"Yeah, but did you notice that we're not up in the air anymore? I landed the plane! And I didn't kill us! Gen, that's *awesome*. I can hardly believe I did that."

She could hardly believe how good he looked with no glasses and his glistening black beard showing off a beautiful smile she'd never really noticed before. His eyes were morning-glory blue. She'd never paid attention to that before, maybe because they were usually bloodshot and covered by smudged lenses.

Then again, maybe he looked better because her vision was off, with one contact missing. She closed her right eye and used only her left. And there he was, still handsome. How amazing.

"Are you winking at me?"

"No. I lost one contact."

"Oh. For a minute there I thought you might be trying to hit on me."

She knew he was joking, and yet there was something in his voice that told her it wasn't totally a joke. . . .

Nerd in Shining Armor

Vicki Lewis Thompson

A Dell Book

NERD IN SHINING ARMOR
A Dell Book / May 2003

Published by
Bantam Dell
A Division of Random House, Inc.
New York, New York

Dell is a registered trademark of Random House, Inc., and the colophon is
a trademark of Random House, Inc.

ISBN 0-440-24116-2

Manufactured in the United States of America
Published simultaneously in Canada

OPM   10   9   8   7   6   5   4

To Pat Warren, who saved this story from a fate worse than death. You are my Friend in Shining Armor.

Acknowledgments:

I'm grateful to so many people that I'd need several pages to thank them all. But my agent, Maureen Walters, deserves special mention for loving my Nerd in the first place, and marketing the book in the fall of 2001 in the second place. She'd intended to send it out the middle of September. She settled for October. Many thanks also to my editor, Wendy McCurdy, for all her perceptive comments, and to Nita Taublib for giving me such a cool chance. I'm also indebted for research help to my son, Nathan Thompson, my daughter, Audrey Sharpe, and my son-in-law, Daniel Garrison. Any mistakes are mine! And finally, to my wonderful husband, Larry, who keeps me steady.

NERD IN SHINING ARMOR

Chapter 1

Ever since Genevieve Terrence's mama had inherited a pair of Elvis's Jockey shorts, Genevieve had been a big believer in luck.

Luck could be good or bad. Granny Neville's luck had been bad when her plane had crashed, killing her dead. But good luck had come out of it when Elvis's Jockeys had passed to Mama, who had sold them for a pretty penny so that she, Genevieve, and Genevieve's little brother, Lincoln, could leave the Hollow and relocate to Hawaii.

Without that famous underwear, they'd all still be back in Tennessee scratching for a living. Instead they were in Honolulu scratching for a living, but at least Genevieve was working for Nick Brogan's company and hoping that Nick would ask her out. Genevieve didn't love sitting there typing boring invoices all day, but that put her in a position for another stroke of luck, an invitation from Nick.

Nick was a far cry from Clyde Loudermilk back in the Hollow, a red-faced boy who used to swat her on the backside and tell her she was built for breeding. Yes, Elvis's underwear had definitely led to progress for the Terrence family. Her brother Lincoln's hair was a different color every month or so, but at least he didn't have a chaw of tobacco stuck in his cheek like all his boy cousins back home.

And her mama had a good number of clients at the beauty salon where she worked as a manicurist, well-kept women who were good tippers.

Life was moving in a positive direction. Genevieve's horoscope this morning had predicted the beginning of a romantic adventure, which was the kind of horoscope she loved to read. It might mean Nick would finally ask her out today. Thinking of that prediction, she anticipated his arrival in the office with more eagerness than usual.

The minute he set foot inside the door, she could smell him coming. Nobody else at Rainbow Software Systems slapped on that purely sinful, strip-naked-for-me aftershave. Nobody else would dare. They couldn't begin to strut in the same barnyard with the likes of Nick Brogan.

She lost her place on the keyboard and &^%$#(&# popped up on the screen. She hit the delete key and hoped he hadn't noticed. Lately Nick had formed the habit of coming up behind her and standing very close to her chair, which she took as a sign of interest. She was definitely looking for signs of interest. Nick might not realize it yet, but he needed her in his life.

Because it suited her goal, she didn't begrudge him a peek down her blouse, either, although her mama would throw a hissy fit if she knew he did that. Mama would claim sexual harassment for sure, but it wasn't, not with Nick. Nick didn't have to harass anybody.

He was gorgeous, rich, and single. And wounded. Not anywhere you could see, but deep in his soul. Once she'd been lucky enough to catch his partner, Matt, in a mood to share confidences, and Matt had told her Nick was an orphan who'd had a rough childhood, so he didn't trust people.

Once she'd learned that crucial piece of information, she could see the lost expression in Nick's brown eyes from time to time. Because she knew what it was like to grow up poor and insecure, she was just the woman to fill the empty place in his heart. Besides, he was a Leo and she was a Gemini. They'd fit together like grits and gravy.

But first she had to get herself invited on one of his business trips to Maui, the kind where he flew the company plane and took one of the secretaries with him, always cautioning her they'd have to stay overnight because the meeting would run late. He had a bad reputation for spending the night with these women and then dropping them the minute they got back to Honolulu the next day. A couple of secretaries had actually quit over it.

Out of the six who currently worked in the business office of Rainbow Systems, two of the rejected ones were still there. They'd both warned the other four not to go to Maui with Nick, because he only wanted a one-night stand.

Genevieve knew that's how Nick's plans would start out, but she intended to break his pattern. She'd felt her chance coming for the past couple of weeks, and she wasn't about to ruin it. But when he stood right behind her chair, he could read her computer screen and see that he made her so nervous she couldn't type straight.

Nervous wasn't how she wanted him to see her. Nervous could get her into trouble, and in no time she'd be sounding like all her relatives back in Tennessee, twanging away like she belonged on the stage at the Grand Ole Opry.

Nobody in this office knew about her roots, and she intended to keep it that way. Savvy, sophisticated, and sexy was what she was going for.

"That's a nice color on you, Genevieve," he said.

"Why, Nick!" Congratulating herself on wearing the peacock blue blouse that brought out the color of her eyes, she turned, as if totally surprised to discover him there. The back of her chair brushed his crotch, which she didn't think was all bad.

She glanced up at him, careful not to oversmile. Her little brother, Lincoln, told her she had a mouth big as a

Mason jar, which was an exaggeration, but she did have a wide mouth and had to be careful not to overdo the smiling. "I didn't even realize you were standing there." Thank the sweet Lord she hadn't twanged once.

"Hope I didn't startle you."

Not possible, she thought, admiring that adorable cleft in his chin. She always knew the minute Nick appeared. He could no more startle her than a hog could lay eggs. "Only a little," she said. "Is there something I can help you with?" He was such a pleasure to look at. Mama would think so, too, once she got a gander at him. He was the spitting image of Cary Grant in *Bringing Up Baby*, Mama's favorite movie. He had the same thick brown hair and irresistible smile.

He used that smile on her now. "As a matter of fact, I do need a favor. I desperately need someone to fly over to Maui with me tomorrow and take notes during a meeting. It'll probably go late, so we'll plan to come back the next morning. I checked with Matt and he said we could spare you for a couple of days."

Praise the Lord and pass the black-eyed peas! If there was ever a time she felt like oversmiling, this was it. At last she was the chosen one. The office grew very quiet, and she realized that all five women in the room were waiting for her answer. She knew they wouldn't like it when she said yes, but that couldn't be helped.

Still, she didn't want to seem too eager, or too available. "Actually I had dinner plans tomorrow night."

From across the room, Sue gave her a thumbs-up.

Nick scowled, though, his eyes darkening like the sky before a gully washer.

His scowl was as sexy as his smile. She loved the way he wore a dress shirt with no tie, and the top couple of buttons undone to show off his tan. "But maybe I can change my plans," she said. From the muffled groans, she knew she'd lost the admiration of all five women as they went back to their typing.

Yet Nick was suddenly bright and cheerful, which made her feel good. His cheerfulness might be all about sex right now, but sex was a starting point with most men, anyway. Soon he'd discover that he'd found the right woman, at last.

"I'd appreciate that," he said. "When can you let me know?"

She glanced at the digital clock in the corner of her computer screen. "Before lunch, I'm sure."

"Good. I—"

"Oh, hey, Nick!" Jackson Farley, one of the company's top programmers, hurried over to Genevieve's desk. As usual, Jackson was loaded down with his laptop and a notebook overflowing with computer printouts. On top of that he was juggling a styrofoam cup of coffee.

Genevieve sighed. Obviously her fashion hints had fallen on deaf ears. Poor Jackson looked like her cousin Harley after a three-day toot. His eyes were red, his glasses smudged, and his dark hair stood out in sixty-eleven directions. To make matters worse, he'd decked himself out in a sweet potato–orange plaid shirt and pants the color of a rotten eggplant. Because he was tall, there was a lot of orange plaid and a lot of rotten purple, and all of it was wrinkled.

People said Jackson was a genius. She'd heard other programmers call him a certified "engine god," whatever that meant. Nobody seemed to care what he looked like so long as he continued creating brilliant software that kept the company riding high on the stock market. But Genevieve cared. He'd never get a girlfriend dressed like that. Jackson Farley desperately needed a girlfriend, if for no other reason than to help pick out his clothes.

"I hear you're flying over to Maui tomorrow," Jackson said. He pushed up his glasses with the hand holding the coffee and sloshed some of it over the rim onto his thumb. "Ouch." He licked at his thumb. "Damn, that's hot."

"Put mustard on it," Genevieve said.

Jackson looked at her. "Really? You mean like regular mustard?"

"Yes. Regular mustard." She'd always been sensitive to other people's injuries, and she could almost feel the sting of the burn. "And go do it soon. It'll take the pain away and you won't blister."

"Thanks. I'll try it. I'm sure I have some mustard packets in my desk."

Genevieve nodded. "I'm sure you do." The man saved everything, and it was all jammed into his desk, sort of like Uncle Rufus's shed back in Tennessee. Uncle Rufus could have a dead body in that shed and nobody would know the difference.

Jackson turned to Nick. "So you are going to Maui, right?"

"Yes. Why?"

"Matt wants me to go with you."

Disappointment spilled all over Genevieve's shiny new prospects. Talk about unfair. Every other secretary who'd gone with Nick to Maui had flown over there alone with him. Just her luck that when it was her turn, Jackson Farley was going to tag along. It would be like taking her brother, Lincoln.

Nick didn't seem any happier about having Jackson along than she was. "What for?" Nick asked somewhat ungraciously.

"Aloha Pineapple is still having trouble with the new software. Henderson's gone over, and Mitchell, but neither one of them has been able to straighten things out. Considering they're such a big client, Matt thinks I should go take care of it."

"Seems like a damned waste of your time," Nick said.

"Does Matt know I wasn't coming back until Friday morning?"

"Yeah. He booked me a room at the hotel, too. It's no problem if I have some time on my hands. I'll take my laptop and get some work done."

Genevieve studied good old Jackson and wondered if she could possibly spend the night in Nick's room and not have Jackson find out. Or if he did find out, if she'd be able to explain that she wasn't going to be just another one of Nick's chickie-babes.

But she needed to be alone with Nick to give it her best shot, and here was Jackson Farley to throw a bucket of molasses into the works. She could tell from Nick's body language that he didn't want to take Jackson to Maui, but he really had no choice. He couldn't very well say no because he'd been planning a roll in the hay with one of the company secretaries.

"I want to be in the air by eight," Nick said. "Oh, and Genevieve's coming with me, to take notes at the meeting," he added casually.

Jackson didn't blink an eye, so apparently he already knew about that. He just glanced at her, his expression smooth as porridge. "Yeah, Matt mentioned she was going," he said. "No problem."

He might seem okay with it, but she knew what he was probably thinking. She felt a blush coming on. Tarnation.

Having Jackson think poorly of her bothered her more than she wanted it to. Who was he, anyway? A genius in terrible clothes. "Go find your packet of mustard," she said, "before that thumb blisters up on you." She winced at her choice of words. *Blisters up on you* was something her aunt Maizie would say.

"Okay, I'll do that. See you in the morning." Jackson ambled off. The tail of his shirt had come untucked from his slacks, which was a constant problem for Jackson because he was at least six-six and regular shirts weren't long enough for him.

Genevieve felt herself becoming more irritated looking at that shirttail hanging out. There were stores that sold extra-long sizes, if Jackson would only take the time to investigate. He could even shop online and not have to leave his precious computer. She felt the urge to erase any lingering effects from that *blisters up on you* remark. "Hasn't Jackson ever heard of *Eddie Bauer*?" she muttered.

Nick laughed. "Don't worry about Farley."

She glanced up at Nick. The way he'd said it, he seemed to be implying that he could work around Jackson during their time on Maui. And he probably could. This was one smooth guy. Sexual excitement curled in her stomach. "Okay, I won't."

"I'll pick you up at seven-thirty," he said. "Assuming you can go." His expression told her he knew she would go.

She lowered her voice. "You wouldn't take off without Jackson, would you?" She didn't want Jackson to go, but she didn't want to leave him standing alone on the tarmac, either.

Nick leaned both hands on her desk, which brought his face very close to hers. "No, but you know Farley. Absentminded as they come and perennially late. I'll bet you a bottle of Dom Pérignon that he doesn't make it on time." He smiled at her. "And I *am* lifting off at eight."

She nearly passed out from the sexy curve of that smile and the lickable shape of his earlobe. Oh, well. Jackson would have to fend for himself. "Aye, aye, Captain," she murmured.

"Mama, will you *please* do my nails? You know how important this is."

Annabelle looked at her daughter sitting across the

kitchen table. All mothers thought their daughters were beautiful, she supposed, but Genevieve really *was* prettier than a speckled pup, as Maizie would say. She'd inherited her father's eyes, a combination of blue and green that had been the primary reason Genevieve had been conceived. Her hair was the taffy color of moonshine whiskey and she had the good sense to leave it alone—a simple cut that brushed her shoulders. No perm or fake highlights to ruin what the good Lord had seen fit to give her.

No wonder some big shot wanted to take her on an overnight to Maui. Annabelle sighed. Worry about Genevieve going on this plane trip had spoiled her appetite for the Big Mac Genevieve had brought her for supper. "I expect you're fixin' to go whether I do your nails or not."

"You bet your bottom dollar I am. And my nails are chipped. You're always telling me that chipped nails are worse than letting your bra strap show. Katharine Hepburn would never have flown to Maui with chipped nails."

Annabelle knew her daughter was playing her like a fiddle whenever she brought up one of Annabelle's favorite stars. It worked, though, because that's what she wanted for Genevieve—the kind of elegant life portrayed in the old black-and-white movies.

Annabelle loved those movies for many reasons, including the fact that the heroines usually took trains and boats to wherever they were going, not airplanes. "Couldn't he charter a boat to Maui? One of those hydrofoils?"

"No, Mama. He's a pilot."

"Who cares? He could take a boat for a change." Annabelle had made but one flight in her life, and that had been because she'd had no other choice if she'd wanted to raise her kids to be something other than backwoods hillbillies.

When Genevieve was fifteen and Lincoln only three, Annabelle had seen plain as day that if she didn't get her budding daughter out of the Hollow where the whole family lived, the girl would soon be pregnant by some mush-brain like Clyde Loudermilk, and she'd sink into the same poverty Annabelle had struggled with all her life. And because Annabelle was the only member of her clan with a regular job, she knew she'd have to go far away, or her relatives might follow her and Genevieve would be as bad off as before.

So Annabelle had settled on Hawaii, partly because she'd always liked *Gilligan's Island*, but mostly because you had to take a plane to get to Hawaii. None of her kin would set foot on a plane after what happened to Granny Neville. Granny Neville had been the first one in the family to take a plane somewhere, and it hadn't turned out well. After the crash they'd found her shoe two hundred yards from the spot they'd picked up her false teeth.

Fortunately, before Granny Neville left for the airport, she'd given Annabelle her most prized possession, a pair of Jockey shorts with *E. Presley* written with a laundry marker right on the label. Those Jockeys had paid for three coach tickets to Honolulu and money to get started in a new location.

But the plane flight to Hawaii had been the most terrifying experience of Annabelle's life. She never expected to get on a plane again and didn't want her children on one, either. Now here was Genevieve with a chance at a real good catch, apparently, and there had to be a plane involved.

"Mama, Nick flies all the time. He's a good pilot." Genevieve spread out her fingers on the worn pine table. "I think French this time, don't you? It's more natural looking and it'll go with whatever I'm wearing."

Annabelle was about to ask what she was wearing, exactly, when Lincoln came in from playing basketball and opened the freezer to take out a red, white, and blue Popsicle. He'd begged Annabelle to buy the Popsicles because they matched his hair, which he'd dyed for the summer in colors that he said suited all the summer holidays—Memorial Day, Fourth of July, and Labor Day.

Working in a beauty salon, Annabelle had seen all kinds of strange hair colors, so she hadn't been as upset as most mothers might have been. And to tell the truth, when Lincoln wanted matching Popsicles, he'd made her laugh because it proved he was still a kid at heart. Besides, hair was minor. What Genevieve was planning, this flight to Maui, was major.

Lincoln bit into his Popsicle and talked with his mouth full. "Hey, Gen, what I want to know is if you're gonna have, like, sex with this dude, since you're staying overnight with him."

"Lincoln!" Annabelle scolded.

"That is none of your business," Genevieve said.

"She's right, Lincoln," Annabelle said. "Go back to the park and play basketball some more."

"No way! This is the most awesome thing that's happened around here in, like, months! Maybe ever! You know Chad, the guy whose dad sells cars? He sold Nick Brogan a Z3."

"I have no idea what that is," Annabelle said. "And I don't give a care, either."

"A convertible," Genevieve said.

"Not just a convertible," Lincoln said. "A Beemer!"

Annabelle tried to make sense of what her son was saying. "You mean like on *Star Trek: Voyager*, where they're always beaming people up and down?"

Lincoln seemed to find this very funny. "A Beemer is a BMW, Mom," he said when he stopped laughing long enough to get the words out.

She was used to having him crack up at things she said, so she ignored his know-it-all grin. "Oh. I've heard of BMW cars." She sort of wished he'd call her Mama, like

Genevieve did, but that wouldn't sound right in front of his friends. Genevieve, being older when they'd left Tennessee, hadn't been able to break herself of saying Mama. Annabelle found that comforting.

"Well, this is a roadster, Mom, and it's really cool and really expensive. That loser Gen used to date drove a Yugo, so she's definitely trading up with this guy. And as her little brother, I have a vested interest in this project." Red Popsicle juice dribbled over his fist and dripped on the floor.

Annabelle glared at him and fought the urge to make him the target for all her fears about rich men who drove Beemers and flew planes. "You're dripping all over the floor. Take that Popsicle outside."

"Okay, but ignoring your kids makes them do drugs. There's ads about it and everything." He sauntered out the kitchen door.

With a sigh, Annabelle stood and walked over to the kitchen cupboard where she kept her at-home manicure supplies. She was barefoot, as was Genevieve. Thank goodness such a thing wasn't frowned on in Hawaii, because after all those years of going barefoot in the Hollow, neither Annabelle nor Genevieve could tolerate shoes except when required, like on the job and in church.

Opening the cupboard, she took down the polish remover and her crystal soaking bowl full of Lincoln's old marbles. Lincoln might wonder about what would happen tomorrow night, but Annabelle knew good and well Genevieve planned to have sex with this Nick person. Her daughter wasn't a virgin, probably hadn't been a virgin when they'd left Tennessee. Clyde Loudermilk would have seen to that. Virginity wasn't really the issue.

She studied her array of polishes sitting neatly on the shelf. "French, did you say?"

"French," Genevieve repeated. "Mama, I know you're scared about this, but it's the chance I've been waiting for.

I've had my eye on Nick ever since I started working at Rainbow Systems, but I didn't say anything because I didn't want to jinx it. You see, he's an orphan and had some terrible times growing up. He needs somebody so much, and I plan to be the one. I expect to marry him."

"Marry?" Annabelle dropped the soaking bowl, which shattered on the kitchen floor. Marbles rolled everywhere.

"Mama, your soaking bowl!" Genevieve leaped to her feet and started picking up the marbles.

"Watch your bare feet with that glass!" Annabelle gazed at the broken glass on the floor and knew it was a very bad sign. Very bad. Of course the bowl wasn't really crystal, only cut glass. Genevieve had bought it for fifty cents at the Goodwill Store for Annabelle's twenty-first birthday. To think that at twenty-one she'd had a daughter in first grade, a daughter who'd sold the tiny creatures she whittled until she had enough to buy that bowl.

And now this girl had her eye on a man who could give her real crystal and a fairy-tale life of fancy cars and clothes and jewels, just like in the movies. Annabelle should be thrilled for her, but the bad feeling wouldn't go away. "Don't fly in a plane with this man, Genevieve." Annabelle started picking up fragments of glass. "It's a mistake."

"Oh, Mama." On her knees searching for marbles, Genevieve paused and glanced up at her. "It's not a mistake. Listen, I know how you feel about planes, but what happened to Granny Neville doesn't happen to very many people. Flying is safer than driving."

Annabelle knew that Genevieve wouldn't all of a sudden listen to her and turn down this opportunity. Genevieve might still live at home, but that was so Annabelle could afford to stay in a nice neighborhood with a good school for Lincoln. The older Genevieve got, the more she treated Annabelle like an older sister instead of a mother. After all, they were only fifteen years apart. Genevieve would go on this trip whether Annabelle wanted her to or not.

"Mama, he looks like Cary Grant."

"Does he?" Annabelle went to fetch the broom and the dustpan so they could clean up the tiny fragments. Meanwhile she tried to push aside her worries and think about Cary Grant flying Genevieve to Maui. That didn't seem so bad.

Maybe she wasn't having her usual premonitions this time. Maybe it was only her backwoods Tennessee raising that made her suspicious of a man who took a company secretary over to Maui and kept her there overnight. He might look like Cary Grant, but it didn't sound like a Cary Grant thing to do.

Genevieve could get her heart broken, but people healed from a broken heart. Annabelle had found that out for herself twice over, once with Genevieve's daddy and once with Lincoln's.

She moved a kitchen chair and started sweeping under the table where some stray slivers had flown. "You're just saying he looks like Cary Grant to soften me up."

"No, he really does." Genevieve stood and dropped the marbles into the mail basket on the counter. "Especially the way Cary Grant looked in *Bringing Up Baby*. You would just melt."

And she might, at that, Annabelle thought, being a sucker for the likes of Cary Grant, Spencer Tracy, and Humphrey Bogart. Each one held a special place in her heart. And as for the women, she'd learned everything she knew about manners and fashion from watching Katharine Hepburn, Lauren Bacall, and Ingrid Bergman. She'd done her best to teach those things to Genevieve.

Genevieve crouched down and held the dustpan while Annabelle swept the glass into it. "I'll get you a new soaking bowl," Genevieve said. "A better one."

"I loved that one," Annabelle said, and her throat tightened up. She swallowed the lump. She'd learned a long time ago that there was no point in crying over what couldn't be changed. She swept the last of the glass into the dustpan Genevieve held. "But I'm sure I'll love the new one you get me, too."

Genevieve stood and dumped the glass into the trash. "Maybe I'll find something pretty while I'm on Maui."

Annabelle searched for a smile to give her daughter and finally managed to find one. "Yes, maybe you will."

Jackson stayed up late driving the Indy 500, and he finished a close third this time. As he'd learned in the past few years, there wasn't much you couldn't do with a computer, with the obvious exception of having sex. Maybe someday that would be perfected. He'd heard of some developments along those lines, but he had a hunch they were a long way from being as good as the real thing.

At least the real thing as near as he could remember it. Lately his fantasies about Genevieve Terrence had become sort of mixed up with his memories of having sex with Diana, his first love, and Cybil, his last love. He was aware that two sexual relationships, even factoring in the AIDS scare, wasn't a very respectable showing for a guy who was nearing thirty.

But relationships were so damned complicated. With computers it was strictly WYSIWYG, What You See Is What You Get, and he loved that. With women you could never tell. Like Genevieve—a perfect example. He'd thought she was way too classy to fall for Brogan's Maui sleepover schtick. Genevieve had always reminded him of a movie star from the forties—Katharine Hepburn, maybe, or Lauren Bacall. His grandma loved those movies, and because he loved his grandma he'd watched a fair amount of them with her back in Nebraska.

Genevieve even dressed a little like the women in those movies. The outfits she wore with the nipped-in waists and flared skirts that skimmed her knees made him want to take her dancing to the sounds of Benny Goodman or somebody like that. Of course he didn't know how to dance, but if he *did* know how, that's the kind of dancing he'd want to do with Genevieve.

Per his usual lack of confidence, he hadn't even asked her out for coffee. Every time he thought he'd worked up the courage, he'd walk into the office where she was typing away and she'd look so together that he'd lose his nerve. One look at her perfect fingernails, her perfect makeup, and her perfect hair, and he'd realize that she'd never want to go out with a guy with zero fashion sense.

During that one humiliating conversation when she'd tried to give him some advice about his clothes, he'd started to tell her about his mild case of color-blindness. Then he'd figured that he didn't want her to think of him as being handicapped in addition to being a nerd.

He was a nerd. He couldn't change that about himself and didn't really want to. Being a nerd paid exceedingly well, besides being what he was best suited for. His two previous girlfriends had also been nerds, and he'd assumed he'd marry a nerd someday. But then he'd flown to Honolulu to interview for Rainbow Systems and had met Genevieve.

She wasn't the first pretty girl he'd ever seen in his life, obviously. He'd analyzed his strong attraction and decided it wasn't totally based on her beauty, although she was beautiful. Something made her stand out from the crowd, and he'd driven himself crazy trying to figure out what that was. Whatever it was, he thought it had something to do with hidden depths. He couldn't help believing that under that polished exterior of hers was a whole other thing going on.

She was a puzzle, and he'd always been fascinated by puzzles.

But apparently when it came to Brogan, there was no mystery. She was just like the other women who had leaped at the chance to go winging over to Maui and leap into a king-size bed in a suite with an ocean view. Jackson hadn't thought much of Brogan from the beginning. Something about the guy was a little off. If Brogan had conducted the first interview instead of Matt Murphy, Jackson wouldn't have considered Rainbow, even knowing he'd be working in the same building with the luscious Genevieve.

By the time he met Brogan, he'd pretty much committed to Matt and started fantasizing about Genevieve. He'd figured with someone like her around, he could tolerate a guy like Brogan. Still, this most recent development made him wonder if he'd be able to tolerate the jerk after all.

When Matt had proposed the trip and explained about Brogan taking Genevieve along, Jackson had nearly begged off. He'd almost been sick to his stomach in the middle of Matt's office, to be honest.

But then he'd had a weird thought—that if he went along, maybe he could be of some help to Genevieve if things went sour between her and Brogan. Okay, so he prayed they would go sour and he'd be around to pick up the pieces. Nobody could blame a guy for wanting to be a hero in the eyes of a woman like Genevieve.

Chapter 2

That night Genevieve used every go-to-sleep trick she knew. She sprinkled oil of lavender on the pillow and took deep breaths until she hyperventilated. Then she lay with her eyes closed and counted jugs of moonshine sitting in a row on her aunt Maizie's back porch in the Hollow.

She imagined the whole scene, with crickets chirping, mosquitoes whining, rockers squeaking, cigarette smoke catching the breeze, and the splat of chewing tobacco in the dirt. She pictured herself sitting on the swaybacked steps with a wedge of watermelon and having a seed-spitting contest with her cousins.

Instead of drifting off to sleep, she worked up a little case of homesickness, though she certainly never wanted to live in the Hollow again. But some things about it were nice for a kid, like almost never wearing shoes and fishing in the crick and catching lightning bugs in a jar. Hawaii had no lightning bugs.

And the birds were all different here, too. Back home she'd been able to name most every bird around. When she'd arrived in Hawaii she'd had to start all over, pretty much. A couple she'd recognized, like the cardinal and the mockingbird, had been brought over from the mainland, according to a book she'd found. But no one had brought over a whippoorwill, and she missed that song.

She didn't miss Clyde Loudermilk, though. That boy had promised her that if she let him do it he'd treat her to the movies every Saturday for a year. She'd given away her virginity for an empty promise, it turned out. Clyde hadn't had the money for a box of popcorn, let alone a whole movie, not even a matinee.

Plus he hadn't understood the first thing about pleasing a woman and he hadn't worried about getting her pregnant, either. At the time she'd been willing to take a chance, on account of the movies, but now she shuddered to think that she could be raising Clyde Loudermilk's kid right now because she'd lusted for a glimpse of Mel Gibson, Tom Cruise, and Harrison Ford. She was no different from her mother—she'd just taken up with a different set of movie stars.

Nick had that star quality, too. But thinking about Nick wasn't going to help her sleep. Thinking about Nick would make her wonder if she'd remembered everything she wanted to take to Maui.

Snapping on her bedside lamp, she sat up and reached for her glasses on the nightstand. During the day she wore contacts, but she kept a pair of glasses beside her bed for when she first got up in the morning. She threw back the sheet and climbed out of bed.

Her suitcase sat on the floor beside her dressing table. She would have loved to take a different suitcase, but she hadn't had time to buy one. She'd known all along she might run into this very problem, but she'd been afraid buying a new suitcase before she'd been asked to go on the trip would jinx her chances for sure.

So she was stuck with the one she'd picked out eleven years ago when her mother had announced they were flying to Hawaii. She'd found it in the Goodwill Store, and it had been cheap, too. Now she understood why. Nobody carried hard-sided, round pink suitcases these days.

Her mother had offered hers, but it wasn't any better. It was also hard-sided, scuffed up, and an ugly shade of tan. Genevieve had decided hers was in better shape, even if it was hopelessly out of style.

She crouched down and lifted the lid to peer at her clothing choices. On top was the outfit she'd wear on the flight back, simple, tailored, and a flattering shade of green. Below that was her best bathing suit, just in case Nick suggested a swim. The next layer included the sexiest underwear she owned, which was blue, not black, unfortunately. And she had no seductive nightgown. Instead of taking a flowered cotton one that made her look like a sweet little virgin, she'd go with the blue bra and panties in bed.

Beneath her underwear she'd packed her flip-flops and six condoms. After her experience with Clyde back in the Hollow, she wasn't taking any chances with anybody. She expected Nick to bring his own, but in case he forgot, she would be prepared. Six was probably expecting too much of Nick, but she had no idea what sort of stamina he had.

She couldn't think of anything else to pack besides her makeup and her curling iron, which would go in last. Her stuff wouldn't take up all the room in the suitcase, which meant it would rattle around in there and wrinkle her green outfit. Then she had an inspiration and went into the hall closet to get her *South Park* beach towel. Lincoln had given it to her for Christmas a couple of years ago. Maybe the towel would make Nick laugh.

After tucking the towel in and closing the lid, she walked over to the windowsill and picked up her latest whittling project, an I'iwi bird. Maybe whittling would relax her.

"I haven't seen you this excited since the night before we left for Honolulu," Annabelle said from the doorway.

Genevieve glanced up and instantly felt guilty for rummaging in the hall closet for her beach towel. She knew full well that her mama heard every little noise that went on in this house. "I'm sorry for waking you up," she said. "I'll turn out the light and be quiet."

"It wasn't your fault. I couldn't sleep, either." Annabelle came over and sat on the bed.

Genevieve looked at her mother, her cheeks rubbed pink from scooching down into the pillow the way she always did when she tried to sleep and couldn't. How young she looked in this light. And after all, she *was* young, only forty-one.

"I hate that you're so worried about this trip, Mama," she said. She put her half-finished whittling project back on the windowsill.

"I probably shouldn't be, but I can't seem to get it out of my mind that something important's going to change."

"That's because it will, and for the better. This is the man for me." She sat on the bed beside her mother. "But I hope you're not scared that I'll run off and get married and leave you to fend for yourself with Lincoln. I would never do that."

"I know, honey." Annabelle reached over and squeezed Genevieve's hand. "You shouldn't have to be thinking that way in the first place, but we've almost got Lincoln raised. Another couple of years and he can get a job to help out."

Genevieve laughed. "Do you think by then he'll have normal hair? I don't think McDonald's will take him looking like Uncle Sam's goofy nephew."

"Oh, that hair is just a passing phase. At least he didn't want to pierce his tongue like Chad did."

"You're right. A stud in his tongue would really creep me out."

"Me, too," her mother said. "I think Lincoln's doing okay, considering."

"Considering nothing, Mama! You've done a super job. We don't need a man around to raise Lincoln."

"Well, that's good, since we don't have one."

But they might soon, Genevieve thought, if matters progressed with Nick. She wondered how Nick would react to Lincoln's patriotic hair when the two got to know each other. Having a guy around would be a real change for Lincoln, for sure. None of Genevieve's boyfriends had paid much attention to him, and Annabelle hadn't dated a man since Lincoln's daddy took off. Genevieve had tried to talk her into dating, but Mama wouldn't hear of it.

"The main thing is, Lincoln's not walking around with a plug of tobacco tucked under his lip," Annabelle said. "If we'd stayed in the Hollow, he'd have his chaw going by now and be measuring how far he could spit. I'm so thankful for the King's undies coming to us. I hate that Granny Neville died, but I'm sure glad I got those Jockeys."

Genevieve glanced at her. "You know, there's something I've always wondered. How would anyone know for sure they belonged to Elvis? Why couldn't a person have written his name on the label for a joke?"

"Because of the little notches."

"Notches?"

Annabelle nodded. "When he was a teenager, instead of a notch in his belt, which his mama would have noticed, he'd cut a little notch out of his underwear label each time he got lucky. The fellow I sold those Jockeys to had a contact from Elvis's early years who said it was true, and the writing matched a sample of his mama's printing." She snuck a peek at Genevieve. "All this time you never asked how Granny Neville happened to have them."

"I always thought she'd found them at the Goodwill Store. You can find some amazing things in that store."

"Well, she didn't find them at the Goodwill."

Genevieve stared at her mother, who had a definite twinkle in her eye. "You're not telling me she was a notch?"

"She would have been, except they heard her daddy coming down the hall, so Elvis grabbed up his pants, shirt, and shoes and dove right out the window. He left his underwear behind."

Genevieve flopped back on the bed and stared up at the ceiling. "Granny Neville almost made it with Elvis Presley?"

"He wasn't famous then, so I'm not sure it counts."

"You haven't told Lincoln this, have you?"

"Now, what do you think?"

Genevieve propped herself on her elbows, resettled her glasses on her nose and looked at her mother. "No, I guess you wouldn't. He'd spread it all over. But he knows about the underwear, and sooner or later he'll start asking questions."

"If I think he's ready to hear it and won't go embarrassing us with the information, then I'll tell him. If he isn't, then I won't."

"It's kind of weird to think of somebody related to us being in bed with the King." Genevieve's curiosity was killing her. "Did she say anything about . . . about what it was like or anything?"

"Only that he was the prettiest boy she'd ever seen and she never forgave her daddy for coming home so unexpected. The women in our family have a weakness for good-looking men." She paused. "Good-looking men who love you and leave you to cry."

Genevieve knew exactly what her mama was getting at. "Nick's different. You'll see."

"I hope you're right. Honey, I hate to ask you this," her mama said, "but will you call me when you get safely to Maui?"

"Sure." Genevieve sat up and gave her a hug. "Sure, I'll

call. Now go on back to bed, and I'll go back to bed, too, I promise."

Annabelle stood and walked to the door. "I'd also like to meet him when he comes to fetch you."

Genevieve hesitated, not wanting to complicate things at this tender stage of the relationship. "I'm not sure we'll have time. He didn't say anything about coming in, and I wouldn't want to make him late for his meeting."

"Okay, then I'll walk you to his car and say a quick hello."

"Well, I'm not sure . . ." Genevieve thought it would be sort of embarrassing to have her mother walk her out, considering the nature of this trip with Nick. Then she saw the concern on her mother's face, and she decided being embarrassed wasn't the worst thing in the world. Leaving her mother to fret because she'd hadn't laid eyes on her daughter's lover would be a lot worse.

"Okay," she said. "Then you'll be able to see that he looks exactly like Cary Grant, just like I was telling you."

Matt Murphy sat at his favorite open-air bar and nursed a gin and tonic while he watched the waves roll in on Waikiki Beach. With the moon shining on the water and a couple of sailboats rocking at anchor, it was a postcard view, and he was tired of having nobody to share it with.

"Last call, Mr. Murphy," said the cocktail waitress, a pretty redhead who was too young for him.

"Then hit me again. I feel sobriety creeping up on me." One advantage of giving Theresa the big house on the hill as part of the divorce decree was that his new apartment was within walking distance of this bar, so he could come down here every night, drink himself silly, and not worry about getting a DUI while he made his way home.

It wasn't a particularly good habit to get into and he

knew it. Yet he hadn't come up with any healthier ways to spend his evenings, so this filled the gap for the time being.

Tonight he was feeling particularly gloomy. He'd never liked the way Nick ran through the company secretaries, and he'd had several arguments with his partner about it. But Nick had rightly pointed out that he hadn't twisted anybody's arm. A woman was free to turn him down with no fear of reprisal.

True as that was, Matt still didn't like Nick's behavior. A few years ago his partner's love life had amused him, but the joke had worn thin. Nick had worn thin, unfortunately. When they'd met in an economics class at Hawaii Pacific, Matt had really liked the guy. But during that period, Matt's judgment of people had been suspect. Witness his marriage to Theresa.

Matt had finally caught on to the self-centeredness of both his wife and his partner, but not until he was very married to Theresa and locked tightly into a partnership with Nick. That aside, Nick had turned into a damn good salesman, and the increasing value of Rainbow Systems was due in large part to his efforts. The company was now worth so much that Matt couldn't afford to buy out his partner even if he wanted to.

During one of their arguments Nick had said they should sell the whole shooting match, retire early, and loaf for the rest of their lives. Matt couldn't imagine such a thing. The fact that Nick could showed how much of a narcissist he'd become. Matt had learned that term during a counseling session prior to the end of his marriage to the other narcissist in his life, Theresa. Matt would have been hard-pressed to hand Nick his share of the company's net worth even before the divorce stripped him bare. Now it would be impossible.

So he was forced to keep his mouth shut as Nick continued his Don Juan activities. Each time Matt prayed that the chosen secretary would tell Nick where he could put his little trip to Maui. But Nick apparently knew how to pick 'em, because no one had turned him down yet. Not even Genevieve.

Matt had thought for sure Genevieve wouldn't fall for Nick's routine, but apparently she had. Having Farley go with them probably wouldn't make much of an impact, but Matt was glad he'd sent the programmer along, for several reasons. Farley would definitely handle the Aloha Pineapple situation, and it was always good for the software creators to see how the actual customers used the product so the programmers weren't working in a vacuum.

Besides, the trip might jolt Farley out of his rut. The guy needed to get a life, and this little trip might help him realize that. There was also the slightest chance that he'd louse up Nick's planned seduction, and no one would be happier to see that happen than Matt.

The waitress came over with his G and T, a lime slice hooked over the rim of the glass instead of a wedge of lime in the glass. A few nights ago Matt had made a comment about liking the look of a lime slice on the glass, and she'd been doing it that way ever since.

"Here you go," she said. "We don't have any other customers. Mind if I sit down a minute?"

"I'd be honored . . . uh . . ." *Cindy? Sherry?* For the life of him, he couldn't remember her name.

"Celeste." She said it with a smile, as if she wasn't the least insulted that he'd forgotten.

"Celeste. Thank you. I'd buy you a drink, except I don't think you could have one while you're working, and you're probably sick of looking at glasses of booze, anyhow."

"I don't drink," she said.

"Smart girl." He polished off the last of his old drink

and reached for the new one she'd brought. "I'm thinking of giving it up for Lent."

She laughed, showing off teeth that probably set her parents back several grand at the orthodontist's. "But this is July. Lent isn't for a long time. Months."

"I know." He squeezed the lime juice into his drink and dropped the slice in with a satisfying plop. "I don't want to be hasty about a big decision like that."

"You're so funny." She gazed at him. "I assume since you come down here so many nights and you don't wear a ring that you're not married."

"Not anymore. We split."

"I sort of thought so. Dating anyone?"

"I think I've forgotten how to date."

"That's too bad."

Any idiot could see where this conversation was going. Might as well nip it in the bud. "Celeste, I'm forty-three years old, and if I'd stayed married I would have celebrated my twenty-first wedding anniversary this year. I don't happen to have any kids, but if I did, I could conceivably have a daughter your age."

"So?" She seemed totally unfazed by his statistical review.

He leaned back in his chair and studied her. Smooth, unlined face, red hair in little ringlets down to her shoulders, perky breasts, small waist, nice legs. "The thing is, I can't imagine what a beautiful young woman like you finds interesting about an old fart like me."

She braced her chin on her hand. "Then I'll tell you. For one thing, you have a very compassionate face."

"Oh, God. You really know how to hurt a guy, don't you?"

She laughed again. "I guess you'd rather hear that you look a little bit like George Clooney."

"Yeah, right. Me and George. Like twins. We both have two eyes, a nose, and a mouth."

"More than that! There's something about the way you grin, and your eyes are that same warm brown."

He sat forward as he realized that, unbelievably, she was edging them toward decision time. "You're really serious about this, aren't you? You're hitting on me."

"Yes, as a matter of fact, I am."

He considered what it would be like to make love to this young sprite, and the concept had definite appeal. He'd been a long time without, and here she was, bypassing all that awkward dating business, something he'd been dreading, thus postponing. But he couldn't imagine what would be in it for her.

Maybe she thought he was rich. "Do you know what I do for a living?" he asked.

"Haven't a clue."

"Well, that's good, because my title sounds very important, but after the divorce I have zero liquidity."

"Mr. Murphy, I'm not interested in your money."

He should turn her down, but damn, this was balm for his bruised ego. "Under the circumstances you might want to start calling me Matt."

"Matt." She gave him a slow, assessing smile. "Matt is perfect for you."

"My name used to be George, but I had to change it because people kept getting me mixed up with that Clooney joker, and that was so annoying."

"See, that's one of the things I find so attractive about you. So many guys my age take themselves too seriously."

"They have to. Nobody else does." He paused, still wondering if flirting with her was such a good idea. "This isn't about you getting ignored by your father when you were a little tyke, is it?"

"Nope." She grinned. "My father dotes on me. So does

my mother. Look, Matt, I'm not hoping to get engaged or anything. I don't even see this as the beginning of a long-term relationship. In two weeks I'm moving back to California. I just happen to be hot for you. I'm available, you're available. I say let's take advantage of the moment."

Amazing. How times had changed since he'd played the dating game. Maybe Nick had the right idea and Matt was the one out of step.

He set aside his drink. "Your place or mine?"

"Oh, mine, definitely. I have the most awesome collection of condoms. I'm guessing if you're recently divorced, you haven't stocked up yet."

"You'd be right about that."

She smiled gently. "First time with a new woman?"

He nodded.

She leaned forward and touched her finger to his mouth. "Then just relax and go with the flow, Matt Murphy. I'm going to be your transition babe."

Genevieve was up an hour before she had to be, which gave her uninterrupted time in the bathroom. She used a new razor on her legs and under her arms. She put on her glasses to check her bikini line and was relieved to discover it still looked good from the last time she'd used hair removal lotion on it.

Her tummy quivering with nervous anticipation, she rubbed lotion everywhere she could reach and misted herself with cologne. Thanks to her mother's coaching, she knew not to put on too much. She switched scents according to the season of the year. Because it was summer, her cologne was called Seaside.

As she put in her contacts, she wondered if Nick knew that she wore them. She thought about tucking a pair of glasses into the suitcase, then decided against it. Glasses made her look like too much of a nerd. She ought to be able to make it from the bed to the bathroom in the morning without bumping into anything.

Next she gave the ends of her hair a touch with the curling iron and did her makeup. Last she put on the dress she'd chosen after much inner debate. It was white with red hibiscus flowers on it, and the color combination made her hair look more blond than brown. With the jacket on, the dress was fairly conservative. But without the jacket, the skimpy little slip dress wasn't even slightly conservative.

Genevieve wore the jacket to the breakfast table, but there was no getting something past her mama.

"Loaded for bear, I see," Annabelle said when Genevieve appeared in the kitchen.

"Once you meet Nick, you'll understand."

"I expect I understand now. I poured you some juice."

"Thanks." She eyed the stove where her mother was cooking up a mess of grits. "Juice is probably all I'm going to have this morning, Mama."

"Some grits will help settle your stomach."

Genevieve smiled. Her mother had said that very thing on so many occasions. She'd eaten her mama's grits before cheerleading tryouts, before final exams her senior year in high school, before her job interview with Rainbow Systems.

"Go on, sit down."

Genevieve sat down and ate a bowl of grits.

The cure worked pretty well. Or maybe it was the calming effect of sitting across from her mother, each of them in the chairs they always used at this table. Annabelle took the chair closest to the stove; Genevieve sat across from her with her back to the wall. Lincoln's chair, nearest to the back door, was empty this morning because Annabelle let him sleep in during the summer.

The fourth chair was usually stacked with things, mail and magazines and the daily paper. Genevieve noticed the front section of the paper was folded back to the weather report. Her mother had been checking on their flying conditions, no doubt.

But Annabelle didn't talk about the weather. Instead she told Genevieve about a client at the salon who was having an affair with a man on the Internet. Genevieve listened to the familiar sound of her mother's voice and remembered that Annabelle used to sing around the house back in Tennessee.

"Mama, how come you don't sing anymore?"

Her mother looked startled. "I don't?"

"If you do, I never hear you."

Annabelle gazed off into space for a few seconds. "I don't know. Got out of the habit, I guess."

"You should get back into the habit. I liked hearing you sing."

Her mother smiled. "We'll see."

Before she knew it, Genevieve had finished her grits. She hurried into the bathroom to brush her teeth and put on her lipstick. As she was carrying her pink suitcase into the living room, she heard Nick beeping the horn out by the curb. Her stomach started to churn again, and for one crazy minute she wondered if this was a good idea.

Then she peeked out the living room window, saw his zippy little black car idling there, and knew she'd be a fool not to go to Maui with him. She hoped Jackson Farley had overslept and wouldn't be waiting at the airfield when they got there. She really didn't want to face Jackson's bad hair and bad clothes this morning. Or his silent judgment of the situation.

Picking up her suitcase by its pink leather strap, she turned to her mother, who was standing expectantly in the living room. "Well, Mama, come on and meet Nick."

"Okay." Annabelle took a deep breath and followed Genevieve out the front door of their rented bungalow.

From the looks of the car, she had an idea what to expect from the man. He would be Genevieve's daddy and Lincoln's daddy all over again.

It seemed her daughter had inherited the family weakness for good-looking men, a weakness passed down from Granny Neville to Annabelle's mama, then to Annabelle, and now to Genevieve. At least Genevieve was twenty-six instead of fifteen or sixteen, the average age the other women in the family had been fooled by a pretty face. And Genevieve carried condoms. Annabelle had checked.

The first thing Annabelle noticed about this Cary Grant look-alike was that he didn't bother to get out of the car. He popped the trunk and let Genevieve put her pink suitcase in the bitty space alongside his sleek leather one. Annabelle reminded herself that in this day and age women didn't want a man waiting on them hand and foot. What used to be good manners was now called patronizing.

Patronizing or not, she thought a man who was fixing to take a woman to bed for the first time might be moved to lift a suitcase for her. Maybe that was old-fashioned thinking, too. Nick Brogan did have a nice dimple in his chin and a good head of brown hair on him. She couldn't see his eyes on account of his sunglasses. He wore a lightweight suit jacket and no tie, which made him look like one of the Kennedys on his way to Hyannisport. Annabelle had seen a passel of pictures like that in *People* magazine.

Genevieve had her suitcase in and the trunk closed in no time. Then she scurried over to the passenger door. "Nick, I'd like you to meet my ma—my mom, Annabelle Terrence," she said.

Nick showed off his pearly whites. *Oh, yes*, Annabelle thought. *I can see what this is all about.* She'd been on the receiving end of that kind of smile before, and it always meant trouble. "Nice to meet you, Nick," she lied. Damned if she'd call this Romeo *Mister* Brogan.

"Same here, Annabelle. Hard to believe you're Genevieve's mom. You look more like her sister."

Annabelle ignored the compliment. "Take good care of her." She knew her daughter would hate her saying that, but she couldn't help it. She also knew it would have about as much effect on this slick character as the No Smoking sign Maizie had tacked up in her cabin had on Rufus.

"Absolutely," Nick said. "Well, Genevieve, we'd better get rolling if we're going to lift off at eight."

"Right. See you tomorrow night, Ma—Mom." She hopped in the little car, waved, and was off.

Annabelle stood on the sidewalk looking down the street until the car turned the corner. If Genevieve stayed around this man very long, she'd break herself of saying mama. Maybe that wasn't much to fret about, but it left a heaviness on Annabelle's heart.

She didn't like Nick Brogan. If he'd had a bad childhood, she was sorry for that, but it had turned him into the sort of man who only cared about himself, and Genevieve wouldn't be able to fix him. Although Annabelle wasn't the type to wish a broken heart on anyone, let alone her only daughter, in this case she hoped Nick broke Genevieve's heart quickly and then went away.

Genevieve would get over it. She was tough, tougher than most people gave her credit for. But then they hadn't known her when she was a scrappy little kid in the hills of Tennessee. You didn't grow up in the Hollow without learning to survive.

Chapter 3

Jackson set two alarms and slept through both of them. Then Mrs. Applegate next door backed her Volvo out of the drive and hit Mr. Applegate's Dodge Ram coming in. If the impact hadn't been loud enough to cause Jackson to leap out of bed, the full-throttle yelling and cursing from both Applegates would have done the trick.

One glance at the clock and Jackson knew he could make it to the airfield if he skipped breakfast—no hardship—and used his portable electric shaver on the way. He grabbed the quickest shower in history and threw on what he hoped was a blue plaid shirt and blue pants. Wallet, keys, glasses, and he was out the door and into his Corolla.

The gas tank needle rode right above the E as he dodged through traffic and prayed he had enough to make it. Halfway there he realized he'd forgotten the shaver. Oh, well. He could pick up a razor and shaving cream on Maui and make himself reasonably presentable before he went to see the Aloha Pineapple folks. Or he could explain to everyone that he was growing a beard. As fast as his grew, they'd think he'd been working on it for several days instead of one night.

His major regret about oversleeping was that he'd set the alarms extra early to allow time for better grooming in honor of Genevieve. He'd planned to shampoo his hair and put styling gel on it. Then he'd hoped to get over to Mrs. Applegate's before she left for work and ask her if his pants and shirt went together. She'd told him he could do that anytime.

He spared a minute of sympathy for Mr. and Mrs. Applegate. Mr. Applegate worked the night shift at a pineapple canning factory and came home about the time Mrs. Applegate left for her daytime job in the same factory's front office. Both of them drove like bats out of hell, and Jackson had been expecting this collision for months. For him, the timing of the wreck couldn't have been better, but he was sorry for the Applegates, who loved their vehicles with a passion.

Parking his car right next to Brogan's Z3, he made a mad dash through the executive terminal and out onto the tarmac. Squinting into the bright light, he spotted Genevieve standing next to the company's twin-engine King Air, a purse over her shoulder and a lightweight briefcase tucked under her arm. As usual, she wore something wonderful, a flowered dress with a snappy little short-sleeved jacket over it. A breeze molded the skirt to her legs and he caught his breath in appreciation. At that moment he hated Nick Brogan, and he'd never hated any human being in his life.

Then the object of his hatred emerged from the far side of the plane, where he'd obviously been stowing luggage. Jackson took note of the designer clothes, the salon haircut, and the healthy tan. On the surface Brogan was everything Jackson was not, everything that a woman like Genevieve would find attractive.

He couldn't blame her for not paying any attention to a disheveled computer programmer when a guy like Brogan showed up and invited her to fly with him to Maui. He couldn't blame her for missing the flaws in Brogan's character, either. For all he knew Genevieve had flaws in her character, flaws he was too smitten with lust to notice.

"Hey, I'm here!" he called out, waving a hand over his head.

They both looked in his direction, and if he'd been closer, he'd probably have been able to watch them roll their eyes. He really needed to get louder alarm clocks. Of course, more time to get ready wouldn't have turned him into a page out of *GQ*, but at least he would have been shaved and his hair would have been combed.

Genevieve gave him a tentative smile when he drew near. "Hello, Jackson." She adjusted her trendy little sunglasses on her nose.

His stomach pitched when he realized that she wasn't really glad to see him. Damn, that sucked. Maybe next week he'd find out if anybody offered makeover classes for guys. Brogan would drop her sooner or later. His kind always did. And then Jackson wanted to be ready.

Brogan was more obvious in his disdain. His lip curled as he looked Jackson over. "Been awake long?"

"No, not long," Jackson said with a cheerful grin. "I'm hoping they serve coffee and a light snack on this leg."

"Sorry." Brogan sounded delighted to be telling him that. Then he glanced around the area where Jackson was standing. "What did you do with your suitcase?"

Suitcase. He knew he was forgetting something when he tore out of the house. He shrugged. "I believe in traveling light."

"All right, then. Let's go. Farley, you take the copilot's seat. Genevieve can sit behind us. She tells me she's not used to flying."

"Okay." Jackson wasn't about to turn down a chance to be in front where the action was. He'd love to take a crack at flying the thing, but he'd be damned if he'd ask Brogan.

Brogan would have to offer, which probably wouldn't happen.

Genevieve looked a little pale as she climbed the small ramp and walked into the plane. She must really want this overnight experience with Studly if she was afraid to fly.

Jackson followed and gave her an encouraging smile before heading to the copilot's seat. He considered offering to sit in back with her and calm her fears, but then he remembered why she was coming on this trip and thought better of it.

Brogan didn't seem particularly concerned about Genevieve's fears. He pretty much ignored her as he made his way to the cockpit and got himself situated. He seemed too damned eager to begin this little trip, in Jackson's opinion. Not only that, but he wasn't even bothering to treat Genevieve with any consideration.

Jackson tried not to think poorly of her for taking that kind of crap, but he couldn't help being a little disillusioned. Oh, well, he needed to squeeze whatever enjoyment he could from this trip. He'd never flown in the King Air. Brogan had talked Matt into buying it a year ago, trading in the single-engine Cessna the company used to own. Jackson thought it was a huge extravagance, a toy primarily for Brogan, but Matt had gone along with the idea.

Jackson thought Matt went along with too many of Nick's ideas, but apparently Matt needed to keep the guy happy. Matt had confided to Jackson that Nick was restless and wanted to sell the company. Matt couldn't afford to buy him out, so there was a stalemate. The bigger plane might have been a bargaining chip for Matt.

As the plane taxied down the runway, Genevieve's voice rose above the roar of the engines. "Is this a parachute back here?"

Jackson turned around to look, and sure enough, there was a parachute on the seat next to Genevieve. He'd been so engrossed in her that he'd missed it. "What's the chute for?" he asked Brogan.

"Oh, just in case," Brogan said. Then he picked up the mike and started talking to the tower.

Jackson thought it was kind of weird to have the chute sitting there like that, and it was having a very bad effect on Genevieve. She'd taken off her sunglasses and her eyes were wide with fear. He hoped she wouldn't throw up or anything.

He turned toward her as much as his seat belt would allow. "Are you okay?"

She nodded, but she didn't look okay. She looked scared to death.

"Have you ever flown in a small plane?"

She shook her head.

"We'll be fine. Brogan's a good pilot." The words tasted like garbage in his mouth, but he made himself say them, so she wouldn't be so scared. Besides, Brogan *was* a good pilot from everything Jackson had heard. The guy might be a lousy human being, but that didn't mean he couldn't be competent in certain areas.

Genevieve didn't look comforted. As the plane barreled down the runway, she squeezed her eyes shut, dug her perfectly polished fingernails into the arms of the seat, and held her breath.

Jackson couldn't stand it. Long arms had their advantages. He reached out to her. "Here. Hold my hand."

Her eyes popped open and she stared at his outstretched hand. Then she leaned forward and grabbed on to it for dear life. Her hands were clammy and her nails jabbed his palm.

He didn't care. He'd put up with the pain if it helped her. She needed him right now, and maybe she'd need him later, after all of this was over. He would have liked to look into her eyes to reassure her, but she'd squeezed them shut again.

Brogan seemed oblivious to her distress as he launched the plane into the air.

"See?" Jackson spoke to her even though she still had her eyes closed. "Piece of cake."

She let out a shaky sigh and seemed to relax a little in the seat, but she didn't let go of his hand.

"We'll be at the Maui airport before you know it." Jackson loved holding her hand, and her skin was beginning to warm. She had such soft skin, and such smooth, perfect nails. He didn't mind a bit that he'd have welts when she let go.

She sighed again, softer this time, opened her eyes and drew her hand away. "Thanks, Jackson. I'll be okay now."

"Sure you will." Damn, he wished she hadn't let go of him. She still looked stiff and scared sitting back there.

But of course she didn't really want to take comfort from him. She wanted to hold Brogan's hand, not his. He leaned back and tried to be philosophical about it all. He failed. Damn it, why did he have to be attracted to her in the first place? She would never have anything to do with him, not even if he had a million makeovers. She liked the Nick Brogan type.

Speaking of the devil, Brogan hung his headset around his neck and glanced over at Jackson. "Ever flown one of these babies, Farley?"

Jackson figured it was a deliberate effort to make him look nerdy and Brogan look cool. "No," he said.

"So I take it you don't have a pilot's license?" Brogan sounded like every cool guy just naturally had one.

"Nope." He probably could qualify for one without a lot of trouble, considering all the simulation software he'd played with over the years. But what was he going to say, that he'd flown a computer? Now, that would impress the

hell out of Genevieve. Oh, sure, she'd think he was quite
the dude if he mentioned that.

"You should try it some time," Brogan said.

It wasn't an invitation to try it now, Jackson noticed.
Brogan wasn't about to suggest he take the controls, because then Jackson might accidentally steal his thunder. "It
doesn't interest me," he said.

Not much. Ha. He'd had a great time with the simulations and had told himself that someday he should try the
real thing, just like someday he wanted to drive a race car,
too. But no matter how many resolutions he made to get
out there in the world and experience things firsthand, soon
another fascinating project would draw him back to his
computer and he'd lose track of time. When that happened,
he barely remembered to eat, let alone schedule a flying
lesson.

Computer-simulated thrills were there whenever he
wanted them, at three in the morning if that's when he
needed to take a break. He was hopeless at keeping a schedule of any kind. That's why he'd bought a home gym instead of joining a club. Plus he'd discovered that he got cool
ideas for new projects while he lifted weights.

But once again, he lifted weights solo. It was a wonder
he had any friends left with all the times he'd stood them up
when they'd asked him to do stuff. Fortunately he'd found
a couple of good buddies at work who'd learned to put up
with him.

Both of his girlfriends had left after failing to change his
forgetful ways. In one case he'd spaced a birthday, and in
the other he'd promised to rendezvous at a glitzy hotel for a
night of wonderful sex. He'd become involved in a project
and left her waiting in that big fancy bed. No wonder she'd
given up on him.

He'd thought a lot about how he'd remedy that if he
ever got lucky enough to date Genevieve. He'd decided if

that blissful day ever came, he'd break down and buy a pager. Then he'd figure out a program that would automatically call him and remind him of his social life. He'd have to remember to take the pager, though. Maybe he could have it surgically implanted somewhere. Like in his foggy brain.

But the way things were going, he wasn't likely to need that pager to keep track of his dates with Genevieve. She didn't even want him holding her hand more than a few seconds, even though she was still rigid with fear of flying in a small plane. Most people took their comfort when they could in situations like that. She must *really* not like him.

Genevieve was grateful to Jackson for getting her through the takeoff, but she sure hoped Nick hadn't noticed her holding Jackson's hand. He probably hadn't. He seemed to be pretty much ignoring her.

That would change once he realized he was dealing with the love of his life. At the moment he was behaving like the wounded man she knew him to be, keeping her at arm's length emotionally. Obviously the other women he'd whisked over to Maui had let him get away with that, but she wouldn't. She'd find a way to break through that gruff shell of his.

She was actually relieved not to be riding in the co-pilot's seat, which is where she'd be if Jackson hadn't come along. Staring at all those little dials would have made her even more nervous.

She hadn't expected to be so terrified of flying in the King Air. Privately she thought her mama's fear of planes was silly. Besides, the flight to Hawaii eleven years ago had been a blast. But she'd been only fifteen then, afraid of nothing, eager for the adventure of their new life.

The two experiences were totally different, she realized now. The plane that had brought them to Hawaii had been humongous, like a movie theater only better, because the food was free. Well, not free, exactly, considering how much those tickets had cost. Still, she could remember being fascinated with the idea that she could have all the Dr Pepper she wanted without ever putting money in a machine.

Yes, totally different experiences. Flying in this bitty plane reminded her of the creaky carnival rides that would squat for a few days in the Wal-Mart parking lot back in Tennessee. She'd squirrel away money in anticipation of those rides and become totally hyper with excitement when the trucks pulled in and started unloading.

The traveling carnival was the biggest thing that came to her part of the woods. Yet every year, when the moment arrived to climb aboard the Tilt-a-Wheel or the Loop-the-Loop, she'd look at the rusty bolts and peeling paint and wonder if the thrill was worth the risk. She was wondering the same thing right now.

She couldn't see rusty bolts or peeling paint, but the plane still seemed very flimsy to be this high in the air. When she finally opened her eyes she looked out, not down, but the scraps of land scattered in an expanse of bright sea reaching out to the horizon didn't make for a reassuring view.

Maybe it was the parachute in the backseat that had spooked her. A parachute in the backseat made her think of bailing out, a horrible thought she hadn't allowed in her brain until she'd seen it. No one would end up bailing out, of course, and they were only island hopping, anyway. Even if they had a problem, they could probably find a place to land.

She glanced at Nick's handsome profile. "How long does the flight take?"

"Oh, not much longer." He didn't look back at her.

She hoped he hadn't noticed how frightened she'd

been, and she really hoped he hadn't noticed Jackson trying to comfort her. She should have pulled her hand away sooner, but she'd been too scared and his steady grip had made her feel safer.

No question, she needed to find Jackson a girlfriend. For all she knew, he could be one of those guys with a natural talent for lovemaking and the misfortune of not packaging himself right. There were enough bad lovers out there as it was, and she hated to see a good one going to waste because he didn't know how to dress.

Jackson could pick up some pointers from Nick, if he'd pay attention. She glanced at Nick again and noticed his jaw was clenched. Poor man. He thought the only way to get rid of his loneliness was with these one-night stands. How wrong he was.

"Hey, Nick," Jackson said. "I may be all wet, but looking at the position of the sun, I would swear we're headed west."

"We are, temporarily," Nick said.

"Why's that?" Jackson asked.

Genevieve noticed Nick's frown and couldn't blame him for being irritated that this man who'd admitted he couldn't fly was questioning their direction. Jackson really was a pain in the butt. She spoke above the drone of the engines. "Don't you think Nick knows how to get to Maui? He's been there a jillion times."

Jackson held his ground. "I realize that, but we've been flying west for some time now. I'm sorry, but that doesn't make sense to me."

"It will," Nick said.

"Of course it will," Genevieve said. "Just sit back and enjoy the ride." Unfortunately, Jackson had brought up a good point, though. The sun was behind them, not ahead of them, so they *were* heading west, which meant Maui was getting farther away with every mile they flew in this direction. She'd been too involved in calming herself down to think about it, but now that she was trying to figure out what was going on, she was having trouble coming up with a logical explanation.

Nick had been worried about getting to his meeting on time. She glanced at her watch to discover the meeting would take place in less than twenty minutes. They should have landed by now.

"Okay, Brogan," Jackson said. "I don't know what you're up to, but by my calculations we're way off course. You may not mind missing your meeting, but Matt's counting on me to spread some goodwill at Aloha Pineapple. That's a big account, and if—"

"Don't worry about Aloha Pineapple." Nick consulted the instrument panel and took off his headset again.

Genevieve's mild uneasiness bloomed into a churning insecurity. "Nick, Jackson's right. Losing that account would be rough on the company." She swallowed. "And since we're not going toward Maui, I'm beginning to wonder where you're taking us."

Nick reached under his seat and pulled out a very black, extremely ugly gun.

Genevieve gasped. The loud drone of the engine blended with the panicked rush of blood in her ears, deafening her.

Calmly, almost tenderly, Nick put the barrel of the gun against Jackson's temple. "Hands behind the seat, Farley." As Jackson complied, Nick pulled a hammer from somewhere beside him.

Genevieve screamed, afraid he was going to bash Jackson over the head. Instead he glanced quickly at the instrument panel before using the hammer on a section of it.

"There goes the radio," Jackson said in a monotone.

"Bright boy," Nick said. "Genevieve, hand me the parachute."

Nick's intention filled her with horror. He was going to bail out and leave her here with Jackson. Leave them to die. But if she didn't give him the parachute, he'd shoot Jackson and she'd be all alone.

Genevieve opened her mouth to ask Nick why he was doing this horrible thing and discovered she couldn't control her vocal cords. Nothing came out but a paralyzed squeak. Why, oh, why hadn't she listened to her mama?

"The chute, Genevieve," Nick reminded her quietly. "And I'd advise both of you not to try being a hero. If either of you makes a false move, I'll pull the trigger and Farley's exceptional brain will be splattered all over this cockpit."

Trembling, Genevieve handed the parachute up to Nick. Then she watched in paralyzed fascination as he put it on, switching his gun to the other hand but always managing to keep the barrel pressed against Jackson's temple. Genevieve tried to think of what she could do, but any sudden move seemed doomed. Nick had obviously thought this out very carefully. Once he started shooting, they'd be worse off than they were now.

"Here's how this will go," Nick said. "The engines are set on idle, so you two will glide quite a distance before you finally go down. We'll all just . . . disappear."

At last Genevieve managed one strangled word. "*Why?*"

"Because it's time for me to get my share."

She struggled with the words, trying to make sense of them. "I don't understand."

"I do." Jackson's voice was tight. "I'll bet he's been stealing from the company and socking it away in some offshore account. Now he's going to fake his death and live the high life under a different name."

Nick smiled, looking proud of himself. "You always were a bright boy, Farley."

"I can't say the same for you, Brogan. Trying to parachute into the ocean isn't very smart."

"I know what I'm doing. I always do."

"You stole from Matt?" Shock still had Genevieve in its grip. She was having trouble assimilating the fact that her dream man, her future husband and father of her children, was a thieving, murdering scum-bucket.

"Matt's in my way, and his financial problems aren't my fault. I never intended to make Rainbow my life's work. However, I have to admit when I planned this, I didn't think Matt would end up losing one of his top engine guys."

"He'll also lose Genevieve, you son of a bitch." Jackson's voice was heavy with anger.

"Well, yes, but there are lots of secretaries in the world. You'll be much harder to replace."

His casual disregard for her life cleared the shock from Genevieve's mind. Damn it, she hadn't made it this far in life to die at the hands of a psycho. She'd handled some rough characters back in the Hollow, guys who got really mean when they were liquored up. Maybe she could talk him out of it.

"Nick," she began, then had to stop and clear her throat. She clenched her hands and tried to stop shaking. "I have a better idea."

"I doubt it. I've been planning this for months, and I've thought of everything." He unfastened his seat belt and eased himself out of the cockpit while keeping the gun trained on Jackson. "Now, neither of you make any funny moves."

"But I do have a better idea," Genevieve said. "Wherever you're going, take us with you."

"I don't need you." He kept the gun on Jackson until

he'd moved between the seats, headed for the door. Then he pivoted and pointed the gun right in her face.

She nearly passed out. "Of c-course you do. You'll n-need a cook, a housekeeper, someone to warm your bed." She gave him what she hoped was a melting look of passion.

"Nice try, but I'll have three million dollars. I think I can find people to do those things." His eyes glittered. "And even if I took you along as my little love slave, I'd have no reason to include Farley, there. I'd have to shoot him after we landed. Would that be okay with you?"

She shrugged. Once they landed the plane, she could figure out how to keep this maniac from shooting Jackson.

"Interesting," Nick said. "It would almost be worth doing, just to see if you'd abandon your friend Farley to save your own skin." He paused. "But I can't risk it, sweet-cheeks." Still holding the gun on her, he glanced quickly at his watch. "Whoops, we're out of time."

Genevieve fought down panic. She had to make him land this plane. "I give great blow jobs!"

Nick laughed. "Wish I had the time to check that out." He continued to aim the gun right between her eyes as he reached behind him to unlatch the cabin door.

"Jackson!" Genevieve shouted above the rushing noise coming from the open door. "We have to do something to stop him!"

"We can't!" Jackson shouted back. "He's crazy!"

"You're going to give up, just like that?" Her opinion of Jackson went down several notches.

"He can't save you." Nick smiled. "But maybe you'd like to treat him to one of those blow jobs. You two will have a little time on your hands. Well, so long!" He jumped.

Terrified, she looked away from the gaping entry into nothingness. This was way too much like a movie with Harrison Ford, except she wasn't in a plane with Harrison, she was in a plane with Jackson Farley, who didn't know jack-shit about flying planes. The bad guy had really left them to die, and they might have to go ahead and die, since this was not a movie.

Her heart pounded so hard she thought it might explode at any minute. If it did, so what? She was as good as dead, anyway.

Chapter 4

At the first sign of trouble, Jackson tried to think his way through this mess. Thinking was hard when Brogan had the barrel of that nasty gun pressed against his temple. Jackson had spent a lot of time sweating.

He'd thought about trying to disarm the guy, but in a small area like this a bullet could ricochet. Genevieve could get shot, even if the gun wasn't pointed in her direction. Wrestling Brogan for the gun didn't seem like the way to go.

Instead Jackson concentrated on the plane's instrument panel. Thank God he hadn't told Brogan that he'd flown simulations, or he'd have a bullet through his brain right now. Instead, he and Genevieve had a chance. Not a big chance, but a chance.

The jerk finally leaped, and Jackson could only hope there was a shark down below with a taste for certified asshole. But he didn't have time to waste thinking about Brogan's fate. He moved to the pilot's seat.

"Come on up here!" he called out to Genevieve.

When he got no response, he turned to discover that she was frozen in place, her eyes buggy with terror. He was pretty damned scared himself, but letting her know wouldn't help the situation.

"Don't worry!" he shouted. "I think I can fly this thing!"

"B-but you said—"

"I know! But I've flown computer simulations!"

She reached out a hand toward him, and he leaned back to grab it. Gripping his hand and keeping her gaze fastened on his, she made it up to the cockpit, but she didn't relinquish his hand as she settled into the copilot's seat.

He decided they needed something to break the tension. "Do you really give great blow jobs?"

She stared at him.

"That was a joke! I know what you were trying to do, and it was a great idea."

"Oh." She swallowed.

"For what it's worth, I think he was a fool not to take you up on your offer."

"Do you . . . really think you can fly this?"

"Yes." He wasn't the least bit sure. The instrument panel was similar to one he'd seen in a simulation, but not identical. All the same, he'd never been in such a perfect position to be a hero in front of a woman he wanted to impress. The stakes were a little higher than he would have liked, but he couldn't do anything about that.

"So you could turn us around and get us back to Honolulu?"

"I'm not totally sure I could do that, but I'll bet I can get us on the ground somewhere." He glanced down at her hand clutching his. "If you turn me loose, that is. I do my best work with my right hand."

"Oh!" She released him immediately and there were red marks on the back of his hand where her nails had been. "I'm so sorry!"

"Not a problem." Jackson flexed his hand and leaned forward to peer at the instrument panel. "Flying out over the Pacific with the gas gauge getting low, now that's a problem."

"It's getting low?" She strained against her seat belt to look where he was looking.

"You have a set of gauges, too." He pointed them out because he'd just realized how distracting it would be to have her hover close like that. Here they were in a life-and-death situation, and he was still mulling over her line about the blow job.

Promising sex to Brogan had been a reasonable bargaining chip, and obviously she'd only said that thing about the blow job to get his attention. It hadn't worked on Brogan, but Jackson couldn't stop thinking about it. He wondered if Genevieve would have said that regardless of whether she was good at the activity. Probably. Then again . . .

"The gas *is* low," she said. "The way Nick was talking, I thought we'd be going along on idle for a long time."

"Airplane gas is expensive." He put his hands loosely on the wheel. "He probably didn't want to waste any more than he had to. We're already far enough out that we'd be hard to find."

"But we're not going down, because you're going to turn us around and get us back to land."

"Yeah." Now was not the time to tell her he'd crashed the simulator a few times.

"We're heading toward some clouds."

"I know." He had to get them turned before they reached the clouds. Flying on instruments was another whole thing, and he'd never worked on that.

"Tarnation, Jackson! You're slower than a coon dog with a full belly. Start flying!"

Despite their treacherous circumstances, he grinned. "What did you say?"

"I said get the lead out!"

"No, I mean the part about me being slower than a

coon dog with a full belly." Okay, he had the basics figured out. He could do this. But he was nervous as hell, and talking about coon dogs helped.

"I suppose we might die together, so it doesn't matter if you know. I spent the first fifteen years of my life living in the backwoods of Tennessee. I mean the back backwoods."

"Really?" Sure enough, he'd been right about her. There was more to Genevieve Terrence than met the eye, although what met the eye was wonderful enough.

"Yes, really. But I'd appreciate it if we could save the discussion of my roots for another time so that you can *concentrate on flying this plane*."

"I *am* concentrating." He took the plane out of idle and gripped the wheel. This was it. He was flying this hunk of metal. "But if you'd talk to me about those backwoods days, it would keep me from hyperventilating while I concentrate."

"Lord in heaven, you're scared."

"Some." He turned the wheel and a gust of wind must have hit them, because the plane bucked.

Genevieve screamed.

"We're okay." His stomach knotted, but he kept turning the wheel a little at a time while he kept adjusting the altitude. "Talk to me, Gen."

"Are we going to die?"

"Not if I can help it. Tell me about Tennessee."

"Granny Neville died in a plane crash. They couldn't find enough of her to fill a casket. They ended up stuffing one of her outfits with old rags so it would look like there was somebody in there during the viewing. They found a picture of her face and stuck that on a honeydew."

"That wasn't the kind of anecdote I had in mind." The right wing cut through cottony wisps of clouds. He was turning barely in time to avoid the muscular-looking clouds they'd been heading toward. "Do you have any stories that don't involve people being dismembered in a plane crash?"

"Well, there was the time Uncle Rufus heard a noise outside his cabin and went out to investigate in his ridge runners. Turns out the—"

"Hold it. What's a ridge runner?" Finally the nose of the plane pointed east, toward the morning sun. He saw a sliver of brown on the far horizon and headed for that.

"Is that land up ahead?"

"Looks like it." He didn't want to think about the landing part of this gig. Landing on a normal paved runway was tough enough for beginners, but landing on uneven ground was damned near impossible for someone who'd never flown a real plane before. "What's a ridge runner?"

"Long johns. They're usually red. At least all the ones my relatives wear are red. Or they start out that way, but eventually they become sort of flesh colored, which is probably what the ones were that Uncle Rufus had on that night. The man hated breaking in a new pair of ridge runners. He claimed the seams rubbed his privates raw."

Never in his wildest dreams had he imagined Genevieve Terrence would have such stories to tell. And they were the perfect thing to keep his mind off the ordeal ahead of them. "So how come you call them ridge runners?"

"Because when the revenuers show up trying to arrest you for operating a still, they like to come in the middle of the night, so naturally you have to take off across the ridges wearing your long johns because there's no time to put on your clothes."

"Your relatives made *moonshine?*" He was totally fascinated, and while he thought about men in red long johns running the ridges of Tennessee to escape the tax man, he nearly forgot that he'd have to put the plane down on the tiny wedge of land that looked too small to handle a helicopter, let alone a plane that had to taxi to a stop.

"They still make moonshine," she said. "From a family recipe. It'll clean out your sinuses and marinate your tonsils."

"I'll just bet."

"You're flying the plane great, Jackson. We're nearly out of gas, huh?"

"We should make it to that island."

"It doesn't look very big."

"No." He glanced over at her. "So what happened when Uncle Rufus went out to investigate the noise?"

She motioned him to face forward. "Keep your eyes on the road. Or on the sky. Whatever. Don't look at me."

He'd rather look at her than at the tiny island they were headed for, and it wasn't as if he had to worry about running into anything up here. But obviously she expected him to look out the windshield while he was flying the plane, so he did that.

"That's better. Why didn't you shave this morning?"

"Got up too late." And it suddenly hit him that if he'd missed this plane, she wouldn't have had a prayer of getting out alive. She barely had one now, but there was a slim chance he'd be able to set this thing down without killing them both.

She sighed. "Jackson, you simply have to pay better attention to your grooming. I'm sure Matt didn't want you going to Aloha Pineapple looking like you just climbed out of bed."

"I was planning to buy a razor and some shaving cream in the drugstore and shave before I went to Aloha." He felt like a little kid being reprimanded, which didn't fit in with his hero schtick at all.

"I'm relieved to hear that. You have a really nice profile, you know."

"I do?" He sat up a little straighter.

"What I can see of it between the bristles sticking out all

over that chin of yours. It's hard to believe you grew those porcupine quills in one night. Looks like they could take the rust off a tailpipe."

He laughed. All these months he'd been daydreaming about a Genevieve who was cool and sophisticated, way too cool and sophisticated for the likes of him. He loved being wrong.

"Um, Jackson, if we're going to land on that sorry excuse for an island, don't you have to start getting lower?"

He did, but the whole concept had him dripping with sweat. He shoved gently forward on the wheel and the nose dropped, giving him a view of more ocean and island, less view of sky. He hated to lose the sky. Flying through it at a steady speed had begun to appeal to him. If the bastard had put more gas in the plane, they could have gone on.

He had no idea what that might have accomplished, without a radio. He'd still have to land all by himself, and in a more populated area he might take out some other innocent folks in the process. No, it was better to land out here. His stomach pitched.

"I don't see anyplace that looks flat." Genevieve's voice trembled slightly.

"Me, either." The island jutted out of the ocean like a chocolate cake made by a six-year-old—brown lava rock with a few decorations of green along the steep sides and near the bottom, where a small crescent beach shone ivory in the sun. The top of the island reminded him of a pitted moonscape. He'd be surprised if it was more than two hundred yards across. There was no sign of life.

"What are we going to do?" The tremble in her voice was more pronounced.

He could only see one option. "Can you swim?"

"Swim?" Panic edged her words. "What do you mean, can I swim?"

"*Can you swim?*" He was yelling, but he couldn't help

it. If she couldn't swim, he didn't know how the hell they'd survive, because he didn't think he could get them both to shore. He steepened the descent and cut the speed. He could see whitecaps now.

"Yes, I can swim! Are you telling me we have to land in the water?"

"I don't see any alternative." He clenched the wheel, clenched his teeth, even clenched his toes. If there was a coral reef just under the surface, they were done for. "I'll try to put it down as close to that beach as I can get without running into the cliff. Once we hit the water, we—"

"Hit the water? Can't you just settle the plane gently down into the water?"

"Look, this is not the fucking *Millennium Falcon,* okay?"

"Don't get all mad at me! I'm not the one who got us into this."

"No, it was your precious boyfriend Nicky, wasn't it? What did you ever see in that slick talker, anyway?" The water drew closer.

"He seemed very nice! I suppose you knew all along that he was a murderer, because you're so *smart.* Tell me, Mr. Smarty-Pants, if you didn't trust him, why did you come on this trip?"

"Because Matt asked me." God, they were coming in too fast, the water skimming along underneath them. He worked with the flaps, hoping that would help. It seemed to, a little. "And because I thought—"

"What? Oh, Jackson, we're going to die, aren't we?"

"I don't know." But he thought they might, so he decided to tell her. "I came on this trip mostly because of you. I thought I might be able to help you when Brogan broke your heart."

"That's so sweet. I take back calling you Mr. Smarty-Pants." Her voice was thick, like she might be crying. "You *are* smart, though, and I admire that. And you've always been nice to me, especially on this trip, when I was scared."

"I'm sorry I'm not a better pilot."

"You're doing your best."

"Okay, I'm going to cut the motor. We'll go down pretty fast after that. Once we're down, get out of the plane as quick as you can and start swimming for the beach. Don't try to find me first. Just start swimming."

"Okay. Same with you. Just start swimming."

"And you're sure you can swim?"

"Yes." She choked back a sob. "Every kid in the Hollow learns to swim."

"Good. Cover your head with your arms." He cut the motor.

Waiting for the impact was horrible, and it seemed to take forever. Genevieve had time for plenty of regrets and prayers and loving thoughts for the mother and brother she might never see again. Would the plane never land?

Then it did, and she wished it hadn't. The water had no give to it, and they hit so hard the windshield cracked. She tasted blood and knew she'd bitten her tongue.

Still, she was alive.

"Let's get the hell out of here!" Jackson shouted.

And thank God, so was Jackson. As water poured in from the open cabin door, she struggled to unfasten her seat belt.

"Come on, Gen!" Jackson shouted again.

"I'm trying!" She concentrated harder on the seat belt as the water level in the cockpit rose almost to her knees. At last the seat belt came free. Then she couldn't think what to do next.

Jackson was already on his feet. "Through the back door, damn it!" He started to lift her out of her seat.

"I'm going!" Shitfire, she didn't want him worrying about her. He'd said it would be every man for himself. She waded through the plane to the open door, took a quick look to make sure she knew where the beach was, and realized she'd lost her right contact. She shut her right eye and looked through her left.

"Go!" Jackson yelled in her ear.

"I'm going!" The beach still seemed much too far away. She was used to swimming for enjoyment, not distance. Oh, well. She launched herself into what she prayed weren't shark-infested waters and starting swimming as fast as she could.

The crawl stroke, her old reliable method of getting herself through the water in a hurry, was twenty times harder while wearing a dress, jacket, and high-heeled sandals. But stopping to take them off could leave her a sitting duck for Jaws and all his relatives. She kept going until her arms ached and her lungs burned. At least the water was warm, but after a while she forgot to be thankful for that because her body was in such agony.

Finally she switched to the breast stroke and squinted through her left eye again. The beach didn't appear to be much closer, damn it. Maybe she should just drown and get it over with. Then she wouldn't care what ate her.

"First one to the beach gets a Starbucks Mocha Frappuccino!"

Treading water, she turned her head and saw Jackson bobbing about two yards away. Without his glasses on. "Can you see?"

"Sort of." He swam a little closer. "At least I recognized you."

"Very funny." Treading water like this let her catch her breath, although she didn't want to think of what could be circling her, waiting to move in and take a big juicy bite. But as long as she was taking a break, she might as well work herself out of her shoes. "Did you lose your glasses?"

"Nope. Tucked them inside my underwear."

She assumed that meant he wore tighty whiteys instead of boxers. Knowing Jackson, that figured. She nudged one shoe off and glanced back to where they'd left the plane. Nothing but water. "The plane's gone." She felt even more vulnerable now that their link to civilization had sunk beneath the waves.

"I know. Come on," he said. "Race you to the beach."

"I'll be lucky if I get to the beach. Couldn't you have landed a little closer?"

"I should have, huh? I totally forgot that the water taxis aren't running at this hour." He grinned at her.

"Jackson, did you take a blow to the head? In case you haven't noticed, we're in a heap of trouble here."

"I suppose."

"You *suppose*? First there's the swim to the beach, where we might either drown or be gobbled up by sharks. Then once we get to the beach we have no supplies, no flares, no nothing." And no shoes for her, now that she'd kicked off the second one. But she was used to being barefoot.

"Yeah, but did you notice that we're not up in the air anymore?"

"Well, sure, but—"

"I landed the plane! And I didn't kill us! Gen, that's *awesome*."

"I guess it is."

"I can hardly believe I did that."

She'd never noticed that his eyes were blue, maybe because they were usually bloodshot and covered by smudged lenses. She'd have better luck finding him a girlfriend if she could get him into contacts. Then again, maybe he looked better because one of her contacts was missing. She closed her right eye and used only her left. And there he was, still fairly date-worthy.

"Are you winking at me?"

"No. I lost one contact."

"Oh. For a minute there I thought you might be trying to hit on me."

She knew he was joking, and yet something in his voice told her it wasn't totally a joke. Before the plane crashed he'd said something about coming on this trip so that he could help her. Was it at all possible that Jackson had a crush on her? Now, that would be awkward.

"Come on," he said. "Let's get moving."

"Okay." Taking a breath, she started swimming toward shore again, and not having her shoes helped considerably. She would make it, damn it.

But distressingly soon her arms began to ache again and she grew short of breath. She switched to the breast stroke and then the side stroke, always aware of Jackson swimming steadily beside her. Whenever she slowed, he slowed. He was keeping pace with her. She just wasn't sure she'd be able to keep pace with him.

They needed to discuss it. She stopped swimming and began treading water again.

He noticed immediately and followed suit. "Need a break?"

She nodded, too winded to speak. But he didn't seem winded at all. She'd never have guessed he'd be in good physical shape. She'd assumed that he spent all his time in front of the computer and never got any exercise.

"You can make it, Gen," he said.

She liked the way he'd started calling her Gen instead of using her full name. It made them seem closer, like buddies, and right now she needed that feeling, because he was her only hope. But she didn't want to put him in more danger because she wasn't up to the challenge.

"It's not much farther," he said.

She glanced toward shore and was even more discouraged when the vision in both eyes was blurry. "I lost my other contact."

"When we get there you can wear my glasses."

His gentleness made her want to cry. "I'm not sure I'm going to get there," she said. "I'm so tired." She looked at him with a mixture of admiration and frustration. "How come a brainiac like you swims like an Olympic athlete?"

He tread water and gazed at her. "Nerds work out, too, you know."

"You belong to a gym?" She couldn't picture it.

"No. I have a whole setup at home. I work out when I'm thinking about a project, and since I'm usually thinking about a project, I work out a lot."

"Well, I don't work out at all, and I'm fading fast. I want you to go on ahead."

"Like hell."

"No, really, Jackson. Don't be noble. You said that when we left the plane we'd both have to fend for ourselves. That's the way it should be."

"That was just to get you started. I never planned to abandon you."

And she didn't want him to, either. But he might have to, for his own good. She wouldn't drag him down with her. "Look, it's stupid for both of us to drown or get chewed on by sharks. You go ahead and I'll either make it . . . or I won't."

His expression tensed. "Do you imagine for one minute that I'm the kind of guy who would leave you out here?"

Until now, she'd never thought about what kind of guy he was, and he was surprising her at every turn. "I know you wouldn't want to, but be realistic."

"Are you done in? Is that what you're saying?"

"Not completely, but close."

"Can you float okay?"

"Jackson, I want you to—"

"Can you float?"

The edge to his voice took her aback. That was twice now he'd shown a tough side she'd never imagined good old Jackson would have. The first time was when he'd demanded to know if she could swim. She was beginning to realize that if she'd said she couldn't, he'd have tried to land the plane on the top of the island, no matter how impossible it had looked. For whatever the reason, he'd appointed himself her protector.

"Yes, I can float," she said.

"Then get on your back. I'm towing you in."

"No. That will take twice as much energy, and I don't care how often you work out, you're going to get tired."

His expression was like granite. "I'm not leaving you. You can either get on your back and let me tow you in or we can stay here and tread water until you're too exhausted to move, and then I'll tow you in, but by then I'll be more tired, so we'll both be at greater risk."

"You're not towing me. I'm swimming." And she set off, although every muscle in her body protested. Damn his noble hide. He was liable to kill himself trying to help her. She couldn't let him do that.

Chapter 5

Jackson swam beside her, painfully aware of her gasping, flailing struggle to make it to shore. But she had grit, and she wasn't about to let him help her until she couldn't move another muscle. Thank God they were getting close to the beach and the swell of the incoming waves lifted them toward the water's edge. They would make it.

Then, without warning, she sank.

He dove under the water, eyes open, and saw her gliding slowly down toward a bed of coral, her muscles limp. He got to her right before she reached the coral, which looked sharp as glass. Hooking an arm beneath her breasts, he surged upward, dragging her with him.

When they broke the surface, they were both sputtering and coughing. He figured as long as she was making noise, she wasn't going to drown on him, so he started swimming with one arm and pulling her through the water with the other. Stupid, stubborn woman.

But she'd been right. Swimming this way was hard, much harder than he'd imagined when he'd suggested it a while ago. If she hadn't pushed herself to go as far as she had, they might have both gone down. As it was he had to call on every ounce of endurance he had to keep swimming.

His soggy clothes felt like the lead apron his dentist laid

over him before she took X rays. Good thing he'd ditched his shoes long ago, and per usual, he'd forgotten socks in the process of getting dressed. That seemed years ago. He stopped to test the bottom with a foot, only to discover it was still over his head.

The third time he lowered his foot, his toe touched sand. With a choked sob of gratitude, he stood in chest-deep water and cradled Genevieve in his arms. Her eyes were closed, but she was breathing. That was all that mattered right now.

He focused on the beach as he started walking through the water. Breaking surf threatened to knock him over. He clenched his jaw and clutched Genevieve tighter, not about to fall down, not about to lose her.

"We . . . made it?"

At the faint sound of her voice, he looked down and saw that her eyes were open, but she looked dazed and disoriented. "We made it," he said, his voice hoarse.

She closed her eyes again. "Thank you . . . Jack."

Jack. He'd never encouraged the nickname because he thought it sounded like a kind of guy who drove fast cars and hung out with glamorous women, the kind of guy who drank whiskey straight up and never let work interfere with pleasure. The kind of guy Jackson wasn't.

But he'd just successfully flown a plane, ditched it in the ocean, and managed to get himself and his lovely passenger safely to shore. The nickname Jack didn't sound quite so inappropriate after all that. If Genevieve wanted to call him Jack, then he'd let her do that.

"You're welcome," he said. About that time he reached the point where the water no longer supported her weight, and he nearly dropped her.

She opened her eyes again and turned her head to look at the waterline only a short distance away. Her voice was unsteady. "You can put me down now. I can walk the rest of the way."

"I'll carry you in." At least he wanted to try. Somebody named Jack would definitely do that.

She looked up at him. "You're panting. You're fixin' to drop me."

"I am not." He noticed that her Tennessee accent was even more pronounced, as if the deeper they got into this mess, the more she was reverting to the little hillbilly she once was. He loved watching it happen, because it made her more accessible.

"Jackson, put me down."

"The name's Jack, and I'm finishing this rescue the way I want to."

"Your name's Jack?"

"Yeah. You called me that a minute ago, and I've decided I like it."

"I probably called you that because I was too exhausted to say your whole blessed name."

He was disappointed to discover that had been the reason, but there was no backing down from the new name now. He felt like a different person, and he might as well be called something different, too. "Be that as it may, I'm going to be Jack from now on." He couldn't feel his arms anymore, but he only had a little way to go.

"All right, Jack it is then. Now put me—"

He stumbled, she screeched, and they landed in a pile at the edge of the water. She came down on her back, her arms flung out to the side, and he ended up on his stomach with his cheek resting on her right breast, his right arm across her stomach and his leg on hers. Neither of them moved as the water ebbed and flowed over their feet.

"I knew it," she said. "I knew you were fixin' to drop me."

He felt boneless, as if he couldn't change positions if his

life depended on it. At least this time it didn't. He wasn't sure if his catatonic state had to do with his absolute, total exhaustion or the miracle of pillowing his head on her breast.

By sheer luck the jacket to the dress had flipped back when she went down, so he had only one thin layer of soaked fabric between him and a part of Gen's anatomy he'd never expected to experience up close and personal. As her chest rose and fell with her breathing, he became convinced she was not wearing a bra.

"I wonder what we should do next," she asked.

"Think," he murmured. Thinking wouldn't require him to go anywhere, and he liked where he'd ended up.

"I wonder how long before they come looking for us."

"They might have started already." He knew they needed to be rescued, but he hoped it would take a few hours. "Depends on how soon the Maui folks called Matt to ask why we haven't shown up."

She lay quietly, just breathing.

He was very happy to have her do that. Eventually she might ask him to move, but until she did, he was staying put.

"You know what I think?" she asked.

"What?"

"I'll bet Nick didn't have a meeting definitely set up, after all. I'll bet he said he might make it over there, and he might not. That way more time could go by before anyone would ask about us. But I did tell my mama I'd call her when I got there. She might think I just forgot, though."

"Well, what about my meeting with Aloha? Won't they call and ask why I'm not there?"

"I don't want you to take this wrong, but they might not call." And then, unbelievably, she began to stroke his wet hair.

He couldn't take anything wrong while she did that. He

closed his eyes and reveled in it, afraid to say a word for fear she'd stop.

"See, you're taking it wrong. Now I've insulted you." She continued to finger-comb his hair. "But you have to admit that you're not the most reliable person when it comes to getting to places on time. Everybody knows that."

"I get distracted."

"I know."

As she continued her gentle caress, he began to wonder if he'd saved them after all. Maybe they'd died in the crash and all of this was taking place in heaven. He could be convinced of that. He could easily be convinced.

"But you weren't distracted today, when we were up against it and trouble was coming at us six ways to Sunday. You focused on what had to be done and you purely did it. I owe you my life, Jack."

"'S okay." Now, there was a brilliant response. Sure could tell he was a magna cum laude with verbal skills like that. But he would trade all his degrees and half his IQ for a kiss from the woman who was touching him so sweetly. He wondered if she'd consider a kiss in return for him saving her life.

"Jack, do you have a crush on me?"

His tongue stuck to the roof of his mouth. He wished to hell she hadn't phrased it like that. A crush sounded like high school. And yet, come to think of it, he had acted like a high school kid with her, hanging around hoping for a little of her time, dreaming of her but never working up the courage to ask her out.

Even now, he was lying here afraid to move because she might stop petting him, like some grateful dog who would do anything for a little kindness. A guy named Jackson would behave like that, but not a guy called Jack.

"You're not saying anything, so I'll take that to mean

yes. And I want you to know that I think that's very sweet, but—"

"I don't have a crush on you."

"Oh." She stopped stroking his hair.

Summoning what little strength he had left, he propped himself up and gazed down at her. Her usually glossy hair was a tangled mess, and the ocean had washed off every bit of her makeup. But her eyes were still that blue-green color that reminded him of a tropical lagoon picture he'd used once as a screen saver. He'd loved the color of the water in that screen saver.

As mesmerizing as her eyes were, though, he couldn't help noticing that her dress was nearly transparent. He tried to keep his gaze focused on her face, but there were her nipples, showing through the material. It was probably the dampness that made them stick up like that.

He wondered what she'd do if he cupped her breast and rubbed a thumb over her nipple. But he wouldn't do that without knowing she wanted him to. Besides, although he loved looking at her and imagining making love right here in the sand, he wasn't certain he had the energy at the moment.

"A crush is for kids, Gen," he said.

She watched him with a wary look in her eyes. "Did I make you mad, saying that?"

"No."

" 'Cause you look kind of like Uncle Rufus's bull when we'd pull his tail and get him riled up."

Nobody had ever described him that way, and he thought it sounded good. Intimidating. Sexy. "I just need you to remember that I'm not a kid."

"I didn't mean you were a kid. I just wondered if you felt something for me."

"I do."

"That's what I th—"

"And it's not a crush," he said, cutting her off. "Let me demonstrate what I mean." A guy named Jack would be at least this bold. He quickly lowered his head and settled his mouth over hers.

She gasped in surprise, but he kept on kissing her. She tasted like saltwater taffy, and at first she was just about as stiff. But he hung on to the image of her lips as a candy treat, and sure enough, they began to soften.

Although he found that encouraging, he didn't for one minute think that he was turning her on. After the first shock of realizing that he was kissing her, she'd probably decided to be nice. After all, she thought she owed him her life. He'd probably get this one chance to kiss her, and then it would be business as usual. He'd only be able to work this hero thing for a little while.

She might not get a whole lot out of this moment, but he intended to milk it for all it was worth. He shifted his angle slightly and got a little more intimate with that warm mouth of hers. Her breath caught again. She obviously hadn't expected him to get serious about this.

He was very serious. He'd been fantasizing this kiss for months, and he'd damn near had to kill himself to get it. At a time like this, a guy named Jack would get tongues involved. So he did.

To his surprise, she let him get away with that. After a very short while, she even began to participate. She must feel *really* grateful. He wasn't about to look a gift kiss in the mouth, so he settled in for more fun and games. He explored and tasted to his heart's content, and the more he did that, the more content his heart became.

The rest of him was feeling pretty darned delighted, too. His cuts didn't sting anymore and his muscles were springing back to life. And oh, yeah, he wished he'd stowed his glasses in a different spot. The earpiece was digging into his expanding penis.

He kept expecting her to pull away, but instead she became more enthusiastic with each passing second. Maybe it was more than gratitude. Maybe the near-death experience had made her want to live for the moment, and for the moment, he was handy. That worked for him. Normally he wasn't very skilled at being at the right place at the right time, but today he was golden.

By now they were both breathing hard, and he thought of a scene from an old movie his grandma loved, where the couple got jiggy on the beach in the surf. *From Here to Eternity.* That was a sentiment he could relate to, kissing Gen this way.

He was so engrossed in the hot, wet taste of her mouth that he nearly missed the fact that she'd arched her back. When he finally received the message she was sending, he nearly passed out from excitement. She wanted him to touch her breasts.

His hand was all sandy, but he wasn't going to reach under her dress, anyway. That would be pushing his luck and potentially ruining his future chances, especially if he sandpapered her soft skin. That's when he remembered that he'd probably already rubbed her face raw with his beard. Instantly he lifted his mouth away from hers. "I'm sorry," he said, panting hard. "I forgot about my beard. I—"

With a moan she grabbed his head and pulled it down again.

Okay! She didn't care about his beard! She didn't care about anything but going for it! A moment didn't get any better than this. Well, it would be a lot better if he hadn't tucked his glasses in his underwear. He hoped he didn't poke out a lens, but he couldn't worry about that now.

Once he cupped her breast, he had absolutely no worries. Not a single one. Kissing and squeezing, kissing and squeezing. He could keep it up forever, especially when she moaned like that. She had some sexy moan. If he could program it into the sound card of his computer, he'd stay permanently aroused.

Her kiss became more feverish, and he wondered if she was losing touch with reality and forgetting who she was kissing. Probably. In that case, he might be able to try . . . anything.

His heart hammered at the idea. But he wasn't quite beyond reason. That might be one of his failings, that he never let himself go, not completely. Someday he might curse himself for not taking full advantage of this situation. But he wasn't going to.

Knowing that, he figured he'd better ease up on the kiss. A guy could be noble for only so long, listening to a woman moan the way Gen was moaning. He changed from full mouth contact to tiny nibbles, and at last, he lifted his head and took his hand, very reluctantly, from her breast.

Slowly she sank back to the damp sand, her eyes closed. He watched her, waiting to see what would happen when she opened those eyes. He had some time to study her face, and sure enough, his beard had given her a case of whisker burn. He wasn't proud of that.

More time went by, and she still hadn't dared to open her eyes, but her cheeks were now an even deeper color, and it wasn't all from whisker burn. She was blushing.

Finally he couldn't stand it any longer. "Gen?"

"I can't believe I let you do that."

So she regretted giving him liberties. He shouldn't be surprised, shouldn't even be disappointed, but he was. "Look, nobody ever has to know. You can trust me."

She opened her eyes. "I know I can. But it's your opinion that I'm worried about."

"My opinion of you hasn't changed." That wasn't exactly true. He'd always wondered whether she'd be cool and sophisticated in bed. Not from this new information.

Too bad this was the first and last time he'd get a glimpse of her passion potential. It had been exciting while it lasted.

"I'll bet you're just saying that to make me feel better. I've acted like a . . . like a tramp."

He decided they both needed to lighten up. "Boy, you sure know how to hurt a guy. I thought it was my manly sex appeal that caused all this."

"You *do* have manly sex appeal, Jackson." She seemed quite amazed by the discovery.

"Jack." He'd hold onto that, at least.

"Okay, *Jack*. I never would have thought so, but with your beard, and—"

"It was rough on your face. I'm sorry about that."

"The beard made all the difference. When you kissed me I felt like a maiden captured by a pirate, a maiden who had been flung down on the sand and . . . well, you know what I mean."

"Ravished?" He liked the sound of that. He'd never been accused of ravishing anyone before.

"I guess *ravished* would be the word. I think what we went through today knocked me off-center, and I plumb forgot who you were."

Ouch. He cleared his throat. "Yeah, me, too." Like he'd ever forget who she was. "Anyway, I enjoyed myself, and I . . . hope you did."

"I did, too, Jack."

He gazed down at her and wished they could do it all again. But they probably wouldn't, because now she'd come to her senses.

"And I want to thank you."

"For?"

"For . . . for everything. I couldn't have asked for a better person to be stranded with than you. You've been wonderful."

He had the definite feeling that with that comment she

was putting the lid on the gratitude jar. There would be no more kisses given because she appreciated all he'd done for her, no more caresses invited because she'd almost died and wanted to vent some of that pent-up emotion with someone she pretended was a pirate. The window of opportunity had been closed and latched.

He smiled at her. Something was better than nothing, and today he'd had more than he'd ever bargained on. "You're welcome," he said.

Genevieve felt marginally better after talking it out with Jack, but she still wondered how she'd face him in the office once they were rescued and had returned to their regular routine. It might take months for this moment to fade from their memories. It might never go away, and whenever he approached her desk or they met at the water cooler, they'd both be thinking of lying on the sand together with his hand squeezing her breast.

She needed to make sure that nothing else embarrassing happened before they were rescued. She didn't know exactly when that would be, but at least by tomorrow people should start looking for them. In the meantime, she and Jack needed to figure out how to make themselves comfy.

"I'm getting up, so I can look around this place. Maybe we'll find something to eat."

He moved to allow her to sit. "Eat? What could we possibly find?"

"I don't know yet. We'll have to look." She got to her feet and dusted off her clothes, which were beginning to dry in spots. In the process she noticed her fingernails were a mess. She held them up close so she could examine the damage better. "Ugh. Mama spent so much time trying to make my nails look good, and now they're a wreck."

"Is that what she does for a living?"

"Yes. She's very good, too. She—" Genevieve stopped talking when she glanced over to where Jack was standing. He'd unzipped his pants and was fumbling around in his underwear. She stared at him. "Jack! What in the name of heaven are you doing?"

"Getting my glasses." He pulled them out, put them on, and then proceeded to zip his pants and buckle his belt.

"You could warn a girl, you know! Even down in the Hollow a guy yells a warning if he's going to unzip!"

"Sorry." His cheeks grew pink. "I didn't think you were looking."

"Well, I wasn't, but then—I mean, anybody would notice. We all grew up fast in the Hollow, but most everybody maintained the common decencies."

His gaze grew less embarrassed and more speculative. "What do you mean, grew up fast?"

She should have known he'd pick up on that. She hadn't meant to say it, especially after the way she'd let him touch her breast a while ago. "My cousin Lurleen was pregnant at the age of twelve." Finally she decided it didn't matter if she told him. Let him think what he wanted. "I lost my virginity when I was thirteen," she said. "Later than most."

"That's still very young."

"People expect that to happen back home." She paused. "I suppose you think that's why I let you . . ."

"I wasn't thinking that."

"Because it's not the reason. I moved here and changed myself. I'm not that kind of girl anymore."

"Gen, I know that."

"You probably think because I was going off for a night alone with Nick that I'm the kind of person who does that, but I don't. I thought Nick was going to be my future husband."

"*Nick?*"

It sounded ridiculous now, so she decided to shut up about it.

But Jack didn't want to shut up about it. "How in hell could you have decided that? Even before I knew he was a murdering, crazy son of a bitch, I knew he was a self-centered, womanizing—"

"I thought that was because of his childhood. Matt told me he had a terrible childhood. I thought that I would be the one who could—oh, never mind! You wouldn't understand!" She turned and started off down the beach.

"Wait." Jack's bare feet thumped through the sand as he ran after her. "Don't get mad, Gen." He caught her arm and turned her around. "I didn't mean to sound critical."

"Yes, you did. You think I'm an idiot for thinking I could find true love with Nick Brogan. And obviously I was."

"No, you weren't. Maybe you were a little too romantic, but that's no crime. You were looking for the best in him, just like you look for the best in everyone, including me. That's what I want to tell you, that I've appreciated the way you've always tried to be friendly, and polite, and give me good advice. You're a very caring person."

"Thank you, Jack. That's a nice thing to say." She gazed up at him. His eyes were getting all smoky again, like they had right before he'd kissed her the last time. She was not about to let that happen again. "Come on," she said. "I think I see a guava tree growing down by that crevice in the rocks. And I'm starving."

Chapter 6

Every time the phone rang in the beauty salon, Annabelle stopped what she was doing and listened to see if it was for her. She was in the middle of a pedicure when the phone rang again, and she was so sure that it had to be Genevieve that she lifted her client's foot from her lap and started to get up.

But it wasn't Genevieve, obviously, because Elena, the receptionist, didn't come to get her. She settled back down and reached for a bottle of burgundy polish.

"Are you expecting a call?" asked her client. Judi was tall, tanned, and covered in gold jewelry. She tipped very well.

Annabelle liked her. She liked most of her clients, and she'd learned not to envy them their privileged lifestyle. "Genevieve flew over to Maui today," she said, trying to make that seem like an ordinary occurrence. "She usually calls."

"Oh, she probably got busy." Judi was at least ten years older than Annabelle, but she'd taken great care of herself, so she didn't look fifty. She had two grown sons living on the mainland. "You know how kids are. They never realize how we worry."

Genevieve realizes. But Annabelle smiled, as if she understood these things as well as Judi. But she didn't. She had a different relationship with Genevieve than Judi had with her Ivy League–educated sons. Annabelle and Genevieve had been through a lot together. Genevieve would remember to call. She might have been rushed right into a meeting, though, so Annabelle told herself to be patient.

"I'm surprised Genevieve hasn't talked about going back to the mainland," Judi said. "That's all Curt and Eric could think about while they were in high school. Isn't it funny that Hawaii is supposed to be paradise, but kids seem just as eager to leave here as they would if we raised them in some dinky little town in Iowa?"

"I guess they have to spread their wings," Annabelle said. She felt guilty that she hadn't been able to let Genevieve do that, but she needed the money her daughter brought in, at least for another couple of years. She hoped money wasn't behind Genevieve's interest in this Nick person. The girl hadn't been raised to covet wealth, but maybe she was tired of working so hard to make ends meet. Nick wasn't the answer, though. Annabelle could tell that the minute she'd met him.

"How's Lincoln doing these days?" Judy asked. "Still with the wild hair?"

"Still," Annabelle said. "He's gone patriotic for the summer. Red, white, and blue."

"Oh, my God." Judi rolled her eyes. "You're very understanding. I'm not sure I would have been able to deal with Curt and Eric dyeing their hair. And their father would have hit the roof." She paused. "Brad and I are getting along better these days, Annabelle. He's mellowed a lot. We're even enjoying sex more."

"That's wonderful." Annabelle smiled again. It always amazed her how much her clients would reveal about themselves. She knew nearly everything about them, and they knew almost nothing about her, except that she was single and had a daughter working for Rainbow Systems and a son in high school who loved to dye his hair crazy colors. They'd never heard about the Hollow, and they never would. She didn't want them to think of her as a hillbilly.

"The menopausal years are tough, you know?" Judi shook her head. "Although you seem to be doing fine. I swear you don't look a day over forty, Annabelle. Maybe more like thirty-five or six."

"You don't look your age, either," Annabelle said, knowing it was expected. "Nobody does these days." She'd always let Judi assume she was older to cover up the fact she'd been pregnant at fifteen. "Are we doing anything special for these toes besides the burgundy polish?"

"What do you suggest?"

"Tiny white orchids might be nice."

"Perfect. You're such an artist, Annabelle. I have a friend from California visiting next week, and I've already told her she has to come in and get a manicure and pedicure while she's here."

"That would be great. I'd love to meet her." Annabelle had learned to say that instead of *I appreciate the business*. She did appreciate the business, but it was better to act as if meeting Judi's friend were far more important than taking her money. In a way, that was true, but she needed the money, too. Lincoln's shoes alone cost an arm and a leg.

"You know, that's one thing about living in Hawaii— the kids decide to leave, but the friends and relatives show up regularly. I don't really mind, but sometimes I feel like I'm running a B and B."

"I'll bet you do."

"You probably find that, too. Do you have a lot of relatives coming over?"

"Not so much," Annabelle said. *Try never.* That part of her plan had worked out perfectly. Every once in a while she missed Maizie and Rufus, but she could bear it, just know-ing that Genevieve and Lincoln were headed for a better life.

After she painted tiny orchids on Judi's toes, she did her fingernails and created a conch shell pattern on those. By the time she was finished, it was nearly noon and still no call from Genevieve. She tried not to be nervous, but she had a gut feeling something was wrong.

She had a half hour for lunch, which wasn't enough time to do what she had in mind. She walked up to the re-ception desk and spoke with Elena. "I'm feeling a little sick to my stomach," she said. She hated lying, but she couldn't very well say she needed the time to drive to Rainbow Systems and check up on her daughter.

"Cramps?" Elena asked, sympathy in her almond-shaped eyes.

"Guess so." She'd never had cramps in her life. She was from backwoods people who didn't believe in such nonsense, and any minor cramps she'd had as a girl had been cured with a nip of Rufus's moonshine. "Would you reschedule my afternoon appointments? Please tell them I'm sorry."

"Sure," Elena said. "Go on home and take some Midol." She winked. "And I've heard that a good session with a vi-brator helps, too."

"Really? I didn't know that." She did, however, know about vibrators. After Lincoln's daddy had left and she'd sworn off men forever, she'd become intimately acquainted with them. She'd discovered that a woman could exist just fine if she had a good mechanic for her car and a vibrator tucked in her bureau drawer.

"See you in the morning," Elena said.

"Sure thing." Annabelle walked out into the summer heat. She could hardly wait for tomorrow morning to come, because by then she should know exactly where her daughter was.

Matt had forgotten what good sex with a willing partner could do to cure depression. After a night spent with Celeste, he felt like a new man. He tackled paperwork that had been sitting on his desk for weeks, and more than once he caught himself whistling. His secretary, Kendra, kept giving him funny looks, and he wondered if she suspected that he'd gotten laid last night. She might. Women were smart about things like that.

Frankly, he didn't care if she suspected. He'd been an object of pity long enough. But nobody needed to pity a guy who had managed to attract a twenty-three-year-old cutie like Celeste into his bed. He still wasn't sure why she'd suggested it, but they'd had a terrific time. She'd had him doing maneuvers he'd only read about in *Playboy*.

Yeah, he was kind of stiff this morning, but it was a good kind of muscle pain. Still, he'd decided not to take Celeste up on another round tonight. He wanted to maintain his image as a stud, and for that he needed at least eight hours of uninterrupted sleep. Tomorrow evening, though, they'd try a few more combinations. He thought the anticipation would do him good. He was a little short of events to anticipate these days.

When lunchtime arrived he'd about decided to go out for a change. Normally he ate at his desk, but the day was gorgeous and he felt like a drive and a shrimp salad someplace where he could look at the ocean while he ate. Before he could act on that plan, Kendra buzzed him.

"Annabelle Terrence is here to see you, Mr. Murphy. She says it's urgent."

Terrence. She had to be Genevieve's mother, and he wondered if she was here to question him about the behavior of his partner. He hoped not. Genevieve and Nick were both consenting adults, and although he didn't approve of Nick's little trips with female employees, he wasn't the guy's keeper. Or Genevieve's, come to think of it.

But he might as well see what the woman wanted. Maybe she was no relation to Genevieve. "Send her in."

The minute Annabelle Terrence walked into his office, he knew she was related to Genevieve, but he assumed she was an older sister. Her hairstyle, facial features, even her curvy figure reminded him of Genevieve. In her flowered sundress that bared toned arms and a graceful neck, she looked like she might be mid-to late thirties. He noticed she wasn't wearing a wedding ring.

Now this was more like the type of woman he should be taking to bed, he thought as he came around the desk. Then he silently reprimanded himself for such a boorish concept. He was supposed to be beyond the stage of seeing every woman in sexual terms. His night with Celeste must have set him back a few years and made him think like a crass young man again.

"I'm Genevieve's mother, Mr. Murphy," she said.

His eyes widened. Either she'd had cosmetic surgery or she'd had Genevieve when she was about twelve. Recovering himself, he extended his hand. "Nice to meet you." He registered warmth and firmness in her handshake. "Have a seat," he said, waving her into the chair in front of the desk. "And please call me Matt. We're not formal in this company."

She smiled, which made her look younger still. "So Genevieve has told me. She feels very lucky to be working here." She sat in the chair and put her little shoulder purse in her lap.

"She's an excellent employee." Leaning his hips against the desk, he found himself holding her gaze a little longer than he should. He liked her eyes, wide-set and a velvety gray. Celeste must have really flipped a switch somewhere deep inside him. Yesterday he hadn't thought that he'd ever be attracted to a woman again. Today he was ready to hit on Genevieve's mother. "What can I do for you?"

"It's about that trip she went on."

Damn, here it came. All thoughts of asking her out disappeared as he prepared to defend his partner's sleazy motives. He hated being put in this position, and he'd have a little talk with Nick when he got back.

"What about the trip?" he asked, realizing for the first time that she was agitated. She hid it well, but he'd become aware of the way she was folding the strap of her shoulder purse into tight little accordion pleats.

"She promised to call me when she got to Maui, and she didn't call."

This was getting weird. Most twenty-six-year-old women he knew didn't call their mothers a few hours after leaving the house. "She probably got busy."

"I thought that, too, but when noon came and she still hadn't called, I decided something had happened."

Wow. This woman was terminally overprotective. And of all things, she seemed to be concerned about the flight itself. In his opinion she should be less concerned about that and more upset about whether Nick pulled his usual trick of dumping his conquest once he brought her home again. "Mrs. Terrence, I'm sure—"

"Annabelle. You said you're not formal here."

That had been when he'd thought this was a social visit. "Sorry. I'm sure Genevieve is fine, Annabelle. My partner is an excellent pilot." *Not such a great guy, but an excellent pilot.*

"Matt, I'm here to beg you to call wherever they were supposed to go on Maui and find out if they arrived."

He swallowed. "Look, I'm sure she'll contact you this

afternoon, or maybe tonight, after the day's meetings are over. I—"

"*Please.*" She was actually quivering now.

And here he'd thought Genevieve had a fairly normal home life. Instead she lived with a paranoid mother. Poor Genevieve. From the terrified expression on Annabelle's face, he had the feeling that she'd break down if he didn't do as she asked. A sobbing woman wasn't going to improve the quality of his day.

With a sigh he moved around to his desk and picked up the phone. "Kendra, would you get me the Maui branch office, please?"

"Right away, Matt."

While he waited until she patched him through, he looked everywhere but at Annabelle Terrence. This was one of the stupidest things he'd had to do in a long while. He should have refused her, but she'd looked so desperate. He was also irritated with her for missing the obvious danger to her daughter. It had nothing to do with Nick's flying. Maybe Annabelle wasn't all that bright.

Finally Ed Modene from the Maui office came on the line to ask what he needed.

"I just thought I'd see how the meeting with Nick was going so far," Matt said, feeling more foolish than ever.

There was a pause. "Nick didn't make it over here."

Matt felt a little queasy. If Nick was using the company plane to conduct his brief affairs without even making a pretense of doing business at the same time, they had a real problem. "I thought he was planning to be there this morning, but maybe I misunderstood."

"We had a tentative meeting scheduled, but he said if he hadn't shown up by nine that would mean he wasn't able to make it, and we'd reschedule for next week. He didn't show, so we canceled the meeting."

"Guess I didn't get the word," Matt said.

Ed chuckled. "Nick's tough to pin down sometimes. Say, when are you coming over for another round of golf?"

"When my game's in better shape," Matt said, trying to sound jovial. "I can't take the humiliation."

"Come over anyway. You can play from the women's tees."

"Thanks a whole hell of a lot. Listen, I have to run. I'll check with Nick and make sure he gets back to you."

"Fine. See ya."

"Right." Matt hung up the phone and stood staring at it while he tried to think what he was going to say to Annabelle.

She beat him to it. "They didn't ever get there, did they?"

He looked up. Her eyes shone huge and bright in a face gone deathly pale.

"I'm sure they're there," he said.

"But—"

"For some reason he didn't go to the meeting, that's all." He didn't want to discuss the reason unless she was sharp enough to pick up on it.

"Call the Maui airport."

He ran a hand over his face. And the day had started out so well, too. "Look, I don't think that's necessary." He could also imagine why Genevieve hadn't called. Nick had been keeping her too busy.

"Then I will." She was on her feet before he knew it and reaching for his desk phone.

"The plane flight isn't the problem, damn it!"

She hesitated, her hand hovering over the phone, and stared at him.

He sighed. Might as well get it out in the open. "The reason you haven't heard from your daughter is that Nick flew them to Maui, checked them in to a hotel room, and . . . well, you should be able to figure out the rest."

"Tarnation! Do you think I have feathers for brains? I know good and well she went over there to have sex with that rooster!"

His jaw dropped. The cultured tone was gone, and in its place was something right out of *The Dukes of Hazzard*.

"I know perfectly well what that scalawag was up to, him and his fancy little black car," she barreled on. "But no matter what they've been doing all morning, she would have figured out some way to call me."

What little patience he had left evaporated. "For God's sake, wake up and smell the coffee! Your daughter, devoted though she may be, is not going to call you in the middle of a passionate rendezvous with a guy like Nick! Maybe things are different where you come from, but in this day and age, girls don't call their mothers during such events!" And if he was a little more outspoken than usual, it might be because he'd been uncomfortably reminded of what Celeste's mother would have thought of his own behavior last night.

"I'm wasting time." She turned and started out of the office. "I'll use somebody else's phone to call the Maui airport. They should be able to tell me if the Rainbow Systems plane landed there this morning or not."

"Annabelle, wait." Remorse hit him as he hurried after her and caught her arm before she reached the door. How could he relate to what a mother might feel at times like this? He didn't even have a father's insight. Damn, but Annabelle's skin was soft. "If I call the airport and the plane landed, will you let it go?"

She turned, her gaze stormy. "Yes."

"I know this doesn't look good, that Nick would behave this way, and I'll handle that situation when they get back."

She faced him, shaking off his grip as she did so. "Genevieve is a grown woman. Her sexual decisions are her own now. I didn't like your partner when I met him this morning, but if Genevieve has to have him, that's up to her. I'm the last person who should preach to her about her choices in men. But planes scare the stuffing out of me, and I need to know she's safe."

He felt like the worst heel in the world. Most everybody had something they were afraid of. He got kind of loony about snakes. With some people it was heights, with others it was spiders. Annabelle happened to be spooked by planes. No matter what was going on between Genevieve and Nick, Genevieve should have called, knowing how her mother felt.

"I'll call right now," he said quietly.

"Thank you."

Walking back to the desk, he picked up the phone again and asked Kendra to get him the Maui airport. Once he'd found out that the plane was on the ground, he could try to make amends to Annabelle by taking her to lunch. She might turn him down, but he'd ask.

If she turned him down, he could always send her flowers. Or maybe he'd take her to lunch *and* send her flowers. He was intrigued by Annabelle Terrence, who had obviously not grown up in Hawaii, or even Middle America. She might try to give that impression, but stress brought out her roots. Maybe over lunch he'd find out more about her.

Only one tiny detail prevented him from proceeding with that plan. The folks at the airport said that the Rainbow Systems plane was not there.

Jack was a fast-food kind of guy. Fruits and veggies were okay once in a while, but this guava tree that Gen seemed so excited about didn't do much for him. Maybe if he'd had a knife to cut them in half they'd have looked more appetizing, but they were kind of mangled by the time he'd used a rock to get them open and they looked sort of like puke. He made his way through a couple of the things, because at least they gave him some liquid and he was getting thirsty.

They'd found a spot in the shade where a ledge of lava rock hung slightly over the beach. Gen had taken off the jacket to her dress and was sitting cross-legged on that, and he'd done the same with his shirt. She looked damned good without her jacket, and watching her suck on those guavas was an experience in itself.

Then there was the matter of the way she was sitting. She had her skirt tucked modestly around her, but still, her thighs were spread, and his imagination was running overtime considering what lay between them. All in all, he didn't regret this experience, assuming they were rescued in a few hours.

"What I wouldn't give for a comb," Gen said as she tossed another guava rind out into the waves.

"What I wouldn't give for a McDonald's." Jack threw his rind and was gratified that it went a little farther out than hers. She had a darned good throwing arm for a woman. Normally he didn't care about such things, but he was getting into this manly man stuff and he liked having an edge.

"And my nails are hopeless." She looked down at the sand. "I wonder if I could take one of those sticky rinds to glue some sand onto and file my nails with it?"

"You might want to put that creativity into figuring out how we can signal to the rescuers."

She squinted at him. "Was that some sort of crack?"

"I just think we have more pressing matters to worry about than your manicure."

"I didn't say my nails were the most important thing. I was just thinking aloud, which I'll be careful not to do in the future, because *goodness*, I might think about something unimportant. I'm sure you always think important thoughts."

He wondered if imagining her topless qualified as an

important thought. It was occupying him quite a lot now that she'd taken off her jacket and he could watch her breasts jiggle when she moved.

"All right," she said. "Let's think about this rescue business. Should we get some rocks and spell out HELP on the sand?"

"We could."

"Do you think there's any chance Nick's still around here somewhere?"

He blinked. He'd been so absorbed in watching her breasts and thinking about how her mouth would taste with guava juice on it that he'd forgotten all about the maniac who had landed them in this predicament. "I doubt it," he said.

"Yes, but would you bet your prize rooster on it?"

He thought about that for a while and decided that if he had a prize rooster, he'd be cautious about making that bet. They might have flown east about the same distance they'd flown west, which could mean that the miniature island they were on could be the same one Brogan had used as a rendezvous point for his pickup men.

"I can see you're thinking along the same lines I was thinking," Gen said. "Nick could be sitting on another part of this island, waiting for his ride. We don't know which direction the boat's coming from, or whether they'd circle around for some reason."

"It's probably a long shot, though."

"Are you willing to take the chance?"

Jack thought about the look in Brogan's eyes when he'd delivered his last wisecrack before he'd jumped. There hadn't been a glimmer of conscience in those eyes. The man Jack had originally categorized as a self-absorbed asshole had turned out to be a full-blown sociopath, a genuine Ted Bundy kind of guy. Like Bundy, he'd perfected his facade over the years. But now that Jack had seen beneath it, he knew Brogan would stop at nothing to get what he wanted.

"No," he said at last. "I'm not willing to take the chance. This island's so small and rocky, I'd bet it's uninhabited, which makes it the perfect rendezvous spot for Brogan. We'd better not try to signal anybody yet. Let's give him time to get wherever he's going."

Gen tilted her head to look up the rocky face of the cliff. "Or we could climb to the top of this place and look around to see if he's waiting somewhere on the other side. Maybe we could get the jump on him and hold on to him until the rescuers come."

That decision was easy. He wouldn't jeopardize Gen's life. "Not in my wildest dreams." Putting her life in danger was enough of a reason that he wouldn't have to admit the other one, that the very thought of going up that cliff, which was high enough to be very scary, made his stomach pitch.

"You do realize that with all that money gone, Rainbow will be in a heap of trouble," Gen said.

"Matt might have insurance on Brogan."

"He might, but we'll have to say he's not dead, so what good is insurance?"

Jack sighed. "Well, not much. And I'm sorry about that, but you know as well as I do that Matt Murphy would never want us to risk our lives for the company."

"Of course he wouldn't, but think of all the people who could lose their jobs. When I think about that, I want to find Nick Brogan and . . . and feed his jingle-jangles to the hogs!"

Jack grinned. "I wouldn't mind feeding his jingle-jangles to the hogs myself. But the guy is too dangerous to fool with. I assume his buddies, when they show up, will have more guns and be willing to follow orders. So let's sit tight on this little beach until we can be reasonably sure he's gone."

Gen licked the guava juice from her mouth. "How long do you think we should wait?"

"To be on the safe side?" He had a hard time being totally logical when she moved her tongue like that and reminded him of what that tongue felt like deep inside his mouth. "If you think you can stand it, we should probably hold out until morning. Someone may come along and get us off before then, but by tomorrow morning I figure we can start trying to get some attention without having to worry about Brogan."

She nodded. "I can hold out, although I'd sure love to have my comb and some lip gloss."

Her lips looked plenty glossy to him. His problem would be spending all those hours with her without getting friendly again. "As long as we're wishing for stuff, I wouldn't mind having a laptop to keep myself occupied."

"This will be good for you, to get away from that blessed computer for a change. I've been meaning to say something to you about that. You need to get out more and away from that screen. Life is about more than staring at a computer screen."

"Would this little adventure qualify as getting out?" His irritation returned. She wanted him to get out and experience things, but she wasn't exactly offering to be part of the deal. "Because if it does, I think this should hold me for about ten years. I happen to enjoy the conveniences of the modern world."

She leaned forward. "I'll bet you grew up playing video games, didn't you?"

"What if I did?"

"I just think that kids need to be outdoors, to play marbles in the dirt instead of spending their afternoons clutching some joystick. We didn't have any electricity back in the

Hollow, so we didn't even know about video games. But we had plenty to do."

"So I gathered." He held her gaze long enough that she began to blush.

"That wasn't what I meant. I meant we made up our own games."

"Uh-huh. At least playing video games didn't end up with girls getting pregnant at thirteen."

"I shouldn't have told you anything about that." She stood up. "I'm going down to the water to rinse my hands off."

He watched her go and wished he hadn't let his irritation get the better of him. In actuality, he was curious about her life back in Tennessee, and he'd like to hear more about it. But when she'd started ragging on his beloved video games and making him sound like a nerdy little kid with no life, he hadn't appreciated it. He *had* been a nerdy little kid with no life, which made him even more sensitive on the subject.

She had a nice walk with a gentle sway to her hips that was sexy without being an obvious bid for attention. She wasn't trying to get his attention, anyway. He was a long way from being her fantasy man.

When she leaned over to wash her hands in the surf, he had a great view of her ass, but he supposed she didn't even care if he was sitting there enjoying the show. He could be her goddamned brother for all she cared. He probably should have made love to her when he'd had the chance, when she'd convinced herself he was a pirate. Women hardly ever got pregnant with a one-shot deal like that, so he wouldn't have been taking that big a risk.

But being the kind of guy he was, he'd had to think of that. Even if she'd been willing to spend all night doing the nasty, he wouldn't, because, oh darn, this island didn't come equipped with a condom dispenser.

She straightened and gazed out to sea, her hand shading her eyes. If she was half as blind as he was without glasses or contacts, she wouldn't be seeing much out there. But he understood the urge to scan the horizon for boats. He'd been doing it, too, whenever he wasn't admiring her breasts or her lips or her toes. He'd discovered a real fondness for her toes, which were especially long and elegant.

Without warning, she whirled and came running back, sand spurting from under her feet. "Jack! Jack, come look!"

He leaped up, heart hammering. "Brogan?"

"No. But I see something out in the water!" She grabbed his hand and started tugging him toward the line of surf. "I need you to come and look with your glasses."

He let himself be tugged. It was the first time he'd been able to touch her since the make-out session lying on the sand, and he loved the connection.

She stopped just short of the waterline. Still holding his hand, she pointed to something bobbing in the waves. "Can you see it?"

Sure enough, he could see something round and smooth out there. "Yeah, but I have no idea what it might be."

"Let me borrow your glasses. I think I know what it is."

He took them off and gave them to her. When she put them on, she instantly looked more serious, and he had to smile. She looked great in glasses, but she probably wouldn't think so.

"They're perfect for me!" she said with some surprise. "We must have the same prescription."

"Could be." He liked that idea. Something, at last, that they shared.

"It is!" she shouted. "It's my suitcase! Oh, Jack, would you fetch it for me?"

"Okay." He squinted in the direction she was staring. Without his glasses the round blob wasn't very distinct, but he could make it out. The thought of going back out into the water was about as appealing as having a vasectomy without anesthesia, but he would do it, for her. She didn't know it yet, but he would do anything she asked of him, on the slim chance that she'd discover that she was once again grateful for his efforts. She was a woman who really knew how to express her gratitude.

Chapter 7

Genevieve stood with the water lapping her ankles as Jack waded out into the surf in the direction of her suitcase. Her round pink suitcase! She'd been so ashamed of it this morning as she'd loaded it into Nick's trunk, and now she'd never seen such a beautiful thing in her life.

She wondered if it had stayed afloat because of its rigid construction. Nick's soft-sided suitcase might have sunk to the bottom. Come to think of it, his suitcase might have been stuffed with newspapers or rags. He couldn't have packed anything valuable in it, considering that he hadn't intended to take it with him in the first place.

Every time she thought of Nick Brogan she wanted to punch something or somebody. But she couldn't punch Jack, because he was the person who had saved the day. He also looked surprisingly good without his shirt. He was pale, though, and already starting to burn. Lucky for him she had both sunscreen and lotion in her suitcase.

And condoms. Why she suddenly remembered that was a mystery. She would not be using them with Jack, that was for sure. She already had enough to live down with that incident in the sand a while ago. One thing her mother had drummed into her head was that you didn't get physical with a man unless you thought he had marriage potential.

Jack would make a sorry husband. Try asking him to bring home a carton of milk and a loaf of bread from the store and see what you'd get. Probably a case of Coke and a package of Gummi Bears. Even those would arrive hours late because he wouldn't even remember to come home in the first place.

Genevieve wanted a man who would be attentive. Nick had fooled her into thinking he'd be attentive, but from the moment he'd picked her up at her house she'd started questioning that. Now she knew why he'd treated her so poorly, not opening doors or helping her in and out of places. He was fixing to kill her, so why bother?

Jack stopped wading and started swimming. His direction was a little off, probably because he couldn't see without his glasses.

She made a megaphone with her hands. "To the right!" she shouted.

He didn't act like he'd heard her, and he probably hadn't with the sound of the surf and the distance. The suitcase was farther out than she'd thought, but she was beginning to realize that distances were tricky on the ocean.

Jack stopped to tread water and look around. He must have spied the suitcase, because he set off in the right direction this time.

As she watched him head for it, her heart did a funny flip-flop. The minute she'd asked him to go after her suitcase, he'd started into the water without a single argument. He hadn't asked her what was so important in that suitcase, and he hadn't told her to wait and see if the tide brought it in.

Now that she considered how willing he'd been to plunge into the water on her behalf, she wondered if she should have asked, after all. He had a thing for her, no question, and it would be cruel to encourage him. Asking him for favors was a kind of encouragement, and she needed to watch herself on that.

About the time she was vowing not to make any more requests of him, she saw the shark fin, gliding like a toy sailboat along the water, a sailboat with a black sail instead of white. It was behind him, and he was concentrating on reaching for the strap of the suitcase, so he wouldn't have any idea what was coming.

"Jack!" Tossing his glasses up on the dry sand, she splashed into the surf, yelling his name and waving her arms. He paid no attention. She launched herself into the waves and swam as fast as she could. Yelling took too much breath, so she stopped doing that.

She switched to the breast stroke so she could see him, and here he came toward her, the strap looped over one arm and the suitcase bumping his back each time he stroked. At first she didn't see the fin and prayed the shark had gone away. But then she saw it again, not far behind Jack. She tried to call out his name and got a mouth full of water instead.

Coughing and sputtering, she sculled the water with one hand and pointed over his head with the other. He must have finally figured out her signal, because he turned his head. Then he started swimming like crazy.

"Leave the suitcase!" she yelled.

But he must not have heard her because he kept the suitcase, which only bumped more frantically against his back. Heart pounding, she tried to gauge whether he was putting any distance between him and the shark. And then, miracle of miracles, the shark turned and started back out to sea. She closed her eyes in relief.

Jack nearly ran her over. Grabbing her shoulder, he shoved her through the water toward shore. She started swimming just to keep him from manhandling her any more. She doubted that he'd understand her if she told him the shark was gone.

They stumbled out of the water together and both fell to their hands and knees, gasping for breath.

"I got"—Jack's chest heaved—"I got it." He slid his arm out of the strap.

"Oh, Jack." She glanced over at him crouching there, water running from his hair into his eyes, and she had the urge to hug him. She didn't, though, because that could lead to more of what had happened before. "I shouldn't have sent you out there."

He pushed back on his haunches and wiped the water from his face. It clung in bright droplets to his bristly beard. "You didn't know."

"I could have guessed. I know these waters are loaded with sharks." She eased to a cross-legged position and tucked her skirt around her legs. She should probably save the effort. The water had made her dress transparent again, so Jack could see about all there was to see.

He was looking, too. Fortunately he didn't have his glasses, so she'd be hazy, just like he was hazy to her. They probably both looked like dream people to each other, fuzzy and soft. But she could sort of see his belly button, so he could probably identify her nipples through the wet dress. She crossed her arms.

"Where are my glasses?"

Uh-oh. "I took them off before I dived in to save you. I tossed them up on the dry sand." She uncrossed her arms and stood, facing away from him as she tried to figure out where she'd been standing when she'd thrown the glasses. "I'm sure they're around here somewhere."

Jack got to his feet. "Let's hope they're around here somewhere. Couldn't you have set them down, like on a rock?"

"How could I think about where to set your precious glasses when I was sure you were going to be gobbled by a shark?" She surveyed the fuzzy landscape and started forward, hoping for a glint of sun off either the lenses or the metal frames.

"Those precious glasses are critical to this operation. Hey, don't walk too fast! You might step on them! Jesus."

Although his tone irritated her, Genevieve paused. He had a point. "What we need is one of those metal detectors. That's how they found Granny Neville's false teeth, with one of those things."

"If you're fantasizing, you might as well ask for something really useful, like a helicopter."

She faced him, no longer caring if her nipples showed or not. "Your mood is getting downright ugly, you know that? You're acting like a pup who got his nose stuck in a knot-hole, and I don't much appreciate it."

"Well, I don't much appreciate that you tossed my glasses into the sand! God knows if we'll find them again, with both of us blind as bats. And even if we do, sand is an abrasive. The lenses will be scratched all to hell."

She lifted her chin. "Oh, kiss my grits."

He stared at her. Then a snort of laughter popped out of him, followed by a chuckle and at last a full-blown belly laugh.

Watching Jack laugh was a novel experience. Now that she thought about it, she might never have seen him laugh like this, doubled over, holding his sides while tears ran down his cheeks. She wasn't sure why he was laughing, though. Maybe he'd finally cracked and this wasn't laughter but hysterics. That wouldn't be so good.

"Jack, are you okay?"

"Yeah." He swallowed and wiped his eyes. "Yeah, I'm good."

"What's so funny?"

He grinned at her. "Kiss my grits. That's what's funny."

"I think the sun is getting to you. There's nothing funny about that. People say it all the time back home."

"I'll bet they do." He continued to smile at her. "Now, c'mon. Let's get down on our hands and knees and crawl around until we find those glasses."

As Jack searched the warm sand for his glasses, he couldn't help glancing up once in a while to watch Genevieve on her hands and knees a short distance away. The woman he saw bore little resemblance to the poised secretary he'd lusted after, but this new version was even more tantalizing than the old.

He'd thought of her as cool and regal. Instead she was spirited and warm and funny as hell. And he'd love to kiss her grits, no matter what part of her anatomy that stood for.

"I found them!" She leaped to her feet, spraying sand everywhere as she waved his glasses by the earpiece. "And they're not broken or anything!" She slipped them on. "Well, okay, they might have a couple of scratches."

He sank back on his haunches and enjoyed his fuzzy view of Genevieve wearing his glasses. Even the prospect of scratched lenses didn't bother him as those wire rims transformed her into a studious sex kitten. He didn't know if there was such a category. If there was, she belonged in it— barefoot, her clothes wet and transparent, and her hair all mussed like she'd just climbed out of bed.

"They're smudged, though." She took off the glasses, breathed on each lens, and then lifted a corner of her skirt to polish them.

"Gen, let—" He clamped his mouth shut before another idiotic word came out. So her skirt was probably full of sand and she'd only make matters worse. She might ruin the damned glasses. But while she polished, he had a blurred but tantalizing view of her thigh.

"What?" She glanced at him.

"Nothing." Worrying about his glasses was a reflex. It

wasn't like he had a computer screen to deal with, so scratch-free glasses weren't a necessity right now, anyway.

"You were about to say something, Jack."

"I was going to say, let's go get your suitcase."

She frowned at him, as if she didn't believe a word of it. "No, you were going to say, *Let me clean my glasses my own self.*" She walked over and held out the glasses. "Here. Clean them however you want. I'm sorry I threw them in the sand."

That reminded him of why she'd done that. She'd seen a shark coming after him and she'd leaped right into the water to try and save him, risking herself in the process. Besides that, she'd had the presence of mind to toss his glasses up on the sand first instead of wearing them into the surf where they would have been lost forever.

He stood. "I'm the one who's sorry. I should be thanking you for coming out to warn me instead of biting your head off about the glasses. That was a brave thing you did."

Her chin lifted. "You think I'd let you get chomped by a shark while you were fetching my suitcase? That would be mighty ungrateful of me."

Ah, the gratitude thing. Maybe that was what made Gen stand out from the crowd—that deep sense of appreciation for whatever good things came her way. The women he'd known had grown up in suburbia where deprivation meant having their allowances docked or being grounded for a week.

He'd never thought of them as spoiled, but compared to Gen, they were. They'd had their choice of Reeboks or Nikes, while she might not have worn shoes until she was a teenager. His other girlfriends had taken their safe, middle-class lifestyle for granted. With her background, Gen never would. Not that she was his girlfriend.

"Well, thank you, anyway," he said. "Not everyone would have jumped into the water like that."

She flushed, almost as if his praise embarrassed her. "No

problem. I reckon we need to take care of one another while we're marooned, right?"

"Right." God, but he loved to listen to that down-home speech of hers. He supposed once they were rescued she'd quit talking like that, and he'd definitely miss it.

"Now take your glasses." She wiggled them at him. "They're scratched, but they're better than nothing."

"No, you take them. You're the one who will be going through your suitcase, not me."

"You have a point." She put on the glasses again. "I still can't get over the coincidence that we have the same prescription. I mean, what are the chances that two people, stranded on a deserted island, would have exactly the same thing wrong with their eyes?"

"It must mean we're soul mates." He said it with a smile, to let her know he wasn't serious. Given his admission that he was attracted to her, she might think he was serious. He wanted to show her he could kid about it, so that when this was all over and they were back to being polite friends at the office, she wouldn't feel sorry for him.

"I thought Nick was my soul mate." She started walking toward her pink suitcase. "Which tells you I'm about as psychic as a jug of molasses. Mama, now, she's psychic. She told me not to go on this trip. I should've listened, but I thought I knew better."

Jack wondered what would have happened if Genevieve had listened to her mother and refused Nick's offer. Nick would have asked another secretary, if there were any left who would fall for his act. Jack could have been stranded here with someone else. He didn't really believe in Fate or premonitions or any of that mumbo jumbo he couldn't quantify. However, having things turn out the way they had seemed exactly right to him.

"Mama must be worried sick by now." Gen knelt by the suitcase and snapped open the clasp. "I promised to call when we landed in Maui. She knows I wouldn't forget, considering she was so petrified of me flying."

"Then she's probably the person who will see that we get rescued." If she had half the determination of her daughter, they'd be out of here in no time. He was happy about that, of course. They had no shelter, no water, and nothing to eat but those damned guavas.

Furthermore, if they wanted to go beyond this little crescent of a beach in search of food and water, they'd have to scale a very high cliff, and that scared the daylights out of him. They were in a tight spot, so he should be looking forward to being rescued. But he also knew that he couldn't expect to be this closely involved with Gen once they were saved. Logic told him they'd go back to the status quo.

She flipped back the top of the round suitcase. "Well, everything's soaking wet, of course, but we can dry this beach towel and use it."

"*South Park*? You like *South Park*?" It didn't fit that she would, but he was thrilled that they might share something as simple as a TV show.

"No, not really." She pushed the soggy towel aside. "My brother, Lincoln, loves it, though. I've watched it a few times with him and he gave me this towel, probably hoping I'd get hooked even more."

So she wasn't an addict. Too bad. He hated to admit that he'd begun weaving fantasies of the two of them cuddled in front of the television with a bowl of popcorn. Okay, he could watch *South Park* with her brother, then. It was a start. "How old is your brother?"

"Fourteen."

"It must be nice to have a brother." His only family was his grandmother, and he'd ended up moving away from her.

"Mostly it is nice, although sometimes he's a pain in the butt." She rummaged through the suitcase. "Oh, look! Mama must have tucked these in here!" She held up four energy bars, two in each hand. "She's always afraid I won't get enough to eat."

Jack's mouth watered, but they were her energy bars. "Now you won't have to depend on guavas."

"Now *we* won't have to depend on guavas. I say we eat two now and save two for later. Which do you want, the chocolate or the peanut butter?"

Chocolate. Oh, God. His stomach rumbled, but he tried once more to be noble. "You keep them. We're not sure how long it'll take for help to come, and you might need them all."

She grinned. "I heard your stomach growling, Jack. And if you think I'm eating these myself after you saved both me *and* my suitcase, you've got another think coming." She waved two different packages at him. "Take your pick. On the house."

"Okay, I'll take the chocolate." He did his best not to rip it out of her hands, but he had the wrapper torn open and half the energy bar gone before he thought to take a breath. He felt a little better when he glanced down and she was gobbling hers just as fast, but he'd totally forgotten his manners. "Thank you," he said.

She answered with her mouth full. "You're welcome."

He finished the bar and was ready for another one. But she was right. They needed to pace themselves. He also wished they had some water, but it looked like guava juice would be the drink of the day.

She held out her hand. "I'll take the wrappers and tuck them back in my suitcase. I wouldn't want to litter."

He smiled as he gave her the empty wrapper. "Too late. We've already dropped a big old piece of metal out in the water."

"Which we couldn't help. That doesn't mean we have to add trash strewn around on the beach." She tucked the remaining two energy bars back in the suitcase. "I sure hope my green suit will be okay once I get it washed. Everything smells of fish, but that'll probably come out with a good soak."

"Probably." He thought it wasn't important what happened to her suit, but obviously she did.

"You know, it's hot sitting here in the sun." She closed the lid and latched it again. "Let's take the whole thing up into the shade and go through it. We can hang things over the rocks to dry, and I'll rub sunscreen on your back."

"That's okay. I can put on my shirt now."

"No, because then you'll get a farmer's tan on your arms, and when you take off your shirt, the rest of you will be lily white. You have a nice build, Jack. You should get a good tan to showcase it."

"What about skin cancer?" He'd noticed her comment about him having a nice build, though.

She gazed up at him, looking so earnest in those glasses. "I'll tell you something. My uncle Rufus was brown as a berry and he never had a lick of skin cancer. What gives you skin cancer is getting all burnt in one sitting. So slop on the sunscreen and work up to the tan slow and natural." She smiled. "See? This mess isn't for nothing, after all. You can get a great start on your tan, which is something that will help you get dates, especially in Honolulu."

So they were back to the makeover discussion. He didn't want dates. He wanted Gen. Obviously that wasn't a possibility if she was still hell-bent on transforming him into a guy other women would want.

She stood, brushed the sand from her knees, and reached for the handle of the suitcase.

"You'd better not pick it up by the—"

Too late. She pulled on the handle and it came off in her hand. "Tarnation."

"Never mind. I can carry it without the handle."

"It broke clean off." She stared at the pink leather strap in her hand. "I can't believe it."

"No problem. We don't really need the strap." Jack leaned down to scoop the suitcase up from the sand. With its waterlogged contents it was very heavy, but that would give him a chance to show off the muscles she'd been admiring.

He'd taken several steps toward the shade of the over-hanging lava rock before he realized she wasn't following him. He turned and discovered her still standing there looking at the broken strap. Then her shoulders quivered.

Good Lord, she was crying. He plopped the suitcase back down on the sand and sprinted back to her. "Gen? What is it?"

"Something stupid." She wouldn't look at him.

"Try me."

"That ugly pink suitcase!" she wailed. "I thought I hated it because it was so old and out of style, and . . . and now it's *broken*."

He thought about his Corolla, which was also old and outdated. Sometimes he cursed it and considered getting a new car, but he hadn't done that, and if it ever got wrecked. . . . He slid an arm around her shoulders. "We'll fix the suitcase."

She looked up at him, the glasses magnifying her teary eyes. "But the metal part pulled right out of the side! I don't think you can fix something like that, Jack."

"I do." He had no idea how, but he'd find a way, once they got back to Honolulu.

"You do?" She sniffed and wiped her hand across her nose.

Suddenly he had no problem picturing her as a little hillbilly, a scrappy kid who nevertheless had a sentimental streak a mile wide. "Sure. Maybe an insert inside to reinforce that part. There has to be a leather shop in Honolulu that could do it."

Although her cheeks were still wet with tears, she began to grin. "Do you realize how dumb that is, to fix this suitcase?"

"Not if it means something to you, and it obviously does."

She sniffed again. "I didn't think so yesterday. Yesterday I was ashamed to take it on this trip, but look what it did for me. It survived the plane crash and came floating in with all my stuff. When I saw it out there in the water, I felt so happy that I hadn't lost it."

"You were ashamed of it? Why?"

"Because it came from the Goodwill, and I thought Nick would see that it was at least fifty years old. I didn't know that it had become a part of my family until I saw it bobbing out there in the waves like a big pink marshmallow."

He stroked her soft arm. "Then if it's a member of the family, it deserves to be fixed. So keep the strap, and that can be the first thing we do when we get back."

"Yeah." She gazed up at him. "You're very sweet, Jack. Did you know that?"

He didn't know how to respond, but he was afraid sweet wasn't a good thing to be if he wanted to make it with Gen. He was better off when she commented on his muscles.

"It's a crime a sweet guy like you doesn't have a girl-friend," she added.

Yep, sweet was a bad thing. It was what she called guys who were nice but boring. He gave her a quick squeeze and released her. "I'll go get your suitcase now." In the process he'd flex his muscles. Then he'd let her rub sunscreen on those same muscles. And even when he had access to a razor again, he'd let his beard grow so he'd look more like a pirate. He might even get contacts, although he hated the idea of putting objects in his eyes.

But tough times called for tough measures. No more Mr. Sweet.

Chapter 8

While Matt Murphy talked to the folks at the Maui airport, Annabelle watched him like a chicken hawk circling the henhouse. His expression gave him away, but then she'd known the plane wasn't there. She'd prayed that she was wrong, but she knew.

Matt hung up the phone. He looked a good ten years older than he had when she'd walked into his office. "I'm sure he's taken it upon himself to land at a different airport," he said. "Maybe he had engine trouble and put down at Molokai."

"Call there, then." But Annabelle didn't think Nick had put down at Molokai. She wished to hell that he had, but they had telephones on Molokai. Genevieve would have called her the minute she had a chance.

Muttering under his breath, Matt picked up the phone again. "Kendra, I want you to contact the airport at Molokai and find out if the Rainbow Systems plane landed there this morning." He paused. "And if it didn't, then check with Kauai and the Big Island. Let me know what you find out." He dropped the phone back in its cradle and stared at it without moving.

"They won't be at any of those airports." Annabelle's heart beat so fast she wondered if she should sit down and put her head between her knees. She couldn't afford to faint. Time could mean the difference between life and death.

He glanced up, his jaw tight. "What are you, psychic?"

"Yes." She didn't usually admit that to strangers, but her daughter's safety depended on Matt Murphy taking her instincts into consideration. "Not as psychic as some of my kin, but sometimes I see things. I saw danger in this trip, but I thought it was my fear of planes talking. It wasn't. Something is terribly wrong and we need to alert whoever can call out the search parties."

Matt's jaw muscles worked. "Until I check with every airport within flying distance of Honolulu, we're not calling anyone. I'm sure there's a logical explanation for this. Nick's a good pilot, and the Sky King's well maintained. The weather's good, and he didn't have far to go. Whatever your Ouija board told you, I'm sure Nick, your daughter, and my top programmer are all just fine."

"If Genevieve's fine, she would have called me!"

"She's young! She could have forgotten!"

"No." She stared him down. "Not my Genevieve."

He met her gaze for several long seconds. Finally he sighed and leaned against his desk. When he spoke again, his voice was gentler. "Maybe she did call. You're here instead of wherever she'd be trying to reach you. Can you check for messages?"

Annabelle flushed. He had a point, although she doubted there were any messages for her at work or at home. Still, she needed to pull herself together enough to find out. "Is there another line I can use?"

"Sure." He punched a button on his phone and turned the instrument to face her before picking up the receiver and holding it out to her.

As she took it from him she reminded herself that Matt wasn't her enemy. In fact, he might turn out to be her most important ally. First she checked the beauty shop. She must have gotten her hopes up, because when Elena told her Genevieve hadn't called, her stomach heaved as if she'd eaten something bad.

Genevieve would have called the shop first, so there was no point in checking at home, but Annabelle did, anyway. Lincoln was at the Parks and Rec basketball camp every afternoon this week, so he'd turned on the answering machine before he left, like she'd told him to. There were no messages.

She was trembling again by the time she put the phone back in its cradle.

"Nothing?" Matt asked.

"Nothing."

The buzzing of his phone made her jump.

He grabbed the receiver. "Kendra? What did you—oh." He paused and cleared his throat. "Okay, let me think."

Annabelle clenched her hands together and waited for what else he planned to say. It had better be the right thing or she was taking over.

"Listen, Kendra, I'm not sure what protocol is here, but start with the Coast Guard." His voice shook. "Yeah, it looks like the plane's missing." He replaced the receiver and squared his shoulders before facing Annabelle again. "We'll find them," he said, looking resolute and determined.

She was encouraged by his air of confidence. Apparently he wasn't the type to fall apart during times of trouble, and she could use someone like that right now. "I know we'll find them," she said.

"We will. And now the best thing for you to do is go home and—"

"Not on your life, Matt Murphy."

He blinked. "Um, you want to stay here? That's fine, of course, but I was just thinking that under the circumstances—"

"You don't have children, do you?"

"What's that have to do with anything?"

"If you had children, you would never suggest that I go home and sit on my hands while everybody goes out looking for my daughter." Power rose within her. She'd felt this kind of power once before, and it had allowed her to conquer her fear of airplanes and take Genevieve out of the poverty-stricken life of the Hollow.

Matt looked sympathetic. "I can understand that you want to do something, but this process is best left to the experts. They may need to talk to you and get a description of Genevieve and . . . what she was wearing this morning."

Annabelle closed her eyes as a wave of grief washed over her. That sexy, flirty little dress. A dress to catch herself a man. Genevieve had been worried about how her nails would look for her grand adventure. Annabelle could still feel the imprint of her daughter's fingers, could almost smell the polish.

"Annabelle, is there someone who could stay with you at home? You're right, you shouldn't be alone. I'd be wrong to send you home without making sure you have some support there."

She opened her eyes and pushed aside the emotions swamping her. She had work to do. "If you think I'm going to stay at home and wait for some word, then you're crazier than my cousin who wears a coonskin cap and thinks he's the reincarnation of Davy Crockett. I'm going to help search. Can you fly a plane?"

His jaw dropped. "No, but I thought you were afraid of flying?"

"Like I said, you've never had children or you wouldn't ask that, either. So you can't fly. Can you handle a boat?"

"That I can do, but—"

"Good. Because I need someone who can either fly a plane or pilot a boat. To be honest, I like the boat better."

Adrenaline poured through her. "Charter one big enough that we can sleep on. We'll need room for you, me, and Lincoln."

He was looking at her as if she'd gone crazy. "Who's . . . who's Lincoln?"

"My fourteen-year-old son. I wouldn't dream of leaving him."

"Listen, it might make you feel better to be out there, but we'd accomplish exactly nothing. You need specialized equipment like sonar."

Her chest tightened up in fear, but she forced herself to breathe through the moment of panic and to look the ultimate horror in the face. "To find the plane under the water, you mean."

He started around the desk. "I shouldn't have implied they were under the water. I'm sure they're fine. Annabelle, maybe you'd better sit down. You're very pale."

"I'm not sitting and I won't faint on you, so don't look so worried. I'm not after your precious plane, either. I aim to locate my daughter, and I'll be better at that than any sonar or radar contraption in the world."

"I'm sure you believe that, but—"

"If you won't rent a boat and take me and Lincoln out there, I'll find someone who will." She felt like Gary Cooper walking down the street at high noon. "And when I rescue Genevieve, I plan to get me a really good lawyer and sue the pants off Rainbow Systems."

Matt didn't seem fazed by that threat. Instead he gave her a sad smile. "That kind of arm-twisting might work with another man, but you're talking to a guy who's been raked over the judicial coals by a very greedy ex-wife." He shrugged. "Bankruptcy doesn't scare me anymore."

She remembered Genevieve talking about the divorce and how tough it had been on Matt in many ways, including his pocketbook. She understood what it felt like to have someone clean you out. It had happened twice with the handsome no-good fathers of her two children. "If you don't have the money to rent the boat, then I'll pay for that." She had no idea how, but she'd manage.

"No, you won't."

Fire blazed within her. "Don't you dare tell me what I can and can't do! I've spent enough time jawing with you, anyway. If you're not fixing to help me, then—"

"I'll help you."

"You will?" She'd about given up on him, and here he was coming around, after all.

"But I think you should have your son stay with someone instead of dragging him along."

"If that's the hitch, then we don't have a deal. Lincoln goes."

"But—"

"You know, it's a good thing you don't have children, if you can imagine leaving one of them behind to wait and worry by himself while his mother's out hunting for his big sister. So thanks, but no thanks. I'll hire a boat my own self." She started toward the door.

"Okay. We'll take Lincoln."

She turned. "Good. Then let's go."

"Now?"

She'd lost all patience with him. "Yes, now! You're not going to be slowing me down like an old mule with the rheumatiz, now are you?"

"No." He glanced at his desk once, then threw up his hands and turned away from it. "Nope. I promise not to act like an old mule with the rheumatiz. Let's go."

"This reminds me of Christmas." In the shade of the overhanging rock ledge, Genevieve sank to her knees in the sand next to her suitcase and flipped open the lid. She didn't know which she was more excited about unpacking, her nail file, her hairbrush, or her lotion.

"Santa brings you suitcases of soggy clothes every year?" Jack crouched beside her.

"Very funny. I meant it feels like Christmas because we have this unexpected treasure to open. I'm referring to Christmas like I remember it back in the Hollow. Nobody could afford store-bought presents, so you never knew what strange and wonderful thing would appear under the tree with your name on it. One year my cousin Festus made me a party dress from corn husks and duct tape."

"Creative."

"It was a little scratchy, but I wore it until the mice ate so much of the corn husks that it was indecent." She tossed her flip-flops into the sand and lifted out the *South Park* towel. "Lincoln made me the cutest bunny out of Play-Doh when he was six. Now he thinks he's too cool to make his own gifts, but homemade presents are the best, don't you think?" She wrung the towel out, letting the excess water drip on the sand beside her.

"I only ever had one homemade present. My grandmother crocheted an afghan for me one Christmas."

"That's wonderful." She hadn't heard much about Jack's family before, and it was good to know he had some kin who cared enough to make him a cherished heirloom. She smiled at him. "I'll bet you were touched that she'd spent all that time making something for you."

Instead of smiling back and telling her that he used that afghan to this day on the foot of his bed, he dropped his gaze. "Actually, I . . . told her I would've rather had Nintendo."

"You didn't!"

" 'Fraid so." He glanced up. "She sold the afghan and a couple more she had around the house, and got me Nintendo."

"That's purely dreadful. I'm flabbergasted that your parents allowed such a thing to happen. Somebody should have tanned your hide for being so ungrateful."

He looked as if he agreed completely. "Unfortunately, Grandma never had the heart to tan my hide, and my folks died when I was two months old, which is why I ended up with Grandma. Years later I realized I'd done a terrible thing by rejecting that afghan, but I never did work up the courage to apologize. I guess I'm hoping she's forgotten."

"Not likely, Jack." She nearly forgave him, considering that he was an orphan and he had that hangdog look on his face. He really had a terrific face, too—squared-off and manly, nicely accented with remorseful blue eyes. A girl could fall for that combo if she wasn't careful.

But he'd caused his poor grandmother to sell what should have been a keepsake, and he shouldn't be let off easy for a transgression like that. "I'm sorry your parents died when you were no bigger than a minute, but I have to say you've treated your grandmother mighty poorly."

"You're right, I did. I'm scum." He glanced at the beach towel in her hand. "Would you like me to drape that over the ledge?"

"Yes, thank you." She handed him the beach towel. "What color was it?"

He stood and draped the towel across the ledge. "What?"

"The *afghan*, Jack. If you're hoping that I'm going to forget, too, you're barking up the wrong tree." She squeezed the water out of her green suit jacket.

"I don't know what difference the color makes to the discussion. It's gone, in any case."

"I just want to picture it, is all." She handed him the jacket. "And I think you should picture it, too, as a fitting memorial to something that has departed from your life forever, because you didn't have the good sense to appreciate the effort involved in creating it."

He arranged the jacket next to the towel. "All right, I admit it was a rotten thing to do, but don't you think you're getting a little carried away with this subject?"

"Nope. I'll bet she spent hours and hours bent over her work, all for love of you, Jack." She squeezed water from the matching skirt and passed it up to him. "She probably even had poor eyesight and arthritis in her hands."

Jack groaned.

"What color was it?" Next she wrung out her bathing suit and held it out to him.

"Orange and yellow, I think."

"You *think?* You paid so little attention to it that you don't even remember what color it was? Your sins are piling up on you, boy."

"Okay, you might as well know the truth. I'm color blind."

"Color blind?" She stared at him in astonishment. "Well, shut my mouth. That explains a heap of things. Why didn't you tell me that a long time ago, when I was trying to do something about your look?"

He shrugged. "What difference would it have made? I couldn't expect you to show up at my house every morning and pick out my clothes."

That idea had more appeal than she wanted to admit. Dressing Jack would be fun, now that she realized he had a decent body. Undressing him wouldn't be a real chore, either. "There is a solution, you know. Wear black." She could see him in all black, too, looking better than those velvet paintings of Elvis that Aunt Maizie had in her front room.

"I'd probably mess that up and get navy or purple mixed in there."

"Not if you asked the salesperson to sell you only black clothes." She gazed up at him. "Right?"

"I guess."

"You don't want the salesperson to know you're color blind, do you?"

When he didn't answer, she figured this physical failing was a touchy subject for him. "Being color blind is nothing to be ashamed about," she said more gently. "It's not like it's your fault or anything. Try being my aunt Nelda, who has six toes on her right foot. That's not her fault, either, but you should see the way people make fun of her every blessed time she goes wading in the crick. She's threatened never to go again, on account of that."

He smiled down at her. "You sound like my grandmother. She used to tell me to be glad I had all my fingers and toes."

"I'll bet I would like your grandmother. Is she still alive?"

"Uh-huh. She lives in Nebraska. I've tried to get her to move over here, but she's very attached to her little house and I don't think she'd ever do it." He glanced at the suitcase. "Anything else to hang up?"

Nothing but her pale blue underwear, and she was feeling a little shy about giving him that. She shouldn't be shy. This was good old Jack, after all. Even so, she couldn't just hand him her panties and bra. "That's it." She unzipped her makeup bag and took out her tube of sunscreen. "Come on back down here and I'll put some lotion on your back."

"Okay." He crouched down with his broad back facing her.

Uncapping the tube, she squeezed coconut-scented sunscreen onto her fingers before laying the tube back inside the suitcase so it wouldn't get all sandy. Then she rose on her knees and smeared the lotion over his right shoulder.

He flinched. "Yikes. That's cold."

"Sorry. It's because your skin's so warm." Warm and smooth. Nice. His indoor-white color was starting to turn pink, but the sunscreen should save him from getting burned. She went back for more lotion, because there was a lot of area to cover.

And she was having a good time. If anyone had asked her before today, she would have said Jack probably had a bony, skinny back, but it wasn't at all. He was firm and very touchable. She made several passes over his shoulders and then got more lotion before heading down toward the waistband of his jeans.

With the way he was crouched, the waistband of his jeans gaped at the small of his back, right where a sprinkling of hair followed his spine down under the elastic of his tighty whiteys. She wondered if he wore Fruit of the Loom or Hanes or Jockeys, like the pair the King had left in her grandmother's bedroom.

Whatever the brand, Genevieve figured Jack would have great buns underneath the cotton. She never intended to find out about that. She'd never find out about what was on the flip side of those briefs, either, although parts of her were acting very interested in that area.

Time for a distraction. "Jack, I have the best idea. I'll teach you how to whittle, and you can make your grandmother something. And when you give it to her, you can tell her how much you regret your behavior regarding the afghan, and this is how you're showing it, by giving her a gift from the heart."

"You whittle?"

Maybe she shouldn't have told him. "I suppose you think that's peculiar."

"No. Well, maybe, a little. I always thought of whittlers as being old guys with beards sitting on a sagging front porch with a hound dog lying beside them and banjo music in the background."

"Picture a barefoot little kid in place of the old guy with the beard, and you've painted it just about right. We always had coon dogs lying around, and I don't know a single porch in the Hollow that isn't slightly swaybacked. My uncle Harley was the best banjo picker in the hills of Tennessee. Or so he always told us." She gave his back one final swipe. "There, you're done."

He stood and stretched, looking way too good doing it. "Thanks."

"Put some on your chest and arms." She thrust the tube of lotion at him.

"Then I'll do you."

She panicked at the thought. "That's okay. I can reach everything that's exposed." If she felt as nice to him as he felt to her, they could get into trouble, with him having a crush and all. And her getting increasingly attracted. She knew it was on account of them being marooned and Jack being her rescuer. Once they were back in Honolulu she'd stop thinking of his hands and his mouth and his . . . other stuff.

She turned back to the open suitcase. There was another reason her thoughts were going in that direction. Six of them, to be exact, lay in the bottom of her suitcase. Now that she'd taken out everything except her underwear and her makeup bag, one or another of those six packets kept slipping into view. She thought the suitcase might have had elasticized side pockets once upon a time, but they'd been ripped out by the time she became the owner.

She shoved the packets under her bra and panties and makeup bag as she listened to Jack rhythmically slapping more lotion on his bare arms. It sounded like two people having sex. Two specific people. People marooned together who wouldn't be discovered for hours and had six condoms.

"Did you bring a knife?" he asked.

"A knife?" She couldn't imagine why he'd ask.

"To whittle with."

"Oh." She'd been so sidetracked by the image of having

sex with him that she'd plumb forgotten about her offer to teach him to whittle. "No, but I have a pair of manicure scissors in my makeup bag. I could make do with those." She turned to glance up at him and found herself having to look past his crotch in order to get to his face. She gulped. "Do you really want to learn?"

"It'd be a way to kill some time until we're sure Brogan is gone for good." His attention veered from her to the blue underwear in her suitcase. "Those look wet, too. Why don't I hang them up?" He leaned over and reached one long arm toward the suitcase.

"Never mind." She spread her hand protectively over her damp undies. "They'll dry in there."

"If you say so."

"I do. So are you ready for me to teach you to whittle? First we have to find some small pieces of driftwood." She had to change her position and change it fast. This view of his male equipment was not helping her mental condition at all. She got to her feet, but in the process kicked the suitcase slightly. The contents shifted.

"Whoa." From the tone of his voice it was obvious he'd seen at least some of the condoms.

She banged the lid shut and avoided his gaze. "Never you mind about that, either." She started toward the beach. "Come on. Let's find something we can whittle."

"Hold on." He grabbed her arm. "You didn't trust that smarm-meister to bring his own, and yet you were willing to go to bed with someone that irresponsible?"

"When it comes to makin' babies, I don't trust *any* man."

His grip on her arm gentled, and a soft light came into his eyes. "You could trust me."

Chapter 9

Condoms. The suitcase Jack had rescued, the one that had nearly turned him into shark bait, the one that meant so much to Gen that the thought of trashing it had made her cry—that same suitcase had contained condoms. And not just one, either. If he'd known the suitcase had condoms in it, he would have dived down to the sunken plane, if necessary. Condoms were even more exciting than energy bars.

This put a whole new light on things. True, she'd brought the condoms on account of Nick, but Nick had been revealed as a murdering, embezzling creepazoid, so Jack could rightly assume she had no more interest in Nick as a sexual partner. She had no interest in Jack as a sexual partner, either, but he had a decent chance to remedy that and absolutely zero competition. Statistically, he was in fine shape.

She smiled at him. "When I said I wouldn't trust any man, I wasn't talking about you."

"Good, because I—wait a minute." What had sounded like a compliment might have been the exact opposite. "Is that because you don't think of me as a man?"

"Well, of course I know you're a man, but—"

"You don't think I'm highly sexed?"

She began to laugh.

"Don't you dare laugh about that." Warmth crept up from his neck to his face. "Don't you dare."

"I'm sorry." She struggled to control herself. "But take a look at the evidence, Jackson."

"Jack."

"Okay, *Jack*." She began ticking off items on her fingers. "You haven't had a date in a coon's age, you pay no attention to how you look, I've never heard you tell a dirty joke, and your head's buried inside your computer for days on end. If sex was that important to you, you'd be spending more time on it."

She had a point. Dating usually wasn't as much fun as writing code, and he'd never had a sexual itch so great that it distracted him from his work until he'd met Gen. He'd have to conclude that sex per se wasn't important to him. Sex with Gen was a different story. He'd fantasized about that ever since coming to work at Rainbow Systems.

"Maybe it's just that I'm very discriminating," he said at last.

Her cheeks turned pink. "See, that's what I'm talking about. You've had a crush on me for a long time. A highly sexed man would have done something about it."

"Being highly sexed and being confident don't always go together."

"So you're trying to convince me that if you believed in yourself more, you'd turn into an animal?" Her color was still high, and she was looking at him with a speculative gleam in her eyes.

"Could be." He wondered how many condoms were in the suitcase. A guy with a low sex drive wouldn't wonder things like that, would he? Of course, he didn't have much else to think about right now. Although he'd fantasized about Gen in the past, it obviously hadn't taken over his whole life or he wouldn't have been able to do his job.

Maybe he didn't have any competition for Gen's attention right now, but then again, she didn't have any for his, either.

He'd always told himself that with the right woman he'd go crazy with lust. He'd felt crazy with lust ever since they'd crawled up on the beach, but maybe being marooned with someone wasn't a very good test. Once he got back to his keyboard he might put the whole idea of sex out of his mind for days at a time, as she'd accused him of doing.

She continued to study him. "You are an original, Jack. I'll give you that." Then she dropped her gaze. "Come on, let's go hunt up some driftwood to whittle."

"Okay." Feeling dismissed, as if he weren't manly enough to capture her attention, Jack followed her to the waterline. He didn't like the status quo, but he wasn't sure what to do about it. Until the discovery of the condoms, he'd abandoned the idea of fooling around, because he wasn't sure he could keep himself in check. Now he was worried that he might be a keep-himself-in-check kind of guy.

Still, the condoms meant all his options were open. He'd been handed a golden opportunity to have the sexual experience of his dreams if he could convince Gen to go along. A guy named Jack wouldn't let that opportunity slip through his fingers.

But what if it didn't turn out to be the incredible experience he'd envisioned? What if sex with Gen, the most beautiful woman he could imagine getting frisky with, was only so-so? Would that mean that he was some sort of eunuch, saddled with a genius IQ and the sexual drive of broccoli? He wasn't sure he wanted to find out the answer to that question. Maybe he was better off living in ignorance of his true nature.

At the waterline, Gen paused to shade her eyes. "Remember those clouds we almost flew into a few hours ago?"

"Yeah." It seemed centuries ago that they'd been up in

the Sky King, terrified that they would both die. They'd made it through alive, which might mean his sexual doubts weren't very important in the grand scheme of things. It was amazing how quickly perspective changed, because now, besides being alive, he also wanted to be a potent sex god.

"They're building up and moving this way."

He squinted toward the horizon. "I'll have to take your word for it."

"Here, use the glasses." She whipped them off and handed them to him.

He put on the glasses and, sure enough, some big bruisers were headed this way. The line of clouds extended eastward, toward Oahu, which meant the entire chain of islands would soon be hit.

"I'd rather be worried about too much sun than have to deal with a storm," Gen said.

"So would I, and not just because we might get rained on."

"I know." She glanced over at him. "Bad weather means they'll have more trouble searching for us, huh?"

"That's exactly what it means."

Her expression grew serious. "I think we'd better find driftwood so we can make a fire. We can worry about the whittling later."

"You have matches in your suitcase?" Maybe the two of them needed to take a careful inventory, and not because they had to count the condoms. She might have brought all sorts of useful gear she'd forgotten about.

"No matches, but we can start a fire with some dry grass and your glasses."

"That only works in the movies, Gen."

"That shows what you know. I've done it plenty of times. When I was a kid that was the only reason I was happy about having glasses. I could start my own little campfires in the woods. You had a peculiar childhood, Jack."

He couldn't help laughing at that. "Fortunately for us, yours was completely normal."

Annabelle noticed that the weather was getting worse as Matt guided the boat he'd rented out of Haleiwa Harbor. She didn't say anything, though, because she didn't care how bad the weather got. Genevieve was out there in the same weather, and Annabelle intended to find her.

Lincoln stood beside her at the back of the boat, both of them watching the frothy wake as they headed out to sea. Lincoln had taken the news of the missing plane as well as could be expected. He'd panicked at first and had made Annabelle promise that under no circumstances was his sister going to end up dead. Annabelle had promised.

Because she'd said it with total conviction, Lincoln had settled down, but she couldn't have left him in Honolulu. He would have gone crazier than a hound with a nose full of porcupine quills if she'd made him stay with a friend while she went off with Matt. She was his security right now, and she knew it.

But to look at him standing in the wind with his earphones and his wraparound sunglasses, anyone would think he didn't need her at all. Whenever Lincoln was plugged into those earphones, he bobbed his head in time with whatever was slowly destroying his eardrums.

Annabelle worried about his hearing, but she wasn't going to bother him about the earphones now. He probably needed the music to distract him from his worry about Genevieve. From this side she couldn't see the little gold earring he'd insisted on having put in last week. She usually tried to approach him from the nonearring side so she could pretend he hadn't done that.

Both she and Lincoln wore orange life vests, although she noticed that Lincoln had unfastened his so that he'd look cool. He hadn't wanted to wear one at all, but Matt had said they weren't leaving the harbor until everyone had on a life jacket, only Matt had called them something else, a set of initials that sounded like BVD but probably wasn't.

The boat was gorgeous, all gleaming wood and sparkling white paint and shiny brass fittings. Quite a step up from Rufus's smelly old rowboat with the outboard motor that hardly ever worked. This was what Annabelle thought was called a pleasure craft. If only she and Lincoln could be going on a pleasure trip. But they weren't, so the wonders of the boat were lost on both of them, which was a shame.

Before they'd left the dock, Annabelle had stored the groceries she'd brought in the boat's tiny kitchen. Matt had called it the galley, so she would try to remember that. And the tiny bathroom, not much bigger than the one in the airplane they'd flown in eleven years ago, was the head. She thought, considering what it was mostly for, that the name was backward.

Their sleeping arrangements would be tight. She'd get the only real privacy—both Matt and Lincoln had insisted she take the little space in the bow, the one sleeping area with a door. The other two beds in the main cabin doubled as bench seats during the day. There'd be no sleeping in for Lincoln, not that she thought he would with his sister missing. Annabelle didn't think any of them would sleep much, but they needed the beds in case someone was ready to drop.

Annabelle didn't care about the close quarters. She'd put up with a lot worse during her years in the Hollow. And although she wondered if Matt minded being crammed in cheek-by-jowl with a strange woman and her teenage son, she didn't really care if he minded or not. By being business partners with Nick, he'd put himself right in the middle of this mess of trouble, and she didn't plan to let him wiggle out of his responsibility.

Now that they were moving out into open water, she needed to focus on Genevieve and establish a mental connection. If she didn't achieve that, she wouldn't be able to tell Matt which way to go once they left the harbor. Lincoln would be a help with that, too. He didn't like to admit that he had a touch of psychic power, but he did. Besides that, he had a powerful bond with his sister.

Lincoln unhooked his earphones and dangled them around his neck. "This is an awesome plan, Mom. I'm glad you talked this Matt guy into renting the boat and going out to look for Gen."

"Call him Mr. Murphy, Lincoln."

"But he told me to call him Matt."

"I know, and I'm telling you to call him Mr. Murphy."

"Don't get all mad at me, just because you're worried about Gen, okay?"

She glanced at him, but he wasn't looking at her. Instead he was staring at the boat's wake, and his jaw was set in that stubborn way that reminded her of Granny Neville. Nothing would be served by the two of them barking at each other.

Yet she didn't want him calling Matt Murphy by his Christian name. He could dye his hair any color he wanted, wear T-shirts with mouthy sayings on them, pierce his earlobes, and let any music he wanted filter through those earphones. He could do all that to his heart's content, but no boy of hers would be disrespectful to his elders.

"I am worried about Genevieve," she admitted. "I reckon you are, too. But we *will* find her."

He continued to study the churning water. "Yeah, I know. I hope it's soon, though."

Annabelle wanted to reach up and touch his cheek,

right where a little downy growth had started coming in. But he wouldn't appreciate that, so she didn't. "Me, too. Lincoln, about what you should call Mr. Murphy, I—"

Lincoln's sigh of protest was loud and dramatic, like most of his behavior in the last couple of years. "If it bothers you that much, I'll call him *Mr. Murphy*, but he's pretty cool, and he's gonna be all *Why are you calling me Mr. Murphy? That makes me feel old*. And I'll be all *Don't blame me. My mom made me call you that.* He is old, of course, but I don't think I should be the one reminding him about it."

She smiled a little at that. If she hadn't been so weighed down with worry, she might have laughed. She thought Matt was a fine-looking man, very much in his prime. He had the sort of handsome face that she'd learned to steer clear of.

If she hadn't desperately needed his help, she wouldn't have had a thing to do with Matt Murphy. With those big brown eyes and great smile, he was much too pretty, and she'd promised herself never to fall for a pretty face again. But all Lincoln saw was a guy with a touch of gray in his hair, a guy on the far side of forty, which made him old and creaky.

"I'll take the chance he'll feel old when you call him Mr. Murphy," she said.

"Annabelle," Matt called above the sound of the boat's motor. "Could you come here a minute, please?"

"Be right there!" She turned to Lincoln. "Want to come with me while I see what he wants?"

"No, that's okay. I'll just stand here and concentrate."

This time she couldn't resist putting a hand on his arm, even if he was four inches taller than she was and thought he was too cool for hugs from his mama. "Are you concentrating on Genevieve?"

"Yeah." He glanced down at her. "You know when we

first moved here, and Gen used to play hide-and-seek with me?"

"I don't remember that."

"Probably because we quit playing. I always found her right away, so she got all bent. She couldn't find me, but I could always find her."

Annabelle squeezed his arm. "That's nice to know. You concentrate."

"I will. I'm listening to that Harry Connick Jr. garbage she likes so much."

"You *are*?" Annabelle liked that music herself, but Lincoln always said he wouldn't pollute his ears with it.

"Yeah. It sucks, but maybe it'll help me think of where she is."

"Thank you, Lincoln. You're a good boy." Before he could see the tears in her eyes, she turned and climbed up the stairway to where Matt was. That part of the boat, where Matt steered, was called the helm. Annabelle liked learning new things, but she would rather be learning under different circumstances.

Matt had one hand on the wheel and the other fiddling with the dials of whatever instruments the boat had. He wore the kind of wire-rimmed sunglasses she'd always liked on a man, and a blue golf cap with "Hanalei Bay Resort" embroidered on the front.

"We need to talk about something," he said.

He was going to bring up the bad weather. She braced herself to hold her ground. "What?"

"The Coast Guard just notified me that they plan to postpone the air search because of the weather. In fact, the weather may interrupt most of the rescue efforts until the storm blowing in passes over the islands."

Annabelle took a deep breath. "I wasn't putting much store in their help, anyway."

He motioned to the swells ahead of them. "Besides that, they've issued a small craft warning."

"We're not so small. This is the biggest boat I've ever been on."

He flicked a glance in her direction. "Trust me, we're still considered small."

"We're not going back. I don't give a care what the weather is doing. We can't go back."

"Hang on. I didn't say anything about going back. I just wanted you to know. We have Lincoln with us."

She turned and looked down at her son bobbing his head in tune with Harry Connick Jr. Surely she wouldn't be expected to risk Lincoln to save Genevieve. "Are we in danger yet?"

"Not yet." Matt leaned over the wheel and peered at the clouds. "But we need a plan. We're headed toward Maui, but I think maybe we should put in at Molokai instead of going all the way to Maui. I should be able to make it there before the water gets too rough."

"I need to ask Lincoln."

Matt's jaw dropped. "Excuse me?"

Too late she realized that wouldn't make any sense to him. Even explaining might not do any good. She had to be careful how much she talked about intuition and psychic connections, or Matt would take her right back to Oahu and call the men with the butterfly nets. "What I intended to say was, I need to ask Lincoln if he wants us to go back to the harbor or not."

Matt shook his head. "You need to decide that for him. A fourteen-year-old won't know whether it's safe to go on. They think they're invincible."

"I meant whether he feels seasick."

"Oh." Matt looked nervous. "Uh, do *you* feel seasick?"

"No." And even if she did, she'd wouldn't let a little

thing like that stop her. "Let me go check on Lincoln, though."

"Listen, if you think there's any chance that he's gonna get seasick, then I think we should take him right back to the harbor. Matter of fact, maybe we'd better all go back. The storm will probably pass over in no time, and then we can—"

"Never mind about Lincoln getting seasick, then." She began to panic at the idea that he might seriously think of turning around. "Just head toward Molokai."

"Look, we're closer to home than to Molokai, and I don't want to be fighting through heavy seas with your kid puking his guts out down below. For all I know both of you are prone to seasickness."

"We're not. And Lincoln will be just fine." She wished she'd never brought up the subject. Come to think of it, her stomach was feeling like she'd just eaten a spoiled batch of crawdads.

"But you just said—"

"He's never been seasick." Which was absolutely true. You couldn't get seasick if you'd never been to sea. She made a shooing motion with her hand. "Let's just go. Pedal to the metal. Or whatever you do with a boat. Just goose it."

He mumbled something under his breath. She figured he wasn't happy, but that was just too bad.

"Hang on," he said as the engine roared and the boat shot forward.

She grabbed hold of Matt because he was the closest solid thing. And he felt wonderful, all warm muscles and broad shoulders. Plus he smelled good. After all her years in a beauty parlor with the perfumes and lotions women liked, she'd forgotten the pleasurable scent of a crisp aftershave. Maybe a vibrator and a good mechanic didn't cover all her needs, after all.

But that wasn't what this boat ride was about. She let go of Matt the minute she found her balance. "Excuse me," she said. "I'll just go talk to Lincoln."

"You do that." He sounded like a bear with a sore paw.

"I will." She hurried down the steps, eager to get away from him. He didn't like her and she didn't care. Just because he felt nice and smelled good didn't matter a hill of beans. All she needed him to do was drive this boat.

Matt had made some dumb moves in his life, but letting Annabelle talk him into renting a boat so they could search for her daughter was the granddaddy of all dumbness. He should just turn the boat around and head for the harbor, no matter what she said. As he considered doing that, a picture of Annabelle staging a mutiny flashed through his head. Yep, she'd be up for that.

She was a fiery woman, and he was inappropriately excited by that. Now wasn't the time to be thinking about sex, and he felt like a first-class sleaze because whenever he looked at Annabelle, that's what he thought about. She was one luscious woman. When she'd grabbed him by the shoulder just now, he'd reacted instantly to her touch. He hadn't wanted her to take her hand away.

Well, he'd better put a lid on those thoughts immediately. If he couldn't, he'd be obligated to take her back to Oahu and find her someone else to ferry her around. He didn't want to do that, couldn't trust that someone else would see this from her perspective and understand why she needed to be out here.

He didn't have any kids, but after the first shock of discovering that the plane was missing, he'd been able to set aside his own fears and imagine hers, which had to be huge. Maybe he was especially sensitized after his night with Celeste. No matter how bold and brash young women like

Celeste and Genevieve pretended to be, they were more vulnerable than they knew. Vulnerability always tore down all his defenses.

So he was out here for Annabelle's sake, and for Genevieve's, but he also was out here because he felt more useful doing something. She'd been right about that—sitting around waiting for word would have been torture. Bucking eight-foot swells with two green-to-the-gills passengers wouldn't be a picnic, but at least he'd have taken some action.

However, under the current weather conditions, they needed to exercise some caution or the Coast Guard would be adding them to the list of the missing. Matt was willing to risk his safety, and Annabelle had the right to risk hers, but neither of them should endanger a fourteen-year-old kid, no matter how obnoxious his hair color. They'd weather this storm in Molokai and then cruise around Maui to see what they could see. Maybe they'd chance upon something. Stranger things had been known to happen.

And he'd keep his libido in check. For God's sake, she even had her kid with her, and yet he still found himself thinking how he'd love to get her naked. He was a sorry specimen.

When it came to Lincoln, Matt thought Annabelle was too lax. Obviously the kid's father wasn't anywhere around or that hair color wouldn't be happening, and the earring wouldn't be winking in his ear, either. The black T-shirt that said *You Got a Problem with That?* was pretty typical—all the kids had attitude these days. But if Matt had a son like Lincoln, the hair situation definitely would be under control and they'd find an alternate way to fly the colors of the flag.

He glanced over his shoulder to where Annabelle and Lincoln were deep in conversation. From their hunched posture Matt figured they had to be freezing their asses off, what with the wind and the spray. When you were out on the water, a summer storm could bring your body temperature down in a hurry.

Finally they must have had enough, because when Annabelle started up the steps toward him, Lincoln followed. The kid looked pale. Nobody enjoyed being seasick, but Matt figured Lincoln would hate it more than most. Spending the first part of the voyage hurling would put a big dent in that macho swagger he had going on. Matt felt a moment of sympathy for him. Being fourteen had never been an easy job, and having your sister missing wouldn't make it a hell of a lot easier.

"Lincoln needs to use the facilities," Annabelle said. "Is that okay?"

"Certainly that's okay. Is he sick?"

"No, I'm not sick. Definitely not sick." Lincoln sounded weak but defiant.

Matt was too busy handling the boat to study him more closely. "Go ahead down below, and just be aware that we're tossing around quite a bit, so hold on to something to keep steady."

"Well, duh."

"Lincoln Roosevelt Terrence! Apologize to Mr. Murphy this second!"

"Sorry, Mr. Murphy."

"No problem." That was some name Annabelle had saddled him with. The kid was supposed to run for high office, apparently. "And call me Matt."

"Yeah, but my mom said—"

"Lincoln, go on downstairs," Annabelle said. "Now."

"And help yourself to some Seven-Up if you want," Matt added. "That sometimes settles a queasy stomach."

"Thanks, but my stomach's good."

"Glad to hear it."

"See you guys later." Lincoln stumbled going down the

steps, but that could have been due to the pitching of the boat.

"Maybe you'd better go with him," Matt said.

She lowered her voice. "He would never forgive me if I did."

Matt nodded. He'd been fourteen once, too. "Okay, but if he isn't back out in a few minutes, you'd better go tap on the door. I don't want him to hit his head and knock himself out in there."

Annabelle drew in a sharp breath. "Then I'll sneak down after I'm sure he's in there, and I'll listen. Oh, and Matt, I apologize for Lincoln's manners. I'll speak to him."

"Don't, Annabelle. He's a lot more polite than most kids I've seen. Don't ride him on my account."

She sighed. "I'm so afraid if I let things slide, he'll get mouthy like his friends, but today it's a little harder to be strict with him."

"Exactly. This is an unusual circumstance. And I can take care of myself. If I think he's getting too much of an attitude, I'll tell him."

"Good. That's good." She hesitated. "Matt, I need to tell you something. Lincoln and I don't think Genevieve's in this direction."

"What do you mean *in this direction*? Nick was on his way to Maui, which is definitely in this direction."

"I know, but we don't think that's where she is. We think we're going farther away from her, not closer."

Matt could smell her perfume mixed with the salty breeze that had been blowing through her hair. He wanted to nuzzle the side of her neck and sniff his fill of that combo. "And what are you basing this on?" He was afraid to ask.

She hesitated. "I don't suppose you'd just take my word for it that we need to turn around."

"Nope. And we're not turning around. Not until this

storm passes over. We'll hole up in Molokai. You can see what it's like out there."

"Yes."

He heard the sound of her swallow, even over the wind and the engine. He gave her a quick glance. "You're about to upchuck, too, aren't you?"

"No."

"Annabelle, go do it. Use the sink in the galley if Lincoln's still in the head. You'll feel better if you get rid of what's in your stomach."

"Will you . . . go the other way once it's safe?"

"You haven't told me why." But he already had a good idea what she'd say. She'd claim some hocus-pocus like her daughter was beaming waves of consciousness at her. Maybe Lincoln was picking up the transmission through his hair.

"I can't explain it so you'll understand! Will you do it?"

"If you don't get below, you're going to throw up all over me." He was demented. Even knowing she was seasick, he still wanted her, right this minute.

"Promise me, Matt Murphy!"

"Okay, damn it! We'll turn around and start back the other way once the storm's over! Now go throw up, will you?"

She was already heading down the steps.

Great, just great. Nothing beat taking a boat ride with a couple of puking, psychic passengers, except having the hots for one of them and knowing he wouldn't be able to do a damned thing about it. When he finally got his hands on Nick Brogan, his partner would have a hell of a lot to answer for.

Chapter 10

Genevieve knew she should be worried about her perilous circumstances, and she hated to think how upset Mama was by this time. But other than worrying about Mama, she was having more fun than she'd had since the days of playing in the mud down by the crick. In the Hollow she'd only had other kids to boss around, but here she had Jack, who did pretty much whatever she wanted him to.

She stood back and admired the three-sided shelter they'd decided to build using the cliff face as one wall and the overhang as a roof. They'd managed to find enough driftwood and lava rocks to put up two more walls. Well, she'd found the materials and Jack had hauled it all over. He'd wanted to do all sorts of elaborate calculating before they started building and kept using words like *schematics*, but the clouds rolling in had finally convinced him to just let her tell him how to do it.

Jack folded his arms over his chest and nodded. "Not bad. Not bad at all. Should provide a fair bit of protection from the elements."

She got a kick out of his man-triumphs-over-nature attitude. A half hour ago he'd been complaining that this would never work. "I'll bet you never built a hideaway when you were a kid in Nebraska."

He paused and adjusted his glasses, as if trying to remember.

"If you have to think about it, then you didn't. I can tell you exactly what my hideaway was like. We dug it out under the roots of this giant tree right beside the crick. Every year we dug out more and added rooms. We had frog races down there and everything. It was great until the year the crick overflowed."

"You're right, I didn't have anything like that. One summer I wanted to put up a tent in the backyard, but I gave up the idea when my grandmother wouldn't let me run the extension cord outside so I could plug stuff in."

She shook her head. "You're not supposed to have *electricity*, for pity's sake." Not that she always had that option in the Hollow, anyway. "You're supposed to act like you're completely on your own, with no grown-ups. You can't have a blessed *cord* running from the house to your hideaway. That's a dead giveway as to where you are."

"So what?" He seemed totally mystified.

"So if the grown-ups can't find you, you can do all the things they would tell you not to." She was beginning to wonder if Jack had taken a single chance as a kid. "That's how I learned to start fires with my glasses. Do you think my mama would have *wanted* me out in the woods doing that?"

"Guess not."

"Bet your britches she didn't. But I did it anyway, and now I can make us a nice fire, lickety-split." She walked over to the small pile of driftwood chips she'd been hoarding during the construction. "Let me have the glasses."

"There's no point in starting a fire when it's going to rain pretty soon."

"That's why we'll start it now, when we still have some sun, and then we'll transfer the fire inside the shelter."

"You can't have a fire in there! You'll incinerate us both!"

"Of course we can have a fire in there." She was patient with him because he was such a beginner at the outdoor life. "There's a nice little gap between the overhang and the wall, so the smoke can get out. And we'll build the fire on sand up against the cliff and put rocks around it, so it can't spread."

"It'll be hot in there," he muttered.

"Not once the rain starts." She gazed at him. "It'll be cozy."

"We'll die of carbon monoxide poisoning."

"No, we won't. Trust me. It'll be real nice."

"Humph." He handed over the glasses, although he still looked worried about the project.

Or maybe he was worried about being tucked into that tiny spot with her, since he had his crush going on and might be afraid he'd forget himself and give in to it. She could see that happening. She should be worried about the same thing, but she wasn't.

Without being real obvious about it, she'd kept her eye on Jack as he'd wrestled with the heavy pieces of driftwood. She couldn't recall the last time she'd had a chance to watch a muscular man stripped to the waist doing physical labor. Clyde Loudermilk had looked good without his shirt, but Jack looked a heap better.

That picture of Jack lifting a piece of driftwood to the top of the wall stayed with her as she knelt on the sand and held the glasses at the right angle to catch the sun. She was a little like this pile of kindling, now that she thought about it. For some time she'd turned down any dates that came her way, thinking she needed to be saving herself for Nick.

What a waste that had been. But the upshot of all that self-sacrifice was that she hadn't done the hokey-poky with a man in a coon's age. Now here she was stranded on a desert island with Jack.

If anybody had told her yesterday she'd be stuck with a guy like him after her long drought, she'd have laughed herself into a case of the hiccups. But after catching his manly display of muscle, she wasn't so sure being plane-wrecked with Jack was such a disaster.

She was beginning to feel very tender toward him. Finding out that he was color blind and ashamed of it touched her. Plus he was an orphan, a fact that always made her want to cuddle that person for all they'd missed. Jack was worth cuddling, too, because he had a good heart and he was very brave. Yesterday she hadn't known any of that about him.

Besides, they needed to find things to do to take their minds off food. She'd already started craving another energy bar, and they couldn't eat those yet.

For another thing, if she had a little fun with Jack while they were on the island, no one would have to know. She could trust him not to tell anyone, and she certainly wouldn't. And the third and best reason for having sex was that she'd be doing him a favor by teaching him how women liked to be treated in bed. He might not know any more about that than he did about making cozy hideaways.

Having sex for Jack's sake instead of her own made the idea seem noble and worthwhile. He might be terrible at it, which would leave her no better off than before. She was taking a big risk, come to think of it, and he should be mighty grateful for the chance to educate himself at her expense. Now that she knew him better, she expected he would be grateful.

A wisp of smoke curled up from the dried leaves and driftwood chips. Genevieve moved the glasses and leaned down to blow gently into the pile.

"I can't believe you're actually getting it to burn."

She blew harder and tiny flames wiggled upward. "You're lucky you have me around, Jack." Leaning back, she waved her hand over the flames until she could feel their heat. "I hate to think of what would become of you if you'd been marooned on this island all by your lonesome."

When he didn't have a comeback to that, she glanced up at him. He was inspecting her the way she imagined he inspected a computer screen that had started flashing warning signals. Well, he'd never get a girlfriend standing around looking like that. He needed a confident smile on his face, not a worried frown. Maybe she could put that smile on his face before they were rescued.

But first she had to get the inside of their hideaway all situated. "Could you tend this fire?" She stood. "I need to fix the pit inside."

"What should I do?"

"Goodness, you don't need an instruction book to—" She stopped when he started to blush. "You really never tended a fire before?" She could see the answer in his eyes. "Never mind. I didn't mean to make you feel poorly about it." She kicked herself for undermining his confidence when she wanted to do the exact opposite.

"I went to a Boy Scout meeting once. We were supposed to learn how to tie all these knots. I couldn't for the life of me figure out why I needed to tie anything except my shoes, so I walked back home."

"You taught yourself to fly a plane, and for that I'll be eternally grateful. Tending a fire's as easy as shooting cans off a fence post. You just—"

"You can shoot?"

"I'm pretty good with a squirrel gun, although I never shot a squirrel, or anything alive. Just cans." She could see she wasn't helping Jack's confidence level bragging on her shooting, either, so she threw in a story on herself. "I tried Uncle Rufus's sawed-off shotgun one time and sprayed lead everywhere. Aunt Maizie had some clothes on the line and I accidentally turned her favorite dress into a peekaboo style."

Jack looked as if he felt a little better after that story. "I'll remember not to hang around when you're toting a sawed-off shotgun. So what should I do with this fire?"

"Just add little pieces of driftwood, but do it one at a time and make sure each one is burning before you put on any more, or you'll smother it."

"I should be able to manage that." He hunkered down next to the tiny blaze and rubbed his hands together.

"Why did you do that?"

He looked up in surprise. "Do what?"

"Rub your hands."

"Huh." He spread his palms and looked at them. "Well, now that you mention it, I guess I rub them like that before I start working at the computer, so it was just force of habit. It's probably a concentration thing, plus it gets the blood circulating in my fingers so I can manipulate the keys better."

By all rights, that shouldn't have sounded sexy to her, but it did. "Oh. Well, I'll go fix up the fire pit." Still thinking about his hands manipulating the computer keys, she grabbed several of the smaller pieces of driftwood she'd collected during the time Jack had lugged the big ones for the wall.

It was the dexterity that had made her think of sex. She deposited her armload of wood inside the enclosure and went back to find a few small rocks. A man who could type well had good control of his fingers, and that kind of skill could be transferred to other matters. Jack might be a little short on experience, but if he had dexterity, all was not lost.

As she gathered rocks and tossed them in through the opening of the hideaway, she peeked over at Jack tending the fire. He picked up a cigar-shaped piece of driftwood. She didn't have to use much imagination to decide what that looked like. According to something she'd read in a magazine, a man's thumb was supposed to give an idea of how big he was. She took a gander at Jack's thumb as he laid the chunk of driftwood in the middle of the fire.

Could be ol' Jack had something besides dexterity going for him.

By the time Gen was ready to transfer some glowing coals to the fire pit inside the enclosure, Jack had figured out how they would do it. He might not have a lot of practical knowledge, but give him a problem to solve and a little time to think it through, and he could usually come up with a solution.

He let Gen consider the problem first, though, in case she'd already thought of something. When she admitted she was stuck on that particular point, he left her guarding the fire and walked down to the beach. As he searched the sand for what he wanted, the last of the sunlight disappeared. Sheets of rain swept the horizon, moving closer to the beach.

They needed to take shelter soon. He felt a rush of adrenaline at the idea of sharing that small space with Gen while the rain came down. Maybe she'd show him how to whittle. They'd need something to do, or he would become way too aware of her and might try something stupid. He had the feeling her thoughts might be going in that direction, too.

That could be a real disaster. Right now he had her friendship, at least. If he tried to take it beyond that and the result was mediocre, any chance of friendship would be gone forever. Whittling was the answer. He'd get her to teach him while they waited out the rain.

Of course, there was still the night to get through. But he could let her sleep in the enclosure and he'd stay outside. She'd be impressed with his chivalry and would never know he was a complete coward.

At last he found what he'd been looking for, what he'd

vaguely remembered seeing while he'd been trolling for driftwood—a piece of a conch shell the size of his palm. Smooth and pink on one side, the curved shell would make an excellent scoop. Then he realized that if he had several of these, they could collect water when it rained and they'd have something to drink besides guava juice. He was getting pretty damned good at this survival business. In fact, he—

A man's bark of laughter made him drop the shells. *Brogan!*

He spun around, his gaze darting everywhere. Nothing. Goosebumps covering his whole body, he started backing slowly up the beach toward Gen. When he was close enough, he called her name softly.

"What?"

"Shh! Keep your voice down. I heard something."

The bark of laughter came again, making the back of his neck prickle.

"That?" Gen asked.

"It's him." Jack began to shake. "And now he's *really* crazy."

"Oh, Jack," she murmured gently. "That's only seals out in the water."

Instantly he knew she was right, and he felt like an idiot. He sighed and rubbed the back of his neck. "Seals."

"Yes." Her gaze was warm with understanding. "But after what we've been through, it's natural to let your imagination play tricks on you."

"I guess." But he didn't think a real hero would freak like that. "Um, I'll be right back." He quickly returned to the waterline.

After gathering the shells he'd dropped, he carried them back to Gen. "One's for scooping up the coals, but we can set the others so they'll fill up with water when it rains." He hoped that bit of creativity would make her forget that he'd been spooked by a bunch of seals.

It seemed to do the trick. She gave him a big smile. "That's brilliant, Jack! And since you thought of it, I think you should be the one to scoop up some coals and carry them inside."

"Okay." He'd figured he would. "First let's set the other shells around. I washed them in the surf before I brought them up here."

"Great." She helped him distribute the shells around on the sand, propping them so they'd collect the most moisture possible. "That should do it. Wonderful idea."

"Thanks." Feeling better about himself, he crouched by the fire to get his shell full of coals.

"Be careful. Don't burn your fingers."

"Right. We don't have any mustard."

"You remembered I told you that!" She sounded very pleased.

Well, duh. He remembered every single conversation that he'd ever had with her, but he couldn't let her know that and reveal how pathetic he was. As for this hot coals transference, he had that down. He'd planned it all while he was tending the fire.

He'd learned something as he was staring at the little flames. Watching a fire could help him think almost as well as watching the shifting patterns on his screen savers. When he got back to Honolulu he might start using the little fireplace in his living room during the winter, if he could remember to buy wood for it. Then again, with his record, he might get involved in work, forget he'd built a fire, and burn the house down.

"Be very careful now." Gen hovered over him, obviously worried about whether he could pull off this important maneuver. "Want me to do it?"

"Nope." Using the piece of shell like a dustpan, he picked up a stick of driftwood and used it to guide several glowing coals up onto the surface of the shell. "I've got it."

He stood carefully, watching to make sure he didn't spill the coals as he carried them into the enclosure. One coal was dangerously close to his thumb and the heat from it was bordering on pain. He had to duck to keep from beaning himself on the overhang. Then he stayed in a crouched position as he turned toward her neat little semicircle of rocks connecting to the rock face of the cliff.

Gen came right in behind him. "Just lay them real easy-like on that pile of kindling."

"Right." He felt like he was in a Hollywood version of the discovery of fire. No wonder somebody had dreamed up the idea of matches. This method was a pain in the butt. Still, he managed to dump the coals on top of Gen's little pile of chips and dried leaves. Then, in the absence of mustard, he stuck his thumb in his mouth.

"Now let me blow on the coals."

He backed off so she could kneel down and blow life into the smoldering coals. Looking at her pursed lips while he continued to suck on his seared thumb reminded him of her boast in the plane, when she was trying to convince Brogan to land and give her a chance to show off her talent for oral sex. Considering she'd lost her virginity at thirteen, maybe she'd been telling the truth. Sex might have been the main source of entertainment in her neighborhood.

Being marooned on this island helped him understand how that could be so. Try as he might to avoid thinking about the subject, he'd been fixated on sex himself. Even learning how to whittle might not save him.

"There it goes!" She sat back on her heels and admired the little burst of flame she'd created. About that time a gust of wind swirled in through the open side of the enclosure and snuffed the flame. "Tarnation!"

"Here, let me work on it." Jack dropped to his knees beside her.

"Thanks. I'm as dizzy as if I'd been inhaling fumes from Uncle Rufus's still."

"Then relax for a minute." Jack was feeling a certain ownership of this fire now, and he wasn't about to let it go out. Rain had begun pelting the hideaway, so he doubted their little fire outside would be giving them any more live coals. He leaned down and blew the way he'd seen her do it, slow and gentle.

"That's good, Jack." She ran her hand up his back.

He nearly fell face-first into the kindling. "Th-thanks." He kept blowing, but it wasn't easy as she continued to stroke her hand up and down his bare back. If he told her to stop, he'd come off as some nervous virgin type. But if she didn't stop, he was going to get an erection. With no good solution at hand, he kept blowing on the coals.

At first she stroked up and down his backbone, but then she extended her territory and began making little figure-eights up and down his back. Only one thing could feel better than what she was doing. Well, maybe two things. Okay, three things, and all of them involved his increasingly stiff friend who wanted to get out of his jeans and party.

"I think that's enough blowing."

"Oh." He opened his eyes and stared down into the fire he'd created. "Guess so." He'd been so absorbed in the way she was stroking his back and the resulting effect on his penis that he hadn't even felt the heat on his face. If she hadn't said something he would have singed his eyebrows clear off in another minute.

"Here." While continuing to rub his back, she reached in with her free hand and gave him a bigger piece of drift-wood. "Put this on."

"Okay." His throat was clogged and he cleared it as he laid the wood across the flames. They licked the wood, which made him think of what else could be licking something critical right now, if he had the guts God gave a goldfish. "How's that?" Except for lifting his head up so he didn't catch his hair on fire, he didn't move an inch.

"Great."

"Are you . . . ready to teach me to whittle?" The instant the words were out, he knew that wasn't what a guy named Jack would say at a moment like this. A guy named Jack wouldn't give a damn about whittling. Instead he'd casually put his hand on her knee, which was right within reach, and give her an encouraging squeeze.

"Is that what you want to do?" She'd begun kneading the muscles in his back now. "Whittle?"

"Uh, well . . . it's an idea."

She handed him another piece of driftwood, a bigger one this time. "It's ready for more."

"Are you sure?"

"Yes." She massaged the back of his neck.

His hand shook as he laid the second piece on. The heat from the fire was making him sweat, but moving away would end the status quo and a decision would have to be made—to whittle or not to whittle.

Then she said his name sort of slow and drawn out, with a question mark at the end.

"What?" His voice squeaked.

"Remember what I told you about hideaways, how they're good for doing secret things?"

He gulped. "Uh-huh."

"Whatever we wanted to do here, we could, and nobody would ever have to know."

"But us." And hers was the only opinion he was worried about.

"Well, naturally *we* would know, but I can keep a secret if you can."

He took a shaky breath. "I know what you're talking about, Gen."

"I surely hope so, Jack. Otherwise, computer genius or

not, I'd think somebody dropped you on your head in the turnip patch."

He had troubled assimilating the information. Genevieve Terrence, the goddess he had worshiped from afar since the day he hired on at Rainbow, was coming on to him. This was the kind of scene he'd fantasized for months, yet like an idiot, he was hesitating. Jack the Confident had left the building, and only Jackson the Insecure remained to face the challenge.

She stopped rubbing his back. "I . . . I thought you were attracted to me."

He turned toward her then, not wanting her to doubt herself for a minute. "I am." Oh, wow, her nipples were making pucker marks in the material of her dress. She wasn't kidding about this. He forced his gaze up to her face. Sure enough, she looked upset. "I am attracted to you," he said again. Major understatement. His equipment was programmed and ready to roll.

"So?" Two little creases formed in her smooth forehead. "What's the matter?"

He could either tell her the truth or have her feel rejected. He settled for the truth. "What if I'm not as good at this as you are?"

The small wrinkles smoothed out of her forehead and she smiled gently at him, almost as if he were some little kid she was humoring. "I wouldn't expect you to be."

"You wouldn't?" He wasn't sure he liked her assumption that he'd be lousy at sex. "I mean, I might be good at this."

She stroked his bristly cheek with the tips of her fingers. "Probably not, Jack. Be realistic. People improve with practice, and I can't believe you've had very much practice."

Her fingertips drove him wild. He wanted to suck on her fingers, her toes, anything that presented itself to him. "So how much practice have you had?" he asked a trifle belligerently.

She seemed taken aback. "Well, not *that* much, but more than you, that's for darned sure."

He thought again about the blow job discussion. He was truly an imbecile not to let her have her way with him. Who cared if he showed himself up as less than studly? At least he didn't have murder in his heart like a former boyfriend he could mention.

"Since I figure you could use the practice," she said, "you can practice on me."

He blinked. "*Practice* on you?" He had an image of a CPR class where everybody perfected mouth-to-mouth resuscitation procedures on mannequins. "What does that mean? You're gonna just lie there?"

"Of course not. But I can give you pointers, Jack. That way, when you get a serious girlfriend, you'll have a better idea what to do."

He jerked away from her and almost landed in the fire pit. "The hell with that! I thought you were looking forward to having some fun, not engaging in tutorial sex!"

"We *would* have fun!"

"Did you plan to draw a few diagrams in the sand first? Or maybe you could write a few instructions on yourself in lipstick. You know, with little arrows pointing to the spot in question."

"Now, Jack, you're getting yourself all riled up over nothing."

"Easy for you to say. You're the proclaimed expert and I'm the proclaimed sexual dunce. Look, I may not be the best lover in the world, but don't feel you have to sacrifice yourself so that I can brush up on my technique!"

"I only thought—"

"That you could teach Jack a thing or two? Well, maybe you can, Gen. Then again, I might surprise you. Believe it or not, in my own bumbling, inept way I have actually succeeded in giving a woman an orgasm. Several times. I suppose she could have been faking, but from my *limited* experience, I don't think so."

She sank back on her heels and gazed at him, her expression filled with dismay. "I'm sorry, Jack," she whispered. "I didn't mean to insult you."

And just like that, his anger disappeared. It wasn't her fault that she didn't see him as a possible boyfriend herself. He'd overreacted because that's how he wanted her to see him, but the fact was, she didn't. "It's okay."

"I'm sure you're a wonderful lover."

"I wouldn't go that far."

She sighed and gave him a tiny smile. "No, you wouldn't, because you're a naturally modest person. And that means if you tell me you're a good lover, you're probably a great lover and I have no business trying to teach you a blessed thing."

"I wouldn't say that, either." He was beginning to regret that he'd lost his temper. She looked very appealing sitting back on her heels, her cheeks flushed and her eyes trying to bring him into focus across the short distance separating them. She'd spread her beach towel out across one wall, probably for them to use as a bed.

Her suitcase sat nearby, no doubt to keep the condoms handy for the activity she'd planned. His penis twitched in frustration. If he'd played along, he might have learned a thing or two, relieved some of that frustration, and had a hell of a lot of fun in the process.

"Jack, I can tell you're just trying to be nice, when the truth is, I've taken a belly flop in the hog pen and ruined the chance of us having sex." She glanced at him. "Want to learn to whittle?"

Nobody was an idiot all of the time, not even him. "No."

"No? I thought you said you'd like to learn?"

"I would." He cleared his throat and gathered his courage. "But I'd rather have sex."

Chapter 11

Annabelle decided she might live to see another day. After some hard thumps and bumps that sounded like the boat hitting up against something, the rocking stopped and the engine was still. She raised her head from the tiny galley sink, grabbed the damp towel she'd been using, and patted her mouth.

The floor felt unsteady, but because the dishes weren't rattling in the cupboards, she concluded that her legs were quivering, not the floor. Rain drummed hard against the boat, but now that it wasn't pitching so wildly, the rain didn't seem as likely to sink them.

"Lincoln?" She sounded like a bullfrog in mating season.

"Yeah?" His feeble response barely made it through the closed bathroom door.

"You okay?"

A pause. "Define *okay*."

Annabelle smiled grimly. "Alive."

"Semi."

"It's a start." She ran a little water in a glass. "Do you want some water?"

"Not yet."

She took a sip of the water, intending to rinse her mouth

and spit it back in the sink. Then she heard footsteps on the stairs and swallowed the water. It wouldn't do for Matt to see her spitting.

He appeared at the bottom of the stairs, his clothes soaked, his brown eyes wary. "How's it going down here?"

"You're all wet!"

"Somebody had to tie us up to the dock."

Embarrassed that she'd been so little help, she straightened her spine. "Well, we're both fine. Thank you for getting us here safely."

He glanced over at the closed bathroom door. "How's Lincoln?"

"I'm fine, too," Lincoln called through the door.

That's my boy, Annabelle thought, more proud of Lincoln at that moment than she had been in a long time. Sometimes the boy had the manners of a government revenuer, but underneath all that swagger he had grit.

Matt didn't look convinced about either of them. "I can get a doctor down here if you need one."

"Absolutely not," Annabelle said. Then she forced herself to say the next part. "How soon can we get going again?"

Matt looked at her as if she'd lost her mind. "Annabelle, you—"

"How soon?"

He shook his head. "Even if you were ready, we have to wait until the storm passes. From the weather reports that'll be a while, and it's getting late. Once it gets dark . . ."

"Maybe the storm will lift early."

"I don't think so, Annabelle." His voice gentled. "I'm afraid we're stuck on Molokai for the night."

Annabelle dropped her gaze so he couldn't read the despair in her eyes. She'd been determined that they'd find Genevieve before dark. The thought of her child out there overnight terrified her.

He continued to speak, his voice calm and soothing. "I can call for a van so you and Lincoln can spend the night in a hotel. You'll be a lot more comfortable there, and then in the morning we can start out again."

She lifted her head and looked at him. "Thank you, but we'll stay right here on the boat. I want to start out at first light. Besides, it wouldn't seem fitting to be lolling around in some hotel room while Genevieve is . . . is . . ." She couldn't put the thought into words.

"She's okay," Matt said. "Nick Brogan may have some unpleasant qualities, but he's a survivor. I wouldn't count out Jackson Farley, either. He can be absentminded, but he's also stubborn, which could be a very good thing under these circumstances."

"Genevieve *is* fine," Annabelle said. "If she wasn't fine, I would know." That was the one thing keeping her going. She had no doubt that if anything happened to either of her children she'd know instantly. Her connection with her daughter remained unbroken, which meant Genevieve was alive. But she might be frightened or hurt, and Annabelle wanted to get to her as soon as humanly possible.

"So you want to spend the night on the boat?"

"Yes, please." She should probably encourage Matt to go to a hotel where he'd be more comfortable, but she didn't want him to do that. Once he was out of her sight, he could oversleep or be held up in some way.

"Then we'll all stay here and leave the minute we can see what we're doing."

She felt like hugging him, but she didn't move. Hugging Matt, considering how he disliked her, would be a very bad idea. "Thank you."

The bathroom door opened and Lincoln stood there holding on to the door frame. His face was the same color as the white streak running down the middle of his hair, and his earphones were hanging around his neck and not plugged into his ears. He looked like he'd been run over by the turnip truck, but he tried to act cocky anyway. "Hey, whassup?"

Matt looked at him. "Not much more, if you're lucky."

Lincoln groaned. "That was heinous."

"Sorry. But you walked right into it."

"Yeah, I did, didn't I?" Lincoln smiled a little.

As Matt looked the two of them over, Annabelle could imagine what he was thinking. She and Lincoln hadn't turned out to be very good sailors.

"I've listened to the weather report for tomorrow," Matt said, "and it's supposed to be a nice day. Neither of you should have this problem tomorrow."

"How come you didn't get sick?" Lincoln asked.

Matt shrugged. "Everybody's different. I grew up here, and I've been around boats all my life. Nothing fazes me. But my brother, he gets sick on the Small World ride at Disneyland. He moved to Iowa so he wouldn't have to deal with water anymore."

"I'll bet Disneyland's cool." Lincoln looked wistful.

"You haven't been there?"

"Not yet." Lincoln glanced over at Annabelle. "I don't know if Mom told you, but planes freak her out. She's all, *If God had meant us to fly he would have given us wings.*" He flapped his hands for emphasis.

"She told me."

"Don't you think that's kind of weird?" Lincoln shot her a quick look. "No disrespect, Mom, but, like, everybody flies these days. It's safer than driving your car."

"But if your car starts misbehaving, you can pull over to the side of the blessed road!" Annabelle said. "It's not like you can park an airplane on a cloud."

Matt cleared his throat. "To be honest, I'm not crazy about flying myself. Only do it when I have to. Now, how about some Seven-Up for both of you? If that goes down, we can move on from there."

"Thank you. That would be very nice." Annabelle was impressed. Even though Matt didn't like her, he'd come to her aid. Then he'd cleverly changed the subject. From her point of view he was not only handsome, but sensitive to other folks' feelings. Either his ex-wife was a very silly woman or Matt hadn't revealed his bad habits yet. Of course he had some—everyone did—but they'd have to be mighty black to offset his good points.

"I guess Seven-Up would be cool," Lincoln said.

Annabelle lifted her eyebrows in warning.

"Yes, thank you," he added quickly.

Annabelle sighed. She had an uphill battle, because if Lincoln was polite around his friends they'd make fun of him and call him a wussy. She'd listened to him belching and wisecracking when he thought she couldn't hear him.

But that behavior wouldn't wash when he was around her. She couldn't let him slide into disrespectful ways or, worse yet, behavior that reminded her of the Hollow. She sometimes wondered if he'd somehow inherited the unpolished ways of the folks in the Hollow. But that couldn't be true, or Genevieve would be like that, too, and she wasn't. She was such a good girl. Annabelle's heart contracted as she thought of her tender young daughter out there in some kind of danger, scared and cold, needing her mama.

Genevieve's heart beat fast enough to keep time with "The Orange Blossom Special." Even though she'd insulted Jack's ability to satisfy a woman, he still wanted to take a shot at satisfying *her*. "I won't offer you pointers or anything," she said.

"Why not?" He took his glasses off. "I don't pretend to be perfect at this."

She swallowed. They were really going to do it. And what was even more amazing, she really wanted to. The steady beat of the rain and the smell of woodsmoke took her back to her days in the Hollow, back when she'd first discovered exciting things about her body. She'd lost some of that thrill along the way, but here, with Jack, the specialness was there again.

Although she knew it wasn't true, she felt like a virgin. "I don't pretend to be perfect, either."

"You'd better put these in your suitcase." He held out the glasses. "And get out—"

"I will." She took the glasses without looking at him. As she'd imagined this event taking place, she hadn't figured on feeling shy. Maybe it was the manly way he'd defended himself when she'd insulted him. In that moment he'd stopped being bumbling Jackson and turned into forceful Jack again. She was beginning to cherish that unexpected side of him, and when he acted like that, she got weak in the knees.

They seemed to be on either ends of a seesaw. If one of them was feeling full of vinegar, the other one turned into a bowl of cornmeal mush. Then, in a little while, they'd trade places. It was the strangest thing. Right now she was in the mush stage.

She took out the condom and then couldn't decide where to put it.

"Just set it beside the beach towel," Jack said, his voice soft.

She laid it in the sand near one end of the towel. Then she reached for another piece of driftwood and gave it to him. "Put this on, so the . . . so the fire won't go out."

"I can't believe we need this fire."

She gathered her courage and looked over at Jack. His skin glistened. Except for the fact that he had chest hair, he looked like a bodybuilder after a workout. "We'll need it . . . later."

He stared at her.

"We will, Jack. You'll cool off eventually."

"I don't think so."

She had a picture of Jack constantly hot, constantly wanting her. It made her tingle all over. "What now?"

"I think we have to make this one up as we go along." He smiled, slow and easy. "It's not your average sex scene."

That smile turned her inside out. Set against his dark beard, his teeth flashed whiter than ever. She wanted him to kiss her, and she wanted it to happen in the next two seconds or she might pass out from anticipation.

"You need to come closer," she said.

"I know. But before I get closer and forget everything—"

"You'll forget everything?" She liked the idea that he'd go crazy with lust and turn into some wild beast. She well remembered the feeling of being ravished when he'd kissed her the first time.

"It could happen. I want you pretty bad."

She looked down at his crotch and discovered he did want her pretty bad. That worked her up even more.

"There's the sand issue," he said.

She wished he'd stop jawing and do something constructive with his mouth. Like kiss her. "That's why I spread out the towel."

"I know, but there's only room for one of us, so the other one has to be on top. All things considered, maybe that should be you. Then you can—"

"Are you fixing to talk me into an orgasm?" As hot and bothered as she was getting, he might be able to do it, but that wasn't what she had in mind. She was thinking about a little foreplay.

"I don't want you to get sand up your—" He gulped as she pulled one strap of her dress down over her arm.

She pushed down the other strap and folded her dress down to her waist. "You were saying?"

He looked like he'd been smacked upside the head with a two-by-four. His mouth opened and closed, but nothing came out.

"You should come closer, Jack. I know you can't get a good view from where you're sitting. You're a little blurry to me, so I must be blurry to you."

Slowly, as if he'd been drugged, he dropped to his hands and knees and crawled toward her. Gradually his face came into clear focus and she could see his eyes. The blue was nearly covered up by pupils wide with lust. Now he was in the bowl of mush stage.

"Don't worry about the sand just yet," she whispered.

He gulped again.

Her heartbeat skittered, knowing that she had the power to make him speechless. "I know I promised not to give you pointers, but now would be a good time to suck on my titties." She cradled her breasts and lifted them toward him. She wanted to feel the scrape of his teeth and the prickle of his beard. "Have a taste."

Making a sound low in his throat that was half animal, half human, he leaned forward and ran his tongue around her nipple. Then he did it again, his tongue warm and wet as a puppy's. He began lapping eagerly, making her nipple go from soft and full to hard and tight.

She closed her eyes. This was more like it. Jack might think he had to plan everything in advance, but some things worked out better by letting nature take its course.

When he sucked her nipple into his mouth, he made an *mmmm* sort of noise, as if he'd just taken a mouthful of pecan pie with whipped cream. He certainly knew how to do this part right—exactly enough pressure to send a signal down below, where the welcome party was being set up. Soon that welcome party would be in full swing, ready to greet the honored guest. Then she'd find out if a man's thumb had anything to do with how he was hung.

But they could have a lot of fun before that moment came. Opening her eyes, she watched him enjoying himself, and that made the sensation even better. His breath fanned her breast as his cheeks hollowed and his eyelashes fluttered closed.

Then he pulled away and rubbed his mouth back and forth across her nipple, wiggling it around with his teeth and tongue until she was almost ready to come, just from that. Maybe it was the crashing surf outside, or the rain, or the cozy hideaway on a deserted island, but she'd never felt this loose with a man.

Before the ultimate could happen, he paused, like a surfer on the crest of a wave. Heart racing, she balanced with him, breathlessly waiting for what he'd do next. It was better than the Tilt-a-Wheel at the carnival.

With his lips parted, he slid his mouth slowly down one slope and up the other. The soft bristles of his beard tickled her skin, and when he closed his white teeth gently over her other nipple, she once again felt like a captured maiden being fondled by a bold pirate. She moaned happily.

Immediately he became motionless. Then he pulled back and looked up at her. "Did I . . . hurt you?" he asked in a hoarse voice.

"Oh, no, Jack. I'll moan if it's good. I'll yell if it's bad."

"You're sure my beard isn't—"

"Jack!" She was losing the pirate image, so she grabbed his head and thrust her nipple into his mouth. "Moans are good, yelling's bad. Now back to business!"

Fortunately Jack wasn't the kind to talk with his mouth full, so that ended the conversation. Now that they understood each other, she was free to moan some more, which she did, because he'd started that nipple-wiggling trick again.

He'd stopped before, but she didn't want him to stop this time. She was wound up and set to chime. Maybe he needed some encouragement. "That's . . . good," she murmured.

He stopped. "What?"

She groaned in frustration. "What you were doing. The . . . the nipple-wiggling thing. I don't know where you learned it, but—"

"I made it up."

"Do it some more."

He settled in again, and before long she was panting. She'd had no idea that she could come this way. Jack was a genius, all right. Only a genius would know how to use his mouth on her until she . . . oh, goodness . . . oh, goodness gracious . . . oh, for the love of all creation! She climaxed, letting out a loud moan and rocking back on her heels. She nearly toppled over.

"Gen?" He sounded worried as he grabbed her by the shoulders, his hands gritty from the sand. "Gen, are you okay?"

"I'm . . . in . . . high cotton," she said, gasping.

"Is that good?"

Still trying to breathe like a normal person, she opened her eyes and looked at him. "That's great! Jack, you made me come just then."

"I did? But I didn't even—"

"I *know*. Isn't it amazing?" She gulped for air. "Whatever that thing is that you do with your mouth, you should get a patent on it."

A slow smile tugged at his mouth. "It was good, huh?"

"Inspirational."

"Wow. I've never made anyone come by just—"

"But you need some follow-up." She'd promised herself not to give him tips, but he needed a teensy bit of help. He had the potential to become really outstanding at this.

"Follow-up?"

"So you move smoothly into the next stage." She took a deep breath. She could hardly wait for the next stage. "You don't want to be gloating about the first orgasm when you could be leading up to the next one." Hint, hint.

"Oh." That lustful expression returned. "*Oh.*"

"Wipe the sand off your hands. You'll be needing them."

While he wiped his hands on his slacks, she reached behind her and unzipped her dress. Then she pulled it over her head, rolled it up, and positioned it at the end of the towel like a pillow.

"Oh, *Gen.*"

"What?" She turned back to him and discovered he was all eyes.

"You're . . . incredible."

"Well, thank you, but I'm really nothing special." She liked hearing him say that, anyway, and she was glad she'd worn her white lace bikini panties today. "You just don't get out much."

He shook his head. "Show me a million almost-naked women and I'd still pick you."

She felt warm all over. No one had ever said something like that to her. "I . . . I'm glad you think so." The way he was looking at her made her feel prettier, like a movie star.

"I know you said I needed to follow-up, but can I . . . just look at you for a minute? The light's starting to fade, and I don't want to miss—"

"You can look, Jack," she said softly. She rose to her knees and slid her thumbs into the elastic of her panties. "In fact, you can have the whole show."

His breath caught as she slid the panties down to her knees. He seemed completely awestruck. "I never thought

I'd see you like this," he murmured. "I never thought you'd want me."

Her heart felt as if someone had put it through the wringer on her mama's old washing machine. He was treating her as if she were some sort of precious gift. No man had ever done that before. Because she had no idea what to say, she cradled his face in both hands and kissed him gently on the mouth.

He kissed her back the same way, and when his fingers slid along her jaw, they were trembling. From the way he slowly explored her mouth, from the tenderness when he combed his fingers through her hair, she would never know that he was going crazy with wanting her. But she thought he probably was, because he'd just told her she was the best-looking naked woman he'd ever seen. Besides, she was going crazy wanting him, so vice versa made perfect sense.

Yet the way they were kissing now was perfect. Perfect. How unbelievable that the sweetest kiss she'd ever had would be from Jackson Farley.

Chapter 12

Heat from the fire blasted the soles of Jack's feet, but he didn't care. Now he understood how a person could walk over hot coals. He could do it if he thought about Gen naked. He could do anything if he thought about Gen naked, even put up with a hard-on the size of a battleship while he concentrated on this follow-up business.

Follow-up should be slow and easy. She'd told him that without saying so, by the way she was kissing him, like she was savoring an expensive dessert. So he'd kiss her the same way, and it was working out great, because he could show her without words how lucky he felt to be here. He was most definitely savoring her.

Most of all, he felt incredibly happy to know that sex with Gen, at least so far, was a big deal for him. There wasn't a single so-so thing about it, which meant that he had as much sexual drive as the next guy, and that was a huge relief. He just needed the right motivation, and the right motivation was, at this very moment, sticking her tongue in his mouth.

And lacing her fingers through his. And guiding his hand down until something feathery tickled his knuckles. His heart boomed like cannonfire when he realized what that feathery stuff was.

Her kiss stopped for a millisecond. "More," she whispered against his mouth. Then her tongue went to work again.

He could do more. He *so* could do more. Jack the Orgasm Man, that was him.

She let go of his hand, probably to see if he could manage on his own. He was up to the challenge, but still, the concept of what he was being urged to do blew his circuits. She wanted his fingers *in there*. He still couldn't believe she was letting him do these things.

Somehow he got past the wonder of it all and shifted a little to the side so he had a better angle. That put his feet closer to the fire, but he didn't care a bit. Any guy whose hand hovered over paradise while his tongue was deep in bliss couldn't let a little thing like hot coals bother him.

He remembered how she'd liked the back-and-forth movement on her breast, so he started by brushing his hand lightly over her springy curls. She started breathing faster, so he figured he was good to go. Resting the heel of his hand just above the border of those curls, he slid his middle finger slowly down until he reached . . . omigod. She was juicy, plump, and furnace hot. His penis ached, his balls ached.

But she hadn't invited him to play that game yet. She wanted follow-up.

So that's what she'd get. What sweet torture. He added a second finger, and the deeper inside he went, the harder his penis became. She moaned. He moaned. And then he got to work, deciding that if this was the order of things for her, he'd follow it or die trying.

As it turned out, he didn't have to work very hard. A few strokes and she threw back her head, gasping and crying out as her spasms rippled past his fingers. As she quivered in the aftershock, he supported her with one hand around her shoulders and the other buried in her center of gravity. Maybe she wanted him to stay right there. Maybe she wanted him to do it again. And he would. Whatever she said, he'd do, even if his equipment ended up with permanent creases from being compacted so long.

"Take off . . . your pants," she said, gulping for air.

Music to his ears. Music to his penis, too. Slowly he withdrew his fingers.

"Ahhh," she whispered, sounding regretful as she closed her eyes.

He didn't want her to be regretful. "I can do that again."

"I know. Maybe . . . later." She sank slowly back on her heels and looked at him with glazed eyes. "I want you to stand up now and take off your pants."

He wondered if he could stand. He was shaking pretty badly. Somehow he managed it, although the sand bit into the tender soles of his feet. He wondered if they were blistered, but he forgot all about that when she reached for his belt buckle. He wondered if she remembered what she'd said in the plane about blow jobs. He would never forget it.

She undid the buckle, worked the button loose, and started unzipping his fly. "I'll bet you're ready to go off like a bottle rocket," she said.

He didn't say anything. He was too busy trying not to go off like a bottle rocket.

"Here's my idea." She shoved down his pants and his penis cantilevered the soft cotton material of his Jockeys so his underwear resembled the prow of a schooner. She glanced at the display and smiled. "I need to relieve that pressure before we settle in on that towel, don't you think?"

His response was a very unsophisticated gurgle of excitement.

"I'll take that as a yes. Now step out of your pants."

He started to follow her instructions and nearly fell on top of her.

She grabbed his hand and placed it on her shoulder just

in time to save the day. "Brace yourself on me. Use two hands."

Beneath his hands her shoulder bones seemed small and delicate. He hesitated to put any weight on them for fear she'd go down.

"Lean on me," she said. "I'm stronger than I look."

He wanted out of those pants, and his passion-clouded brain couldn't think of alternatives, so he used her for support while he extracted his feet from the jeans. She held under his weight.

"Good." She gazed up at him, looking directly into his eyes. "You might want to keep hold of me, to steady yourself." Her cheeks grew pink. "It could get a mite intense."

He nodded. Nodding was the best he could do under the current circumstances. His blood hammered in his ears and he wondered if he might pass out from excitement. There was only so much a guy could stand. But passing out would be such a lame thing to do when he was about to have the most excellent experience of his entire sexual life.

Dropping her attention to those misshapen briefs, she tugged them down in one bold move. "Bless my ever-loving soul," she murmured. "Thumbs don't lie."

He didn't understand what thumbs had to do with anything, but who cared if she made sense? Who cared if she started speaking in pig Latin? But she didn't speak at all. Instead she wrapped both hands around his penis. She looked like a rock star holding a mike, ready to belt out that first note.

If she didn't hurry up, it would be a very short song.

When she started playing around with quick swipes of her tongue, he gasped and clutched her shoulders, sure it was all over. But by gritting his teeth he managed to stave off a climax that might have blinded her. Ah, this was incredible. He had to make it last somehow, so he closed his eyes and started reciting the square root table in his head.

That worked until she slipped her mouth down over the tip. He had only a nanosecond to warn her. "Gen—"

She tightened her grip on the base of his penis, which staved off the inevitable a second longer. Slowly she slid her mouth free. "It's okay," she whispered, her breath cool on his wet skin. "Let go. I've got you." Then she was back, just in time, holding him firmly in one hand, stroking his balls with her other hand.

He emptied his lungs in a roar as he emptied his come into her mouth. He saw stars, planets, the entire universe. If he hadn't been anchored so firmly to her wonderful mouth, he would have taken flight, rising into the sky like a helium balloon.

Gradually his head stopped buzzing, but his legs were like licorice whips and even her support soon wouldn't be enough to keep him upright. Fortunately she released him about that time, because he needed to get down on his knees before he fell.

Kneeling on the sand, he was still weaving a little as he held on to her shoulders and stared into her beautiful face, the face of a goddess. "Th-thank you."

She smiled. "Kisses make a nice thank you, too."

What a terrific idea. He leaned forward and touched his lips to her mouth, the very mouth that had sent him to Pluto and back. Hot damn, she tasted of sex, and what started out as a thank-you kiss turned into a wet, sloppy tongue-fest that soon had him stroking her breasts and her fondling his penis again.

In no time at all he was recharged and ready to take that *South Park* beach towel for a magic carpet ride. He'd never rebounded that fast, not even at seventeen. He was a stud. He was a manly man. He was Jack.

He lifted his mouth a millimeter away from hers. "Ready to unwrap one of those condoms?"

She laughed softly and squeezed his rigid penis. "I guess you've been saving up."

For you, he wanted to say, but thought better of it. "You bet. Just hoping I'd be stranded on a desert island with a willing woman and a suitcase full of condoms."

She laughed again. "Next you'll be telling me Nick did you a favor."

"He did." He cupped her breast, memorizing the silken weight of it so he could have memories in his old age. "But the thing is, he meant to kill me, so I don't think I'll bother to thank him." There, that was a good comeback, the kind of comeback that a guy by the name of Jack would make. "And that's as much time as I want to waste talking about Brogan."

Goddamn sonofabitchin' rain! Nick Brogan huddled inside a crevice that wasn't nearly adequate to shield him from the storm. It wasn't bad enough that his pickup men hadn't shown up on schedule, or that he was fucking starving to death, or that he'd lost his Ziploc bag before he could get the gun inside.

No, he also had to put up with getting rained on. He used to be dying of thirst, too, but now that was solved. He could tilt his head and open his mouth and have all he wanted to drink. Too bad it wasn't raining Scotch.

Quenching his killer thirst was the only good thing about this damned rainstorm that had blown in without warning, totally not part of his brilliant plan. He should be well on his way to sipping Dom Pérignon instead of sucking drops of rainwater out of the sky. God knew where the idiots were who were supposed to show up hours ago.

Probably lost, wandering around clueless, the jugheads. He'd known they weren't the sharpest knives in the drawer when he'd hired them. Initially that had worked to his advantage, because they'd been too stupid to ask a bunch of questions he didn't care to answer. They didn't even know his name and they had no idea what he was up to.

They'd seemed perfect, needing money to fix the broken radio in their boat and buy new fishing gear so they could continue to take out charters. Even the busted radio had played right into his hands, because he hadn't wanted them to communicate with anybody during this exercise.

He hadn't expected a lot out of them, but he'd hoped that even their midget IQs would enable them to find this beach again once he'd pointed it out. Apparently not, and from the size of the waves hitting the shore he'd bet the Coast Guard had issued a small craft warning by now. Besides being dumb as sand fleas, his pickup men were also cowards, so once they heard of a small craft warning, they'd scuttle all plans of looking for him until the weather cleared.

Whatever he'd agreed to pay them, it was too damned much. Not that he'd planned on actually giving them the money. Shooting them and dumping the bodies overboard was a hell of a lot cheaper and less risky.

Before this caper began, he'd wondered if he'd have the nerve to kill anyone, after all. Now he knew the answer. Nobody was getting between him and that three million. Nobody.

So he'd be safer to eliminate the pickup guys from the equation. Even stupid men might end up saying the wrong thing to the right person, although that wouldn't have been a big worry if everything had happened the way he'd envisioned. He should have been gone by now, on his way to Tokyo via a rattletrap cargo plane whose pilot wouldn't ask bothersome questions.

Now he was late, and he wasn't sure how to fix that little glitch. He hadn't wanted to risk using a cell phone on this operation, for fear the signal would be picked up by somebody he didn't want listening in. So here he was, pinned down on this lousy scrap of real estate, helpless until the brainless morons he'd hired managed to stumble upon him.

On top of all that, his gun had salt water in it now. Maybe he should use some of this blasted rain to wash out the gun. Yeah, he'd better do it, although that might screw up the chamber even more. He hadn't anticipated this and didn't know for sure what to do about the wet gun. They hadn't covered that during his gun owner's course last month.

He hated it when things didn't go the way they were supposed to. At least the deal with the plane had come off like a dream. The only two people who knew that he wasn't at the bottom of the ocean were dead. From that standpoint, the plan had worked to perfection. Now he just needed to get the hell out of here.

Matt made a pig of himself eating baked ham, turnip greens, and mashed sweet potatoes. He hadn't had a home-cooked meal in forever, and besides being sexy and damned good to look at, Annabelle was a great cook. It was a bonus to the trip he hadn't counted on, and he was looking for all the pluses he could find.

On one hand he felt guilty chowing down on the food Annabelle fixed, because she wasn't eating much of it, but on the other hand he reasoned that it would be an insult not to enjoy her cooking. And he wasn't alone in the glutton department. Lincoln's appetite had come back and he seemed determined to replace everything he'd upchucked a couple of hours ago.

Matt was reasonably sure Annabelle wasn't still seasick. No, she was simply heartsick. Lincoln might be worried, too, but he didn't have the burden of responsibility that his mother had, and besides, it took a hell of a lot to cause a normal fourteen-year-old boy to go off his feed. Watching Lincoln eat made Matt feel better, so he could imagine how it cheered Annabelle. Some things, at least, were the same.

Lincoln reminded Matt of how he'd been at that age— a bottomless pit. Sitting next to Lincoln on the longer side of the L-shaped bench seat, Matt had a chance to observe the kid up close and personal. Under the constant scrutiny of his mother down at the end of the table, Lincoln made a real effort to mind his table manners, but he still ate like a teenage boy, wolfing his food and washing it down with milk. Matt wondered if the food remained on his tongue long enough for all the wonderful flavors to register. Probably not. But then, he might not see this meal as anything special, considering that he ate his mother's cooking all the time.

Matt spent the meal asking the clichéd questions most adults asked kids—about school and sports. Lincoln responded with good grace, although Matt wondered if he was mentally rolling his eyes. Annabelle added a few bits of information that Lincoln might rather have kept under wraps, like the poetry contest he'd won last year and the part he'd been asked to play in the school musical. Oh, and by the way, Annabelle had said casually, Lincoln was on the honor roll.

"It's no big whoop to be on the honor roll." Lincoln broke into her litany. "Everybody's on it."

"Everybody most certainly is not," Annabelle said. "You're the only one of your friends who made it."

Lincoln shrugged. "I got lucky."

Annabelle opened her mouth as if to contradict him. Then she closed it again, glanced at Matt, and smiled. "Then you must be a mighty lucky boy," she said.

Matt smiled back, enjoying the cozy moment in which he and Annabelle silently shared the knowledge that Lincoln was trying his hardest not to be labeled a nerd who cared about grades. Funny how this little meal in the cabin of a rented boat felt more homey and comfortable than any Matt had shared in that big old house with Theresa. Twenty years ago he'd thought it was reasonable to want a nice wife, maybe a couple of kids, and a job he could enjoy.

The job had turned out okay, but Theresa hadn't been a nice wife. Kids only would have mucked up the situation, so he was glad they hadn't had them. But that meant he didn't have a fourteen-year-old basketball player/poet around the house. Multicolored hair aside, Lincoln was the kind of boy any man would be proud to call his son. Matt was curious as to where the guy was who had that right.

Finally Matt had stuffed in as much as he could hold. Maybe the food comforted him, too. He wished he could figure out a way to comfort Annabelle short of holding her, which wouldn't be happening.

He placed his napkin beside his plate. "That was delicious, Annabelle. Thank you."

She gave him a brief smile. "I'm glad it set well with you."

"It did. Great meal."

"Uh, Mom?" Lincoln eyed the food still on her plate. "Are you going to eat that, or what?"

"You probably should try," Matt said. He wanted to say something about keeping her strength up, but that sounded too dire, so he didn't.

Annabelle shoved her plate toward Lincoln. "You go ahead and have it."

"You're sure? 'Cause if you're gonna eat it, then—"

"I'm not, so no sense in letting it go to waste." She gave the plate another little push in her son's direction. "Go on. Otherwise I'll scrape it in the garbage."

Full as he was, Matt would have finished her meal rather than see it go in the garbage. Once he was convinced she wouldn't eat it, he was relieved when Lincoln pulled the plate in front of him and dug in.

Lincoln was chewing away, his mouth full, when he glanced up and apparently realized that both his mother and Matt were sitting there watching him eat. "Hey, like talk among yourselves, okay?" he said.

"Lincoln, don't speak with your mouth full!" Annabelle recoiled in horror.

Lincoln swallowed loudly. "Somebody has to talk. You're freaking me out, like watching me eat is the entertainment." He glanced at his watch. "I know what! The TV works, right?"

"It should," Matt said.

"Then let's watch the Cubs and the D'Backs. I almost forgot the game was on."

Matt stood. "I'll see if we can bring it in." He flipped on the television mounted in a wall cabinet opposite the table. He even knew the right channel, because had the evening turned out differently, he would have watched the game himself. Considering he'd decided to take a break from Celeste, he couldn't very well go to the bar tonight, so that had left cozying up to the TV.

"Oh, wow, a triple!" Lincoln said. "Gonzo is so totally awesome."

"He's good." Matt watched Luis Gonzalez pull off his batting glove as he stood on third.

"Yeah. My friends are all *Gonzo's the bomb*."

"I'll start on the dishes." Annabelle slid from her seat and started collecting plates and silverware.

"No, you won't." Matt turned away from the television and walked back to the table. "I'm not much of a cook, but I'm a damned good dishwasher."

She met his gaze. "It'll give me something to do," she said quietly. "I'm not much of a baseball fan."

He understood her reasoning, but he didn't like the

idea of turning her into some kind of galley slave, while the two guys bonded over baseball. Too bad he couldn't invite her for a little walk, but it was raining. Or was it? After crossing back to the television, he turned down the volume and listened. No rain.

Matt adjusted the volume again, then located the remote and handed it to Lincoln. "Tell you what. You keep tabs on the game, and your mother and I will take a walk on the dock. We won't go far, so if you need anything, just come out and get us."

"Sure." Lincoln nodded, his attention focused on the screen. "Oh, geez. They *stranded* him."

Matt didn't spare a glance at the TV. Instead he looked at Annabelle, who stood with the dishes still in her hands as she stared at him in obvious shock. "Wouldn't you like a little fresh air?" He tried to make the suggestion sound casual, although he didn't feel at all casual about it.

She hesitated, as if making a really tough decision. "I . . . I reckon I would," she said at last.

He could get used to that little hillbilly twang that crept into her voice now and then. "Gonna take the dishes with you?" he teased, to see if she'd lighten up any.

She looked down at the dishes as if she'd never seen plates and forks before. "Uh, no." She turned to set them on the kitchen counter, but not quickly enough to hide her blush.

That splash of color in her cheeks was the best thing Matt had seen all day. He'd actually succeeded in flirting. He couldn't remember the last time he'd tried to flirt with a woman. By the time he and Theresa had split the sheets, they'd been years past the flirting stage. As for the episode last night with Celeste—she'd done all the flirting while he'd gone along for the ride. He also thought it would take quite a lot to make Celeste blush.

No matter how much an evening with a twenty-something woman had stroked his ego, he'd never felt completely comfortable with Celeste. Annabelle was his generation, his value system. She might be a tigress when it came to her kids, but she wasn't bold with men. If anything, she seemed wary. He kind of liked that, because that probably meant she wasn't any more sophisticated about the game than he was.

But he was way ahead of himself. She'd agreed to a walk along the dock, not a romantic rendezvous. Damned if he wasn't looking forward to having a little time alone with her, though.

She rinsed her hands in the sink and dried them on a towel. Then she walked toward Matt, ducking when she came between Lincoln and his ball game. "You're more than welcome to start on the dishes after you get finished eating," she told her son.

"Huh?" Lincoln glanced up, clueless. "Did you say something, Mom?"

"I . . . oh, never mind. I guess we can worry about it when we get back."

"Okay. Whatever." Lincoln turned back to the game. "You kids have fun."

Matt chuckled, but Annabelle stopped in her tracks and stared at Lincoln. *"What?"*

Lincoln looked at her with a sly grin. "I've been waiting at least a trillion years to say that. But you, like, never go out, so I'm all, *When can I ever use that line?* I figured this might be my big chance."

Annabelle seemed to be at a total loss for words, so Matt jumped into the breach. "Okay, we'll take off now. And don't try to sneak a beer while we're gone. I counted the bottles."

Lincoln gaped at him. "We have beer on board?"

"No, but I've always wanted to say that, and I've never had a kid to say it to, so I guess we're even, huh?"

Lincoln laughed, obviously pleased with the little interchange. "We're so even, dude. Later."

"Later." Matt motioned for Annabelle to go ahead of him up the steps to the deck.

They didn't speak until after he'd helped her climb from the stern to the dock, which was shiny with rain in the soft mercury lights lining the row of berths. The night was warm and moonless, and the only sounds came from the creak of boats whenever a swell rolled under the dock.

"You're being mighty kind to my son." Annabelle lifted her gaze to his. "And I thank you for it. This is a sorry mess we're in, but you being nice to Lincoln helps."

"He's a good kid. I'll admit when you insisted he had to come along I wasn't looking forward to it, but I'm getting a kick out of him, multicolored hair, earring, and all." He gestured to their right. "Why don't we walk down to the end of the dock and back? We'll be able to see the boat the whole way."

"All right." Annabelle fell into step beside him, her arms crossed over her middle, as if feeling the need to protect herself.

He hoped she didn't feel the need to protect herself from him. "Are you cold?" The line came right out of his college dating days, back when he'd looked for any excuse to put his arm around a girl. In the pale light, Annabelle looked like a college girl, and he wouldn't mind having a reason to put his arm around her.

She glanced at him, a hint of a smile in her eyes. "I'm okay. Thanks."

He knew she'd recognized the line for what it was. "That meal was awesome." He hadn't been able to say that in college, where they'd all lived on fast food. "Thank you."

"It's the least I can do. I, um, enjoyed watching you eat it."

Hey, that was progress. She'd acknowledged paying attention to him. "Did you notice the total rapture on my face?"

This time a real smile appeared. "I did. You reminded me of Lincoln when he's looking at Britney Spears on TV."

"I'd take that meal over Britney any day." *I'd take you over Britney, too.* But he didn't think that was the thing to say. Not yet.

"Well, thank you. I miss cooking for a—" She caught herself and cleared her throat. "Another grown-up."

"I miss eating dinner with a beautiful woman." He looked over to see how she was taking that.

She was staring off across the water, like he'd gone too far and she was thinking how to change the subject. "You mentioned Lincoln's hair a while back. You probably think I should have put my foot down about that."

He didn't want to push her, so he went along with the switch in topic. "I did think that at first. But he has such a good attitude compared to a lot of the kids I see that I'm revising that opinion. Maybe if you give kids a chance to rebel in the small ways, they won't feel so determined to rebel in the big ones."

"That's what I hope." She sighed. "But when you're doing the raising by yourself, sometimes it's hard to know what's right."

"Then Lincoln's father isn't a part of his life?"

"No." She stopped walking and turned to him. "Listen, maybe we should get something straight."

"Uh, okay." The tone of her voice told him that the ground he'd gained earlier was slipping away. Her closed expression didn't give him much hope, either.

"I think, with us sharing space like this, we need to talk plain to one another."

"I agree." If he were to talk plain to her right now, he'd say he wanted to kiss her and see if he could get past that barrier she'd thrown up. At least he couldn't take her chilly behavior personally, now that Lincoln had announced she didn't date. "You hate men?"

"I wish I did. But it turns out I love men."

That was nice to hear. "From a distance?"

Still she wouldn't look at him. "Oh, no. I've enjoyed them up close, too. Genevieve and Lincoln are the evidence."

"I just meant—"

"You see, Genevieve's daddy made me pretty promises and then left me pregnant. I did without men for a long time, but then Lincoln's daddy showed up, and it was the same cock-a-doodle-doo, different rooster."

Matt couldn't help smiling, but he quickly controlled himself. She was deadly serious about this, and she didn't think anything was strange about the little expressions he found so endearing. Plus, the last thing he wanted to do was make her self-conscious about the way she talked. "Sorry to hear that," he said.

"Not as sorry as I was, believe me. After that man hightailed it out of the Hollow, I made a vow that I wouldn't have sex again until after my childbearing years, and I'm not there yet."

Matt swallowed. Now that was a challenge any red-blooded man wouldn't be able to leave alone. "Annabelle, do you have something against birth control?"

"Yes." She looked at him, finally, and her eyes held no sign of compromise. "It's not guaranteed."

"Well, no, but the percentages are in your—"

"Then there's that other problem."

"Other problem?" He couldn't believe they were standing out here discussing sex. And even in the dim light he could tell that her cheeks were getting pink again.

She took a deep breath. "When a man strikes my fancy, I lose all common sense. If he wants to do it right now, I do it. I don't think about babies and scraping for a living because my man ran out and left me in the family way. It's a failing, pure and simple. So it's easier to do without."

Matt was getting extremely agitated. Okay, he was getting horny. "It shouldn't be all up to you. It's a guy's responsibility, too." And last night he'd been unprepared. Celeste had taken care of the problem. He was still unprepared. So much for taking responsibility.

She held his gaze. "You see where counting on that has landed me."

"Annabelle, all men aren't like the two you hooked up with. In fact, most men aren't like that. They try not to get a woman pregnant, but if an accident happens, they do what's right and help with the kid."

She regarded him silently, her set jaw indicating that she wasn't buying a word of it.

"Let's move the discussion to a personal level. I would take every precaution so that a woman wouldn't get pregnant, and if she happened to, I would be there every step of the way, supporting her and the baby in any way I could." He would welcome the chance. Until spending time with Lincoln, he hadn't realized how cheated he felt because he'd never had a kid.

Annabelle's expression had no give to it. "That's what they all say."

Chapter 13

Annabelle stood on the dock waiting for Matt's comeback. Sure as shootin' he'd have one. They all did.

Anytime she ended up alone with a good-looking man, some version of this conversation took place. Once they realized she didn't have a husband around, they usually wanted to get friendly. Then she'd tell them how the cow eats the cabbage, and they'd take that as a personal challenge to be the one to break down her defenses.

Once Matt had dreamed up this stroll on the dock, she'd known that sooner or later they'd get around to this subject. She really didn't mind. Arguing with Matt about her decision not to have sex, other than the battery-operated kind, helped fill the pit of worry she was threatening to sink into.

But instead of arguing with her, Matt sighed. "I suppose it's just as well that you feel this way, for a couple of reasons."

So he was giving up. Well, that was good. One less complication to worry about. "What reasons?"

"First of all, this is the worst possible moment to be thinking of romance, with you worried sick about your daughter. I'm worried, too, although I don't claim to be in your league."

She nodded. He was right about the bad timing. He also sounded more sincere than any man she'd come across. She didn't trust her judgment when it came to that, because being attracted to a man always fried her brains. But having a man like Matt hold her during a time of crisis didn't seem like the worst idea in the world. It probably was, though.

She'd never known a sailor before, and she had to admit Matt looked good standing on the dock, his hands shoved in the pockets of his slacks, while in the background were all those expensive boats. In this light, she and Matt could be characters in a classic black-and-white movie, two doomed lovers saying their last good-byes while the waves lapped away under their feet.

"What's the other reason?" she asked.

"I have no business getting involved with anyone, no matter what the circumstances. I let something that happened last night fool me into some magical thinking, but the truth is, I have nothing to offer right now."

Her mouth fell open. "Nothing to offer?"

"That's right." He met her gaze. "Theresa cleaned me out. More than cleaned me out. When the court ordered me to pay her a quarter of the value of Rainbow, I went into debt up to my eyeballs. I may not get out of debt in this lifetime. I can't ask any woman to get involved in a mess like that."

Annabelle was flabbergasted. Being broke had never stopped a man from trying to seduce her. Both Genevieve's and Lincoln's daddies had seduced her and taken every nickel she'd put aside, to boot.

Then she thought of something else. "I shouldn't have asked you to rent the boat. I didn't know you were up against it, and this morning I might not have cared. But now I do. Let me know how much they charge you, and I'll pay you for it."

"No, you won't." He took her by the shoulders. "I—"

As if suddenly realizing he was touching her, he let go and backed away. "Sorry."

She stepped toward him and put her hand on his arm. "It's okay, Matt. Don't feel funny about doing something that comes natural. You're a decent man, and I know you're not trying to take advantage of me."

He glanced down at the spot where her hand rested on his arm. "Oh, but I'd like to, Annabelle." He raised his head and looked into her eyes. "You see, that's the problem. I would love to take advantage of you."

Her pulse skittered around like a drop of water on a hot griddle. She should move her hand, but she liked the feel of his warm skin, and she really liked the way he smelled. "What happened last night?"

"You don't want to know."

Her grip on his arm tightened. "Yes, I really do."

"Okay, but I'm not bragging about this, just so you know. The only reason I brought it up is that maybe that's why I'm thinking along lines I shouldn't be. Or maybe it's not. I might have wanted you regardless of last night, but—"

"Great balls of fire, are you going to tell me or not?"

"I was propositioned by a twenty-three-year-old."

"*Oh.*" She drew her hand back.

"See, now you think I'm a dirty old man."

"No, I don't." She was thinking he was a mighty fine specimen, to be attracting the attention of a girl that young. "Did you—"

"Yes, I'm afraid I did. So you can see how I might be all full of myself today, thinking I'm some kind of stud and forgetting I'm basically the same middle-aged, penniless man I was yesterday."

"Surely you don't think a man should be measured by the size of his bank account."

He shrugged. "That's the way Theresa measured me. As for Celeste, she's young, moving back to the mainland at the end of the summer to finish college, so she doesn't care if I have money or not."

"How did you meet her?" Annabelle had taught herself not to envy others, but this very minute she desperately wanted to be Celeste, a girl who used men for what she wanted instead of letting them use her.

"Who, Theresa or Celeste?"

"Celeste. Theresa doesn't sound worth wasting our breath on."

Matt smiled. "You've got that right, but come on, Annabelle. You can't really be interested in this."

She was fascinated, but if she let on, he might figure out she was softening toward him. "It's a dang sight more interesting than a baseball game."

He studied her for a moment and finally nodded. "Okay, I can see your point. If my midlife foolishness entertains you, so be it. I've been wishing I had someone to talk to about this, because I've been trying to figure out if I should feel guilty or not. I mean, she's young enough to be my daughter."

"But she started it, didn't she?" That was the part that captured Annabelle. She'd always been a sitting duck, waiting for a smooth-talking man to come along. Maybe if she'd done the choosing her life would have turned out different. Not that she regretted having Genevieve or Lincoln. Never that. But it would have been nice not to have to work so danged hard all the time.

"Yes, she started it," Matt said. "I tried to talk her out of the idea, but I didn't work very hard at it. Theresa had demolished my ego, and having this sweet young thing hot for my body was more than I could resist."

"Matt, I can't imagine any red-blooded man who wasn't getting any being able to resist a prospect like that. Unless he was one of those holy men you read about. I guess they could resist Dolly Parton dancing buck-naked with a rose in her teeth."

Matt laughed, the sound rolling up from his chest in a satisfying wave. "Now, there's a picture. Well, I'm no holy man, Annabelle. Not by a long shot."

"I don't know any holy men myself." She'd made him laugh, and that pleased her no end. A good sense of humor got to her every time, but she hadn't had much call to check out Matt's. They'd been involved in too much anxiety to have cause to laugh together. "But you still didn't tell me how you met this Celeste person."

"While I was up to no good, as usual." Matt's smile lingered. He was obviously having a better time now that they were joking around a little. "She's a cocktail waitress, and she'd watched me coming in every night to drown my sorrows."

"So you knew each other, then." Annabelle didn't drink hard liquor and watched out for those who made it a habit. Growing up around moonshine had made her careful. But she had to believe Matt wasn't a natural-born drinker, or he would have brought some on this trip, crisis or no crisis. People sometimes tried to cure unhappiness with a bottle, and she wasn't one to judge.

"I was a customer of hers, and that was about it. I'm not sure exactly what caused her to decide to change the relationship."

Annabelle had no trouble picturing what caused that. If she'd watched a man like Matt night after night, seeing how lonely he looked, she would have thought of the same exact idea. That was another good reason to work in a beauty parlor instead of a bar.

"Maybe I was an interesting challenge for her," he said. "Maybe she wanted to see if she could take a stodgy older guy who'd had nothing but married sex for twenty years and teach him a few new tricks."

One fact stood out in that statement of his. "You were faithful to your wife all that time?"

He looked puzzled. "Why wouldn't I be?"

She thought of all the tales she'd heard over the manicure table and began to understand what a rare duck Matt Murphy was. Rare and wonderful. "From what you've said, your wife wasn't very nice to you."

He didn't deny it. "That's no excuse for cheating. I probably should have asked for a divorce years ago, because you're right, she wasn't nice to me. But she had me convinced it was my fault because I spent too much time at the office."

"Did you?"

He rubbed the back of his neck and stared into the darkness. "Yep. I could say it was in order to afford all the material pleasures she wanted, but that wouldn't be fair. I didn't know her well enough to marry her, and when I got to know her better, I didn't much care for her."

"So you hid out in your office."

He nodded. "I had a ball building that business, and I tried to bribe Theresa into being happy by giving her stuff instead of my time." He blew out a breath and glanced at Annabelle. "I've never admitted that to myself, let alone someone else. I've been playing the victim, pretending Theresa didn't love me enough, when the fact is, I didn't love her enough."

"Now, don't go putting all the blame on yourself." She shouldn't take sides when she didn't know his ex-wife at all, but the woman had to have a head full of straw. Any fool could see Matt was the kind of man who didn't come along every day, a man worth hanging on to. Annabelle would have met him at the front door wearing nothing but an apron if that would have made his home life more interesting. Surely he hadn't been all that hard to please.

"Not all the blame, but my share. People get in ruts and

they can't get out. She didn't want kids and I went along with that. I shouldn't have, but she brought up all the disadvantages—the late-night feedings, the teething stage, the terrible twos, finding decent baby-sitters, teenage rebellion, paying for college."

"All those things are real enough," Annabelle said. "I couldn't pay for college for Genevieve, and I don't think I'll be able to pay for Lincoln, either. I regret that."

"But you have these two great kids, and you've been able to watch them grow up. Wasn't that an amazing thing to do?"

Annabelle smiled. "Yes. Yes, it surely was. I've had my share of worry, but it's been worth every minute." She paused, thinking about the past few hours of misery. "Even counting today."

"We'll find her," Matt said. "And she'll be fine."

"I know." Annabelle looked at him and knew what she wanted right now. It wasn't much to ask. After all, young women of twenty-three were bold enough to ask for a lot more. "I don't mean to start any trouble, Matt, but I was wondering if you could see your way clear . . ." She hesitated, drained of courage.

"What is it?"

"I sure could use . . . a man's arms around me, just for a little bit. Because I know we're going to find my Genevieve, but that doesn't mean I'm not powerful scared."

Without a word, Matt opened his arms, and Annabelle stepped inside. As his arms closed around her, she sucked up all that male strength, all that warmth and comfort. She didn't pretend there was nothing sexual about it, because there was a lot sexual about it, and that was comforting, too. She closed her eyes and sighed. Surely this wasn't a terrible thing to do, just to hold each other like this.

"Mom!" The dock shook as Lincoln came running toward them. "Stop hugging and come inside! They're talking about Gen on TV!"

Annabelle ran down the dock, nearly slipping on the wet surface. *Somebody had found Genevieve.* Leaping to the deck of the boat, she nearly fell, but when Matt tried to help her, she shook him off. All she cared about was getting down into the cabin to see what was on that TV.

Gasping for breath, she grabbed the edge of the table and stared at the screen. There was a picture of Genevieve, the high school graduation picture Annabelle had given the authorities before heading out to this boat to meet Matt. And there was a picture of Nick, and the computer guy, Jackson Farley.

The blood rushed in her ears so fast she had trouble hearing, but at last she made out the female announcer's words.

". . . still missing. The private plane disappeared on its way from Honolulu to Maui. Search efforts will resume at dawn, according to a spokesperson for the Coast Guard."

The three pictures were taken off the screen and replaced by the anchor desk and the red-haired woman Annabelle recognized as a regular on the news show, although she hardly ever watched it. *"In other news,"* the reporter said, *"gas prices continue to rise and more people in Honolulu are taking to bicycles. We'll have more on that when we return."*

Annabelle gripped the table and stared at a commercial for some drug that was supposed to cure anxiety. She could never understand that. If you had anxiety, then something must be wrong, and you didn't want to take a drug that made it so you didn't care about whatever was wrong.

Matt had asked her if she wanted to see a doctor about taking some tranquilizers before they left. She'd said no. She hardly ever went to doctors and surely wouldn't go to one now, when she needed all the anxiety she could get to keep her sharp. But as the news report echoed in her ears, she wished, for the first time ever, that she drank hard liquor. From listening to Uncle Rufus, she'd learned that a quick snort could dull pain. Not much, but enough so that a body could stand it.

Jack awoke to pale light filtering into the hideaway. His stomach growled like a disk drive gone bad. He and Gen were down to one energy bar, plus the guavas, and he had to admit the thought of guavas sounded better this morning than it had yesterday. All the sex probably had made him hungrier than he would have been without it. But he didn't care. He'd gotten it up four times during the night. No, five, counting the blow job.

Gently untangling himself from Gen, who was still zonked out on the beach towel, he crawled out of the hide-away wearing nothing but his glasses. During the energy bar break halfway through the night, he and Gen had sampled some of the rainwater they'd caught in their various shell containers. On his hands and knees in the doorway of the hideaway this morning, he surveyed what was left and knew it wasn't enough to last the day, so he told himself he wasn't all that thirsty and ignored the water.

Instead he'd toddle down to the surf and heed nature's call. But when he tried to stand up, he let out a yelp of pain and promptly sat down, not caring if he got sand in his privates. The soles of his feet hurt like hell. Examining them one at a time, he discovered that he had several blisters the size of quarters on both feet, compliments of keeping them so close to the fire while he carried on with Gen. Well, he had no regrets about the blisters, either, but he really had to pee, and going in the water was the gentlemanly thing to do.

So he'd crawl down to the waterline. Why not? Gen was asleep and the island was, well, *deserted*, which was why they were in this fix in the first place. The crawling took a while, but eventually he reached wet sand. Deciding that might not feel so bad on his blisters, he eased himself to his feet.

Sure enough, the cool sand felt kind of good. Not wonderful, but better.

Inching down closer to the incoming waves, he stood with the water caressing his toes and aimed his stream out over the waves. Actually this was kind of fun, being nature boy and peeing into the ocean. Except for the bottoms of his feet, he felt like a million bucks. Oh, he had a few stiff muscles here and there, but he wasn't going to complain about the workout. He'd forgotten how great sex could be. No, that wasn't accurate. He hadn't forgotten, because sex had never been this great, which was why he hadn't made it a priority in his life.

If he had Gen to have sex with, it would become a top priority. He might have serious trouble meeting his deadlines at work. He'd have to make sure he worked when she worked, because whenever she was free, he'd want to be in bed with her. Of course, she might not feel the same way. Well, she probably didn't feel the same way. She'd probably had sex with him all night because there was no TV and the sleeping arrangements weren't exactly top drawer.

Thinking about how Gen viewed all this put a damper on his good mood, so he decided not to think about it. The sky had taken on a deeper shade of what he had to assume was blue, and as he watched, the first rays of sunlight flickered on the water. The air smelled salty and fresh, and his blood sang happy songs this morning as it rushed to all parts of his body, proud to be pumping through such a studly specimen as he was.

So this was what dawn was like. He wasn't all that familiar with sunrise, or sunset, either. In order to hit it right you either had to be lucky or have some sense of time. When he was deep into writing code, he lost that. He'd probably also discounted the importance because he was color blind, so sunrise and sunset weren't such a big deal to him.

But as he noticed how the water sparkled with the rising

sun, he wondered if maybe it should be a bigger deal. He lived in Hawaii, for crying out loud, but he might as well be living in Cell Block 46 for all the benefit he'd derived from his location. Maybe he couldn't see the tropical colors, which was ironic considering that Hawaii was all about color, but he could watch the shifting light and breathe in the aroma of paradise. He could feel the warmth of the sun on his shoulders and the tickle of surf dredging the sand out from under his feet.

He could, but he hadn't bothered. Now it was the only game in town, so maybe once he set himself in front of his monitor again he'd lose this newfound urge to experience his natural surroundings. Once he didn't have dynamite sex with Gen to wake up all his nerve endings, he might go back to living in his head. But this morning, as he stood naked by the ocean, he didn't want to let that happen.

The air reverberated with the high-altitude drone of a jet, and he glanced up to watch it draw a white line across the sky. He had the silly thought of jumping and waving his arms, although he knew the jet was too high and commercial airline pilots wouldn't be on the lookout for anyone in the first place. The fact that he was naked didn't dawn on him until later. He probably should crawl back up to the hideaway, put on some pants, and start thinking of the best way to attract the attention of rescuers.

He should, but he hesitated. Standing here bare-assed in the surf made him feel connected to all that had happened last night. Putting on his pants might be a kind of signal that their Fantasy Island interlude was over.

Continuing to have sex with Gen or trying to get rescued. It was a tough choice. True, the condoms would run out eventually, but they hadn't run out yet. Still, now that they'd gone all this time without any sign of Brogan or his pickup boat, they could reasonably expect he'd left the area, so they were free to attract major attention. Working on that program was the sane thing to do.

With a sigh of resignation, he turned around and saw Gen coming toward him, the beach towel wrapped around her like a sarong. He didn't have much practice at the morning-after routine, so he wasn't exactly Mr. Smooth when it came to this particular social skill. Usually the sight of a woman he'd been to bed with the night before tended to inflate his penis. Because of the incredible sex he'd had with Gen, the flag went up even faster.

Being naked with her in the dim hideaway was one thing, but facing her in the bright sunlight wearing only his morning wood took more guts than he had. He backed quickly into the surf, lost his footing and plunged into the water, landing on his butt in the shifting sand as an incoming wave crashed over him. Instinct made him grab his glasses.

Coughing and sputtering, one hand holding his glasses against his face, he scrambled to his knees. Come to think of it, she didn't have the glasses, so she might not have seen his erection. As he was contemplating his overreaction, a second wave caught him from the back and knocked him down again. Not quite the manly image he was trying to project, but at least the erection problem had been solved. Nothing like complete humiliation to douse the flames of passion.

While trying to right himself a second time, he felt something grab him by his right elbow. Expecting his arm to be severed by the chomp of razor-sharp teeth, he nearly fainted. Then he pulled, and his arm came free, or he hoped it had as he scrambled out of the water, still clutching his glasses in his left hand. Maybe endorphins had kicked in, making him oblivious to the fact that his arm had been severed at the elbow and he was going to hemorrhage all over the lovely white sand.

At last he was out of reach of the waves. With a sense of

dread, he sat up and looked at his right arm. All there. Then he looked around for Gen. Not there. *The shark!*

"Gen!" he bellowed, tossing the glasses aside as he staggered to his feet, prepared to go back into that water and pull her from the jaws of death or die in the attempt.

"Right here!" Her head bobbed where she was treading water several feet beyond the surf line.

"Gen, get out of there!" He dashed into the waves. "Something's in the water! It grabbed me!"

"That was me! I was trying to help you, but you wouldn't let me."

His forward momentum had carried him right up next to her by the time her explanation penetrated his panic. What was deep water for her was only chest deep for him. "That was you?"

"Yeah." Her hair was all slicked back from her face, and although she was a little blurry, she looked wonderful. Kissable. "Sorry if I scared you, Jack, but you looked like you were having problems, and I knew you didn't want to break your glasses, so I thought maybe I could help. Then I decided I was more hindrance than help, so I left you there and came on out into the water."

"Why?"

"I . . . um . . . because."

Then it occurred to him that she'd have the same needs he had the first thing in the morning, and as a woman, she couldn't exactly stand on shore and aim out into the water. "Oh." His cheeks grew warm. "Right."

She edged a little closer to him and lifted her face. "I was flattered that you were so glad to see me this morning."

His blush got worse. She'd noticed his morning wood.

"Don't be embarrassed, Jack." She grabbed hold of his arm and pulled herself in close, close enough that he could feel her breasts bobbing against his diaphragm, which was chugging in and out like a fireplace bellows. "It's a compliment to get that reaction first thing in the morning, know-ing I must look like a bag lady after all we've been through."

His tongue felt thick, and so did the recently deflated penis. "You look beautiful."

"So do you." She wound both arms around his neck. "Lift me up, Jack. I want to kiss you."

He wrapped his arms around her and she wrapped her legs around him. A little wiggling on either of their parts and he'd be positioned to connect up all the relevant parts. "Gen, maybe you'd better not—"

"Oh, we're not actually going to do it." She lifted her-self up and over his now totally rigid penis. "But there's nothing wrong with a few water aerobics, is there?"

He groaned as she settled her delicious behind right on top of him. He fit perfectly in that little groove.

"Good morning, Jack," she whispered, pulling his head down for a kiss.

Of course he had to kiss her. With her mouth hovering so close, kissing her was a given. Then using tongues seemed the next logical step. Soon all sense of his surround-ings faded, dissolved by the heat of her mouth and the sug-gestive motions of her tongue.

Gradually he became aware of another part of her mov-ing. Buoyed by the water, she was sliding her bottom back and forth, gently riding his penis and adding to the subtle current that already swirled around his balls. *Holy Oceanic Orgasms, Batman*. As long as she'd started the program, he decided to participate. Cupping a cheek in each hand, he urged her on, a little faster, and a little faster yet, until they were churning up the water like an outboard motor.

She shifted her hips, bearing down a little more on the front part of his shaft, and he figured she might be getting some action, too. Sure enough, she started to whimper, the sound muffled by their intense lip-lock.

When she came, he managed to keep them from

capsizing, but when he came, they both went under. As they both floated lazily to the surface, he decided this was another Hawaiian thing he'd been missing—water sex. He wondered if condoms stayed on under water. Maybe they should test it.

He cradled her gently while he grinned like an idiot. "What a way to start the day."

"Mm." She stroked the drops of water from his beard. "Your bristles are softer already."

"Oh, God, I didn't give you a rash, did I?" He peered down at her face, which looked a little pink, but not too bad.

"You've been very considerate." She continued to stroke his face. "Probably too considerate, seeing as how I've had fun pretending you're a pirate."

He liked that. Glowering at her as fiercely as he knew how, he tried to think how a pirate would talk. Rough and tough, that's for sure. "Aye, and a randy pirate I be, too, lassie," he said in a gravelly voice. He clutched her breast. "Methinks I'll carry you off to my cave and have my way with you."

"Again?"

"And again, and again! I can't get enough of you! You drive a bloke crazy!" Then he plunged his face into the water and sucked vigorously on her nipple as she shrieked. When she continued to shriek and struggle, he held her tighter, lifted his head for a breath and went for the other nipple.

"Jack!" She yanked on his hair, hard.

"Hey!" He jerked upward. "I'm trying to play pirates, here."

"Shark, Jack!"

With one mighty heave, he threw her as far toward shore as he could. Then he leaped after her without looking behind him. As they both scrambled onto the packed sand above the waterline, panting but unharmed, he revised his views on water sex. From now on, he was only doing it in a swimming pool, and that was final.

Chapter 14

Annabelle didn't really want to sleep and take a chance on having bad dreams about Genevieve, but she had to admit the cozy little bed and the slight rocking of the boat was powerfully soothing. She kept herself awake by thinking of Matt in the very next room, probably wanting to come in here and keep her company. He wouldn't, of course. He had more common decency than any man she'd ever laid eyes on.

But Matt had sex on his mind—she wasn't blind to that fact. They'd passed some time last night playing gin rummy, and Lincoln had tarred and feathered the both of them. All during the game, Matt had been watching her with that certain look in his eye. Annabelle knew that look. On some men it gave her the willies, but on Matt it gave her tingly feelings.

Despite all her efforts to stay awake, she must have dozed off sometime after three, because the next time she looked at the small digital clock beside the bed, it was after five. She'd had no dreams that she could remember, no nightmares and no messages that would help lead her to Genevieve.

She'd showered before going to bed, bumping around in the tiny space and nearly tripping over the ledge when she climbed out. This morning all she had to do was dress, wash her face, brush her teeth, and comb her hair. She'd left all her makeup at home, just bringing lotion. A search and rescue wasn't the place for makeup, and it wasn't like she was trying to attract a man.

Well, she'd attracted one anyway. He didn't seem to care that she wasn't wearing lipstick or mascara. To a woman of forty-one who thought she needed a little help to look pretty, his interest in her plain old self felt nice.

Once she was ready, she peeked out the door. The tiny galley was empty. Beyond that, she heard a twin set of snores. Lincoln and Matt were still sawing logs.

Antsy as she was to get under way, she thought maybe they needed a little more sleep. The three of them had stayed up until one in the morning playing cards, as if nobody had wanted to face bad dreams. A few more minutes of peaceful rest would be good for Lincoln, who was a growing boy, and Matt needed to be alert to steer the boat.

But she desperately needed her morning coffee. Within three minutes she had it perking in the galley. Soon afterward she poured herself a full mug, tiptoed between the two bench seats where Matt and Lincoln slept, opened the cabin door, and climbed the steps to the small deck in the back of the boat. The *stern* of the boat, she reminded herself, wanting to get the words right.

Not another soul was about in the gray mist, and the cool, damp air smelled fishy. Annabelle leaned against a little cupboard that Matt had called a hatch and stared down the line of docked boats as she sipped her coffee. It was Kona coffee because she'd insisted on bringing her own, not trusting Matt to provide a good brand. She firmly believed that anything in this life could be faced if a person had a strong cup of coffee before starting the day.

She'd finished half a cup when a noise made her turn.

Matt came up the steps, a steaming mug in one hand, a

long box of store-bought sugar doughnuts in the other. "Morning." His voice was still roughened with sleep. He'd dressed for the day in a polo shirt and slacks, but he hadn't shaved. His stubble made him look more like a seaman than ever.

"Morning." Annabelle cleared the huskiness from her throat. Hers had nothing to do with the time of day and everything to do with how glad she was to see Matt. He'd slept wrong on his hair, giving him a cowlick, which only added to the tenderness she felt for him.

He held up the doughnuts. "Seeing how picky you are about coffee, you probably don't want these, but you might as well know I have a weakness for preservative-filled junk. You're welcome to share."

She wondered why it mattered whether she knew his habits. The only reason she could think of was that he intended to keep on with her after they found Genevieve. Unfortunately, nice man or not, he could be trouble. A man coming off a divorce wasn't a good bet. Either he wouldn't want to get serious or he would, but it would be too soon. And Lincoln was already getting stuck on him, which was dangerous.

He hesitated. "Maybe you wanted to be alone out here. I should have thought of that, instead of barging in on your privacy." He turned to go.

"No, wait. I'd like some company."

He glanced back at her. "You're sure? Because I can take my evil doughnuts and disappear. Poof."

There was something to be said for a man who could make a body smile even in the midst of heartache. "I'd even like one of your evil doughnuts."

The sparkle returned to his eyes as he swung around and came back toward her. "Each one shortens your life by twenty-three minutes. They've done studies." He held out the box and flipped it open with his thumb.

It was a snappy gesture, and she was a sucker for those. She'd first noticed Genevieve's father because of the smooth way he'd vaulted a fence. "You sound like Lincoln. He makes up studies all the time." She picked a doughnut from the box.

"You think I made that up?" He pretended to look hurt. "I'll have you know I'm a font of useful information, a waterfall of statistics, a roaring river of—"

"Baloney?"

He grinned. "That would be the delicate way to put it. And I already know you don't like swearing, so we'll leave it at that." He set the box on the hatch and plucked out a doughnut for himself. When he bit into it, powdered sugar drifted onto his navy polo. "Messy, too."

"That's okay." But she leaned over when she took a bite of hers, so the sugar would fall to the deck instead of on her pink shirt. She hadn't brought a lot of clothes, thinking that packing too many would seem like they would be out here for days. She wanted to be back home by nightfall, with Genevieve.

"Damn, but this really is good coffee. Oops. I mean, *golly gee*, but this is one fine cup of coffee, Mizz Terrence."

She licked the sugar from her mouth. "The doughnuts are fair to middlin'. And they're perfect with the coffee. But you're making me out to be a fussbudget, and I'm not."

"Aw, I'm just teasing you a little." He gazed at her mouth, then brought his attention back up to her eyes. "I think it's great that you're setting such a good example for Lincoln. He's one smart kid. A world-class gin rummy player, too."

She wondered if telling him how Lincoln won would help or hurt. Finally she decided it might help. "I can tell you how he wins."

"He cheats? Because if he does, he's damned—dog-gone—good at it."

"I guess you could call it cheating. If he really concentrates, he knows what cards everybody has and what's coming up in the deck."

Matt stopped chewing his bite of doughnut and gave her a long look. Then he finished chewing, swallowed, and took a sip of his coffee. "He told you this?"

She nodded. "A long time ago, when he was six. He thought everybody could do that, and he finally asked why Genevieve and I would make such dumb plays and let him win all the time. After I told him that it was kind of unusual, what he could do, he kept quiet about it. You know how kids hate to be different from their friends."

"Wow. Well, after last night, I can't dispute it. I've never taken such a shellacking in my life."

"I told you that for a reason. When we head out today, I want you to take us in the direction Lincoln says. He can find her." She held her breath and waited.

Matt gazed at her silently for several seconds. "Okay," he said at last.

She sighed in relief. "Thank you, Matt. I know you don't hold with such things, but where I come from, it's natural as can be. And Lincoln has the gift."

"If I hadn't played cards with him, I might give you more of an argument, but anything's worth a try." He paused. "Where *are* you from, Annabelle?"

"Tennessee."

"Whereabouts?"

"You wouldn't have heard of it."

"And you don't want to tell me, do you?"

Annabelle looked into his eyes. Then she glanced down the line of boats. "I guess it doesn't matter. I used to think that if I closed that door once and for all, nothing bad was going to happen to my children. Stay in the Hollow, and all kinds of bad things could happen to them. But Genevieve is missing, so keeping a lock on the past didn't guarantee anything."

"I just . . . I'd like to get to know you better."

She felt more than saw that he'd moved closer to her. "I'd like to get to know you better, too, but I can't." She met his gaze. "Lincoln's never had a daddy. You can see he's hungry for one. If we started seeing each other, he'd start making plans for you, plans that might never come true. I won't put him through that kind of misery."

Matt studied her for a moment longer. Then he stared into his coffee mug and swirled the contents. "I can see your point. This is all new territory for me. All I know is that some carefree young thing like Celeste is fine for a night or two, but I don't intend to make a career of twenty-something women. Logically, most of the single women my age are going to have kids. And you're absolutely right that kids shouldn't be pawns in the whole dating game." He glanced up at her. "Any suggestions?"

She didn't want to make suggestions. She didn't want him to move on and find some other lucky woman, but she wasn't free to take a chance on him. "You could look for a person who doesn't have kids. Put an ad in the personals."

Matt groaned.

"I have customers who do it." And she could probably find Matt a bushel basket full of dates in one week of doing nails. But there were limits to this helping business.

"Okay, but aside from being phobic about the personal ad thing, I like kids and wish I'd had some. If I date women without any, that probably means I'll never even have stepkids. At least now I have a shot at that."

"Then make sure you don't meet the kids or get involved with them at all until after you're convinced that you and this person are right for each other."

"Meaning it's too late for you and me?"

The cabin door opened. "Hey, like, where is everybody?" A head of red, white, and blue hair appeared. "I woke up and I was all, *They've left me all by myself on this boat, abandoned like that kid in* Home Alone, *and*—hey, dude, are those doughnuts? Cool." He leaped the rest of the way up the steps and snagged one out of the open box. "Totally my favorite. I know Mom didn't buy these, so thanks, Matt. You're awesome." Then he shoved half of it in his mouth.

Annabelle glanced over her son's shoulder at Matt. "I think that answers your question."

Genevieve stood by the edge of the surf and used a shell to scoop water and wash off the sand sticking to her. Her heart rate was nearly back to normal, but she still got cold chills whenever she remembered looking over Jack's shoulder and seeing that dark fin coming toward them.

But even taking the shark into consideration, she was having a heck of a good time being marooned. She was also beginning to figure out why. The very skills that branded her a hillbilly back in Honolulu were exactly the skills she needed to survive out here. For the first time in eleven years, she could be herself, all of herself and not just the more civilized parts. What a relief.

Even better, Jack didn't think less of her for her backwoods raising. He seemed to get a charge out of it. Maybe that was another reason the sex between them had been so outstanding. She wasn't afraid of forgetting herself and revealing her roots. Jack already knew about her, so she had nothing to hide.

She wondered if she had the courage to stop covering up her background once she got back to Honolulu. Mama would advise against it and tell her she'd never attract the right man if she reverted to countrified ways. But Genevieve was thinking that if she felt free enough to have great sex with a man, he might not care whether her voice twanged when she talked.

Maybe she should ask Jack his opinion. Then again, maybe not. She was a little worried that all the sex they'd had was giving Jack ideas about a relationship when they got home. But it would never work. During the night she'd asked him about his horoscope sign and sure enough, he was a Taurus. Besides being a genius who would make a very forgetful husband, he was the wrong sign for her. She'd find his steadiness boring and he'd find her wild imagination irritating.

She appreciated his steady tendencies at the moment, though. He'd found his glasses and stationed himself right beside her to keep an eye out for Jaws.

"I don't think he'd leap out of the water to get us," she said, although she didn't mind having Jack nearby as a precaution.

"I'm not taking any chances. And we're not going back in that water."

"That's hunky-dory with me. But it means we can't have fish for breakfast."

"Fish?" He frowned at her. "We don't have anything to fish with."

She splashed a shell full of water over her breasts. "We have my curling iron. I'll bet if I waded out in the water with it sprung open and moved really fast, I could snap it shut on a fish." That was the kind of thing she never would have thought about if she hadn't grown up in the Hollow.

"Eeww."

She laughed and scooped up another shell's worth of water. "I can tell you never caught crawdads down by the crick."

"Fortunately not. Gross."

"You'd sing a different tune if you were starving to death."

"Let's hope it doesn't come to that. I like my food un-recognizable. I was thrilled when they came out with square hamburgers, because they don't look like anything that ever used to be alive."

"Well, don't worry, because I'm not going wading in shark-infested waters with nothing but a curling iron to pro-tect me." She washed off her thigh. "You know, I'll bet it was all that churning around in the water that got him in-terested. I didn't think of that."

"I just didn't think, period. No blood to the brain."

She glanced at him and couldn't help smiling. "I liked your pirate imitation."

"You did, huh?" He shot her a quick look before going back on sentry duty with a cute little grin on his face. "I liked your little maneuver, too."

"It didn't turn out too bad. Except for the shark."

"Next time we'll have to try a private swimming pool."

She started to agree with him, but then she realized what he'd said. In order for them to have sex in a private swimming pool, they'd have to keep dating once they got home.

Besides the obvious problem of continuing a doomed relationship, she hated to take this magic time and try to transfer it to real life. Having sex in somebody's swimming pool wouldn't come close to what had happened out there in the ocean. Even the shark coming along had added to the thrill. She could say that now that they hadn't been chomped.

He cleared his throat. "Then again, maybe not."

She looked over at him. His jaw had tightened up and a cord stood out in his neck. He looked . . . dashing. Then she remembered how he usually presented himself in the of-fices of Rainbow Systems, with his mismatched clothes and distracted look. "Jack, I just don't know if it's a good idea to think beyond—"

"Exactly." He gazed out to sea. "Forget I said anything. I lost my head."

Now the mood was ruined, but she was afraid to say anything encouraging about what might happen after they were rescued. She didn't want him to get his hopes up.

"You know, I've been thinking that they may not even be looking for us way over here," Jack said.

She was more than willing to change the subject. "Why not?"

"Because Brogan was scheduled to go to Maui, so unless somebody was tracking us on radar for some reason, they'd have no idea that he abandoned the flight plan and headed off in the opposite direction. He sure as hell didn't announce it on the radio before he smashed the devil out of it."

"You might be right." She'd gotten rid of most of the sand. "I'm pretty much cleaned off. Want me to be on look-out duty while you wash the sand off?"

He brushed at his arms. "I'm fine."

"Jack, you still have a ton of sand on your arms, and your back, not to mention your butt. You should—"

"Just don't mention my butt from now on, and I promise not to mention yours, okay?"

Stung, she stepped back a pace. "You're mad at me."

He turned, his expression fierce, a lot like the pirate he'd pretended to be earlier. "You're damned right I am. First you make it seem like—" He stopped and stared at her. Gradually the anger left his eyes. "Ah, don't look like that, Gen."

She swallowed, surprised that she'd be so bothered that he was upset with her. "What . . . what were you going to say?"

He shrugged. "It's not important. This is my problem, not yours." Leaning down, he picked up the beach towel she'd tossed aside when she'd jumped into the water with him. "Come on. Let's go back to the hut and split the last energy bar. Then we'll figure out our next move."

She held her ground. "First I want to get something straight. What's happened between us meant something to me. I wasn't just playing around because you were the only guy available."

He looked at her, his face expressionless.

"Okay, Jack. Do you honestly think that's why I had sex with you, because you were convenient?"

When he didn't say anything, she marched right over and gave him a good punch on the arm.

"Ow!"

"Serves you right, if that's what you think of me, that I would have slipped those condoms on whoever's noodle was handy!" She pulled back her arm to punch him again.

"No, you don't." He caught her wrist. "I'm not going to stand here and let you beat up on me. I have a feeling you could do a pretty good job."

"Then take back what you said!"

"But I didn't say anything!"

True, he hadn't. "Then take back what you were thinking!"

His mouth twitched, like he was trying not to laugh. "First I'd have to find out what you thought I thought."

"You know good and well. You're making me madder than a treed polecat, standing there smirking!"

"Smirking? I don't smirk."

"Oh, yes, you do so smirk! You're a first-class smirker!" She wound up with her free arm.

He looped the towel around his neck and grabbed her other wrist before she could land a blow. There was a pirate's gleam in his eye. "I'll tell you what I'm thinking right now. You brought up the subject of condoms, and I'm thinking that there are two left. No matter why you had sex with me, I can see that once we leave this island, that will be the end of Gen giving Jack a little nooky. So I say let's use up the supply."

"Oh, that's *so* romantic."

"Isn't it?"

"See? Now *that's* a smirk if I ever saw one. And I'm not going to cooperate, so there."

"I think you are." With one quick lunge, he lifted her over his shoulder, her head hanging down and her bare bottom pointing up at the sky.

She struggled and kicked, but she was careful not to kick him anywhere that she'd do damage. The more she struggled and wiggled against him, the more she liked his idea. But she didn't want him to know that yet. "You put me down, Jackson the Smirker Farley!"

"The name is Jack, and I've always wanted to do this." He started to move.

"Jack!" She pretended horror, when in fact she was delighted. No man had ever tried such a John Wayne trick with her, not even in the hills of Tennessee. Her head buzzed from being held upside down, but a much stronger reaction was developing right where she was draped over his shoulder.

"Yell all you want. Nobody's around to hear you, so I'm in charge."

"You're going to force me to have sex with you?" She was in a perfect position to watch his cute hiney in action as he trudged up the beach to the hideaway, and seeing those muscles bunch was a very arousing spectacle.

"It won't be forced and you know it."

He had a point. "Then could we . . . pretend it's forced?"

His laugh was breathless. "Sure. One ravishing coming up." Then he yelped.

"What's wrong?"

"This sand is sharp, that's what. Ouch! Ouch, ouch, *ouch*."

"Ravishers don't say ouch, Jack." She hated anybody being in pain. "Maybe you should forget this idea and put me down before you hurt yourself."

"Nope." Panting, he ducked through the opening of the hideaway.

She appreciated that, because otherwise he could have knocked her cold, which would have interfered with her enjoyment of the ravishing. He set her on her feet, and while she was still feeling dizzy from hanging over his shoulder, he caught both wrists in his long fingers. Holding her one-handed, he flipped open her suitcase and grabbed the curling iron cord.

"What on God's green earth are you doing?"

"Restraining the prisoner." His eyes glittered as he wound the cord around her wrists and tied it. "Much better than using it to catch fish," he said as he clipped the curling iron securely to a piece of driftwood embedded in the wall of the hideaway. "If you pull on that, you might make the whole shelter give way, so I wouldn't, if I were you."

Her heart pounded with excitement. "Don't you think you're carrying this a little far?"

He leaned down and cupped her chin in one hand. "You tell me." Then he kissed her hard, thrusting his tongue possessively into her mouth.

With her hands bound and the possibility of bringing the whole hideaway down on their heads if she moved, she could do nothing but stand there and let him kiss her. Well, she could do one other thing. She could moan. Which she did.

Breathing heavily, he lifted his mouth from hers. "Just as I thought. You love it."

Chapter 15

Jack made a very good pirate, and Genevieve discovered that she loved the role of "prisoner," at least with a guy she could trust the way she trusted Jack. After several maneuvers that certainly expanded her idea of sexual excitement, they collapsed on the beach towel again, exhausted and extremely satisfied.

But when the glow of good sex began to wear off, Genevieve remembered she was very hungry. Jack snored softly in her ear, but she was too hungry to sleep. Their food wouldn't last much longer, either. One energy bar and a few guavas wouldn't do it, especially the way they were burning energy, going at it like bunnies.

With a shark taking up residence in their little lagoon, she wasn't keen on fishing, but they might have to reconsider and try it, anyway. A well-aimed rock might bring down a tern, but she hated that idea. Wild birds had been her friends since childhood.

She managed to slip out of Jack's arms and stand up without him even knowing. Gazing down at him, she thought about how talented he was in the sex department. Not having a steady girlfriend meant he was going to waste. When they got home, she should make a greater effort to fix him up with someone.

That someone should be a nerd like Jack, somebody who would understand when he lost himself in a computer project and forgot her birthday. The woman for Jack needed to be much more flexible about things like that than Genevieve was. Unfortunately, the idea of Jack having sex with someone else gave her a tummyache. Or maybe she was just so hungry that anything would give her a tummyache.

Kneeling down beside her suitcase, she took out the last energy bar, sat back on her heels, and unwrapped it. She was almost drooling.

"You can have the whole thing."

She glanced over toward Jack and discovered he was wide awake and watching her. She could eat the whole thing and that wouldn't put a dent in her hunger. She could eat three of these and still be hungry. "No way." Breaking the bar in two, she held out both halves. "Because I split it, you get to choose."

He smiled. "I can't see which is bigger without my glasses. You take the biggest."

Holding the two pieces close to her nose so she could see them clearly, she handed over the one that was a teensy bit larger. Jack weighed more than she did, so it stood to reason he'd need more food.

Although she bit into hers immediately, he laid his half on a corner of the beach towel. "You know what? I think I'll save it for later."

She talked around the mouthful of energy bar, unable to stop eating long enough to be mannerly. "You eat it right this minute." She glared at him. "I don't want you passing out on me on account of running low on vittles."

"I don't really like this kind, anyway." He held it toward her. "Look, you've already finished that half. Here's the rest."

"No!" She swatted his hand away and the rest of the

energy bar sailed into the air. She butted heads with him as they both tried to catch it, but without glasses, neither of them could see well enough and the bar dropped into the sand.

"Gen, I'm sorry!" He scrambled to his knees and cupped her face in both hands. "Where did I get you?"

"Right here." She rubbed the side of her head. "Where did I get you?"

"It doesn't matter." He looked miserable as he leaned over to kiss where she was rubbing. "I wouldn't hurt you for anything. Do you think you'll have a bump there? I'm so sorry."

"It's really okay." But she thought it was very touching the way he was fussing over her. Remembering the sexy way he'd taken control earlier made his sweetness even nicer. He knew when to be bold and he knew when to be tender, and that made him special. "We'd better find the other half of the energy bar, though."

"Yeah." With one last kiss to the side of her head, he reached in the suitcase and took out his glasses. "One of us needs to eat the thing." He looked around and finally found it with sand sticking all over the chocolate. "But not until we wash it off. I'll go do that. He stood up and winced.

"Jack, is something wrong with your feet?"

"I'm fine." He started out of the hut.

"Wait!" She lunged forward and grabbed him around the knees.

"Whoa. Titty tackle. Can't say I've ever had that sensation on the backs of my legs. I like it."

She adjusted her position and held on, even though he was trying to distract her with naughty talk. "Never mind that. I want to see the bottoms of your feet."

"Trust me, they're not half as sexy as you might think. I can suggest about ten parts of me that will turn you on much faster than the bottoms of my feet." He tried to pry her hands loose but she'd locked them together. "Come on, let go and I'll go wash off your energy bar."

"*Your* energy bar. Now, Jack, I know you don't want to keep walking and make me fall down and hurt myself. And I won't let go until you lift up your foot so I can take a look."

"What are you, kinky?"

"That's it." She rubbed her breasts over the backs of his knees. "I want to suck your toes."

"Stop it, Gen."

"Just lift one foot, and I will."

"This is ridiculous."

Tired of arguing with him, she slid her arms up higher and used her natural coordination to quickly grab hold of his balls.

"Yikes!"

"Don't make me have to get rough." She squeezed gently.

"I, um, guess you're really serious about this."

"Uh-huh." She enjoyed cupping the weight in her hands. Only extreme hunger kept her from turning her hold into a caress and asking if he wanted to use up that last condom. That and the fact that she sort of wanted to save that one, keeping it like money in the bank, for when they really needed it.

"I just have a few blisters on the bottoms of my feet," Jack said. "No big deal."

"Blisters? How in tarnation did you blister up your feet?"

"Well." He cleared his throat. "Last night, when I was . . . when you first took off your clothes and let me . . ."

"I remember that, Jack." Most likely she'd remember it for the rest of her natural days. He'd made her come by sucking on her nipples. That was a landmark event, for sure. "But near as I recollect, you weren't using your feet at the time."

"They were a little close to the fire."

She released him and sat back on her heels, totally amazed. "Your feet were frying like green tomatoes in a skillet and you didn't *tell me*?"

"Uh, no." He kept his back to her.

Even without glasses, she could see that his neck was getting red, and it wasn't from sunburn, either. She'd never been paid such a strange and backhanded compliment in her life. He'd scorched his feet rather than take a chance on missing out on sex with her. Or else, even more unbelievable, he'd been so taken with the enjoyment of her naked body that he hadn't even felt the heat on the bottoms of his feet.

"So now you know how pathetically eager I was," he said.

He was embarrassed that she knew, and now she felt bad for making him tell her. "Jack, I was eager, too," she said softly.

"But I'll bet you wouldn't have blistered your feet."

"Well, maybe not, but—"

"I'll go wash off the energy bar now." He started to leave.

"I'll go with you." She hopped to her feet and picked up the beach towel. "I would go in your place, but you need to soak your feet in the salt water. That will help you heal up those blisters. And while you're soaking your feet and eating your half of the energy bar, I'll pick us some more guavas."

He ducked out of the hideaway. "You can go pick the guavas, then. I'll go down to the water by myself."

"Then take this with you." She hurried to catch up with him. "Slow down a minute, Jack. It'll feel better if you sit on the beach towel while you're soaking your—" She stopped as she glimpsed the reason why he was charging off so fast. He was stalking down to the waterline sporting a full-blown erection, and he wasn't happy about it.

He still needed the towel, though, so she walked faster to try to overtake him. The sand felt hot under her feet, so she could imagine how it affected him. "Jack, when I grabbed you by your privates, I didn't mean to cause a problem for you."

He gestured toward his bobbing penis. "You mean this problem? I might as well get used to it, because all I have to do is look your way and I immediately rise to the occasion."

"It's because of being stranded like this," she said. "I—"

"Speak for yourself. There were times at the office when I considered wrapping a roll of duct tape around my Jockeys so I wouldn't embarrass myself when I saw you. You've affected me this way ever since I met you. You just didn't know about it."

The idea made her head buzz. Jack had been having sexual urges toward her for months? He'd admitted having some interest in her, but she hadn't taken that to mean he could barely control himself. How incredible. And exciting, too. Still waters really did run deep, after all. "I thought . . . I thought all you cared about were your computer programs."

"Think again."

"You always seemed to have a one-track mind."

"I do." He stepped into the shallow water and glanced over at her.

She returned his gaze, and a shiver of sexual excitement ran through her at the look in his eyes. He certainly didn't look like a nerd today, with his beard glossy black in the sunshine and his hair ruffled by the sea breeze. He'd had a good body to begin with, and now his skin was beginning to turn brown, which set off his muscles to good advantage.

She knew what those muscles felt like, knew what his fingers could do, and his mouth, and his . . . That part still stood out, proud and free, announcing that he found her irresistible. She was beginning to understand how lucky she was, because ever since they'd splashed down near this beach, his one-track mind had been focused on her.

Staring at a man's penis wasn't ladylike. Her mother would have a hissy fit if she had any idea her daughter could do such a thing. But Jack's penis was a work of art.

"You're not helping matters," he murmured.

She dragged her attention back to his face. "Sorry. But I keep thinking of you being affected this way, and me never suspecting a thing. You mean, even when we'd happen to meet over by the water cooler, you'd be getting a—"

"We never just *happened* to meet. I'd do my best to run into you, even though it was torture for me."

She looked into his eyes for a long time. "When we go back . . ."

"I have no idea how that's going to work." He cleared his throat. "I might have to quit."

"No! Rainbow will have enough problems after what Nick did. If you quit, that could sink the whole company, which means I wouldn't have a job, anyway."

"Maybe I could find him a replacement."

"Jack, you will do a tom-fool thing like that over my dead body. I've heard how they talk about you. You're a genius. Do you think there's a genius hiding behind every banyan tree? Hardly. You're one of a kind, and you belong right where you are, doing whatever it is you do, which I don't pretend to understand."

"Then maybe I could work at home most of the time. There's no reason why I have to—"

"Stop it, stop it, stop it!" Genevieve couldn't explain why this was upsetting her so, but it was. The idea that he would stay home to avoid her, that their nice little friendship was ruined and now she wouldn't see him walking around in his mismatched plaids with his hair sticking up, was too much for her. "I *like* having you in the office, and I'll bet everybody else does, too."

"Yeah. Comic relief."

"That's not it! You're . . . you're *real*, Jack." She blinked away the moisture in her eyes. "So many people in this world look like they came right off the assembly line in some people factory. They wear what everybody else wears and they talk like everybody else talks." *Like she'd been trying to do herself.* The idea shook her. "But not you," she said, wondering if she could learn a thing or two from Jack about being real. "If I thought I was the reason you had to hide in your house and work by some sort of remote control, I would never forgive myself."

"Then I won't do that," he said gently. "And thank you, Gen. That might be the nicest speech anybody's ever made about me."

She sniffed. "You're welcome. But I have to warn you, I can't quit, either. Mama needs my income until Lincoln graduates, and he has three whole years left."

"Don't worry." Jack's expression was tender. "We'll figure something out."

"I hope so." But she had no idea what. From now on, every time she saw Jack at the office, she'd know he was doing battle with his penis. And knowing that, she'd start thinking about what had happened on this island and get all worked up herself. Maybe she should have considered that before she allowed herself to get so carried away by lust.

At any rate, the depressing conversation had taken care of Jack's problem for the time being. Now instead of looking like an actor in an X-rated movie, he looked like the statues standing around in fancy museums.

He leaned over and swished the sand-coated energy bar through the water. "Let me wash this off so you can finish it."

"*You* are going to finish it."

"I'll eat guavas."

"You hate guavas." She wasn't too keen on them herself.

She'd tried to pretend they were okay, back before her suitcase had come drifting in with an alternative food source.

"I love guavas now." He held the dripping energy bar out to her. "Take it."

"Nope." She backed up a step.

"Come on, Gen. Your mother packed these for you, not for me. Besides, you need your strength."

"And you don't?"

"I'm used to going without food. Sometimes when I'm writing code I forget to eat for a day or more. I'm not even that hungry right now."

"Liar."

"Gen, let me do this for you. Please."

"Why? Why not let me do this for you? Sure, my mother packed these in my suitcase, but you're the one who landed the plane without killing us dead. If you hadn't done that, nobody would be eating these energy bars. I want you to have half."

He sighed. "In all my life, I've never felt like somebody's hero before. Yesterday was the first time that I was a . . ." He flushed. "It sounds dumb."

"A knight in shining armor?"

"Yeah. Something like that. I want to keep that feeling a little bit longer. I know this isn't much, but it's something I can do, something heroic. Take the energy bar."

"Okay." She stepped closer and took it, knowing that he must be even hungrier than she was. "Thank you, Jack. You really are a knight in shining armor."

He smiled. "Don't overdo it."

"But I mean it. You are." As she started to take a bite, she saw the yearning in his eyes. Taking it back out of her mouth was a challenge when she was so ready to devour it, but she managed. "I'll go somewhere else to eat this."

"No, eat it here. I want to watch you enjoy it."

"But you looked at it with so much longing. Now I feel really bad that I agreed to take it."

"It wasn't the energy bar I was looking at."

"Oh." She felt warm all over when he said things like that.

"Now eat it."

She bit into the bar, and although it was salty, and sand he hadn't been able to wash off crunched when she chewed, she'd never eaten anything so wonderful in her life. And she was absolutely certain that no man had ever given up so much for her as Jack had just now, by sacrificing his half of the very last decent thing they had to eat.

Annabelle felt like the most selfish person in the whole wide world. Matt and Lincoln were getting along great, and Matt had even let Lincoln drive the boat. Lincoln was eating up the attention.

Annabelle had kept herself a little apart, hanging out near the stern of the boat so the men could bond. And they were bonding to beat the band, which made Annabelle feel even worse about her son. Out of fear that she'd pick another loser, she'd deprived Lincoln of a daddy. She'd deprived Genevieve, too, but for a boy it might make more of a difference. Then again, maybe not.

Once they'd arrived in Honolulu all those years ago, she should have gone on a manhunt for a nice, respectable father for them. If she'd made sure that he wasn't very exciting in bed, then he wouldn't have been as likely to run out on her.

It was the exciting ones you had to watch out for. The boring ones were grateful to get any woman at all and so they stayed put. She'd just never thought of going after a boring man in order to provide for Genevieve and Lincoln's development.

Unfortunately, Matt might not qualify in the boring

department. Every time Annabelle looked into those big brown eyes, she knew exactly why the cocktail waitress had wanted to take him home to play Count the Bedsprings. The fact that he'd caught the waitress's attention pretty much put the guaranteed-to-be-exciting label on him. Annabelle had better steer clear of Matt Murphy.

But Lincoln sitting up there driving the boat, proud as could be, was heartwarming, and she'd never forget the sound of Matt laughing at something Lincoln had said to him. She could imagine how that made Lincoln feel, getting a man like Matt to laugh at those one-liners of his. Annabelle tried to be a good audience for him, but she knew he probably craved the sound of male laughter. Shoot, she craved it, too.

Now wasn't the time to be thinking of things like that, though. Now was the time to concentrate on Genevieve. Much as Annabelle liked knowing that Lincoln was enjoying himself with Matt, she sincerely hoped he wasn't allowing himself to be distracted. He needed to be concentrating on his sister.

With that thought, she reluctantly decided to interrupt the little rooster party they had going on in the cockpit of this boat. She steadied the binoculars with one hand so they wouldn't hang loose around her neck by the strap and bang against her breasts as she climbed the steps to the cockpit.

Matt noticed her first. Even without being able to see his eyes, she could tell he felt guilty about something, too.

"Hi, Annabelle. Listen, I don't want you to think that I was up here laughing because I've forgotten what this trip is all about."

"No, Mom, he wouldn't forget," Lincoln said quickly. "Like, we were just trying to relieve the tension."

She didn't know which amazed her more, that Matt was afraid she'd disapprove because he'd been laughing or that

Lincoln was sticking up for him. "I never thought for a minute that you were forgetting anything."

"Mom, you should try driving this boat. It's unbelievable. The guys are gonna be all, *You got to drive a boat?*"

Matt picked up on the suggestion right away. "Sure. Take a turn, Annabelle."

"I didn't come up here so that I could—"

"Aw, come on, Mom." Lincoln's voice turned sing-songy and coaxing, like it did when he'd tried to get her on a roller coaster. "It's very cool. If you don't, then later you'll be all, *I wish I'd tried it.*"

"All right. And while I'm driving, maybe you could put your earphones on again and see if anything comes to you regarding your sister."

"Uh, sure. Sure, I will." Lincoln sounded eager to please as he started to get up. "Matt, maybe you'd better take the wheel while Mom and me are switching places."

Annabelle noticed that her son was using Matt's Christian name again, and decided not to bring it up. She'd kept Lincoln from ever being able to call a man Daddy, so maybe she shouldn't be so particular about what he called his new friend.

"Can I have the binoculars?" Lincoln asked as he slipped out of the captain's seat.

"You'll have to ask Mr. Murphy. They belong to him."

"He's welcome to use them," Matt said. "And I wish both of you would call me Matt. I think the situation puts us all on a first-name basis."

Lincoln gave her a look that said plainly *See there?*

Annabelle wasn't in the mood to argue. "I suppose you're right." She lifted the strap of the binoculars over her head and stood on tiptoe to put it around Lincoln's neck.

"Mo-om. I can do that."

"I don't want you to drop them. No doubt they cost a pretty penny."

"I'm sure he'll be careful," Matt murmured.

Annabelle felt the two males closing ranks on her, which made her feel out of place. She began to wonder if that had been another reason she hadn't wanted to invite a man into the family. When it was her and Genevieve and Lincoln, the females had the advantage. Well, she hoped she hadn't been that unsure of herself.

"Go ahead and sit here and take the wheel," Matt said.

"I do believe I will." Annabelle settled into the driver's seat and immediately felt better. She'd always been one to steer her own course.

At Gen's suggestion, Jack sat on the beach towel and soaked his feet in the salt water.

"I'll pick us some guavas and be back," she said.

Jack watched her go, glad he'd kept the glasses so he could enjoy the free way she walked around this beach without a stitch on. When she reached up to pick guavas off the tree, she could have been Eve in the Garden of Eden.

Yeah, but once Adam had eaten the little treat Eve had brought him, things hadn't worked out so good. Jack wondered if Adam had enjoyed the kind of amazing sex with Eve that he'd just had with Gen. If so, being booted out of the Garden must have been a real bummer. Jack could relate.

Gen came back toward him holding three guavas in her cupped hands. Her breasts swayed gently as she trudged through the sand. Jack wondered if this was the picture he'd superimpose over Gen the next time he met her coming from the copy machine with a stack of papers.

She dumped the guavas on the towel beside him. "This time we'll use my manicure scissors to peel them. I'll be right back."

"Okay." Turning to watch her walk up to the hideaway would definitely be ogling, so Jack faced the ocean instead.

Some kind of seabirds soared overhead, but he'd never learned their names. He'd bet Gen would know. He loved that she was so tuned in to the natural world.

Sunlight sparkled on the water, but there were no fins. That didn't mean the shark wasn't out there like a submerged submarine, though.

Jack shuddered every time he thought of the times he and Gen had tempted Fate by splashing around in that water. Why the shark hadn't grabbed one of them when they'd swum in from the plane was a puzzle. So far they'd been incredibly lucky. Jack knew from his statistics class that the odds couldn't keep going in their favor.

He caught Gen's scent before he heard her steps in the sand behind him. She'd put on some more of that coconut suntan oil. As he turned his head to smile at her, he discovered that wasn't all she'd put on. She was wearing a light-colored bikini.

"Now I feel underdressed," he said. He wondered if the bathing suit was a signal that they wouldn't have sex anymore. If so, it wasn't a very good signal, because those little scraps of material would come off in no time. He'd always thought that was the idea of a bikini—gift-wrapped sex.

"I put this on for a reason. I have a plan, but first you need some more of this lotion on your back and shoulders. You're starting to get a little red."

"Okay, thanks." He wasn't about to object if she wanted to rub her hands all over his back. "What's the plan?"

"Well, I've been thinking." She knelt on the sand behind him, snapped open the lid, and squeezed out some lotion. The slurping sound made him think of sex, and the strong scent of coconuts made him think of sex. When she started smoothing the cool lotion over his back, he had to casually splash water over his penis to keep it subdued.

"About what?" He listened to her breathe, trying to tell if she was the slightest bit turned on. He couldn't tell.

"About what you said before, that they wouldn't look for us down here." She re-capped the lotion, and gave a couple more swipes over his back; then she swished her hands through the water before sitting cross-legged on the towel beside him.

"They might not."

"I agree with you." She picked up a guava. "They'll be down around Maui, because that's where Nick was supposed to be headed."

"I'm afraid so."

"Then we need to do something to get a lot of attention if we expect to be noticed." She licked the guava juice from her hand.

"Probably." Jack thought Gen in a bikini licking guava juice from her fingers should do the trick, or at least it would for him.

"I think we need to climb to the top of this rocky cliff and use my clothes, and whatever you can spare, to make a big X that a plane could see."

He'd been considering the same thing, although the thought of scaling that cliff turned his insides to water. But as scared as he was to make the climb, that wasn't the worst part. Once they left their little section of paradise here on the beach, they wouldn't climb all the way back down again. Their interlude would be over. That was the worst part.

She handed him a juicy piece of guava. "What do you think?"

He knew exactly what Adam had felt like when faced with that apple. The poor sap had known he was screwed, but he'd had no choice. He was going to be kicked out of paradise. "I think you're right," he said, and took the dripping piece of fruit.

Chapter 16

An hour later, Gen stood beside the hideout with Jack. Leaving this spot felt a lot like leaving the Hollow. In many ways being marooned here had been like a trip back home, and she was glad for that. The girl who had left Tennessee at fifteen still lived inside her, and Genevieve wanted to renew the acquaintance. Maybe she wouldn't go back to being a hillbilly, but she wouldn't be so ashamed of her roots, either. They'd helped her survive.

"We did a pretty good job of making a hideout," Jack said.

"I wish I had a camera to take a picture of it. If we ever come back here, it will probably be gone."

"You never know. It's pretty sturdy."

"It's a wonderful hideout, Jack." She could tell he was proud of having built it and hated to leave it to the elements, as she did. But if they ever hoped to be rescued, they had to climb to a high spot and concoct a signal that a plane would see. "But it's served its purpose and now we have to go."

He gazed at her for a long, silent moment.

She wasn't as psychic as her mama or Lincoln, but it didn't take a psychic to read what was going on in Jack's genius brain. He was thinking of a very specific purpose the hideout had served. They still had one condom left, packed into her pink suitcase along with six guavas, their clothes, and the last of the rainwater. They hadn't discussed it, just packed it in with the other stuff.

All in all, she thought they'd made good use of the materials at hand. They'd rinsed out her shampoo bottle and funneled the water into it using Jack's cupped hands. Because she'd ripped the original handle off the suitcase, she'd had to come up with a way for Jack to lug it along with them. She'd cut the cord off her curling iron and put that through the holes made when the handle had pulled out.

The cord was long enough to loop over Jack's shoulder and across his chest so the suitcase sat against his right hip. While they'd rigged that up, she kept thinking about how he'd hog-tied her with the cord. From the look in his eyes and the jut of his fly, he most certainly remembered it.

He cleared his throat. "Guess we'd better get started. Sure you don't want to use the glasses first?"

"No, you first. You're leading the way." He looked like such a manly man right now, if you didn't count the pink suitcase attached to him by the curling iron cord. She'd made cutoffs out of his pants, and although he was still wearing his belt, he'd decided against a shirt. The women at Rainbow wouldn't recognize him now. If she could take a picture of him looking like this, without the suitcase, of course, he'd have about a million dates in no time.

He gazed up at the rocky cliff. "Yeah, like I know how to do this."

"You don't?" So maybe he looked more manly than he was. Once again, she'd made the mistake of thinking he'd had a normal childhood. She'd assumed he'd want to lead this expedition. "You've never climbed a ledge before?"

"Nope." He started toward the rocks. "But there's always a first time."

"Wait." She admired his grit, taking on the challenge

without having a lick of experience. "I don't want you to fall down and break your leg. You'd better give me the glasses."

"I suppose you're a climbing expert."

"No need to take that tone with me, just because you're feeling testy."

"I'm not feeling testy."

"Oh, yes, you are, mister. You're ready to bite my head off because I might know a little bit more about the outdoors than you do." Her mood wasn't the greatest, either, come to think of it. The good sex was over and now they had nothing but climbing and signaling and trying to survive on guavas.

"Well, then, take the damned glasses." He whipped them off and shoved them at her.

"Thank you, Your Prickness." She took them, glared at him, and put them on. "You'd think some people could be a little more grateful, instead of starting a fight with the very person who is about to save their sorry—" She paused as he began to grin, his teeth white against his beard. She frowned at him. "*Now* what?"

"It's the glasses."

"What about them?"

"They just don't go with that hot little bikini of yours. You look like a cross between Jennifer Aniston and my high school English teacher."

She thought the Jennifer Aniston part was a nice compliment, but she wasn't sure about the rest. "Did you like your high school English teacher?"

He didn't answer her, and his grin softened as he continued to gaze at her. His eyes got sort of dreamy, too.

"Jack?"

"Gen, I suppose there's no guarantee about how this will turn out. I don't think we'll be stranded here forever, but . . . the thing is, I just want you to know that I—"

"We most certainly won't be stranded here forever. Not

if I have anything to say about it. Come on. I'll show you how we're going to shimmy up these rocks in no time." She headed off toward the most likely spot for hand- and footholds. If they stayed there another second, Jack was going to say something embarrassing, something he'd never be able to take back.

That would be bad enough. The trouble was, she might say something just as embarrassing in return. They needed to get themselves rescued before she gave in to that temptation. It was only being stranded here together that was making her think that she was falling for Jack. She'd figure that out once she got herself back to Honolulu.

"I need a boost, Jack."

Jack gazed up at Gen's bikini-clad bottom hanging about two feet above him. He didn't dare look down. The only way he could deal with this climb was to pretend that the sand was exactly the same distance away that it had been twenty minutes ago.

"Hey, you down there!" she called again. "A little help, please! I can't quite reach the next handhold."

"Uh, wait a sec."

"How long of a sec?"

"I'm assessing the situation."

"Assess this, boy genius. I'm holding onto a piece of rock no bigger than the hind tit on a sow, and if you don't give me a boost in the next two seconds, I'm liable to lose my grip, fall down on top of you, and send us to the bottom, which is about a hundred feet. How well do you bounce?"

"A hundred feet? We're five stories up?" He saw spots in front of his eyes.

"God bless America. Are you informing me at this late date that you're afraid of heights?"

"What if I am?"

"You could've opened your trap and told me, is what! Here I am needing a boost, and you're afraid to let go and give me one. A fine kettle of fish this is. I should be carrying the suitcase, too."

"You mean in case I don't make it, you'll have the supplies?" The sweat poured down his back. His hands were sweaty, too, but he didn't want to think about what might happen if they got too slick to hold onto the lava rock.

"No, that is *not* what I meant. The suitcase is adding to your problems, maybe throwing you off balance a little. You could probably climb better without it."

He hadn't really thought of that, but now he started sweating even more. She was right. The suitcase could be the death of him.

"Listen, Jack, if it's you or the suitcase, I want you to take that thing off and drop it."

"No way." He hadn't forgotten how much she loved the silly thing. "I couldn't take it off now, anyway. I'd fall for sure."

"You're not gonna fall."

"Right." He swallowed hard.

"Forget giving me a boost. I'll just stretch a little higher and get that handhold."

He had a sudden vision of her stretching, missing, and falling on account of him. "Don't stretch! I'll do it! Give me a couple of seconds to psych myself up, okay?"

"Do you want me to pass you the glasses? Would that help?"

"Hell, no, I don't want the glasses! The only thing that's saving me is that I can't see what I'm doing."

"We're almost to the top, Jack. I can see it from here. About two more handholds and I'll be able to pull myself over the edge."

"And then we'll be six stories up." Jack thought he might be sick to his stomach.

"Don't think of that. Think of . . . think of the last condom. What do you say, Jack? When we get to the top, wanna use that last little raincoat?"

As diversionary thinking, the concept was a real winner. His prize was right above him, but he wouldn't get it unless he let go of the rock and boosted her up. But if he let go of the rock, he'd be able to cup his hand around one of her firm little butt cheeks.

If he didn't give her a boost, they would both fall five stories and die. It should be an easy decision. "Are you serious about the last condom?"

"Just get me up there and I'll show you how serious I am."

Filling his mind so full of sex that he didn't have room for any images of going splat on the sand, he peeled his right hand from the chunk of black lava rock that had been his security, got a handful of Gen, and pushed upward.

"Yee-haw!"

Heart pounding, he latched onto his rock again and stared after her with lust in his heart. She scrambled the rest of the way to the top and disappeared over the edge.

He felt instantly desolate. "Gen?"

Her head popped over the edge. "Right here, big boy. Come and get me."

He wished she'd taken that last part a little slower. He'd been used to putting his hands on the same outcropping where she'd had her feet and pretending they were rungs on a ladder. Now every outcropping between him and Gen looked the same.

"Come on up, Jack," she called again more gently.

He tilted his head to look up. Nothing showed but her head against the bright sky. She was very blurry and very far away.

Looking at the rocks right above him, he searched for a place to grab on to. Once he found a handhold, his feet usually took care of themselves. But nothing looked good. Five stories up. Five fucking stories up. His stomach pitched.

"Okay, I can see you need a little motivation. Hang on." Her head disappeared, then popped back into view. "That was a joke, Jack. *Hang on*. Get it?"

"Sorry. Can't laugh. Might go splat."

"Poor Jack."

He should have been insulted by that, but he was too scared to be insulted.

"Here you go. This should help take your mind off your problems." Gen reappeared over the edge. "Ouch."

"What happened?"

"It's just that these rocks . . . ouchy . . . aren't exactly comfortable, but what the heck." She wiggled closer so that her shoulders came into view. "Are you looking at me?"

"Yes."

"Good. Concentrate on these babies, and climb on up to mama."

Jack blinked. Surely she wasn't dangling her bare boobs over the ledge to entice him up there.

"Hurry up, Jack. There's a piece of lava rock making a permanent dent between my ribs. Or maybe my twin beauties don't turn you on the way they used to, now that you've seen me prancing around the beach in my birthday suit most of the day."

His tongue stuck in his throat, but finally he managed to croak out his question. "You're hanging naked over that ledge?"

"Correction, I'm hanging topless over this ledge. But since you're not moving, I must be using the wrong fishing lure."

Two things finally penetrated the fear holding him flattened to the cliff. She really would have sex with him when he climbed up there, and with all the adrenaline surging through him, it was going to be one hell of a ride.

"I'm moving." Gritting his teeth, he reached up, trusting his hand would find the right spot. The indentation wasn't huge, but enough. He moved his other hand, then a foot. The suitcase banged against his hip.

"Jack, Jack, he's our man! If he can't do it, nobody can!"

He glanced up again and she was wiggling her breasts at him. The sweat still rolled down his spine, but saliva pooled in his mouth, too. Apparently he wasn't scared spitless. He located another indentation in the lava, and another.

"Give me a J, give me an A, give me a C, give me a K! Gooooo, Jack!"

He drew closer, focusing on those shimmying breasts.

"Two tits, four tits, six tits, a dollar. All for Jack, stand up and holler!"

Smiling grimly, he came within six inches of reaching one bobbing nipple.

She scooted back out of reach, out of sight. "All the way, big boy, all the way!"

Panting, he fumbled for the top of the ledge.

"That's it," she called. "Come on up."

A little more. Just a little, and—his foot slipped. Gen's scream stabbed his eardrum as he clutched at the rocks and she latched onto his arm.

Her fingernails dug into his skin as she hung on. For one long, agonizing second, he thought he'd pull them both to a dusty death. They'd be swallowed up by the sand, like a scene out of *The Mummy*. And he would no longer be her knight in shining armor.

That thought alone gave him the strength to grip the rock with his free hand and shove his feet into places that probably weren't even places. "Look out!" he bellowed. "I'm coming up!"

He wasn't even sure how he did it, but moments later he was lying facedown at the top of the cliff, his cheek pressed against a very sharp rock.

Gen's breathless voice came from somewhere above him. "Move away . . . from the edge." She dragged at his arm.

He managed to struggle to his hands and knees and crawl a few feet before collapsing again. The suitcase bumped along with him.

"Jack, are you hyperventilating? Roll over so I can see."

With a groan, he rolled to his back and the suitcase flopped onto his stomach. "Just . . . ventilating. Nothing hyper." He closed his eyes against the sun's glare.

"Here, let me take that thing." She managed to work him free of the suitcase. "Thank you, Jack. Thank you for bringing that all the way up here."

"You're welcome."

"It's so strange, you being scared of heights, when you aren't scared of flying."

Gradually his head stopped spinning. "And you're scared of flying but not of heights. Go figure."

"I guess it's a good thing we're both not scared of the same things, huh?"

"Guess so." He opened his eyes and used his hand to shade his face as he looked up at her.

She was kneeling beside him, her breasts still bare, her hair tousled, and his glasses perched on her nose as she gazed down at him with concern. "That was too close for comfort."

No other woman could look so adorably sexy and so earnest at the same time. He thought of the way she'd instinctively grabbed him, hanging on even though she didn't know if he'd eventually pull her over the edge and down with him. His stomach lurched again. "You shouldn't have tried to catch me."

"You would have done the same for me, and you know it."

That much was true. Still, he didn't want her sacrificing herself. "I think you saved my life. If you hadn't grabbed me, and I hadn't been so scared that I'd pull you with me, I might have given up."

"I wouldn't let that happen." And then she did the most amazing thing. She cupped his bearded chin in both hands, leaned over him, and kissed him soundly on the mouth. It was a quick kiss, one he'd barely registered before she leaned back and took her hands away.

He stared at her, dazed by the affection in that kiss. It hadn't been about lust. Well, mostly it hadn't been about lust. There had been a slight hint of tongue there. "What was that for?"

"I'm, um—" She cleared her throat. "I'm glad you didn't go splat, is all."

"So am I." And suddenly he didn't want to use the last condom, after all. He wanted to save it, in case they spent another night marooned on this island. He wanted to have one more time to look forward to. But he wasn't sure how to explain that to her.

She glanced at the suitcase, as if she might be thinking of the condom, too.

"Let's save it," he said, hoping she'd understand.

She looked back at him and nodded. "Yes, let's," she said softly.

"It's so rocky here, and I'd like the last time to be . . . special. Not rushed."

She swallowed. "Me, too."

"There could be another beach, with a slope down to it instead of a cliff."

"I guess there could be another beach, Jack."

"Absolutely." His heart thudded in anticipation. Something was happening between them, and he shouldn't get his hopes up, but he was doing it anyway. She was hoping for another beach.

She pushed herself to her feet and retrieved her bikini top from where she'd thrown it onto the rocks. "We might as well look around before we make our big X."

"Might as well." He sat up and gave himself the pleasure of watching her put on the bikini top, arching her back as she fastened it between her shoulder blades. He liked the idea that she'd put it back on, because it would give him great pleasure to take it off again.

When he finally struggled to his feet, he longed for the sand instead of this rocky surface. It was about the size of four football fields, and from here he couldn't tell if there was a gentle slope anywhere. He sure hoped so, because he wasn't going back down another cliff like the one he just climbed, no matter how inviting the beach.

Nothing grew up here, but the view was incredible. Scary, too. The ocean stretched endlessly all around them, unmarked by land or boats. Even a whale spout would have been welcome. Nothing.

Way off to the east he thought he could make out another island, but it could be shadows from the clouds hovering near the horizon. He glanced over to where Gen stood looking around, her mouth hanging open.

"Jack," she said, almost whispering. "We are out in the middle of the frigging *ocean*."

"I know it looks like that, but there has to be land to the east of us. We didn't fly west for *that* long. My best guess is we're on one of the Leewards."

"The Leewards. I read about them in a bird book. There are some interesting birds out here." She glanced around. "If we're lucky, we might even see an albatross."

"If we're even luckier, we'll see an airplane." Jack started walking gingerly over the rocky terrain. It was hell on his blistered feet, even with the saltwater treatment he'd given them this morning.

"Your feet still hurt, don't they?"

"It's not so bad."

"Your mouth is all scrooched up like a catfish, so I know they hurt."

"Don't yours, walking on these rocks?"

She shook her head. "I've gone barefoot all my life. What I hate is putting on shoes to go to work. This is heaven."

"Could have fooled me."

"Then why don't you just sit on the suitcase and let me look around?"

"Because then you'll think I'm a wuss."

"No, I'll think you're smart to take advantage of the strengths of your partner."

Partner. He liked the sound of that word. And his feet were killing him. "You talked me into it." He hobbled over to the suitcase. "Are you sure it'll hold me?"

"It'll hold you. It may not be stylish, but it's tough. I'm surprised the handle came off, but I guess those wet clothes weighed more than a full barrel of moonshine."

Jack eased himself down on the suitcase, and when nothing seemed to be giving way, he put all his weight on it and stretched out his legs.

"Perfect." Gen smiled. "Now relax and I'll go out on patrol."

She was the best-looking patrol he'd ever seen as she strolled the perimeter in her tiny bikini. He'd let her keep the glasses, and she should have them since she was doing the walkabout instead of him, but he wished he could see her better. It wasn't every day you watched a goddess walking barefoot on the moon.

On the far side of the plateau she turned and made a

megaphone of her hands. "Jack, guess what? There *is* a beach on this side, and the way down isn't bad at all!"

"What's your definition of *not bad*?"

"There's a sort of trail running down it! You'll be fine!" She started back in his direction.

A trail. Hot damn. They could make their giant X on the top of the island and saunter back to the beach. And this time, when they used the last condom, he planned to make it about more than sex.

A grayish bird perched on a rock at the edge of the water. Nick wasn't sure what kind it was and didn't much care. Whatever it was, it was a dead bird. He crept up slowly from behind, a baseball-size rock in his hand. He'd tried and failed so many times to kill one of these damned things, but this time he'd make it.

At first he'd thought maybe he could grab a fish with his bare hands. Then he'd tried using his shirt as a net and had accomplished nothing but ripping his shirt on a piece of coral and gashing his toes on a seashell. So no sushi for him.

If only his .357 were dry enough to risk firing it, he'd have a meal in no time. He hoped to hell it was dry by the time the idiots picked him up, *if* they ever picked him up, or he'd have to swipe one of their guns in order to kill them both. It was an added glitch, but not insurmountable. He could always fake it with his gun until he could trade for one of theirs. In the meantime, he had to get something in his stomach, or he'd be too weak to outsmart even those morons.

At first the thought of eating raw meat hadn't appealed to him, but as the day wore on, he got a lot less picky. This bird was going to give his all for the cause. Nick eased closer, his arm cocked. He'd been a decent pitcher in high school. He could do this.

Taking aim, he held his breath and hurled the rock as hard as he could. The effort threw him off balance. As he landed facedown in the sand, he heard two things—the splash of a rock falling harmlessly into the waves and the vigorous flapping of wings. This was turning into a really shitty day.

Then he heard a woman scream. At least that's what he thought he heard. Maybe the sun was frying his brain. Or maybe one of the birds flying around this godforsaken place made a noise that sounded like a woman screaming.

Spitting sand, he got to his knees. Lack of food was making him a little dizzy. He'd found a puddle in a rock that had captured some of the rainwater from the night before, but he'd long since finished that off. He barely had enough spit to rid his mouth of the sand.

His pickup men had to show today. Maybe he should forget about food and conserve his energy for when they arrived. They'd have water on the boat, and probably some food, too. Once they plucked him from the island, he'd be on his way to a perpetual feast. He couldn't lose sight of the goal. He—

A shout immobilized him. That was no bird. Chills ran through him as he heard a shouted reply. He'd thought this little piece of volcanic rock was too isolated to attract anybody. Besides, he'd intended to be long gone by now.

They could be hikers. Or bird-watchers. They'd have a boat. They'd have food. And once he'd taken charge of both, he'd have no need of the people. He got quietly to his feet and moved to the spot where he had his .357 drying in the sun.

Chapter 17

Annabelle hadn't counted on how much she'd love steering that boat. As she sent it plowing through the waves to rescue her daughter, she felt like the whole blessed cavalry riding in to save Gary Cooper from the Indians. Once Matt turned over the driving to her, she didn't want to give it up.

Having Matt stand behind her seat so she could breathe in the scent of him was part of the thrill, of course, but she would have enjoyed herself without him being there, too. Maybe *enjoy* was the wrong word. She couldn't very well enjoy anything until Genevieve was back home safe and sound.

But driving this boat . . . she hadn't felt this powerful since the day she'd stepped off the plane in Honolulu eleven years ago. At the time she'd promised herself to find more challenges—not in the area of airplanes, which were completely unnatural—but she'd thought about taking one of those classes where folks broke boards with the side of their hand.

She wasn't sure what all the kinds of martial arts were and she got the names mixed up with Chinese food. Kung fu sounded like something you ate and Kung pau sounded like breaking boards with your hand, but she thought maybe she had that backward. At any rate, she hadn't done it, or any of the other projects that had flitted through her mind, like going to one of those karaoke bars to see if she could still sing like she used to be able to back in the Hollow. Then there was tap dancing. She'd always dreamed of being able to tap dance like Donald O'Connor or Gene Kelly.

Oh, she could try blaming it on lack of money. Honolulu was an expensive place to live, and she'd struggled to make ends meet. But Lincoln had a friend who could break a board with the side of his hand, and one of Genevieve's girlfriends from high school was a tap dancer. Annabelle had gone to a school musical to see her perform. Those kids would have taught Annabelle the basics if she'd had the nerve to ask.

Instead she'd let herself get into a rut, and that was the truth of it, pure and simple. She'd moved from one rut in the Hollow to another rut in Honolulu. It might be a fancier rut, and at least her children had more to work with here, but as for Annabelle herself, she hadn't grown a lick. Once they found Genevieve, she'd do something about that.

She couldn't expect to be allowed to drive boats, though, no matter how much she believed she'd found her second calling. Boats were for rich people, and she never expected to end up in that category. So she'd have to make the best of this chance.

Matt leaned down close to her ear. "You look like you were born to do that."

"Hardly. If a body is born to do something, don't you think the good Lord would provide a way for them to actually do it?"

"You're doing it right now, aren't you?"

"This is a special circumstance, and you know it."

Matt chuckled. "Are you saying that you know when

the good Lord has a hand in something and when he doesn't?"

He had her there. But she hoped the good Lord hadn't seen fit to create this problem with Genevieve just so Annabelle could drive a boat. In that case, she would need to have a talk with the good Lord.

"Well, just keep doing what you're doing," Matt said. "You're a natural at driving a boat. I'm going to confer with Lincoln and see if he's getting any Genevieve signals from Kauai. Because if we're going beyond that, we need to fuel up so we're at full capacity when we leave there."

"You believe he's getting signals?" That would comfort her some, if Matt was convinced about Lincoln's special abilities.

Matt hesitated.

"Then you don't believe it." She hadn't really expected him to, so she shouldn't be so disappointed.

"At this point, I don't know what to believe," Matt said. "And I'm—"

"Just playing along?"

He sighed. "No. I have a feeling you wouldn't allow me do that."

"You've got that right, mister."

"I'm trying to keep an open mind, is what I'm doing. Can you live with that?"

"I don't have much choice, now, do I? I can't very well climb into your head and shine a light into your brain, can I?"

"You know, Annabelle, sometimes I think that's exactly what you've done. When I look at you, it's like somebody turned a floodlight on in my head."

"That sounds downright unpleasant." It was a long way from saying *you light up my life*, and she'd always wished a man would tell her that. She thought it sounded so romantic, and it was one of her all-time favorite songs. Telling her that she caused a floodlight to go on in his brain wasn't the same.

"That's the best way for me to explain it," Matt said. "You make me look at things differently, like when I was talking to you about Theresa, I finally figured out that I'd just never loved her enough to be a good husband."

"Well, I guess that could explain why Genevieve's daddy and Lincoln's daddy both took off so quick. Maybe they just plumb ran out of love. And here I thought they were irresponsible, selfish good-for-nothings."

"They were." Matt said it with such feeling that it warmed her heart. "And I was selfish, too, hanging on to a woman and not giving her the love she needed. But leaving you with a baby . . . I would never do something like that."

"I believe you. You didn't have to rent this boat, and now that I know you're not rich, I can see it was even more of an imposition. And I'm going to pay you back, if it takes me—"

"No, you are not."

"Oh, yes, I surely am."

"I don't want the money. But there is something I do want from you."

Annabelle's heart started thumping faster. She lowered her voice. "If you want sex, then I take back all the nice things I've ever said about you."

Matt leaned closer, his breath tickling her ear. "Annabelle, if I didn't want sex, there would be something seriously wrong with me. But I respect your reasons for not getting involved. So I'm wondering if we can be friends, you, me, and Lincoln. After this is over and we've found Genevieve, I don't want to go our separate ways."

Annabelle didn't want that, either, but she had her rules, and Matt was too good looking to be only a friend. "You want to come over for supper and gin rummy? Is that what you're thinking about?"

"I'd love to. I'd also like to take a boat out for the fun of it again, and I'd like you and Lincoln to go along. You could practice driving."

No fair. He'd picked the one thing that she couldn't do on her own. He was the only person she knew who could teach her all about boats. "Why should I care about driving a boat? I have as much chance of owning one as a mule has of winning the Kentucky Derby."

"You don't know that. You don't know what the future has in store for you. And you love being at the wheel of this boat. You might as well admit it, because it's written all over your face."

"I do love it," she said softly. "I didn't expect I would. I only took the wheel so Lincoln would get back to concentrating on Genevieve, but . . . there's something about being out here on the ocean, like we're dancing over the waves."

"I feel that way, too. Let me give you a chance to really enjoy it."

She hesitated. "Are we still talking about driving the boat?"

"Why?" There was laughter in his voice. "What else could we be talking about?"

Annabelle lifted her chin. "I may be a hillbilly, but I wasn't born yesterday. I know all about those double meanings."

"I'm sure you do." He cleared his throat. "I was talking about driving the boat. Let me teach you."

"I'll think about it."

"Good. That's a start. Now I'll go talk to Lincoln about our heading for the next few hours."

"I hate to see you ripping up your clothes," Jack said.

"I don't. This is about survival." Perched cross-legged

on the *South Park* beach towel next to Jack, Genevieve opened a side seam on her dress with the hibiscus pattern on it and tore the dress apart without a single regret. Back in the Hollow she'd never worried about clothes. After this, she wouldn't let herself worry about them again. She had a whole new perspective on things.

Jack worked on the seams of his shirt. "Maybe we should have brought driftwood up to build a fire, instead."

"Oh, sure. I barely got *you* up here, let alone a bunch of driftwood."

"See, you think I'm a wuss."

"I do not. I think you're an idiot for not telling me you were scared of heights. You could have stayed on the beach and I would have come up here to make the X." She demolished the dress's other side seam.

"I couldn't let you do that."

"Why not?"

"I don't know—there could have been something dangerous up here."

"Like what?" She sneaked a glance at him. His protective urges were so cute.

"Well, isn't an albatross kind of big?"

She bit her lip to keep from laughing. "Pretty big. Almost a seven-foot wingspan."

"Holy shit!" He looked up in the sky as if afraid one could be dive-bombing them at this very moment. Then he shuddered. "See what I mean? If some bird the size of a Learjet came swooping at you—"

"I don't think there's ever been a report of an albatross attack."

"That doesn't mean it couldn't happen. You could have a rogue albatross. Damn, are they really seven feet wide?"

"That's what I've read. I've never seen one."

"Well, if there are any hanging around here, it's good there are two of us. They wouldn't feel so free to mess with two people." He finished ripping apart his shirt and picked up the jacket to her dress. "I don't see any point in tearing this. It's as big as it's going to get."

"I suppose you're right." She knew their situation was a little uncertain, and she should probably be more worried than she was. But it was hard not to feel optimistic sitting here beside Jack, a most excellent lover, and enjoying an outstanding 360-degree view.

"I really liked this dress."

"Me, too, but I don't care about it now. We have to be practical. We want the X to be as big as possible, so—"

"Bigger than a freaking albatross," he muttered.

"Jack, you really don't have to worry about those birds."

"Oh, yeah? What do they eat?"

"Fish."

"My point exactly. Meat eaters. For all we know, a herd of hungry albatrosses, or albatrossi, or whatever, could be headed this way. And we are a whole lot more accessible up here than fish swimming underwater. There's this old Hitchcock movie about—"

"Now, stop it. I saw that movie on TV and it made me mad. Birds aren't like that."

"Says you."

"When it comes to birds, I am the expert on this island." She pulled her pale green skirt out of the suitcase.

"You're going to ruin that, too?"

"Yep." She cut through the waistband. "So what? You've already sacrificed your shirt and the bottom half of your pants."

Jack laughed. "Yeah, but I think we've established that's no big loss."

"True." She grinned at him. "Except now I'm getting kind of sentimental about your style of dress. It's you, after all."

"Don't get too attached to that look. I'm going for all black when we get home."

"I'll probably barely recognize you." And wearing all black, he'd start attracting women. That's what she'd hoped for, of course. She reached into her suitcase and handed him her blue panties. "Tear these along the side, okay?"

"Okay."

She pulled the skirt apart. "I wonder if you really will buy an all-black wardrobe. You might get back to civilization, start thinking about computer programs, and forget all about your clothes and what we talked about. Right now you don't have your computer stuff to distract you."

When he didn't answer, she looked over to find him sitting like a statue while he stared at her panties. "Can you rip those by yourself, or do you need me to start you off by snipping some of the threads? The stitching's small. Do you want the glasses?"

He glanced at her, as if coming out of a trance. "No, I can do this without the glasses. Actually, I was thinking how much more fun it would be to rip them off you."

She gulped. Just like that, what had been a friendly discussion exploded like a cherry bomb. To think that thoughts of having sex with her had sent him into a trance. Now, that was exciting. "You . . . you know what ripping panties off of me would lead to."

"I know," he said in a cocky, very-sure-of-himself way.

His tone gave her delicious goose bumps. If a guy started out talking that way, like he was God's gift, then everyone knew he was a jerk. But Jack had started out with a low opinion of his sex appeal, and his brand-new self-confidence really turned her on, maybe because she'd helped him get to this point. She was proud of her contribution, and almost ready to suggest changing into those panties.

Then he tore them neatly across the side seam. "And for

the record, Gen, I won't forget a single minute of the time we've spent here." He tossed the panties onto the pile of torn clothes and looked her straight in the eye. "The question is, will you?"

"Of course I won't."

"Then it seems to me we should reminisce together."

His suggestion made her heart hurt. She wished he hadn't brought up the subject, but maybe they needed to get it out of the way. "It won't be the same, once we're back in Honolulu."

"Why? Because you can't see yourself dating a nerd?"

"That's not it. Well, that's sort of the problem, but not what you think." She didn't suppose he'd understand the astrology obstacle, so she brought up the other important issue. "You need to find somebody who's willing to play second fiddle to that computer screen you're so attached to. I'm not."

"Goddammit!" He lurched to his feet and started to pace. Then he winced and stopped. "Goddammit," he said again, softer this time. "I've told you I won't forget a minute of the time we've spent together. What makes you think I'll get involved with my computer and forget about *you*?"

"Because you're a genius! And there's some woman out there ready to make allowances for that, but I know myself, and the first time you forgot about me because you were so fascinated with your beloved computer program, I'd feel like you'd lost interest. I would hate that, Jack."

"I wouldn't allow such a thing to happen."

"You couldn't help it."

"I could! I could program my computer with a timer, so it would beep a signal when it was time to see you. Hell, I could program it to shut down completely, and then—"

"Don't you see?" It was good they were having this talk, because it pointed out exactly the problem she was so worried about. "I don't want you to have to set a timer. I want a man who's so crazy about me he remembers on his own, without being reminded."

"I'm pretty sure I would remember! But just in case, I could have a backup system."

She shook her head. "Pretty sure isn't good enough." How she wished Jack was a normal guy, with a normal nine-to-five job. But then he wouldn't be Jack. "What we've had on this island has been very intense."

"You're telling me."

"I think part of that's the danger, don't you?"

"I think part of that's me finally getting you naked."

Her cheeks grew warm. "And part of it's because we have no distractions."

"Personally, I think Rainbow should be worried that I'll be less productive now that I know what I've been missing in life. I think that's a lot more likely than me ignoring you."

"I just think, after what we've had on this island, that anything back home would be a letdown. For both of us. This isn't exactly your normal date, Jack. I mean, don't you think going out for pizza and a movie would seem dull after this?"

He gazed down at her. "Not if you consider what we could do when we came home from the movie."

When he talked like that, she got very hot and bothered. Then again, she was still on this island, which felt like being back in the caveman days. She was afraid that four walls and a regular bed wouldn't give them the same thrill. And she couldn't stand the idea of a watered-down sexual experience with him. Not after what had happened here.

"I just don't think it would work," she said at last.

"It won't if you're not even willing to try."

She gazed at him in silence.

"Okay, then." He gave her a long look before reaching

into the pile of clothes. "I might as well start tying what we have together while you keep tearing things apart."

"Was that some sort of loaded remark?"

His glance flicked over her. "Take it any way you want."

"I think it was a loaded remark. I'm not tearing us apart." She started to take out the seams of her suit jacket. "I'm trying to keep us from ruining the magic."

"Don't do me any favors, okay?" He tied the end of her bra to her panties. "I think the magic would transfer to Honolulu just fine. It would be like saving it on a disk and putting it into another computer. The files would all still be there."

"You're wrong." She ripped the sleeve from her jacket. "Stuff would be lost. Or scrambled."

"Now you're talking about my specialty." He tied a length of her hibiscus dress to her panties. "I'm an expert at retrieving lost files and unscrambling messed-up ones. I could straighten us out in no time."

"Maybe so, if you weren't in the middle of some exciting new software project, which is what you would be the minute we get back. You'll be behind and have to work overtime to catch up." She removed the other sleeve and started ripping the jacket's side seams.

"You have it all figured out, don't you?"

"I believe I do." She finished taking the jacket apart and got to her feet. "That's the end of the clothes. Are we going to use the beach towel, and should I start cutting it down the middle?"

He stopped tying and studied her. "Is that a trick question?"

It was. Once she destroyed the beach towel, they'd have nothing to lie on and would have a tough time using that last condom. He wanted a relationship after they got home. She didn't. She thought he should be the one to decide if he wanted to have sex with her again or start keeping his distance.

"Don't cut up the towel," he said.

"You're sure?"

"I'm sure." He smiled at her. "I want one last chance to change your mind."

"You won't, Jack."

"Since you've made such a point of me being a genius, and I do score that way on certain tests, let me remind you of the single-mindedness part of that profile. Once I decide a problem is worth solving, I don't give up until I solve it, no matter how long it takes."

Now, that kind of statement made little squiggles of anticipation run through her. For a moment she allowed herself to imagine being pursued by Jack and letting him catch her. But once he did, once the challenge was gone, he'd be back in front of his computer screen, sure as hound dogs have fleas.

But she folded up the beach towel and put it in the suitcase, anyway. She wouldn't mind having sex with Jack once more, because that would probably be the last time she'd have 100 percent of his attention.

Because of Jack's tender feet, Genevieve did most of the work creating the X. Then she weighed it down with rocks. Every once in a while she scanned the sky, hoping to see an albatross, but the birds overhead were smaller, mostly terns.

Finally they'd done the best they could with what they'd had to work with. After they shared one of their store of guavas and sipped a little water, Genevieve led the way to the trail she'd found, the one that ended up at another white sandy beach.

The trail was rocky, and she kept looking back to make sure Jack was behind her. "I feel like I should try to carry you," she said. "Or at least carry the suitcase. This must be murder on your feet."

He flashed her a toothy grin. "I'm keeping the suitcase. It has the important supplies in it. Besides, I'm not thinking about the pain. I'm thinking about what I have waiting for me at the bottom."

She pretended not to know what he meant. "Another soothing saltwater bath for your feet?"

"That, too."

She could hardly wait, either, but she couldn't resist teasing him a little. "You know, maybe we shouldn't, after all. Now that we've made a signal up above, we wouldn't want someone to fly in to rescue us right when we're—"

"I'm willing to take that chance. But maybe you aren't."

She laughed. "I'm willing to take that chance. After all, we only have one condom left." She touched soft sand with her feet. "You're almost there, Jack. Only a little more."

"I'm counting the steps."

She turned back to watch him hobble the last couple of yards. "Good job."

He glanced up. "It's all in the reward. I—" Then his eyes widened. "Gen! Look—"

Before he could finish, before she could turn to see what had startled him so, an arm came around her neck and something hard pressed against the side of her head.

Chapter 18

Jack wanted to throw up. This couldn't be happening, not twice in two days. They'd survived this madman yesterday, and damned well, too. He was supposed to be gone forever, off to spend the millions he'd embezzled.

Flushed with fear, Gen stood trembling in Brogan's grip, her eyes huge behind the lenses of Jack's glasses. She still couldn't see who had her.

"And I so hoped you were dead, Brogan," Jack said, to clue her in.

"Nick?" Gen sounded terrified, and Jack didn't blame her one damned bit. This was the stuff nightmares were made of.

"I had hoped the same thing about you two," Brogan said. "But here you are, anyway, so I'll have to kill you again, apparently."

"Nick, why are you here?" Gen's eyes were wide, as if she was in shock.

"There's always a snake in paradise," Jack said. He hated hearing Brogan's first name coming out of Gen's mouth, hated thinking about the plans she'd had for the slimeball. Once his nausea passed, rage moved in. Even without his glasses, he was sure he'd be able to find the exact spot on Brogan's throat where his thumbs needed to go. Choking him to death would be easy, and oh so satisfying.

"I'm not any happier to see you two than you are to see me," Brogan said. "I was hoping you were a couple of bird-watchers, somebody who would have a boat. Somebody with food and water."

Jack thought of the small amount of water and the five guavas in the suitcase. There was no reason for Brogan to think they had anything to eat or drink, and Jack planned to keep it that way as long as possible. "Sounds like somebody ruined your little party."

"Stupid assholes are probably circling one of the other islands and wondering why I'm not there. They have the brains of termites."

"It's so hard to get good help these days." Although Jack's dearest wish was to rush the guy and grab the gun, he couldn't guarantee Gen wouldn't get shot in the process. He remembered what it felt like to have a gun barrel shoved against his temple. He didn't want to make any moves that would scare her even more.

Brogan nodded toward the suitcase. "I see you still have that dorky suitcase. How in hell did you make it out alive, let alone save that ridiculous suitcase? You couldn't possibly have landed the plane."

"Ha! Jack *did* land the plane." Gen's fire seemed to be returning. "And then he saved my suitcase. And don't you dare insult my luggage, you murdering, lying—"

"Oh, you can't call me a murderer yet, Genevieve." Brogan tightened his arm around her neck. "You're both still alive. But I'll be taking care of that detail shortly. I just need a little more time."

"Time isn't going to help," Jack said. "Your whole pro-gram has been shit-canned, and you know it. You can't leave behind a couple of dead bodies with bullets in them that could be traced to you."

"I always knew you were a genius, but I'm no slouch myself. I figured that one out, which is why you're both still breathing the cool salty air."

"You're looking a little ragged around the edges, Brogan." Jack's vision might be blurry, but he could see that the guy's presentation had taken a hit. His Italian shoes were gone, probably kicked off during his swim to shore. He must have deep-sixed his jacket for the same reason, because it wasn't in evidence, either. His imported silk shirt and slacks were ripped and stained.

Brogan stiffened. "Nothing that a few days in Fiji won't cure."

Jack detected a little bit of belligerence, a crack in Brogan's layer of suave confidence. Gen might be right about this grooming thing affecting how people thought of you, because Jack had trouble believing that Brogan, looking the way he did, would end up on a beach in Fiji sipping an umbrella drink.

Without the advantage of Gen's sunscreen, the guy's face was all blotchy except for a few bristly patches of hair. Apparently Brogan couldn't grow much of a beard. The previously *GQ*-worthy babe magnet resembled something the cat had dragged in. By comparison, Jack felt like a stud.

While this pleased him no end, he decided not to make any more remarks about Brogan's appearance. The maniac's vanity might override his logic and Jack would end up with a bullet in his brain because he was sporting a better look.

"Tell you what," Brogan said. "Let's move this little party down to the beach, so I'll be able to see if and when those two morons show up. Farley, you first. If you try anything, Genevieve becomes one dead secretary. Disposing of the body is a problem, but not a huge problem, so don't test me."

"Hey, I'm a computer geek, not a hero." Jack stepped

onto the sand and gave Gen a reassuring glance as he moved past her.

"I've been counting on that," Brogan said. "Which is why I can't figure out how you landed the—hold on. You've flown simulations, haven't you, you son of a bitch!"

"He was wonderful," Gen said. "He kept his head and saved our lives."

"Temporarily," Brogan said.

"I was lucky that I didn't kill us both in that plane." As much as Jack enjoyed having Gen sing his praises, he didn't want Brogan to think of him as a threat. The chances of catching Brogan off guard were better that way.

"It was more than luck," Gen said. "I don't know many folks who could have done what Jack did. He was cool as a lemonade jug floating in the crick."

"I was a basket case," Jack said. "It's a miracle I held onto the controls."

"So it's *Jack* now, is it?" Brogan said, a sneer in his voice.

"All my friends call me that."

"Not that I ever heard. How interesting. And, Genevieve, you're sounding like a little hillbilly! I always wondered if you were what you pretended to be. Seems a little of the polish has worn off."

"I'd rather be a hillbilly than a slimy excuse for a—"

"Now, now." Brogan tightened his grip on her neck. "Better watch yourself, little girl. I'm sure Jack doesn't want you dead any sooner than necessary. I have the feeling you two have become *much* better acquainted since I last saw you."

Now there was a subject Jack *really* didn't want to get into. "Are you kidding, Brogan? Do you think a good-looking chick like Gen would have anything to do with a nerd like me?"

"Good point. I suppose she's grateful that you saved

her life, but not *that* grateful. Right, Genevieve, sweet-heart?"

"A man like Jack is a darn sight preferable to a toad-sucker like you."

"Well, damn." Brogan's laugh had a crazy edge to it. "I guess this means the offer of a blow job has been re-scinded."

Gen made a noise low in her throat.

Jack was afraid she might let her temper get the better of her, so he decided to change the subject. "What kind of boat do your pickup guys have?"

"Why, you gonna help me keep a lookout? How Christian of you."

"In case you hadn't noticed, we're stranded on this is-land, too," Jack said. "Getting picked up by a couple of stu-pid bad guys is better than not getting picked up at all."

"Or so you think. Okay, what the hell. They have an old beat-up trawler, dirty white with green trim. I thought a fishing boat would be less conspicuous, and they looked like they could use the money."

"And they had the conscience of a cockroach, just like you," Gen said.

"Well, I guess the romance is definitely over between us," Brogan said. "Okay, we're close enough to the water-line now. Genevieve and I will sit on this lava rock and make ourselves comfy."

Jack tried to think of some way he could get Brogan to point the gun away from Gen. He came up blank.

"Farley, you stay right there and open the suitcase so I can find out if there's anything useful in there."

"There's not a blessed thing in there that you'd want," Gen said.

"There must be something of value, Daisy Mae, or you wouldn't have asked Lil Abner to haul it all the way from the other side of the island."

"Maybe we happen to like this suitcase," Jack said.

"Well, that figures with a couple of losers like you. And I have to tell you, Farley, that wearing it like an oversized purse does nothing for the castaway look you have going."

Oh, what a great opening for a slam. Jack had to really control himself. He wished Gen could get a gander at her former dreamboat, but Brogan kept a tight arm around her neck and the gun right up against her temple.

"Dump the stuff on the sand, Farley."

Jack lifted the cord over his head, held the suitcase against one hip, and snapped it open, all the while trying to think what he might do with the contents to get the edge on Brogan. He could throw a guava at the guy, but that would just make a mess and might get Gen shot. The curling iron was a better weapon. Gen had insisted on packing it, even with the cord cut off. To leave it, according to her, would have been littering.

If Jack was thinking of throwing something, he had to factor in his aim, which would be lousy considering Gen was wearing his glasses. He'd have to get close enough to jab Brogan in the eye, but that wasn't likely, and there was still the problem of Brogan firing the gun.

Every possible move Jack could make carried that danger. He could toss the beach towel over Brogan's head, but Brogan could still shoot Gen.

"Dump the damned suitcase, Farley!"

"There's a small bottle of water," Jack said. "It could get br—"

"*Water?* Shit, leave the rest of it right there and bring the water. And don't try anything, or I'll shoot your girlfriend."

"She's not my—"

"Bring me the fucking water!"

Jack pulled out the lotion bottle with water in it and

dropped the suitcase to the sand. Then he started toward Gen and Brogan.

"Hold it."

Jack stopped walking.

"This is damned inconvenient," Brogan said. "If I let go of Little Miss Muffet to drink the water, one of you is liable to get some stupid idea of escaping. But I have to have that water." He sighed. "Leave it right there and go take that ridiculous cord off the suitcase."

Jack put the water down and started back to the suitcase.

"And make it snappy, or I'll just shoot Genevieve and reduce my problems by half."

Jack ripped the cord out, making the holes in the suitcase even bigger. He hated to, but he completely believed that Brogan would shoot that gun without hesitation. According to what Jack had read on the subject, sociopaths didn't much care what happened to the people who got in their way. With the cord in his hand, he turned back to Gen and Brogan. "Now what?"

"You're going to walk over here nice and easy, and hand the cord to our Playmate of the Month. Then you're going to lie down with your back to her while she ties you up. If you make even one suspicious move, she's history."

Jack did as he was told. He tried to communicate some hope to Gen as he handed her the cord, but at this point he couldn't figure out how to get around the damned gun. Moving slowly, he lay down in the warm, gritty sand, his back to them.

Brogan directed the operation, instructing Gen to tie Jack's hands behind his back and then loop the cord around his right ankle, so he was trussed up like a calf in a rodeo. She did a good job, because Brogan had threatened to shoot her if she didn't. He felt the quiver of her hands each time she touched him. He wished this was a game they were playing, like last time. But this was no game. So much for catching Brogan off guard.

"Okay, now, sweet peach," Brogan said when she was done. "I want you to go get the water and bring it to me. I'll have the gun pointed at the back of your hero's head the whole time, so keep that in mind."

His cheek resting on the sand, the barrel of the gun pressing against the base of his brain, Jack had a fuzzy view of Gen's legs as she walked to the water bottle, picked it up, and came back.

"Take the top off," Brogan told her.

Jack was getting very thirsty himself, so when he heard Brogan gulping the water, he groaned softly.

"Don't drink it all!" Gen said. "Then we—you disgusting nightcrawler! You drank every blessed drop!"

"Kiss my ass," Brogan said. "Now go get the suitcase and dump it over here so I can see what else is in there."

Once again Jack watched as Gen walked across the sand, hefted the suitcase, and walked back. When she dumped it, a guava rolled past his nose and lay three inches from his mouth.

"Guavas, huh?" Brogan said. "How thoughtful. Let's see, in order to eat one, I'll need to have both of you tied up." He paused. "Genevieve, be a good little secretary and take off Farley's belt."

Gen walked around in front of Jack and knelt down on the sand. "You okay?" she murmured as she fumbled with his belt.

He thought of the last time she'd unbuckled that belt. "Yeah. You?"

"Yeah. I—"

"Shut the hell up!" Brogan said. "And, by the way, how come there aren't any clothes in this suitcase?"

"We used them to make an X on top of the lava plateau," Gen said.

"Goddammit! You people are way too much trouble. Now I have to worry about going up there and taking that apart. All I need is for some Coast Guard helicopter to spot that." Brogan sounded frazzled.

A frazzled bad guy could be a good thing or a bad thing, in Jack's estimation. He might get careless, but he might get an itchy trigger finger. It could go either way.

Gen pulled his belt free of the loops. She didn't seem quite as shaky, so he was hoping maybe she wasn't so scared. Well, the gun was pressed against his head now, not hers. He'd rather have it that way, although if Brogan killed him, there would be no one to watch out for Gen.

She stood, her toes not far from his face. Such nice toes. Everything about Gen was nice. The idea that something bad could happen to her made him sick to his stomach all over again.

"Come around here and loop the belt between his crossed hands," Brogan said.

Gen and her nice toes walked away. Then Jack felt the belt slide over the spot where his wrists were bound with the curling iron cord.

"That's right," Brogan said. "Now put the belt through the buckle. Okay, now put both your hands through the loop."

The warmth of Gen's wrists touched his. Then came a sharp yank, and the belt tightened, pinning their wrists together. The belt leather snapped a couple more times, and Jack figured out that Brogan was weaving it in and out of the binding so it wouldn't pull loose.

"Okay," he said at last. The pressure of the gun barrel against Jack's head eased and then was gone. "Now I can eat one of the damn guavas. But any funny moves from either of you, and I'll just shoot you both. I could almost do it with one bullet, you being trussed up and cozy."

Jack got to listen to Brogan slurping eagerly while the

other guava remained almost within reach of his tongue. Gen was being forced to listen to Brogan eat, too, and she had to be just as hungry and thirsty as he was. Jack hated to admit it, but as her knight in shining armor, he sucked.

After they left Kauai bearing northwest, Matt took the helm. Lincoln's inner radar was guiding them toward the Leewards, a string of islets, shoals, and reefs that were very tricky to navigate and could catch an experienced sailor unaware, let alone beginners like Annabelle or Lincoln. Matt's gut was in a big old knot.

The optimist in him had wanted Lincoln's radar to beam them to some lavish resort in Kauai where Nick and Genevieve were kicking back, drinking mai-tais. In this scenario the two lovers had convinced Jackson to be a pal and go along with their little game of hooky. Nick had bribed somebody at the airport to say the Rainbow Systems plane hadn't landed there.

Although Matt would have been furious to discover all of that was true, he'd rather uncover that kind of hanky-panky than to be headed toward the most remote part of the island chain. Any plane that went down out there was in very serious trouble. Except for a couple of wildlife stations, the area was uninhabited until you got to Midway. Matt was no pilot, but he couldn't believe there would be viable places to land until Midway, either. And that would put Nick more than a thousand miles in the wrong direction. Not possible.

This boat didn't have that kind of range. Matt hadn't said so, but he'd decided privately that they'd go as far as a small piece of land about three hours away, a place so small it barely qualified as an island. By then the light would be starting to fade, anyway. They could anchor there for the night, but then they were heading back. Enough was enough.

If Matt had been worried before, he felt dry-mouthed with terror now. He was afraid to ask either Annabelle or Lincoln if they still "knew" that Genevieve was alive. Even if she'd survived some kind of crash landing, she and the others would be stuck with no food, no water, no shelter of any kind. They could be injured and have no way to tend their injuries. The more Matt thought about it, the more scared he got.

Lincoln was still in the cockpit with his earphones on, doggedly listening to Harry Connick Jr. Annabelle had gone below to make them an early dinner that Matt couldn't imagine being able to eat. While they'd taken on fuel in Kauai he'd treated them all to fast-food hamburgers while he'd tried to talk them into going back to Honolulu.

He'd had no luck selling that program. Lincoln had insisted they had to keep going this way. The kid had said it with such urgency that Matt finally had agreed, for the time being. If the plane was out here somewhere, time would be of the essence. Yet he couldn't imagine how they'd ever find it, despite Lincoln's radar.

Before Annabelle appeared in the cockpit, Matt could smell the coffee she was bringing him. He could fall in love with her because of her coffee alone. Theresa made bad coffee, partly because she didn't drink it herself, so she didn't know good from bad. Matt should have taken over the job, but he'd accepted the bad coffee the way he'd accepted all the other disappointments in his marriage.

Now that he was on his own he'd still been wimpy about his coffee, buying a bargain preground instead of pricey beans and a grinder. After tasting Annabelle's coffee, he was ready to make the switch.

"Here you go." Annabelle handed him a mugful of heaven.

"Thank you, Annabelle." He said her name because he liked using it. You could smile and say her name at the same time. He'd never known an Annabelle before, and he couldn't imagine the name suiting anyone else.

"You're welcome." She looked so serious. No smiles for her.

He'd tried not to communicate his concern, but she was no dummy. She had to know this was a desolate place for a crash landing.

He longed for some way to make her feel better. "You make the best coffee."

"Thanks." She handed Lincoln a can of Coke.

Maintaining his cool-guy slouch, he took it and thanked her.

Matt wondered if posture was another thing Annabelle had decided not to hassle the kid about. Every time Matt noticed the curve of Lincoln's spine he fought the urge to tell him to sit up straight. That was probably another reason Annabelle didn't date, so she wouldn't have to deal with guys thinking they could step in and demonstrate their own brand of parenting.

"I'll be back with the rest in a minute," Annabelle said. "I made ham sandwiches so you could eat and drive at the same time."

"Perfect." Matt vowed he'd choke down that sandwich. Not eating it would let her know that worry had taken away his appetite. That could only upset her more.

While she was down in the galley getting the sandwiches, he sipped his coffee and allowed himself a small escape from reality. In his world, he'd have married someone like Annabelle the first time around, someone who cherished good coffee and understood kids. Then Matt would be sitting here with his son, Lincoln. His son of the wild and crazy hair and the gentle heart.

Genevieve didn't fit into the picture very well, though.

Annabelle had admitted during lunch that she'd had Genevieve when she was fifteen. Matt had been raised not to get fifteen-year-olds pregnant. He'd always heard that teenage pregnancies screwed up everything and everybody, yet Annabelle and Genevieve seemed to be fine, so there went that theory.

This time as Annabelle climbed the steps to the cockpit, Matt smelled her perfume and got hard. Certainly inappropriate under the circumstances, and yet emotions were running high with all of them. Sexual urges could be closer to the surface now, at least for him, maybe even for her.

He glanced over at Lincoln, afraid that the kid would sense something and check out Matt's fly. Having an adolescent around as a chaperon meant no public displays of lust. Knowing the adolescent could be psychic ruled out private lusting, too. Matt started reciting baseball statistics in his head and finally got his erection under control right before Annabelle approached with her plate of sandwiches.

"Can you manage a sandwich and your coffee?" she asked.

"Sure." He set his mug into a cup holder and picked up a sandwich.

"Yikes!" Lincoln bolted upright. "What is *that*?"

Annabelle dropped the plate of sandwiches. "What, Lincoln? What?"

Heart pounding, Matt looked in the direction Lincoln was pointing.

"That big freakin' bird! It looks like a seagull on steroids!"

Matt gazed up at the large gray and white bird gliding in the sky just ahead of them. Then he sank back against the seat and gulped for air. "It's an albatross. They're more common out here in the Leewards than back in Honolulu, so I guess you've never seen one before."

"Lincoln, you got us all excited about a blessed bird?"

Annabelle sounded all choked up. "I ruined this whole plate of sandwiches for a gol-danged *bird*?" Then she turned and ran down the steps.

Lincoln pulled off his earphones and looked miserable. "Aw, geez. I didn't mean to—"

"Go after her." Matt couldn't leave the cockpit, couldn't even slow the engine and let Lincoln take over.

"But I didn't think she'd—"

"Go after her, damn it! She's hanging on by a thread, and I think the thread just snapped. She needs somebody to hold her and tell her it's gonna be okay. I can't do it or we're liable to end up on a reef somewhere with a hole in the side of this boat. So it's up to you."

"Right." Looking shaken, Lincoln headed down the steps.

Left with sandwiches underfoot and an albatross flying ahead of the boat as if showing the way, Matt shivered as a chill ran down his spine.

He'd picked up the old superstition about albatrosses from his father and his father's sailor friends. It wasn't logical, and it wasn't modern, but many old salts still thought of the big birds as the reincarnated souls of dead seamen. Matt had been indoctrinated early, and the sight of the bird always gave him the creeps. He wished to hell they hadn't run across this one.

Chapter 19

Genevieve wished Nick would choke to death on the guavas. He'd already eaten three of the five they'd brought in the suitcase. He reminded her of a hog with his snout in the slop bucket. To think that she'd once thought he was the spitting image of Cary Grant. Right now he looked like Frankenstein.

He didn't scare her as much as Frankenstein would, though. When he'd first grabbed her, she'd about jumped out of her skin, but she'd found out that a person couldn't stay scared forever. Sooner or later the feeling wore off, and now she was busy calculating how to get out of this fix.

Cousin Festus down in the Hollow used to like to jump out and grab folks like Nick had, until the day Lyda Mae kicked him in the balls with the heel of her army-issue boots. Genevieve had meant to practice that move herself, but she'd left the Hollow and forgotten all about it. She could have used that move when Nick grabbed her.

Except Cousin Festus never came at anybody with a gun. Maybe kicking Nick in the balls wouldn't be such a good idea. But she needed to think of something, because once he figured out how to dispose of their bodies, he'd kill both her and Jack. He could feed them to the sharks, but Genevieve had seen *Jaws* and she knew you couldn't count on a shark to eat everything. A shark could leave the exact body part with a bullet in it that would incriminate Nick.

No, if Nick was thinking straight, which he might not be, the only way to dispose of two bodies was to tie a rock on them and sink them out in the ocean. That would require a boat, so logically Nick shouldn't decide to kill them until his pickup men arrived.

Genevieve was worried that Nick might not be logical, though. When she looked into his eyes, which she mostly tried not to do, he reminded her of Uncle Rufus's old hound dog Sour Mash, who got bit by a rabid skunk.

Anybody using logic wouldn't drink all the water and eat all the food. All three of them could be stuck here for a while, and although Nick certainly didn't care if she and Jack died of thirst, he ought to have sense enough to save something for himself. Genevieve thought maybe the strain of being so close to getting all that money and not being able to finish the job might have affected Nick like the skunk bite had affected Sour Mash.

Sure enough, Nick ate the fourth guava, and all that was left was the one that had rolled in front of Jack's face. Grabbing his gun, Nick stood up, probably to walk around and get it.

A moment later, Jack cursed softly.

"Hey!" Genevieve struggled against the belt holding her wrists. "Whatever you're doing to Jack, cut it out!"

Nick came back into her line of vision and grinned, revealing the guava seed stuck in his teeth. "You have a thing for Farley, don't you, Genevieve?"

She started getting scared all over again. Nick had that crazy look in his eyes, and if he thought she cared about Jack, he might start torturing Jack just to pass the time. "No, I don't. Just like you said, he's a computer geek. Not my type."

"Maybe, maybe not." Nick's gaze swept over the two of

them. Then he glanced down. "Well, look at that! If it isn't a condom!" He stuck the guava in his pocket and scooped the condom from the sand.

"So what?" Genevieve tried to look bored with his discovery. "I always carry one in my suitcase, for emergencies."

Nick tossed the condom in the air and caught it again. "I don't believe you for a minute. You brought this in case you needed it on Maui. And with all the rumors about me, I doubt if you only brought one. So I ask myself, what happened to the rest of them?"

"She only brought one," Jack said. "She knew you were a one-shot-and-it's-over kind of guy."

"Fuck you, Farley." Nick walked back over in front of Jack.

From the sound of it, Genevieve figured he'd kicked sand in Jack's face. "Jack, shut up." She nudged him from behind. "I did have more condoms," she said. "And we used them to . . . to hold rainwater. Which we already drank." They could have used them that way, she realized now, but they hadn't thought of it. The condoms had been too precious to think of using them for anything besides their intended purpose.

"Considering what a geek Farley is, I can picture you doing that. Better to have something to drink than to waste a condom on somebody who can't get it up unless he's looking at pictures on a porno site, isn't that right, Farley?"

"I guess you know all about that," Jack said. "I'll bet you get off calling nine-hundred numbers from the office."

"*Jack.*" Genevieve clenched her jaw and punched him hard in the back. He was going to get himself shot any second, talking that way.

"You weren't by chance hacking your way into company records, were you, Farley?"

Jack laughed. "No, just a lucky guess."

"Yeah, well, I'm beginning to realize that you're a dangerous guy to have around. With your computer skills, you might be able to figure out how I cooked the books when I made my withdrawals. I'd planned to kill you anyway, but the urge is getting stronger by the minute. Time to say bye-bye, Farley." Nick crouched down and aimed the gun at Jack's head.

"No!" Genevieve screamed.

"What's the matter, Genevieve?" Nick kept his attention on Jack. "Maybe you're more attached to this nerd than you think. That's a little joke, there. *Attached*. Get it?"

"Nick, you don't want to shoot Jack." The blood whooshing in her ears was louder than the surf. "You said yourself that you can't let somebody find either of us with a bullet that could be traced to you. Jack's feeling a little cranky tied up like this, so that's why he's—"

"A little cranky?" Jack said. "Try pissed as hell! You eat our food, you drink all the damned water, and then you throw sand in my face and insult me! I've had it with you, Brogan!"

"And I've had it with you, asshole!" Nick pressed the barrel of the gun to Jack's forehead.

"Stop it, both of you!" Genevieve couldn't *believe* that Jack was being so stupid. "Nick, you can't shoot Jack right now, and you know it, so quit acting like you're going to! And, Jack, shut your trap! We're in enough trouble already without you making it worse."

"I'll shoot Farley if I want to!" Nick said. "No secretary is going to tell me if I can shoot somebody or not. And I really feel like shooting this guy. I'll worry about what to do with him later."

"Brilliant," Jack said. "Act now, think afterward. You're a regular mental giant, Brogan."

"Whatever. I have the gun and you don't. Any last words, boy genius, before I blow a hole in that super-size brain of yours?"

Genevieve's fingers brushed the inside of Jack's wrists, where the blood pumped fast. One bullet, and that blood would stop pumping. She didn't know how to stop Nick, with Jack egging him on, acting more like an idiot than a genius. "Nick, don't," she said.

"Give me one good reason."

"You're not a murderer yet. If you don't kill anyone, this could all be cleared up. You could plead temporary insanity. I'm sure Matt—"

Nick's laughter cut her off. "And give up my three mil? Not likely, sweetheart. Nope, you two are in my way. Time to get rid of one of you, at least." The soft click as Nick pulled the hammer back with his thumb seemed to echo in the lava rocks surrounding the beach.

A large shadow passed over them, and Genevieve looked up quickly, praying it was a plane or a helicopter, although she knew immediately it couldn't be, because there was no engine noise. In the sliver of time she recognized the albatross soaring above them and instinctively went for the diversion.

"Omigod!" she yelled. "Look out!"

Nick's head jerked upward. He leaped to his feet and raised the gun.

Frantically Genevieve tried to squeeze one hand out of the belt loop.

Before Nick could register the fact that what was circling overhead was only a harmless albatross, he had reflexively pulled the trigger.

There was a click, and nothing.

"Son of a bitchin' gun!"

Genevieve worked harder, like a fox in a steel trap, not caring if she tore the skin from her hand if she could work it free. She and Jack had just gotten lucky. Something seemed to be wrong with Nick's gun.

Another loud click echoed in the rocks.

"Fucking thing's loaded, it's dry, and it won't fire. Stupid fucking gun."

Genevieve tore one hand loose, skinning it good in the process. Then the other hand came free. She glanced over in time to see Nick point the gun at the sand, pull the trigger, and then howl in pain. Somehow he had managed to shoot himself in the foot.

"Help—I'm shot!" he yelled hysterically.

"I wish I could help you," Jack said. "But I'm all tied up at the moment."

Genevieve murmured to Jack, "I'm free. Here—" She began to work on the knots she'd tied so well earlier, but her fingers were shaking so badly she was having trouble. And the hand she'd forced through the belt loop was bleeding.

She struggled with the knots, but the blood dripping on the curling iron cord made it slippery.

Fortunately Nick was hollering loud enough to drown out the Mormon Tabernacle Choir, plus he was so busy ripping up his shirt to use as a bandage that he didn't seem to be paying them any mind.

Finally Genevieve loosened the last of the knots and unwound the cord from Jack's hands and his ankle.

"Oh, thank God." He started to unbend his leg.

"*Don't*. He might figure out you're loose."

Jack groaned but stayed where he was. "We need to get him over here so we can tackle him and get that gun away from him," he whispered.

"Right." Calling to Nick felt like splashing around in the water to get the attention of a shark, but at least he was a wounded shark. Genevieve got back in position beside Jack, as if she were still tied up. Before speaking, she had to stop to clear her throat. "Nick!" she called.

He was moaning so loudly he didn't seem to hear her. She tried again. *"Nick!"*

"I got a problem over here!" he yelled back. "Oh, Sweet Jesus, it won't stop bleeding."

"You need to put more pressure on it, Nick! And make sure it doesn't get infected. I have some antibiotic ointment in my makeup bag. It's the little flowered thing with the zipper lying over here about a foot from me."

"Why would you care what happens to me?"

"Because if that bullet wound gets infected, and you pass out and leave us tied up like this, we could all die."

Nick was silent for a moment. "So you're turning into Florence Nightingale because you need me?"

"I reckon that's true. If you'd untie me, I could help you with that gunshot foot."

"Nice touch," Jack murmured.

"Hell, I'm not that stupid! But I'll use the stuff in your makeup bag. That's a good idea."

"He stuck the gun in his waistband," Jack said, his words covered by Nick's loud cussing as he limped toward them.

"Damn." Genevieve had hoped he'd leave the gun behind.

Jack flexed his fingers behind his back. "I'll get it," he said softly.

As Nick approached, Genevieve remembered that she had the glasses and Jack didn't.

In the next second Jack had launched himself at Nick and made a grab for the gun. Being half blind, of course he missed.

Yelling, Nick toppled to one side and got his hand on the gun. As Genevieve lunged forward, Jack finally got hold of the gun barrel, which wouldn't do him much good if that blessed gun went off.

Genevieve latched on to Nick's injured foot, but she couldn't tell if Nick had his finger on the trigger of the gun or not. "Let go of the gun!" she hollered, banging down on his wound with her fist.

Nick's animal yowl of pain was followed by the click of the gun's hammer.

Jack rolled to one side. "I've got it!" He held the gun aloft and scrambled to his feet.

"I'll kill you!" Nick screamed, reaching for Genevieve. "I'll kill you both!"

She jumped out of range and got to her feet. "Kiss my grits, Nick!"

"I've got this gun pointed right at your head, sucker," Jack said. "It didn't go off last time, which means it might next time."

"Damn it, my foot hurts! Can't you do something?" Nick said, appealing to Genevieve.

Genevieve gulped for air. "You got your own self into this fix, Nick. I know you had a rotten childhood and all, but that's no excuse for trying to kill folks." She went to stand beside Jack and sight down the gun barrel. Jack's aim was way off. "Better give me the gun," she said, "since I have the glasses."

"No, you give *me* the glasses."

"First tell me who pulled the trigger a minute ago."

"He did."

"Are you sure? With you being so all-fired smart, you could have figured out it would have been self-defense."

Jack blew out a breath. "Gen, I promised I wouldn't kill him, and I don't break promises."

"Okay, then." She took off the glasses and handed them to Jack.

Jack slipped them up over his nose and blinked. "Oh, *there* you are." He moved the gun barrel a good three inches to the right. "You looked ugly before, but now that I can see you better, you look downright disgusting."

"He definitely looks better without the glasses," Genevieve said.

"Very funny," Nick said, his shoulders sagging.

"Now, Nick," Genevieve said, "if you promise not to try anything, I'll cut some material off your pants and make a pressure bandage for your foot."

"And if you move a muscle in her direction," Jack said, "I'll shoot. I'll try to hit your arm or something you can live without, but I've never shot a gun before so I make no guarantees."

"I won't try anything. I promise. I—" And then he passed out.

"Uh-oh." Genevieve started to rush toward him.

"Wait." Jack grabbed her arm. "It could be a trick."

"You're right." She approached slowly, Jack right beside her, the gun cocked.

Nick didn't move, not even when Genevieve kneeled down and started to unwrap the blood-soaked bandage from his foot. "I'll bet he's gone into shock," she said. "That's dangerous."

"What can we do about it?"

"I think you're supposed to wrap the person in blankets."

"We have the beach towel."

"That will help, but we might need to do more than that."

"Like what?"

"Like while I try to stop the bleeding, you can hug him."

Chapter 20

Jack grabbed the beach towel and tried to convince Genevieve that wrapping Nick in the towel and *then* hugging him was a dandy way to handle a basically icky situation. But she didn't think that was good enough. She said Nick needed a quicker warm-up, which meant skin to skin. Jack's skin next to Nick's skin.

"No friggin' way."

"Do you want him to die?" she asked as she snipped off the bottom of Nick's pants leg with her manicure scissors.

"Yes. Yes, I do. Especially if it's really not our fault because he shot himself in the foot."

"Well, I don't want him to die." She folded the pants material and pressed it hard against the bleeding, which seemed to be concentrated around Brogan's big toe.

Jack still held the gun pointed at Nick's head, just in case he suddenly popped up and started any mischief. "I don't see why not. He's a wart on the backside of humanity."

"That's true, but if he dies out here, that's too easy. I want him to go back and get what's coming to him. Besides, if he's alive, there's some chance of Matt getting his money back. If he's dead, there's no chance."

As usual, Gen made a lot of sense. "Okay, if I have to do

this, then you get the glasses." He tossed the beach towel down beside Nick and pulled off his glasses. "This project definitely requires fuzzy vision."

She took the glasses from him. "And I'll do a better job with his wound if I can see. I think he only shot off the tip of his big toe, so once I get the bleeding stopped, he'll probably be okay."

With a sigh of resignation, Jack lay down next to Nick. He continued to point the gun at Nick's head as he edged closer. "This is grossing me out."

"Would you rather have me do it and you hold the pressure bandage on his toe?"

"No, I would not." The only thing worse than wrapping his arms around this creepazoid was having Gen do it. After sliding one arm under Nick's head, Jack transferred the gun to that hand. Good thing he had long arms so he could keep the barrel shoved into Nick's ear. Then he managed to pull the beach towel around both of them while he slung his other arm over the guy's clammy chest.

"Closer," Gen said.

"He feels half dead already."

"See? That's why you have to warm him up."

"If he so much as moves a pinkie, I'm outta here."

"I hope he does move pretty soon. If he stays unconscious, that's not so good."

Jack rested his chin on Nick's shoulder. "If I have to snuggle with him, unconscious is my preference. Matter of fact, I could use a little unconsciousness myself."

Gen didn't say anything for a couple of minutes. Finally she turned to him. "Jack, we're in kind of a mess."

"Gee, do you really think so?"

"Once I get this bleeding stopped, maybe I should go back for more guavas while it's still light out."

"I pretty much hate that plan. How's this? We tie up psycho-man and go over there together."

"That's crazy." Gen lifted the bandage. "Damn, he's still bleeding."

"What's crazy about it? If we tie him up, he sure as hell isn't going anywhere."

"He's lost a lot of blood. One of us needs to keep an eye on him, and you're terrible at going up and down cliffs. If we're not rescued soon, we'll need some kind of liquid. It doesn't look like rain."

Despite the clammy body he was gripping, Jack was starting to sweat under the beach towel. Sweating meant he was losing water, and he was already thirsty as hell. They definitely needed more guavas, but he didn't want Gen going over there alone. Yeah, he would be scared going back down the cliff and then climbing it again, but thinking of Gen doing it by herself scared him more.

"Okay, Gen, I've hugged Brogan like you wanted, and I haven't pulled the trigger on the gun because you asked me not to. If you take everything that's happened before this into consideration, I think you'd have to agree I've been more than reasonable."

She gazed at him. "More than reasonable."

"I'm through being reasonable. If you go for guavas, I'm going with you."

"Jack, it makes no sense. I—"

"I don't give a damn if it makes sense or not. If you go, I go. Brogan will have to take his chances." He gave her his sternest glare, even though she looked so cute wearing his glasses, so adorably serious and intense.

"Okay," she said finally.

He heaved a sigh of relief. If she hadn't agreed, he'd have to go anyway, and they'd fight, and he didn't want that.

"I suppose we should go together," she said. "That's how we've done everything so far, so we might as well keep on doing what's been working."

"Exactly. And I promise not to get so freaked out about the cliff."

She gave him a small smile. "I think it's kinda cute, you being afraid of heights."

"Where I grew up it was very flat."

"It looks like it in any pictures I've seen."

"I'm thinking of going back there for Christmas. I . . . um . . . want to ask my grandmother if she'll crochet me another afghan." As hot as he felt cuddled up to Brogan, an afghan didn't sound very appealing right now, but by winter it would.

"That's nice, Jack. But first you'd better grovel. If I happened to be your grandmother, I'd expect you to beg my pardon from here to next Sunday before I'd even consider making you another afghan. You were mighty ungrateful, to say the least."

"I'll grovel." There was more to this Christmas plan of his, but he hesitated. Oh, what the hell. Nothing ventured, nothing gained. "Would you like to come with me?"

"To Nebraska?" Her eyes widened behind the glasses.

"Yeah. I could show you where I grew up, and you could show me all the things I missed—the hideouts I could've built, the trouble I could've gotten into if I hadn't spent so much time inside with my Nintendo. And you could meet my grandmother. I think the two of you would get along great." His heart pounded with anxiety as he waited to see what she'd say.

"That's a nice idea, but I don't have the money for a plane ticket to Nebraska. Between helping Mama with the rent and paying the gas and insurance on my car, I don't have a lot left over."

At least it wasn't a flat no. "My treat." Jack often wondered what he'd ever do with the money that kept piling up in his bank account. He'd been meaning to buy a new car, but he kept forgetting about it, and he liked the car he had, anyway. He could certainly afford a couple of tickets to Nebraska.

"Oh, Jack, that's sweet, but I couldn't accept something that expensive from you."

Still not a no, but yes was getting farther away. "Why not?"

"If I let you pay for my plane ticket, then you might think . . . well, it's only natural for you to expect—"

"More sex?"

She flushed. "Am I wrong?"

"Yes." Not that he wouldn't love to have more sex from her, but that was a separate issue. "Damn it, what kind of guy do you think I am, the kind who expects you to trade sex for a plane trip?" Then he lifted his head and glanced at the unconscious slime-bucket he was helping nurse back to life. "You think I'm like Brogan?"

"No, of course not! It's just that—when men buy things for you, they usually have other *things* in mind. And maybe that's fair. I've had to count pennies all my life, so I know what it means to get your money's worth. After all—"

"Whoa right there. Maybe a lot of guys do think like that. I don't. To me, it's very simple. If I'd like you to go somewhere with me, then I should pick up the tab. If you want me to go somewhere with you, then you pick up the tab. Having sex doesn't have anything to do with it."

"But the only tab I could afford to pick up would be for an ice-cream cone. Most guys can buy dinner, movie tickets, a weekend trip. Don't you see? It's not equal."

"Trust me, for any guy lucky enough to have you go along, it's equal. So, will you come to Nebraska if I promise there's not a sexual surcharge?"

She grinned. "Sexual surcharge. That's funny."

"I'm a regular laugh riot." She still hadn't answered him, but he was afraid to push it for fear she'd say no. That would be very depressing, and he didn't want to be depressed besides being hungry, thirsty, and overheated.

"Getting back to the subject of sex," he said. "You need to know something. I would love to have sex with you after we get back to Honolulu. Not connected with me buying something. Just because it's so amazing between us."

"Jack, it wouldn't be the sa—"

"I know you've said that, but I can't believe it. I think it's worth at least a try."

"And if we try and it turns out bad?"

Never in a million years. "It won't."

She shook her head. "You can't guarantee that."

"Sure I can. I—"

Brogan moaned.

Jack pulled away from him so fast he damned near squeezed the trigger on the gun. With the size of the gun, he might've blown a hole in Brogan and himself with one shot. Shaking, he scrambled to his feet and pointed the gun at Brogan's head.

"Oh, Jack, for heaven's sake."

"I do not want him to wake up while the two of us are all cuddly-wuddly."

"You had a gun barrel in his ear. That should protect your manly reputation."

Brogan moaned again and his eyes fluttered open. Then they closed again.

"What do you think?" Jack murmured.

"The bleeding's about stopped," Gen said. "And his skin feels warmer, so I think he's doing better. You'd better go get the cord and we'll tie him up before he comes completely awake."

"Good idea." Jack walked over, picked up the blood-encrusted cord, and remembered how it got that way. He hurried back over to her. "Gen, let me look at your hand."

"It's okay."

"Let me see it." He crouched down beside her and took her left hand in his. Even with blurry vision, he could tell it was a mass of dried blood. "Shit. Stop nursing this maniac so we can go down to the water and soak your hand."

"There's no time." She pulled her hand away. "Let's roll him over and tie him up so we can get another load of guavas before dark."

"I'll tie him up. You go rinse your hand in the water."

"It's all r—"

"Gen, do it." When he saw all that blood on her he wished like hell that he could choke the life out of Brogan. He didn't trust the gun to finish him off, but choking would be an excellent alternative if the gun failed. Too bad he'd promised Gen not to kill the guy. He had promised, though, so Brogan got to live a little longer.

He tied him up good and tight, yanking on the cord a little harder than necessary, because it made him feel better.

"Jack!"

He glanced up to see Gen running back toward him. He leaped to his feet. "What's the matter?"

She was panting. "I just saw that scruffy old trawler. Nick's pickup men are coming this way."

Although still far from land, Matt had to slow the boat considerably so he didn't run up on any submerged reefs. The albatross got way ahead, and he wasn't sorry to see the bird go. This trip was already spooky enough.

Eventually Lincoln returned, looking subdued.

"How's your mom?" Matt asked.

"Okay, I guess. She's all, *I'm fine, I'm fine. Go back up to the cockpit and get the sandwiches while I make some new ones.* But she's, like, still freaked. And it's my fault."

Matt took pity on the kid. "Don't be too hard on

yourself. I can see why you got so excited about the albatross. I flipped out the first time I saw one."

"It's a big honkin' bird, isn't it?"

"Yep." Matt decided not to go into the bad luck thing.

"Well, I'd better get the eats shoveled up. At least Mom didn't, like, break the plate."

"I think it's that stuff that doesn't break, but it wouldn't have mattered if it broke."

"Easy for you to say. I'm all, *There goes my allowance if it breaks*." He started tossing ham, bread, and lettuce back on the plate. "Can I throw this over the side? For the fish?"

"Why not?"

Lincoln picked up the last of the spilled food and stood. "Isn't there something spooky about an albatross? Like a superstition or something?"

Matt glanced at him. "Seamen believe it's bad luck to kill one."

"Well, duh. It should be. They're beautiful. But it's not bad luck to, like, see one, is it?"

"I don't think so. And at least we know there's land not far away, even if we can't see it. That's kind of reassuring."

"Yeah." Lincoln glanced around. " 'Cause we're like a toy boat in the middle of a freakin' big ocean."

"I know where we are, so don't be scared."

"I'm not scared, dude." Lincoln tried to look cocky. "I was just asking about this albatross deal."

Matt was guessing the kid was at least slightly scared. "Well, an albatross is kind of like a black cat. Some people say they're bad luck, but personally I like black cats."

Lincoln nodded. "Me, too. I wish I could have a cat. Or a dog. But Mom's all, *Nobody's home enough to take care of a pet*, which is true."

"What you do is get two cats, so they keep each other company."

"Yeah, that's what *I'm* talkin' about." Lincoln sighed. "But that's twice as much food and stuff."

Matt's thoughts leaped ahead. He and Lincoln could get a couple of kittens at the pound. Matt would keep them, so Annabelle wouldn't have the bother or cost, but Lincoln would have visiting privileges whenever he wanted. Then again, Annabelle would probably nix the whole thing.

"Guess I'll go dump this over the side," Lincoln said.

"Okay." Matt glanced at the sun and estimated about two hours of good light remained, just enough time to make it back to Kauai. They needed to turn around and abandon this wild-goose chase. Nothing was here. The only other vessel he'd seen was an old trawler, which shouldn't be fishing because it was a protected area. But Matt didn't have time to play wildlife cop. Other than the trawler, which he'd spotted about thirty minutes ago before it motored out of sight, they were alone.

They'd checked around a couple of tiny deserted islands and found nothing. Now there wasn't even one of those in sight. Like he'd told Lincoln, he wasn't lost. But he still felt isolated. "Lincoln, come here a sec," he called.

"Yeah?" Lincoln climbed the steps, his plate empty.

"Are you still picking up vibes, or whatever it is you're going on?"

"You think I'm, like, making this up, don't you?"

"No, not exactly, but I—"

"Hey, never mind. That's cool. I don't expect you to believe me. But we're getting closer."

"How much closer?"

Lincoln shrugged. "I dunno, dude. Just closer."

Matt gazed at him in frustration. "That's all you can tell me? You're not picking up anything more specific than that?" He couldn't believe he was actually asking such a question, but Lincoln was all he had.

"Not on that deal, but I can, like, tell you something else."

"What's that?"

"Mom thinks you're hot."

Genevieve knew they had about two minutes to decide how to handle this new development.

"You're sure it's the pickup men?" Jack asked.

"It has to be. It's an old green and white boat, just like Nick described. Who else would be roaming around? I guess they finally figured out where to go to pick him up."

"This might be our only shot at getting rescued for a long time," Jack said.

"That's what I'm thinking."

"Okay, so we tell them Brogan tried to kill us and see if we can get them on our side," Jack said.

Genevieve shook her head. "Too risky. Nick will try to say otherwise, and they might believe him, considering that he gave them money to begin with."

Nick opened his mouth, and his voice was a harsh croak. "What's . . . going on?"

"Nothing," Genevieve said. "Jack, stuff my makeup bag in his mouth and use your belt to hold it there. Then throw the towel over him. I'll go down to the beach and wave them in."

"Wait! We haven't figured out what to do!"

"We're out of time."

"Then at least take the gun!"

"Oh, sure. They'll definitely want to row in if they see me waving a gun. No, I'm using the bikini as bait. And let me do the talking." She didn't have the foggiest idea what she'd say, but she had a little while to think about it.

She ran down to the beach and started jumping up and down, hoping she looked like a star on *Baywatch* instead of a sunburned chick with bad hair. The thing to remember about these guys was that they were in need of money.

Money. She turned and ran back up to where Jack was draping the towel over Nick. "Go into his back pocket and fetch his wallet. See if he has any cash."

"Oh, *man.*"

"Come on, Jack. This is no time to turn homophobic on me." She ran back down to the waterline and continued her *Baywatch* jiggle.

The trawler chugged within about two hundred yards. Because she was still in possession of Jack's glasses, she was able to make out the two men on board. One stayed behind the wheel while the other one watched the bottom, obviously looking for reefs.

"Cut the engine!" the guy in front yelled. Then he busied himself with the anchor. Apparently her *Baywatch* imitation had worked, because once the anchor was lowered, they dropped a little motorboat about the size of Uncle Rufus's into the water and pointed it toward the beach.

Jack came up beside her. "A hundred bucks in twenties. Looks like he took it out of the ATM before he left."

"That's *it*? I thought he was planning to pay these two off."

"I think he was planning to bump them off and use their boat to get to his next rendezvous point. Why waste cash when bullets are so cheap?" Jack patted his back pocket. "But we're okay. I have a little over three hundred, so that's four hundred all together. That might get their attention, at least."

Genevieve gazed at him in astonishment. "You have three hundred dollars in your wallet? Why?"

Jack shrugged. "I didn't know if you might need it."

"*Me?*"

"Well, yeah. I thought you might get fed up with Brogan and want to catch a commuter flight back. I wanted to have enough cash that I could give you the plane fare and I wasn't sure what it would run, being a last-minute reservation."

Unexpectedly, her eyes filled with tears. Fortunately, because she had the glasses, Jack probably couldn't see well enough to notice. "That is the sweetest thing any man's ever done for me. Thanks, Jack."

"But the money turned out to be useless."

"Maybe not. Maybe it'll be enough for these guys." It was hard to tell. They didn't look all that smart, but looks could be deceiving.

Both of them wore dirty white T-shirts and stained work pants. One, obviously the older, had a gray-streaked beard. The other one just looked like he hadn't bothered to shave. Both were on the paunchy side and wore mirrored sunglasses.

"From the looks of them, ten bucks would be a vast improvement."

"They do look pitiful. Now that we know Nick planned to kill them, I almost feel sorry for them."

"Don't." As the boat drew nearer, Jack lowered his voice. "If grungy bad guys had a union, they'd be card-carrying members."

"They remind me of some of the good ol' boys back in the Hollow. All they need is a chaw in their cheek and Red Man gimme caps instead of those cheap tourist ones."

As if to prove her point, the younger guy spit a stream of tobacco into the water.

"Oh, boy," Jack said. "You'd better let me do the talking. Uh, what are we going to say?"

Genevieve almost laughed, but she stopped herself in time. She didn't want these two men to think anything at all was funny about their situation. And it really wasn't, but Jack still made her smile. "Seeing as how you don't know, you'd better let me do the talking. Just go along with whatever yarn I spin, okay?"

The prow of the boat crunched on the sand and the younger guy climbed out.

"I don't know about this," Jack said. "I think—"

"Hi, there," Genevieve said, walking toward the boat. "Are we glad to see you!"

Chapter 21

The younger guy, his teeth stained with tobacco juice, leered at Genevieve. "You looked very glad, jumping up and down like that."

She stuck out her hand. "I'm Gina and this is Jeff. What's your name?"

"I'm Sl—"

"That ain't important." The older guy climbed from the back of the boat and jumped awkwardly to the sand. With a grunt, he tugged the boat a little farther up on the beach. "We're lookin' for a guy who said we should meet him here. Seen anybody around?"

"Here?" Genevieve pretended to be amazed. "Out in the middle of nowhere?"

"That's right," the older guy said. "He's about my height, brown hair, nice dresser. Real educated type. Easy to talk to."

Uh, oh. Nick charmed them, she thought. "Gee, we haven't seen anybody who looks like that, have we, Jeff?"

"Nope. And we've been all over this little island. Nobody like that here."

"Well, shit." The younger one spit into the sand. "I'll bet he drowned, Merv. I think we're outta luck."

Merv scratched under his beard. "Damn it all, Slick, I

always thought this was a dumb idea. I shouldn't of let you talk me into it. I shoulda known the minute I saw that albatross flying around the boat a while back that this was a huge mistake."

"Maybe not," Genevieve said. "Maybe Jeff and I can keep this from being a wasted trip for you. The thing is we're on our honeymoon, and we took a boat for a little sail. We got way off course, and the boat sank. We're marooned here."

"Is that so?" the younger guy said. "You got any money?"

"Some," Genevieve said. "And we'd be glad to pay you to radio for help. Just one little message, so the Coast Guard or the—"

"Sorry, lady," Merv said. "Our radio's broke."

Genevieve stared at them, unable to believe they'd be stupid enough to come out here with no means of communication. "You must have something."

"Nope."

She felt dizzy with disappointment.

"Then we'll pay you to take us to Kauai," Jack said.

Genevieve spun to face him. "Ja—Jeff, is that a good idea, honey?" She couldn't imagine how they'd get Nick on the boat without causing themselves problems, and if they left him behind, he might die on them.

"It's the only idea, *sweetheart*."

"But—"

Jack grabbed her arm and steered her away from the two men. "Excuse us for a minute. We need to have a private conversation."

Genevieve leaned in close and lowered her voice. "Are you out of your mind? What about Nick?"

"We send somebody back later," Nick muttered.

"He could die in the meantime!"

"So could we! Listen, we can't let—"

"Uh, folks?" The older guy, the one named Merv, interrupted. "I'm afraid me and Slick can't take you with us."

Jack turned back toward them, his expression intense. "Why not?"

"We, uh, don't have no extra room." His gaze flicked up to the lump that was Nick under the towel.

They know something's going on, Genevieve thought.

"We don't need extra room," Jack said. "Listen, we have four hundred dollars. We'll give you that if you'll take us to Kauai."

Merv was already backing toward his boat. "That's okay. We'll tell somebody to come and get you. Yep, we'll surely do that."

"Merv!" Slick said. "If the people want to give us four hundred dollars to take them to Kauai, I say let's—"

"Can't do it, Slick." He started shoving the boat back in the water. "Now help me get this tub afloat."

"Wait!" Jack said. "We'll give you more money after we get there! Name your price! A thousand! Two thousand!"

Slick looked really upset. "Listen, Merv, what's it gonna hurt us to take—"

"Into the boat, lamebrain."

"Can you spare us some food, at least?" Genevieve didn't think they'd get aboard that trawler now unless they used the gun, and she and Jack weren't the type to pull off that sort of maneuver.

"Don't have no extra food, neither." Merv yanked the cord to start the outboard motor.

"Water, then!" Jack shouted above the roar of the engine. "Have some common decency and leave us some bottles of water!"

Merv didn't answer as he headed the boat out toward the anchored trawler.

"Damn it!" Jack stared at the departing boat. "Damn it to hell!"

"Something spooked them." Genevieve glanced back at Nick under the towel. She could see him moving. Probably Merv had seen that, too, and he didn't want any part of whatever was going on. She couldn't blame him, considering he and Slick were already working on the wrong side of the law and had something to be spooked about. But now she and Jack were in a terrible pickle.

"I thought of going up to get the gun, to see if I could force them to take us," Jack said.

"Me, too, but I decided we weren't the type."

"I should have done it, anyway."

Genevieve turned to him. "No, you shouldn't. Be true to who you are, Jack."

"Even if it means we won't make it?"

"We'll make it." She couldn't think otherwise. "And goodness, you offered them your life savings! What were you thinking? Two thousand dollars, indeed!"

His laugh was hollow. "Are you kidding? It would be worth twenty thousand, or twenty million, if I had it, just to make sure you're safe." He gazed at her, and his throat moved. "God, I want you to be safe."

The tenderness and longing in his eyes was so strong, so potent, it nearly hypnotized her. She didn't believe any man had ever looked at her like that. She could get hooked on Jack's brand of adoration. But she couldn't expect it to last. He'd forget her when he was able to return to his true love, computers, and she'd be left hanging like a ham in the smokehouse.

"Gen," he said. "Listen, I—"

"Here's your water! Three whole bottles!"

Genevieve turned, and sure enough, Slick was in the boat, a bottle of water in one hand.

"I'll toss it to you!"

Genevieve ran to the surf line just in time to catch the first bottle as it sailed toward her.

"Give it here," Jack said.

She passed it off and darted forward to catch a second one. After lobbing it back to Jack, she had to leap in the air for a third. Then she raced toward Jack. "Water! We have water!"

"Yeah." He was grinning.

"We need to go check on Nick. Even if you don't want to, we have to give him some of this water."

"I know. But let's each have one swallow first. We worked damn hard for this." Carefully he set down one bottle and twisted the cap off the other.

Genevieve followed suit. "We have water. Thank you, Jack."

Jack smiled at her. "Here's lookin' at you, kid." Then he raised his bottle in her direction.

In that moment she felt something happen to her heart, like it was swelling and might just bust out of her chest like the crick when it flooded its banks. She hoped it wasn't love.

Annabelle could tell that Matt wanted to turn around. He'd warned them that he wanted to save enough daylight to head back to Kauai, and they were pushing that limit now. She sat on a bench seat in the cockpit next to Lincoln, who was plugged back into his earphones. Annabelle used the binoculars to scan the ocean.

About two minutes ago she'd noticed an island glimmering on the horizon, almost like a mirage. She wanted to see what was on that island, but they weren't going that far.

Matt had vetoed the idea of anchoring there for the night after he'd looked at his charts. Too many submerged reefs surrounded the island. A sudden storm could push the boat and cause the anchor to drag along the bottom. The coral beds would rip the hull to shreds. Besides, the island wasn't big enough for a plane to land on it.

Standing up, Annabelle brought the island into focus. Imagining Genevieve was on that island was probably only wishful thinking. She wasn't giving up hope, would never give up hope, but any fool could see that the odds were not good out here.

Then she saw a boat coming toward them from the general area of the island. "Matt, should we stop that boat and ask them if they've seen anything?"

"Let me take a look."

Annabelle lifted the strap from around her neck and handed the binoculars to Matt. When their fingers brushed, the warmth of his skin reassured her. At a time like this, a person needed a human touch.

She had a feeling Matt knew that and would have comforted her even more if he could. He'd probably sent Lincoln after her when she'd lost control a while back. She hadn't liked having Lincoln see her cry, but his firm hug had helped her pull herself together.

Matt handed the binoculars back. "I'm not sure it's a good idea to flag them down, Annabelle. I have a feeling they might be up to something illegal, like fishing in protected areas. I don't know how they'll react to being stopped."

Annabelle trained the binoculars on the boat. "What makes you think they're breaking the law?"

"Their speed, for one thing. I saw them earlier going in the other direction. Either they're not worried about the reefs out here or they know these waters a heck of a lot better than I do. They really move out."

"It's about time for us to turn around and go back, isn't it?"

"Yeah. I know you don't want to, but—"

"I'd feel better about it if we tried to talk to the people on that boat. At least they've been as far as that island."

Matt gazed at the boat as it rapidly closed the distance

between them. "Okay, but I'm keeping my distance.
They're probably fine, but I'm not taking any chances. Pirates still exist, you know."

"They *do*?" Annabelle's heart beast faster as she studied
the boat through her binoculars. "I don't suppose they fly
the skull and crossbones to warn a person about their inten-
tions, either."

"Not if they're smart pirates."

"Pirates?" Lincoln pulled off his earphones and stood
next to Annabelle. "You think that boat might have pirates
on it?"

"I thought you couldn't hear us with your earphones
on," Annabelle said.

"I can't, but I can read your lips." He glanced at the
oncoming boat. "I don't think they're pirates."

"I hope not." Her heart quieted after he'd said that,
though. She probably counted on Lincoln's intuition more
than she should, but he was so often right that it was hard
not to rely on it.

Matt slowed the engine and tooted a signal on the
boat's horn. At first it seemed that the green and white boat
wouldn't answer, but then it tooted back. As the distance
closed between the boats, Annabelle sized up the two men
through the binoculars. Lincoln had better be right, because they surely looked like pirates to her. All they needed
was a patch over one eye and a knife between their teeth.

With the engine on idle, Matt called across the water.
"We're looking for three people! My partner, a guy about
forty, left Honolulu in a private plane yesterday morning,
and now the plane is missing."

"That's too bad!" a guy with a beard yelled out. "You
looking for them?"

Annabelle felt relieved that the guy sounded reasonably
normal. He hadn't waved a gun and told them to prepare to
be boarded, or whatever it was pirates said.

"Yes, we're looking!" Matt shouted across the space between the boats. "My partner had two people with him, a young woman, light brown hair, pretty, and a tall guy with dark hair and glasses."

Annabelle had to admit it sounded crazy to be out in the middle of nowhere asking if folks had seen so-and-so, like you were strolling through a friendly neighborhood. But she held her breath and waited for the answer, anyway, even though she didn't expect to hear anything promising.

"Sorry," the guy with the beard called across the space. "We ain't seen nobody." Then he tugged on his ear. "Sorry about that," he said again.

"Thanks, anyway." Matt gave a wave and revved up the engine. Then he let out a breath and turned to Annabelle as the other boat took off. "We might as well turn around."

She gazed at him, hating to agree with him, yet knowing he was right.

"Mom, she's still out there." Lincoln's plea was quiet, but there was a desperation about it, too.

Annabelle turned to him. "I know. But it's too dangerous to stay out on the water looking."

"I don't care! She's here! I can feel it!" Lincoln's eyes filled with tears.

Annabelle put a hand on his arm and fought to control her own tears. "Lincoln, try and understand." Her voice shook. "I can't risk you to try and find her."

Chapter 22

Jack wished he believed that Frick and Frack would actually notify somebody to come out and pick up a couple of castaways. As he and Gen kept guard over Brogan, occasionally taking out his gag to give him some water, Jack watched the light fade and tried to tell himself help was on the way. He wasn't convinced.

The seals had started communicating from wherever they were, but this time Jack didn't mistake the barking and bleating for human laughter. Last time he'd heard the seals, he and Gen were on the brink of a wild sexual adventure. Tonight neither of them had mentioned the one remaining condom. Jack had pocketed it, not wanting anyone to find it. If nothing else, he'd have one hell of a souvenir.

They were down to a half-bottle of water each, including Brogan. They'd eaten the guava, giving a little of that to the sleazeball, too. Jack figured Gen had to be starving, since he was ready to start munching on sand himself. They'd decided not to go after more guavas, though, and risk being on the wrong side of the island when help arrived. *If* help arrived.

Gen, however, was the eternal optimist on that subject. On most subjects, come to think of it.

"Those guys gave us water, so they'll also send help,"

she announced with confidence. Then she gave Brogan another sip of water before stuffing the makeup bag back in
his mouth and tightening the belt to keep it in place.

Jack was glad to see that Gen had no sympathy for
Brogan. She just wanted him alive so Matt could maybe get
his money back. Jack pretended Brogan wasn't even there,
so he could try to enjoy the rest of this time alone with Gen.

"Are you going to be okay getting on a helicopter if
that's what they send?" he asked her. "It's even scarier than
the Sky King."

"I would climb on the back of an albatross if that's what
it took to get home again."

Jack smiled. "That bird sure showed up at the right
time."

"Sure did. I'm really glad Nick didn't kill it, though. I
would have felt terrible about that."

"Yeah, me, too." Jack took another drink of his water.
"I seem to remember reading about an albatross in school.
A guy with one around his neck or something like that. An
albatross was bad juju, at least in that story."

"Birds are never bad luck for me." Gen stretched her
legs out in front of her. "In the Hollow folks think an owl
hooting means somebody will die, but I don't. I used to
love sitting on the porch listening to an owl. Or a whippoorwill."

"Tell me more about what it was like back there."

"You're sure you're not bored?"

"Positively sure." As she described the backwoods area
where she'd spent the first fifteen years of her life, Jack
couldn't take his eyes off of her. He'd asked to have the
glasses again, making up some excuse about wanting to see
if he could spot the seals. All he'd really wanted was a clear
view of Gen before they lost this intimacy, maybe forever.

He'd taken a gazillion mental pictures of her sitting on
the sand, her skin brushed with light from the setting sun,

her hair loose around her shoulders. He'd made love to this goddess. He, Jackson Farley, had held her in his arms and made her moan.

"I'm through being ashamed of my raising, Jack," she said at last.

"Good. Because you shouldn't be."

"I realize that now." Then she fell silent and gazed off into the distance, as if talking about the Hollow had put her back there.

Jack liked hearing about her childhood, but he didn't want her drifting away from him. He decided to broach the subject nearest and dearest to his heart. "Gen, you've said you don't want to take a chance on having sex once we get back because you think it wouldn't be as good as it was here."

She turned to look at him, her gaze cautious. "That's right."

"You're so optimistic about everything else, why not be optimistic about us?"

"It's one thing to be a positive thinker. It's another to ignore reality completely."

"You don't know what the reality would be. You won't even give it a chance."

She sighed. "I've watched you for months at Rainbow. Once you get excited about a project, you forget everything else, and don't tell me you don't. You'd stand me up, Jack. You think you wouldn't, but you would."

Jack didn't believe for a minute that he'd stand her up, but this didn't seem to be an argument he could win. "How about if we test that theory with something really small? What if right now, we make a date to go out for ice cream?"

She licked her lips. "Ice cream sounds *wonderful* right now."

Brogan moaned, but Jack ignored him. "It does, doesn't

it? Two scoops on a sugar cone. Double fudge and strawberry cheesecake."

Gen closed her eyes. "Fresh peach and cappuccino."

"We'd have to eat fast, because it melts quick in the
summer."

She kept her eyes closed. "But I'd try to eat it slow. I'd
want the cappuccino on the bottom and the peach on top.
But even if the peach drips on the cappuccino, that's okay.
Those flavors go great together." She licked her lips again
and sighed.

"So, is it a date?"

Eyes still closed, she smiled lazily. "Oh, yeah." Then her
eyes snapped open. "Wait a minute. You tricked me into
that."

"You said it. You said yes. This is just for ice cream.
Nothing else. No big deal. If I can't even show up for an ice
cream date, then you're right, I'm hopeless. I won't bother
you ever again."

She shook her head. "This is ridiculous. You're setting
yourself up for failure. Once we get back, you'll have tons of
work. If we had a really big date, and you thought we'd
have sex afterward, you *might* remember, but not just a little ice cream date."

"Then it's a perfect test. Three nights from tonight, I'll
be at your house at seven-thirty."

"No, you won't."

"Yes, I will."

"I tell you, Jack, you won't. But if you want to think
that you'll—" She stopped talking and grew very still.

"What?"

"Shh. What's that noise?"

Jack listened. Was that a motor?

Gen's voice shook with excitement. "I think it's a
boat."

Jack stood and gazed at the ocean. With dusk coming

on, visibility wasn't very good, but the chugging grew louder, and then he saw it. "It *is* a boat!"

"The same one?"

Heart pounding, Jack squinted to make out the shape and color of the boat. If it was those two goons coming back, that wasn't a good sign. Not a good sign at all.

"Is it the same boat or not, Jack?" Gen made a grab for the glasses.

He held her wrist so he could keep them. "Just a minute. Let me make sure it's not those guys. If it is, we might need the gun."

"It can't be them. It just can't."

"Well . . . it's not! Definitely not! There's no green on this one! And it's shaped all different. It looks newer." He clutched her arm. "God, Gen, this is it. I'll bet they'll have a working radio. This is it, Gen."

"Let me see, damn it!" She jerked the glasses off his face and almost poked his eye out. "What a beautiful boat. Bless my soul, what a beautiful boat." She started to laugh, but her laughter turned into sobs. "Oh, Jack."

He put his arm around her and drew her close to his side as they watched the boat, Gen sniffing and Jack's heart pumping like crazy.

"C'mon, c'mon, c'mon," Jack chanted softly.

"Do you think they can they see us?"

"*Oh.*" He'd forgotten it was getting dark. "Maybe not!" Releasing her, he ran back to Brogan, snatched the towel off him, and began waving it like a giant flag. "We're here!" he shouted. "We're here!"

Gen started yelling and jumping up and down, and between the two of them, they made enough racket to fill a football stadium. Jack carried on until he was hoarse.

Then the boat's horn blasted through the twilight.

"They see us!" Gen's voice had become a croak. "They see us, Jack!"

Dropping the towel, Jack ran back down and stood beside Gen as the boat came closer still. "Can you tell who's on board?" Between the shadows falling and having no glasses, he was barely able to see the boat, let alone any people.

"There's somebody on the front of the boat, holding onto those guardrail things. He's . . . oh, Jack." She gulped for air. "He has red, white, and blue hair. It's Lincoln. It's my baby brother, Lincoln. He found m-me." Then she dissolved into tears.

"It's okay. It's gonna be okay." Gently Jack took the glasses from her. She was crying too hard to make use of them. With a lump the size of Nebraska in his throat, he watched as Matt Murphy lowered a small dinghy from the back of the boat. Then he helped a woman down, a woman who looked like Gen's older sister but had to be her mother. Then Lincoln climbed into the boat, and Matt started the small outboard motor.

As they headed toward the beach, Lincoln made a megaphone of his hands. "Gen!" he shouted. "You're it!"

Three days later Gen sat at her desk at Rainbow, typing invoices. It was her first day back at work, and nothing about being here felt real. But it was real, she told herself. She was using her same keyboard, the one where she'd nearly worn off the T, and she had her same chair, blue upholstery that was slightly faded in the seat and casters on the bottom that squeaked.

So if sitting at her neat little desk was real, then the events of the past week must all be a dream. No matter how hard she tried to blend one with the other, they kept separating like oil and water. She couldn't hold both in her mind at the same time.

At least Nick was locked away. While they were still on the island, Matt had radioed for a helicopter to pick him up and haul him to a hospital, where he'd stayed for the past two days, under guard. She hoped he was being guarded real good.

She hadn't seen Jack since Matt had dropped her, her mother, and Lincoln off at their house in the wee small hours two mornings ago. She hadn't had a chance for a proper good-bye, with Matt eager to head off for Jack's house. She wasn't even sure what a proper good-bye would be, under the circumstances. A handshake hadn't seemed like the way to thank a person who had saved your life, and a kiss would have caused too much speculation.

Right before Matt had driven away, Jack had told her that he'd see to getting her suitcase repaired. That reminder of what they'd shared had choked her up so badly she hadn't been able to say another word.

She'd taken that day and the next off because her mama wouldn't hear of anything different. Lying on the couch and eating the food Mama kept bringing in, she'd enjoyed an elaborate manicure and pedicure, watched Lincoln's taped collection of *South Park*, and played endless games of gin rummy with Lincoln and Mama.

Her family deserved every second of the time she spent with them. If her mama hadn't told Matt that she thought ear tugging might be a sign Merv was lying, and if Lincoln hadn't thrown a hissy fit and insisted they turn the boat around, Gen and Jack might not have survived.

But while she was being pampered by Mama and teased by Lincoln, she felt like she was missing something critical, like an arm or a leg, without Jack around. She'd called his house, gotten the machine, then called Matt at the office to discover Jack was already back at work, trying to get caught up. Gen had arrived at her desk this morning with a sense of excitement, thinking that Jack would stop by to see her soon.

She wondered if he'd shaved off his beard. He wouldn't

have taken time to shop for black clothes, though. She'd prepared herself for him to look like a nerd again. In fact, she'd rather see him looking like a nerd, because she was fond of that picture. She missed him desperately.

But the man who approached her desk wasn't Jack. In spite of that, she gave him a big old smile, because Matt Murphy was her third favorite guy after Jack and Lincoln.

"Are you sure you feel good enough to be working?" Matt said. "I don't care if you want to take more time off."

"If Jack can come back and put in all those blessed hours, I surely can hold up enough to do a little typing." True to what she'd promised herself, she no longer tried to keep the backwoods expressions out of her conversation.

"Jack? Oh, you mean Jackson."

"It was easier for us to use nicknames on the island," Gen said. "Now I can't get myself to change back."

"I'm sure that's true. That was quite an ordeal." Matt shook his head. "Anyway, I've tried to get Jackson, or Jack, to relax a little, but he won't. He's convinced this new software in development could be a lifesaver for the company, and he's determined to whip it into shape."

As much as Gen loved hearing that Jack was busy saving Rainbow, the news only confirmed what she'd expected. Jack had put her completely out of his mind. "I'm still hoping Nick will tell you where he banked all that money," she said.

Matt gazed at her. "I don't think he will. Not after I turned down his deal."

"What deal?"

"In the middle of all the commotion, while you were reuniting with your mom and Lincoln, Nick called me over and said he'd give back all the money if I wouldn't turn him over to the authorities. But if I turned him in, he'd carry the info on his Swiss bank account to his grave."

"That low-down, dirty, rotten, slime-sucking—"

"Yeah, I've thought all those things, too. But you know what? It's done. We're never getting the money back, and Rainbow will be a little shaky for a while, but I'd rather be me, with a business to rebuild, than Nick, who will never be anything but a criminal—and a failed criminal at that. I've decided not to waste time being angry with the guy. He'll soon get what's coming to him."

Gen sighed. "I suppose you're right. But Jack and I worked hard to keep him alive, and now I hate to think of him breathing the same air we do."

"I doubt he's having any fun. I was curious enough to find out how he was doing in the hospital and how bad the infection was in his toe. They said he still can't walk, and he screams bloody murder every time they make him get out of bed and try it."

"He could be faking. He knows sure as shootin' that once he leaves the hospital he'll be locked up tight."

"Maybe, but he's as good as locked up now. A guard's watching him twenty-four seven." He frowned, his voice filled with regret. "I was such a naive fool to trust him the way I did. I should have seen the signs of his instability a long time ago."

Genevieve's insides twisted. "Don't feel like the Lone Ranger."

Matt's gaze snapped to hers. "Genevieve, you have nothing to feel bad about. I'm the one who's known him the longest, the one with the responsibility to this company and its employees."

"And you've had a hay wagon full of troubles on your mind these past few months. You have no cause to feel guilty, either."

"My personal problems are no excuse." He scrubbed a hand over his face. "But dwelling on my shortcomings won't make anything better, either."

Genevieve smiled. "Now you're sounding like my mama."

"I wouldn't be surprised. Your mama is one of the smartest women I've ever met. Good thing I have Lincoln to vouch for me, or she wouldn't give me the time of day. Which reminds me, you're invited for our boat ride this evening, you know. I have to warn you, though, that I've promised Lincoln he can drive, and the boy has the soul of a hot rodder."

Genevieve laughed. "He said the very same about you. Not exactly those words, but close enough."

"I enjoy that kid." Talk of Lincoln seemed to lift the shadows from his eyes. "But do you think there's any chance he'll have normal hair someday?"

"Someday." Genevieve was really happy for Mama and Lincoln, because Matt looked like a stay-around kind of guy. Her mama would put him through his paces, but Genevieve thought the ending would turn out happy for everyone.

"So do you want to come with us?" Matt asked. "I'll let you drive, too, if I can pry Lincoln's fingers off the wheel."

"Thank you, but to tell you the truth, I could use some time to myself." And that's probably what she'd get. Seven-thirty would come and go without Jack showing up to take her out for a double-dip sugar cone. She didn't expect him to remember, but just in case a miracle happened, she wanted to be there to answer the door.

"I can understand that," Matt said. "I'm sure your mama's been hovering."

Genevieve rolled her eyes. "You can't even imagine. I'm grateful you're taking her somewhere so she'll stop fussing over me."

"Don't be too hard on her. She was pretty darned scared. We all were."

Genevieve looked up at this kind man and hoped her

mama wouldn't hold him off for too long. "You really care about her, don't you?"

He grinned sheepishly. "It shows, huh?"

"Yes, but it looks good on you. If you need another person to vouch for you to Mama—"

"Whoa." He held up a hand. "Thanks, but no thanks. I think one kid campaigning is plenty. If you both start in, she'll think we're ganging up on her. I don't want her to feel pressured. Everything will be fine. I'm a patient guy."

Genevieve lifted her eyebrows.

Matt grinned. "Okay, semipatient. It'll work out."

"I hope so." She smiled at him. "You deserve each other, and I mean that in the nicest way."

Genevieve had a harder time convincing her mama that she didn't want to take the boat ride. Annabelle obviously didn't want to let her out of her sight. But finally, after Genevieve explained that if she didn't get some time alone she would go crazier than a bedbug in a cornhusk mattress, her mama finally agreed to go off and leave her.

Genevieve really did think she might go crazy, but not from too much company. She'd had too little company—of the Jack variety. It truly puzzled her that she could miss him so much she hurt. But that was the sad situation she found herself in.

At six o'clock she made herself a turkey sandwich, ate half, and put the other in the refrigerator. Lincoln would eat it tonight—he could be counted on to finish off any and all leftovers.

She'd dressed in the kind of clothes that said *Oh, did we have a date for ice cream? I barely remembered.* Her white shorts were clean but she'd bought them last summer, so they weren't special. Her cropped tank top was from a shopping trip two summers ago. It was red, which wouldn't matter to Jack, who wouldn't be able to tell if it was some flattering color or not.

Although she hadn't bothered with shoes, she'd combed her hair and put on a little makeup. She'd left off her lipstick, though. Fresh lipstick was a dead giveaway that you were expecting company, that you were eager to see someone. Which she surely was, damn it.

To pass the time until seven-thirty, she picked up her whittling, the same little I'iwi bird she'd been working on the night before she'd left with Nick. The person she'd been then seemed so much younger than the person she was now. Surviving an experience that nearly killed you could have that kind of effect on someone, she decided.

Because it was still light outside, she took her carving out in the tiny backyard. They had three plastic chairs back there with faded cushions on the seats and a round plastic table where they ate sometimes. She sat in one of the chairs and started working on the little bird's beak. Her next-door neighbor was playing a boom box outside, so she wouldn't hear Jack drive up, but from this position she could see the street. She wasn't likely to miss him.

Of course he wouldn't arrive. At this very minute he was probably hunkered down over his blessed computer screen, writing a brilliant program for Matt, so that Rainbow wouldn't go into bankruptcy. To expect him to run over here and take her out for ice cream was selfish, in a way.

Except he'd promised, and he knew how much was riding on that promise. At least he'd known when they were back on the island. Now, though, he didn't seem to remember that she existed.

A phone call would have been nice. It wouldn't have killed him to stop by her desk today, either. He had to have lunch sometime, and they could have eaten together, if he'd thought about her at all. Well, it wasn't like she hadn't predicted this exact thing.

As she sat whittling away at the bird's beak, it came to her that maybe she was asking too much of Jack. Come to think of it, by leaving this date up to him, she'd abandoned him to totally take care of himself. She knew good and well that when he was preoccupied with his work, he wasn't good at that. Rather than demand that he drop everything and pay attention to her, she'd be a whole lot better person if she'd take some ice cream over to him.

Unfortunately, she didn't know whether he was at work or at home, and he might not answer the phone at either place. When Jack concentrated, he *really* concentrated. Matt would know where Jack was, but Matt was out on a boat with her mama and Lincoln.

Shoot. The more she thought about it, the more she realized that she'd take Jack any way she could get him. Maybe he wouldn't always know she was there, but once she got his attention, he gave her a hundred and ten percent. That more than made up for the times he might forget all about her. She was even willing to fly in the face of astrological wisdom and link up with a Taurus. Jack had that kind of hold on her.

Okay, it was decided, then. Tomorrow she'd use her lunch hour to track him down. She'd take him his two favorite flavors of ice cream, double chocolate fudge and strawberry cheesecake, and she'd tell him no more tests. She got little squiggly feelings in her tummy as she thought of what she and Jack might do with that ice cream. Maybe she should take it to him after work instead of during lunch.

Something rustled behind her. She put down her knife and started to turn, thinking it was the neighbor's tabby cat. "Hey, Lillibeth," she called. "Are you—"

An arm snaked around her throat, cutting off her wind.

Chapter 23

The way Jack saw it, he had three priorities: getting the new software program ready for testing, fixing Gen's pink suitcase, and making sure he took her out for ice cream. Sleep wasn't a priority, so he didn't bother much with that.

By six-thirty on the night he'd promised to pick up Gen, he had the software project in decent shape. Not perfect yet, but he was on the right track, and he could afford this break. Gen's suitcase, the handle neatly repaired by a shoe shop, sat by his front door. He trimmed his beard, jumped in the shower, and dressed in the white shorts and white T-shirt Mrs. Applegate had bought for him.

She'd heard about his adventure and had come over wanting to do something to help, so he'd given her a shirt and a pair of slacks for size and asked her to go shopping for him. He'd explained the black program that Gen had outlined and given Mrs. Applegate a wad of cash.

His neighbor was a careful shopper, and he couldn't believe how many things she'd walked in with last night. She'd followed his directions about buying a lot of black, but she'd also bought him some white stuff, which she said would be much more comfortable in the summer and would look good with his tan. He'd decided that she was right about wearing white in the summer, and white seemed like the right color for an ice cream date, as long as he was careful with the double chocolate fudge.

About four this morning he'd taken a break from writing code to make a test run over to Gen's house so he'd know how long the trip would take. Fifteen minutes, but he'd add another five to allow for more traffic. At four in the morning her mom's house had been dark, and Jack had parked outside for a few minutes, thinking about Gen inside, sound asleep.

While he was deep into his project he hadn't missed her quite so much, but this morning he'd ached so badly he could barely stand it. If he'd known which bedroom window belonged to her, he might have thrown stones against it to wake her up. But he hadn't known, and he still had plenty of work to do on the Rainbow program, so he'd forced himself to drive home again.

Tonight would be an ice cream date—nothing more. Even if Gen acted like she wanted it to turn into more, Jack was going to do his best to resist her. He wanted to impress upon her that he was a man of his word when it came to this relationship. His track record with women had been terrible, so now he had to prove that he could be reliable. If he was very careful about coming through on all his promises to Gen, he might have a chance with her.

At ten minutes past seven he left his house. At twenty minutes past seven he ran out of gas.

After the first moment of terror, which Genevieve thought would happen to anybody grabbed suddenly from behind, she got furious. She was sick and tired of Nick Brogan running around trying to kill innocent folks.

So when he hauled her up out of the chair by the neck, she tried to stomp on his bad foot.

"Stop it!" he yelled. "I've got your knife! I'll slit your throat if you don't stop it!"

"You will *not*." She kept struggling and stomping, wishing she had on shoes. She tried to get an elbow in his stomach, but he pulled her up hard against him, and he was stronger than she was. She tried screaming a little, but decided that was a waste of time. Nobody would hear her over the rap music blasting away next door.

Nick smelled like disinfectant and sweat, not a good combo. Having such close contact with his body made her skin crawl. "Look out, Nick. I'm gonna throw up."

"I don't believe you." He was breathing hard, but he must have recovered his strength in the hospital because his arms felt like iron around her neck and ribs. "We're going in the house now."

"No, we're not." She brought her heel down as hard as she could on his bad toe.

His yowl of pain was the most unholy sound she'd ever heard. She struggled out of his grip and started for the house. She was inside, gasping and fumbling with the lock, when he crashed through the door, flinging her against the wall.

He lunged for her, his face a mask of pain and fury. She fought him off, hitting, kicking, and scratching, but he got his hands around her throat.

She tried to pry them loose, but rage must have made him even stronger. His thumbs pressed against her windpipe. She couldn't breathe, couldn't . . .

Jack looked at the gas gauge and wondered why he hadn't run out long before this. The needle had been on empty when he'd driven to the airport to meet Nick and Gen. Matt had taken him to the airport yesterday to get his car, and Jack hadn't given the gas situation another thought, not even early this morning when he'd taken his test run to Gen's. Maybe Gen was right, and he didn't deserve a classy woman like her.

He had no gas can. Even if he ran to the station, bought one, got gas, ran back, and put it in, he'd lose too much time. Damn it all. Damn it to hell.

No, by God. He wasn't giving up. If he went on foot, he could cut through some areas he'd otherwise have to drive around, so the trip would be shorter. By sprinting all the way there, he might only be a couple of minutes late. They could take her car for ice cream.

Arriving panting and sweaty wasn't how he'd planned to begin this date, but Gen would have to give him credit for trying his best. Abandoning his car, he pocketed the keys, grabbed her pink suitcase, and started running.

When Gen came to, she tried to lift her hands and discovered they were tied to the back of the kitchen chair she was sitting in. Nick had ripped up one of Mama's favorite dish towels to do it, the one with pretty seashells on the border. That infuriated Genevieve.

She was also tied to Mama's chair, the one Mama always used, and that infuriated her even more. She never sat in this chair. Neither did Lincoln. This was Mama's seat. Nick sat in Lincoln's chair, eating the other half of her turkey sandwich, the part she'd saved for Lincoln. She wanted to wring his worthless neck.

When she swallowed, her throat hurt, but she wanted to know a few things, sore throat or not. "Why are you messing with me, Nick Brogan? You must have got loose from the hospital, so why aren't you hightailing it out of here?"

He smiled at her. "Ah, we're awake." He took another bite of the sandwich, chewed and swallowed before answering. "In order to *hightail it out of here*, my little hick from

the sticks, I need some help. You're my bargaining chip."
He surveyed her from head to foot.

She was suddenly cold, even though it was close to
ninety degrees in the house. "You'll never get away with it."

"I think so. People seem to think a lot of you. They
wouldn't want you to end up dead. And now I want you to
make a phone call to Matt Murphy."

She used Jack's line from the island. "Gee, I would love
to, but I'm all tied up."

"I'll dial the phone." He picked up the cordless where it
was lying on the table beside his plate. "You just talk. Tell
him I want safe passage to Fiji for you and me, and once I
get there, you'll be sent back, unharmed."

"I'm so sure he'll believe that, you toad-sucking
weasel."

"He'll have to take his chances. I know Matt, and he's
already riddled with guilt because he put you and Farley in
danger. He won't want to take any chances on getting you
killed, especially now that he's sweet on your mother. If
something happened to you, that would put a real crimp in
his romantic plans." He picked up the last of the sandwich.
"Incidentally, good sandwich. Much better than hospital
food."

"If I'd known you were coming I would have made it
even better. I have some yummy rat poison I could have
mixed in with the mayonnaise to give it some zing."

"I didn't think you'd expect me to show up. I like to
keep one step ahead of people."

"That must be hard, seeing as how you shot yourself in
the foot."

He grimaced. "I blame you for that, Genevieve. And
just like I promised you back on the island, you'll pay for it,
along with all the other things you've done to me. I used to
think you were sweet, but you're not."

"I used to think you were human, but you're not." She

glanced at the kitchen clock. Seven thirty-two. Not only was she being held hostage by a maniac, Jack wasn't coming to buy her ice cream. Under the circumstances that was a good thing. She didn't want Jack getting mixed up in this. Still, it was kind of sad, thinking that he'd forgotten his promise. She didn't blame him—that's the way geniuses acted. When she got out of this current mess with Nick, she'd tell Jack it was okay that he'd forgotten about the ice cream.

Nick swallowed the last of the sandwich and picked up the phone. "Time to let Matt know we have a new ball game, new rules."

"You won't get him. He's not home."

"And you would know this because . . . ?"

"He took my mama and Lincoln for . . . dinner."

"Then I'll try his cell."

"I heard him tell Mama he'd turn it off, so they could have some peace and quiet."

"You're just saying that." Nick punched in a number and held the cordless to his ear. "Shit. He never turns that cell off."

Genevieve was so glad that Mama hated cell phones. "They'll be back any minute. You need to get out of here, Nick. If three people walk in the door, you can't control all of them."

"I can if I have a knife at your throat."

"That little whittling knife?" She knew even a whittling knife could do her in, but she tried to pretend she wasn't worried. "Don't make me laugh."

"Not that one, although it would have worked." He reached down to the floor and held up her mama's ten-inch butcher knife. "I was referring to this little knife."

"Oh." Although she was trying to stay mad and not get scared, looking at that knife, which Mama kept razor sharp, bothered her more than she wanted him to know. "You wouldn't kill me. Then you wouldn't have a hostage."

"True, but you never want to test a guy with nothing more to lose. One way or another, I'm not going to prison. It's Fiji or Hell for me."

Something in his eyes told her that he meant what he said. Now she had to hope nobody came—not Jack, not her mama, Lincoln, or Matt. She had to think of a way out of this before anybody else showed up, or somebody was bound to get hurt.

At seven thirty-five, the doorbell rang.

Genevieve knew it was Jack, sure as shootin', and she didn't want him in here. "That's probably my Avon lady," she said. "Don't answer the door and she'll go away."

Nick looked at her with a cold smile on his lips. "That's not the Avon lady. That's Jackson Farley, come to pick you up for ice cream. Who would have thought? I was sure you were right about him, and he'd forget completely. Well, Jackson will have to come in and join us, I'm afraid. He expects you to be here, and if you're not, no telling what he'll do."

"Jack!" Genevieve screamed. "Nick's here!"

Nick cursed and leaped up, placing the blade of the knife against her throat. Then she heard the front door crash open. That lock never had been any good.

"He's got a knife!" Genevieve yelled.

"And it's right against your girlfriend's throat," Nick said. "So come on in, Farley."

Jack appeared in the kitchen doorway, breathing hard, the shoulder of his shirt flecked with paint from the door he'd knocked off its hinges. He held her pink suitcase by its strap, which meant he'd had it fixed. After his first glance at Genevieve, he started toward her.

"Stay back, Farley."

Jack swallowed. "I'm sorry, Gen. I wasn't thinking. I should have found a phone and called the police."

"It's okay, Jack. I'm not sure if the police can help us.

Nice outfit, though. And you fixed my suitcase." He still had his beard, and although he hadn't dressed in black, he'd managed all white, which turned him into a hottie. He should wear shorts more often. "And you remembered the ice cream date."

"Of course I did. I would have been here at seven-thirty, but my car ran out of gas, so I had to cover the last part on foot."

She noticed his shirt was all sweaty. He must have been running. "I shouldn't have made it a test. I don't care if you forget sometimes, Jack. I really don't."

"Oh, please," Nick said. "Would you two cut it out."

"How the hell did you get away, Brogan?" Jack asked. "Matt said they were guarding you twenty-four seven."

"They were, but as long as people are in charge, you always have to make allowances for human nature. First of all, I pretended I couldn't walk without horrible pain."

"I knew it!" Genevieve said. "I told Matt that you'd play possum like that, but he said it didn't matter, on account of the guards."

"Well, they had a male guard, of course, me being such a terrible criminal and all, and most of the nurses were women. All I had to do was set up a romance between the best-looking of the guards and the cutest single nurse, and before you knew it, they were paying so much attention to each other they didn't notice that I'd left the bathroom and was AWOL. Hospitals have plenty of places to hide, and patients hang their clothes right in the room, so eventually I found something that would fit."

"You'll never get away with it," Jack said. "They're out looking for you. They're bound to try here."

"Well, as I explained to your girlfriend here, I've got nothing to lose."

"Okay, I lied to you about when my mama and Matt are coming home," Genevieve said. "They won't be home for hours. They went on a boat ride with Lincoln, and they'll be out until way past dark, cruising around and looking at the lights."

"Without his cell on?"

"Mama doesn't like cell phones."

"Shit." Nick sounded very unhappy. "I need Matt to be in on this. He's the guy who can make sure I get to Fiji. I can't count on the cops for that, but Matt will try to do it, just to save you."

"It won't save me," Genevieve said.

"Nobody knows that for sure, now, so don't get excited."

But she knew for sure. Once Nick was positive he wouldn't be followed, he'd dispose of her. She was too dangerous to keep around. She had to get out of this pickle now or never.

Nick started to say something else, but then he paused and sniffed the air. "Now what? Damned if it doesn't smell like something's burning!"

Genevieve realized he was right. In a flash of guilt she remembered her brand-new, super-duper curling iron. She'd decided to curl her hair for Jack, then changed her mind, and never bothered to unplug the iron. Being so distracted about Jack and all, she might have left it close to a towel.

And maybe . . . maybe instead of it being a terrible mistake, this could be her salvation if she worked it right. "I'll bet it's my curling iron," she said. "I think I left it on by accident."

"I smell it, too," Jack said. "Those things are dangerous. The label says right on it that you shouldn't leave it plugged in next to something flammable."

"You left a curling iron plugged in?" Nick shouted. "How could you do that? Talk about irresponsible!"

Genevieve thought this was a definite case of the pot

calling the kettle black, but all she did was shrug. "Stuff happens."

"You are *so* much trouble."

"Listen, you'd better send Jack to check it out. This is a rickety little old house. If a fire started in the bathroom, it would spread fast. We have good neighbors. They'd call the fire department, and then you'd have a hard time maintaining your hostage situation, with the house burning down around your ears."

"The smell's getting stronger," Jack said.

"Damn it all." Nick cleared his throat. "Okay, Farley, I'll give you ten seconds to go check the bathroom and report back. If you're not back in ten seconds I'll cut off one of Genevieve's fingers. Got that?"

"Twenty seconds," Jack said.

"Ten."

Jack ran down the hall, and Genevieve started counting, Mississippi one, Mississippi two, Mississippi three.

"There's a fire!" Jack yelled from the bathroom.

"Put the damn thing out!" Nick screeched back at him.

Jack appeared in the doorway, looking scared. "Can't. It's too far gone."

And sure enough, Genevieve could see the smoke now.

"Shit, look at that damned stuff," Nick said. "Farley, go put it out."

"I can't. It's spread too far."

"Damn it! Now I gotta take Genevieve and get out of here!"

"Along with the chair?" Genevieve hoped the house wouldn't burn down along with everything in it, but she supposed Mama would prefer that to having her daughter's throat slit.

"No, not with the chair." Nick tried to keep the knife against her throat while he fumbled with the knots he'd made with the dish towel, but as he worked on the knots, the smell of smoke got worse.

"Farley, you stay right where you are, or so help me, somebody's gonna get hurt."

"You don't have to worry about a geek like me," Jack said. "I'm no hero."

"Good. Don't step out of character and try to be one."

Genevieve's gaze locked with Jack's, and she knew he was going to try something if Nick ever took the knife away from her throat. But she didn't want Jack to get stabbed, either.

Be careful, she mouthed.

He gave no sign that he'd understood, or that he was worried about being careful. He had that intense expression that meant he was concentrating all his considerable brainpower on the problem. He'd also picked up the suitcase again, although she didn't think it would make much of a weapon.

The smoke got worse, and there was a terrible smell along with it. She thought of her collection of carvings in her bedroom, but it wouldn't matter if they all burned up if she and Jack survived.

As Nick continued to fumble and cuss, she glanced down. There was no way he'd be able to untie her one-handed, and the knife was sharp, but not sharp enough to cut right through a section of terry-cloth dish towel. Sawing would do it eventually, but that would take too long.

She held her breath, waiting for him to finally put down the knife. At last he set it right by his knee and wrenched at the knots.

Jack lunged, swinging the suitcase and bashing Nick in the face. Nick fell backward, away from the knife and up against the cabinets. Wood splintered. Then Jack dropped the suitcase and leaped on top of Nick.

As the thump of body blows and grunts of pain filled

the small kitchen, Genevieve scooted her chair around so she could pick up the knife with her toes. Going barefoot all her life, she'd become very good at using her toes.

Holding the handle tight, she lifted her leg around the back of the chair. She had to grab it by the blade, and the sharp edge nicked her palm, but she was able to finally get hold of the handle with her other hand.

She slid the blade between the chair leg and her wrist and started sawing. The men had rolled away from the cabinets and Nick had his hands around Jack's throat. Jack's glasses lay crumpled over by the stove. Genevieve prayed as she'd never prayed in her life, and kept sawing.

Jack managed to throw Nick off just as she got one hand free. After slipping off the chair, she untied the second piece of towel and leaped to her feet.

Nick had Jack down, a knee in his chest and his fist raised to punch Jack in the face. Genevieve did the only thing she could think of—she grabbed the pepper shaker off the table, wrenched off the lid, and tossed the contents into Nick's face.

As Nick gasped and choked, Jack managed to roll on top of him. A couple of blows from Jack's fists, and Nick was out cold.

Breathing hard, Jack staggered to his feet. "Good . . . good thinking, Gen."

"We . . . should call 911." She picked up the phone off the table, dropped it once, and picked it up again. She dialed 811, hung up and dialed 711. Finally she managed to hit the nine.

She gave her name and address, and said there had been an assault and the house was on fire. They asked if she could stay on the line, but she said no and hung up.

"Gen, I'm going to stay by him and make sure he doesn't come to. You'd better go see if you can turn on the shower and put out the fire. It should all be contained in the tub."

She ran down the hall, waving away the smoke and stench. Once inside the bathroom, she found a tub full of smoldering ashes and a partially melted plastic shower curtain. The curling iron was in there, too, but it had only burned a small hole in one of Mama's hand towels.

From what she could tell, Jack had used the packet of matches Mama kept next to a scented votive to start a fire in the wastebasket. Then he'd put the wastebasket in the tub. That fire had been the one to get Nick's attention. She turned water on the whole thing, making a bigger mess, but at least it was all in one spot.

She hurried back to the kitchen. "You're a genius," she said.

"I know. Which is what worries you."

"Not anymore, Jack." She walked over and sat down on the floor beside him.

"What do you mean, not anymore?"

"This may not be the time or place."

"If you're going to tell me to get lost, there is no good time or place."

"Not get lost," she said. "I want you to stay found."

He gazed at her. "Come closer. You're blurry."

She scooted in until her thigh touched his. "How's that?"

"Better. Now say that again."

"Jack, I've missed you something terrible the past few days. I've come to the conclusion that we go together like grits and gravy."

"You have?"

She nodded. "I decided that if you didn't remember the ice cream date, I wasn't going to hold it against you."

"But I remembered."

"I know. Which makes you perfect."

"Gen, I'm sure not perfect. I—"

"Perfect for me." She leaned over and kissed him lightly on the mouth. Then she drew back. "That's to hold us over until we can be alone again."

He swallowed. "God, Gen, I—"

The sound of sirens cut him off.

"They're here," she said.

"Gen, I love you more than life itself."

"Well, I love you even more than *that*, so there."

"That's not logical." But Jack smiled as he said it, which made him look real cute, so she decided to kiss him again.

Later on, she realized that they must have given the officer who came into the kitchen quite a start. Down at the police station the officer admitted that he didn't often come on a scene where folks were making out next to an unconscious perp.

Fortunately, once the whole story came out, and Matt and Mama and Lincoln showed up to add their two cents' worth, neither Genevieve nor Jack had to hang around the police station.

Which was a good thing, because they had double-dip cones to buy. And a happily ever after to take care of.

EPILOGUE

On the morning after their wedding, Genevieve sat with Jack on the *South Park* beach towel to watch the sun come up over the rim of the ocean. They'd wrapped themselves in Genevieve's favorite wedding present, an orange and yellow afghan. Turns out Jack's grandmother hadn't sold it, after all. She'd only told Jack that she had, hoping someday he'd grow up and realize his mistake.

They were honeymooning where it had all begun, except the hideout had been spruced up a tad. Genevieve, busy with wedding plans, hadn't been a part of the improvement project. Matt and Jack had come out several times in Matt's financed-to-the-limit new boat. Much beer had been consumed, some construction materials had been added, and now the hideout was reasonably watertight and had new fixings like straw mats on the floor and a canvas flap for the door.

Even so, it was only a temporary honeymoon cottage. Genevieve and Jack had a special permit to use the spot for this weekend, and then the hideout would be torn down. Genevieve thought that was fitting. Besides all the ecological stuff to think about, she wouldn't want someone else staying in it.

Matt had ferried them out here yesterday after the

wedding. On the way Genevieve had tried her best to learn whether he was fixing to pop the question to Mama. Matt wouldn't tell, but Genevieve thought he might be working up to a proposal. Even though he was never getting back the money that jailbird Nick had embezzled, he surely realized that Mama didn't give a care whether he had money or not. Besides, Jack believed the company would be in high cotton before long, once the new software program came out.

Genevieve hoped that Rainbow would recover, because she and Jack both needed jobs. But sitting here on the beach watching the sunrise, she couldn't seem to worry about such things. She'd just finished telling Jack about Elvis's Jockey shorts. Mama had said she could, once Jack was officially in the family.

This was as official as it got, with Genevieve wearing a diamond the size of a black-eyed pea on the fourth finger of her left hand. She'd tried to talk Jack into something smaller, but he had a pile of money in his savings account, enough for the ring plus a down payment on a house. Genevieve had been worried about moving out of Mama's house and leaving her shy of the rent money, but Matt had told Genevieve not to fret about that. She considered it more evidence that Matt would propose to Mama very soon.

"That's some story about the notches and your Granny Neville," Jack said.

"You can't tell Lincoln. Mama doesn't think he's ready to hear this yet."

"Was his hair really purple yesterday? Because it looked black to me."

"Trust me, it was purple." Genevieve smiled as she remembered Lincoln walking her down the aisle in his rented tux and purple hair. "Mama thinks as long as he goes on doing that, he can't hear about the Jockey shorts. He might spread it around school or something."

"Okay, I won't tell Lincoln." Jack hugged her closer as he gazed at the horizon. He had on his extended-wear contacts for the honeymoon, but he'd promised to keep his glasses forever, for the sentimental value. "What color are those clouds?" he asked.

"Bright pink. Fuchsia." In the weeks since finding out he was color blind, she'd invented a way to help him "see" the colors. "Let's say you're moseying down the highway, enjoying the scenery in your Corolla. That would be your garden-variety pink. Then let's say you come to a straight patch and decide to go lickety-split, pretending you're in one of those Formula 1 cars on your computer. That's fuchsia. It's chock-a-block full of excitement."

Jack laughed. "Or let's say you give me a little kiss on the cheek. That would be your ordinary pink. But if you rip off my clothes and throw me down on the sand, that would be fuchsia."

"Actually, that might be fire-engine red." Genevieve began to heat up like a kerosene stove. They'd had a real jamboree of a honeymoon night, but that didn't mean they couldn't have a mud-wrestle on the morning-after, too.

Jack turned to her and gave her his best pirate's leer. "It's fire-engine red I want, then, lassie."

"Then it's fire-engine red you'll get!" Tossing aside the afghan, she grabbed the hem of his soft T-shirt and ripped it right up the middle. She'd always had a hankering to do that.

Jack's eyes bugged out a little, as if he hadn't expected such goings-on, but it didn't take him long to start popping the buttons on her shirt. Jack was really learning how to jump in and enjoy the moment.

As they proceeded to get quickly naked, she took a second to make a wish that they'd be ripping each other's clothes off for a long, long time to come. Of course that wouldn't happen all by itself. It would take a heap of love and buckets of luck—the good kind.

The love was a sure thing. And bad luck was just a part of living, like boll weevils and chigger bites. But she had to say that good luck had been following her around like a hungry coon dog most of her life. She had no reason to believe the next fifty years with Jack would turn out any different.

Can't wait to join Vicki Lewis Thompson in her
next sexy, dazzling adventure?

Read on for a preview of . . .

Hanging by a
G-string

late spring 2004

Chapter One

"At work my mommy wears teeny-tiny, sparkly clothes." Dexter looked up from the chessboard, his glasses huge on his four-year-old face. "With pink feathers. Didja know that, Mr. Harry?"

"Uh, huh." Harry Ambrewster, MBA, Stanford, Class of '92, didn't have a lot of experience with baby-sitting. Still, he didn't think baby-sitters normally discussed teeny-tiny, sparkly clothes that a parent was wearing *right this minute*. Thinking of Lainie Terrell in her skimpy outfits made his palms sweat.

He wiped them on his Dockers. After two nights of staying with Dexter while Lainie pranced on the Nirvana Casino stage, Harry had learned that baby-sitting involved lots of floor time, even when the kid was a bonafide genius. Consequently he sat cross-legged on one side of the coffee table, balanced on his knees on the other side, sandwiched between the table and the couch.

Dexter picked up his knight and moved it within striking range of Harry's queen.

Harry decided to give the kid a break. "Do you really want to move your knight there?"

"Yep." Dexter leaned his chin on both fists. "Have you seen my mommy dance?"

"Sort of." Lainie performed in four out of six numbers staged nightly at the Nirvana Casino. Harry had watched her so many times he had the numbers memorized, although he sat at a back table and hoped she had no idea he was such a regular. She might laugh. Better that she only know him as the boring accountant from payroll who also happened to be a neighbor in her apartment complex.

"I wish I could see her dance."

Harry tried to redirect Dexter's attention. "You do realize I'm going to capture your knight."

"I know." Dexter sighed. "But I really, really want to see the show. Mommy won't let me."

"Mm." Harry picked up Dexter's knight. He hated to beat the kid, but if Dexter didn't learn to pay attention, he'd get his ass whipped whenever he sat down at a chessboard, genius or not. "Well, she shouldn't let you go. The show is for big people." Or big people with infantile obsessions like Harry's.

He wasn't proud of giving into his craving as often as he did. He should volunteer to be Dexter's permanent babysitter, because then he'd be forced to spend his evenings playing chess with a four-year-old instead of secretly lusting after the kid's mommy.

Although Harry liked Dexter a lot, he wasn't ready to make that sacrifice and give up his reserved spot at that back table. Not yet. He was only filling in for the regular sitter this week because if he didn't, Lainie would miss too much work and get her long-legged self fired. Then she might leave Vegas, and Harry wouldn't be able to watch her dance anymore.

Logically, that would be a good thing. His fascination

with her was doomed on many levels. For one thing, she was far too cool ever to be interested in an accountant. He was all ledgers and calculations, while she was all fire and rhythm. His favorite dance number was called *Fever*, where she wore fishnet stockings and red satin rose petals over her—

"Check."

Harry blinked. "Son of a b— bucket. How'd you do that?"

"I just—"

"Okay, okay. I see it now." Talk about embarrassing. The kid might have more brain cells than the Sahara had sand, but Harry was no slouch in that department, either, and he had the kid by twenty-nine years. Plus, Harry had only taught Dexter the game two nights ago.

"I didn't checkmate you. You can still get away."

"Right." Harry made the necessary defensive move as he vowed to take his own advice and concentrate on the game instead of letting his mind wander to Lainie. Chess was one of the few activities in which he was the alpha dog, and he'd obviously underestimated his opponent.

Dexter leaned over the board, and Harry noticed that his curly dark hair needed combing. Dexter had his mother's hair, but hers was long enough to reach her waist when she wore it down. And she had such a tiny waist. And such generous—

"You're not mad, are you, Mr. Harry?" Dexter lifted his head, looking worried.

Harry stared at him, astonished. "Mad? About what?"

" 'Cause I almost beat you."

"Good grief, no! Maybe I was mad at myself for not giving my full attention to the game, but I would never be mad at you for doing your best. That's what you're supposed to do."

"So you'll keep playing?" He seemed very anxious.

"Of course." Harry had decided the boy's gray eyes came from his father, because Lainie's were a mesmerizing shade of blue.

Dexter flopped back against the edge of the couch. "Whew. What a relief."

He sounded so adult that Harry couldn't help smiling. A faint memory of his own childhood drifted in. He used to have trouble holding on to playmates for the same reason. "Do people wimp out on you a lot, Dexter?"

The little boy nodded.

"Your mom?"

"Not really, but she doesn't like to sit still a lot."

"Ah." Just as Harry had suspected. High energy all the time. A guy like him would bore her silly.

"She likes it when we go play in the park, though," Dexter said loyally. "And that's fun."

"I'll bet." Theoretically Harry was all for playing in the park. But as a kid he'd never worked up any enthusiasm for slides and monkey bars, preferring to sit under a tree and work on logic puzzles. Lainie and Dexter had been coming back from the park, their eyes bright and their hair tousled, the day he'd stopped to talk to them on his way to his own apartment. Lainie had confessed her baby-sitting crisis and he'd leaped into the breach.

"But Mrs. Flippo won't play *anything* with me anymore, not even Chutes and Ladders. I even said I'd let her win, but nope." He tugged at his hair. "And who wants to watch TV all the time?"

"Indeed." Harry felt himself weakening on the baby-sitting thing. This little guy was starving for mental stimulation. Harry could relate. Maybe that's why his own mother had given up on regular baby-sitters all those years ago and brought him to work with her.

Unfortunately, work for her had been exactly like work was for Lainie, and Harry had spent his formative years backstage at a casino just like the Nirvana. Doing his homework surrounded by flowery-smelling, nearly naked women, he'd been marked early, set up to want what wasn't good for him. In his twenties he'd gone through an all-showgirls-all-the-time phase. He'd discovered if he drank plenty of booze, he'd get goofy enough to be considered cute.

He'd pulled out of that nosedive before permanently damaging his liver, and he'd thought he was way over showgirls. To prove it he'd dated several women with ordinary bodies who couldn't dance a lick. He'd meshed with them on an intellectual level, but as for sex . . . lackluster would be too good a word. He'd been able to perform, but not with enthusiasm. He blamed it on not finding the right woman.

Then Lainie had come to work at the Nirvana and moved into his apartment complex. And just like that—recidivism. But he'd conquered his obsession before, and he would again, because his children would not have a Vegas showgirl for a mother. Once he mastered his infatuation with Lainie, he'd resume looking for Ms. Right.

"Check."

Harry snapped out of his daze and discovered he was in a worse pickle than the last time. Unless he brought all his powers to bear on this chess game, this little sprout might actually beat him.

"While you're thinking, I'll get the cookies, okay?"

Harry nodded, still studying the board. Because he wouldn't take any money for baby-sitting, Lainie had baked cookies for him. First came peanut butter, then oatmeal, and tonight, the most seductive of all, chocolate chip. She couldn't know his weakness for chocolate chip.

"Here you go, Mr. Harry." Dexter set a plastic plate loaded with cookies next to the chessboard.

Harry couldn't believe how distracting the scent of chocolate and cookie dough was. His mouth watered, and he couldn't keep his mind on the chess game. Lainie had made those cookies, and that was part of the problem. He smelled them and imagined her bustling about the kitchen in her snug jeans and tight T-shirt, bending over to slip the pan into the warm oven, pausing to lick the spoon. . . .

Dexter picked up a cookie and leaned over the board as he bit into it. A crumb fell on a black marble square. "Whoops." He wet his finger and picked it up. "Whatcha gonna do?"

Harry surrendered to his urges and picked up a cookie. "Eat one of these." The cookie was incredible. Some people over-baked them and burned the chocolate chips, but this one was totally perfect, the outside a little crunchy and the inside soft and gooey. He moaned with delight.

"My mommy makes good cookies, huh?"

Harry talked with his mouth full, something he never did. "She sure does."

Dexter took another bite of his cookie and studied the chessboard. "I think it's time for you to castle, Mr. Harry."

Harry had come to the same sad conclusion. And he wasn't even sure that move would save him. The kid had him on the ropes. "As soon as I finish the cookie."

"Want milk?"

"Not yet, thanks." Oh, what the hell, he might as well castle and be done with it. Then Dexter would edge in with his king, and in a couple of moves, it would be all over.

Harry glanced at the clock, wondering if they had time for a rematch before he tucked Dexter in at eight-thirty.

Just as he'd picked up the rook, someone banged on the door. They hammered on it with a lot of force, like they were ready to break it down. Startled, he dropped the chess piece and scrambled to his feet, adrenaline pumping. This couldn't be good.

He started around the coffee table to get Dexter, and Dexter met him halfway, grabbing him around the legs. Harry lifted the little boy into his arms and held him tight. "It's okay," he said, not believing a word of it.

"Open up!" yelled a guy with a nasal twang to his voice. "I wanna see my son!"

Dexter moaned softly in distress. "It's Daddy," he whispered.

Harry gulped. Lainie had never mentioned a daddy. From the way Dexter was trembling, there was a good reason for that.

"A man deserves to see his boy!" Dexter's father bellowed. "Dexter! Come on out and let me see how big you are!"

Dexter shrank away and buried his head against Harry's neck.

Harry figured the guy had to be drunk, and he'd probably come here now because he knew Lainie would be working. Maybe he thought a baby-sitter would be intimidated into opening the door to him. Harry decided not to respond. Letting this cretin know that the baby-sitter was a man might rile him up even more.

"Damn it, I know you're in there. The law's on my side, y'know. A woman can't take a man's son away. Let me in, damn it!" Dexter's father pounded on the door, making it rattle in the frame.

Dexter winced with each blow and tightened his grip around Harry's neck.

Harry leaned down and murmured in Dexter's ear. "Don't be afraid. I won't let him get you."

More pounding. "If you don't open this door, so help me, I'll bust it down!"

Harry wished he had more confidence in the door. He wished they were on the first floor instead of the second. And he wished he'd taken that karate course he'd always thought about. First thing tomorrow he'd check it out. But that didn't help him right now.

Maybe he should dial 911, but Dexter's daddy could be through that door before a squad car pulled up. Besides, even if the police arrived in time, Harry didn't know if Lainie might be a mom on the run. Judging from this performance, she had reason to run, but the courts could still put her in jail for it. Harry wasn't about to take that chance by alerting the cops.

"Okay, you asked for it." The door reverberated with a heavy thud, as if the guy had just rammed his shoulder into the wood.

Keeping his eye on the door, Harry retreated down the hall toward Lainie's bedroom at the back of the apartment. He'd never been in there, but her floor plan matched his. People usually had heavy dressers in the bedroom, and that could serve as a barricade until Harry decided what to do next.

"I'm scared," Dexter whispered.

"Don't be. I'm right here." Even though Harry's blood was pumping wildly, he tried to keep his voice calm. Lainie had obviously made a terrible mistake five years ago by letting this neanderthal close enough to father her child. But Dexter shouldn't have to pay for that by being terrorized.

"He's a lot bigger than you," Dexter said.

Not what Harry wanted to hear. "Well, I'm smarter than him." That was a reasonable guess. Harry doubted that Dexter had inherited his IQ from the imbecile trying to break down the front door.

"So what are we gonna do, Mr. Harry?"

"Think." Somehow it didn't seem like enough. The moment called for boldness and daring. Harry wasn't the bold and daring type. Inside Lainie's darkened bedroom, he glanced around and found a dresser, but it was made of flimsy white wicker. Considering the drawers were probably full of lacy underwear, the dresser lost all potential as a barricade.

Another thud, louder than the first, echoed through the apartment.

"We could go out the window," Dexter said.

"Uh, we're on the second floor." Harry glanced at the double-paned window. There was a good-sized tree outside, but the thought of climbing out the window and down the tree while holding Dexter made him queasy. If he dropped the kid . . .

"We could climb down the tree. Like Spider-Man."

The crack of wood splintering narrowed Harry's choices. Lowering Dexter quickly to the floor, he closed and locked the bedroom door. Then he dragged the wicker dresser in front of it, for whatever time it might give them. Checking to make sure his car keys were in his pocket, he unlocked the window and shoved it up. A cold blast of air hit him in the face, and he realized he was sweating.

As he punched out the screen and it clattered to the ground below, he realized he didn't have a coat for Dexter, but he didn't have time to worry about that. "Okay." He took a deep breath and crouched beside Dexter. "We're going to climb out the window and go down the tree, like you suggested."

"What if he chases us?"

"We'll take my car. Don't worry. We'll lose him. Are you with me?"

Dexter nodded so hard his glasses jiggled on his nose.

"I want you to climb onto my back, wrap your arms around my neck and your legs around my waist. Then I want you to hang on like Velcro. Got that?"

"Yep." Dexter glued himself to Harry's back and got a choke hold on his neck.

Harry adjusted the little boy's grip so his windpipe wasn't in danger of being totally closed off. Then he stuck one leg over the windowsill.

"After we get down, where are we going?"

Harry doubled over so he could work both of them through the opening. "To see your mommy."

In the midst of a dressing room filled with laughter, nakedness, and efficient movement, Lainie wiggled into her red rose-petal outfit for the *Fever* number. Halfway though the night's entertainment, the other dancers rode the crest of a performance high. Lainie wanted to throw off her uneasy mood and ride it with them. The crowd was friendly, sweetened up by the comedian the casino had recently hired. Jack Newman had turned out to be a good complement to the musical part of the show.

He'd also indicated an interest in Lainie. Years ago Jack would have been exactly her type, but ever since tangling with Joey Benjamin, she steered clear of boisterous men. More accurately, she steered clear of all men. She had a son to raise, and she lived in fear that somebody, some day, would try to take Dexter away from her. If anyone should challange her custody, her profession could count against her. A boyfriend might make the picture even worse.

She'd been thinking of potential custody battles ever since last night, when out of the blue, Joe had called her at work. If only she knew what he was up to. Six months ago he'd seemed more than happy to let her move from Atlantic City to Vegas. When she'd told him she'd waive her rights to child support, he'd seemed even happier. After six months of silence, she'd dared to think she'd cut Joey out of her life, and more important, out of Dexter's life.

And now, this phone call. She wonderered if he'd gone through the phone book or if he'd used some of his father's money to locate her. Maybe it didn't matter. What mattered was that he'd begged her for another chance. The thought sent a chill down her spine.

He hadn't mentioned Dexter, hadn't even asked how he was. That didn't surprise her. When told about the pregnancy, Joey had suggested an abortion. When she'd refused, he'd said *don't make the mistake of thinking I'll marry you, sweetheart.*

She'd said *don't make the mistake of thinking I'd have you, sucker.* The relationship had degenerated rapidly after that. But for Dexter's sake, because she'd missed having a father growing up, she'd tried to keep things civil. Then Joey's drinking had gotten worse and he'd started to scare Dexter with his loud voice and threatening gestures. She'd had to rethink her strategy.

The dressing room door opened. "On stage for *Fever*," called Tim, the stage manager.

Lainie hurried out with the rest of the ensemble.

"Where's your accountant been keeping himself?" asked a blonde named Gina as they filed onto the curtained stage during the intro.

"He's not exactly mine."

"Sure he is. He never takes his eyes off you, and he's been at that back table almost every night, except just recently. I wonder if he's sick or something."

Lainie shrugged. Explaining that Harry was home watching Dexter would start all kinds of rumors, and she didn't need rumors right now, not with Joey popping up again. Harry might not want anybody to know what he was doing, anyway. Although he seemed to have a crush on her, he'd never asked her out, and he'd had plenty of chances.

Harry might be shy. She certainly hoped that was the problem. Unfortunately, shyness might not be it. He could be like a lot of guys—including Joey—who thought showgirls were exciting but not the sort of woman they'd take home to momma.

Lainie would hate to find that out about Harry, because he seemed nicer than that, but the evidence was there. She wouldn't go out with him, of course, but he didn't know that. She wouldn't have minded being asked, for the record.

"Curtain," Tim murmered from the wings.

Lainie smiled automatically, gratefully. As always, when the curtain swished open, it swept her worries into the wings where they belonged. For the few minutes of the number, nothing existed but the joy of moving to the music, sensing the approval of the audience, feeling the rhythm in every cell of her body.

How she loved this! Dancing before a live audience gave her a thrill greater than sex, which was a good thing, because she wasn't getting a smidgen of sex these days, unless she counted solo sessions with her vibrator. She'd created quite a fantasy life for herself during those sessions. Recently, because there was a rebellious streak in her, she'd thrust Harry, so to speak, into the role of her fantasy lover. Wouldn't he be surprised.

About the Author

Essentially a wuss, Vicki Lewis Thompson stumbled upon a career in fiction because her first two choices—high school English teacher and journalist—rivaled *Fear Factor*. Now instead of trying to rescue a dangling participle or cover a skydiving event *from the open door of the plane*, she sits in her cozy office and lets her characters take all the risks.

She lives with her husband in Arizona, a place with fewer natural disasters than almost anywhere in the world. Well, okay, she did come upon a rattlesnake in the backyard not long ago, which means she now spends more time in her cozy office and less time in the backyard.

Don't miss any of these delightful romances from

Emily Carmichael

Finding Mr. Right
___57874-X $5.99/$8.99 Canada

A Ghost for Maggie
___57875-8 $5.50/$8.50

Diamond in the Ruff
___58283-6 $5.50/$8.99

The Good, the Bad, and the Sexy
___58284-4 $5.99/$8.99

Please enclose check or money order only, no cash or CODs. Shipping & handling costs: $5.50 U.S. mail, $7.50 UPS. New York and Tennessee residents must remit applicable sales tax. Canadian residents must remit applicable GST and provincial taxes. Please allow 4 – 6 weeks for delivery. All orders are subject to availability. This offer subject to change without notice. Please call 1–800–726–0600 for further information.

Bantam Dell Publishing Group, Inc.	TOTAL AMT	$_____
Attn: Customer Service	SHIPPING & HANDLING	$_____
400 Hahn Road	SALES TAX (NY, TN)	$_____
Westminster, MD 21157		
	TOTAL ENCLOSED	$_____

Name _____

Address _____

City/State/Zip _____

Daytime Phone (_____) _____